Caroline Cauchi also writes as Caroline Smailes and her acclaimed novel *The Drowning of Arthur Braxton* was adapted into a film starring James Tarpey and Johnny Vegas. It won Best UK Feature 2021 at Raindance film festival. Matt Haig called the novel, 'magical, weird, wonderful'.

Caroline worked as a lecturer for several years before turning her hand to fiction. She lives in Liverpool with her husband and children.

<u>carolinesmailes.co.uk</u>

twitter.com/Caroline_S
instagram.com/caroline_smailes

T0109857

MRS VAN GOGH

CAROLINE CAUCHI

One More Chapter
a division of HarperCollins*Publishers*
1 London Bridge Street
London SE1 9GF

www.harpercollins.co.uk

HarperCollins*Publishers*
Macken House, 39/40 Mayor Street Upper,
Dublin 1, D01 C9W8, Ireland

This paperback edition 2023

First published in Great Britain in ebook format
by HarperCollins*Publishers* 2023

A catalogue record of this book
is available from the British Library

ISBN: 978-0-00-864153-5

Kugina, this one's for you. I'll never not miss you.
(Dr Jacqueline Azzopardi, née Cauchi: 1969–2016)

'For in the routine of daily life there is so little time to reflect, and sometimes days go by when I don't actually live, but let life happen to me, and that's terrible. I would think it dreadful to have to say at the end of my life: "I've actually lived for nothing, I have achieved nothing great or noble"...'

Johanna Bonger, aged seventeen (March 26, 1880)[1]

The Woman Behind Vincent van Gogh

Sunday June 17, 2018

Since Vincent van Gogh's death on July 29, 1890, it has been widely assumed that the renowned artist committed suicide. Indeed, speculation about his death has persisted for over one hundred years. Yet with most of the public not even knowing his name until decades later, why is it that little thought is given to what happened to the Post-Impressionist's art after his passing?

Today Van Gogh is among the most famous and influential figures in the history of Western art. Some would never now consider that a name that is synonymous with art sold one or two paintings during his lifetime, and instead favoured exchanging his work for food and alcohol. Of course, other artists in Van Gogh's social circle appreciated his paintings, but most of the public only learned his name decades after his death.

But how did that shift in public awareness occur? What happened to Vincent's art after his death? Who took it upon themselves to introduce Van Gogh's paintings to the world?

A Mrs Van Gogh happened. And aside from Vincent's artistic talent, she is entirely accountable for making Van Gogh a name that everyone recognises.

Yet what do we actually know about this Mrs Van Gogh?

Chapter One

EMERGE

Summer 1888

PARIS

Railway Carriages

'Sister.'

One word and I'm transformed into an ugly, sobbing mess outside the Gare du Nord. Lord knows what the other travellers must think; small trunk dropped to my feet, tears decorating my cheeks. I think I even release a tiny mew-like whimper. My handkerchief's pushed too far past the tight cuffs of my bodice for me to reach, but really I'm no longer trying to get it. I see him. My brother: tall, bowler hat in hand thrust above the crowd, calling me, fighting against the stream of passengers from the train.

I stand still, watching as he weaves past the stone columns outside the station. Other travellers rush along, porters wobbling behind, straining to juggle too many travel cases. Hustle, bustle, shouts of *au revoir*, bowler hats and beggars. Bonnets, laughter, top hats and barefooted children. Ladies raise their parasols to prevent the sun from touching their skin, and some even have fans, desperate for a breath of air; I have nothing to protect me from the afternoon sun. Languages I know, dialects I don't quite recognise. It finally feels real: *I'm in Paris.*

'You're here,' I say, the words stuttering out with my gulps.

'Oh my, such heat,' he says. He dabs at his forehead with a silk handkerchief. Andries has what others consider a youthful face: oval in shape, blemish free, overly prominent ears, the end bristles of his moustache wishing to curl. 'Were you waiting long? I'd have been here earlier, but Mamma's letter only arrived a few hours ago and there was so much to organise…'

'So, they've told you?' I ask. Andries nods, his eyes jumping to each passer-by, not meeting mine. That starts me off again. Snot and tears galore. The shame, the embarrassment, the huge mess I've made of my life. I lift the sleeve of my blouse to wipe my eyes but Andries thrusts his silk handkerchief at me. I take it, dab at my eyes and cheeks, then blow my nose so hard that it toots like a trumpet. I hold out the handkerchief to my brother but he shakes his head.

Andries pulls me to him. He plants a kiss on my forehead before placing his arm around my shoulder. 'It'll be all right,' he says.

'I can never go back to teaching,' I say. A young porter collides with my huge bustle, the small travel case in his teetering bundle falling to the pavement with a clump.

'*Pardon, mademoiselle,*' he says. Eyes down, he bows slightly and that makes the remaining cases topple forward. He pulls back to steady his load. The boy is flustered, young, closer to a babe than an adult. 'My first day,' he mumbles in rapid French. I can't help but smile.

'Mine too,' I say in Dutch, but I don't think he understands.

'This bustle. It's too large for Paris,' I say grudgingly. 'I swear people are pointing and laughing.' I turn to show Andries. It juts out like a shelf, making my silhouette appear like the hind legs of a horse. The station's clock strikes four o'clock as Andries bends and picks up the fallen luggage, balancing it back on the leaning tower of leather cases, before the boy lurches off.

'Do you hate me?' I ask.

'Don't be silly,' he says. 'You're my favourite person in the world.'

'Pa does. He says I've thrown away my education and brought shame upon you all.'

'There'll be other occupations,' my brother says. He picks up my trunk and nods for me to follow him back through the crowd.

6

'My reputation is ruined. Eduard Stumpff will see to that.'

'He wrote to Pa,' Andries tells me as he manoeuvres through the crowd. 'Says you pursued him, blames you for him being caught in a *compromising* embrace. Said it was a one-off though.' His pace is a little too quick, his bowler hat in hand thrust above the crowd. I'm having to skip to keep up.

'What?' I say. 'It'd been going on for three years—'

'It was a one-off,' Andries repeats, his voice stern, his eyes fixed ahead. I nod; he doesn't see. It seems my history has been rewritten during the long train journeys from Amsterdam to Paris. All blame is on me. The official stance has been made. 'Pa's already negotiated an "honourable discharge on health grounds" from teaching, with the proviso that you stay away from Stumpff.'

'I'd like to tell them all the truth. He was a dissembler—'

'You should have resisted him, Jo,' Andries says.

'But he's a novelist,' I say, as if that's explanation for my inability to say no.

Eduard flashes before my eyes. His dark hair falling across his eyes, one hand grabbing my waist, the other pushing me up against the blackboard, chalk in my hair. *I love you, Jo. We'll be together soon.*

Andries stops, and the vision dissolves as I collide with his back. The noisy streets of the 10th arrondissement fill my ears once more. He turns to look at me.

'What were you thinking, Jo?' I can hear the disappointment in his words.

'I clearly wasn't, but he's no saint. He—'

'Come,' he says, stepping off again. 'We'll fix it together. I thought we'd catch a *fiacre* to my apartment. Save you the walk today.'

We move towards the line of horse-drawn carriages outside the station. Heaps of manure decorate the cobbles and the stench invades my nostrils. I hold Andries' handkerchief over my nose and lips, but it does little to dispel the stink. I wait as he discusses our location with the coachman, the smell not seeming to bother either of them. The coachman's whip is the longest I've ever seen and his top hat far taller than the style worn back home.

Paris is bigger and bolder than Amsterdam. Already everything here feels extraordinary; I'm convinced that even the sun blazes brighter and stronger.

Two sprightly boys, orderlies I guess, scurry about on all fours, a scoop in one hand and a brush in the other, trying to pick up the rounds of muck. Defeat is scribbled all over their faces, their scoops too little, the piles too big.

Their negotiations finished, Andries hands the coachman my trunk, then offers his hand to help me inside the carriage. I remove his handkerchief from my face, holding my breath as I manoeuvre my bustle up the three steps and through the narrow door into the hooded transport. Once inside I exhale; it feels like I've been holding my breath for the last three years. Perching on the edge of the leather seat, I adjust my ridiculous bustle to the confined space as Andries steps in behind me and closes the door.

He shouts to the coachman and a cry of, '*Hé, la-bas!*' is heard as the *fiacre* lurches forward over the cobbles.

Shelter On Montmartre

F ive minutes in silence, with us both watching Paris life through the carriage windows, then my brother asks, 'What did the cook do when she caught you?'

'Screamed hysterically until the headmaster arrived,' I say.

'I'm not surprised he dismissed you on the spot.'

I nod, unable to stop the prickles of heat rushing up my neck and to my cheeks. 'Yet Eduard kept his position.' I watch my brother, waiting for reaction: nothing.

'And word had reached Amsterdam before you arrived home?' Andries asks, his eyes looking out of the window, not at me.

'Pa was waiting at the station. He was furious, yelling and slapping me about the head and face. I imagine it'll be the talk of the neighbourhood for weeks.' I can't help but lift a hand to my cheek. The sting lingers.

'How did you expect him to react?' He looks at me now.

'With kindness,' I say, my words almost a whisper. 'I made a mistake, got carried away, but isn't that what humans do? I didn't even know what would be waiting for me here.'

'Oh Jo,' he says, reaching over and squeezing my hand. 'I'll always welcome opportunity to spend time with you.'

'Eduard said that he loved me, that he'd make it official, that we'd be together just as soon as his novel was published.'

Andries snorts and shakes his head. I'm not sure if he mocks me or if my words have amused him, but I know he's not angry. 'You fool. You're an adult. Twenty-five years old,' he says. 'You should know better.'

'Pa wouldn't let me explain myself. He didn't even allow me one night at home, instead I was packed off here on the next train.'

My brother squeezes my hand again.

I'm safe now.

'You gave that man everything he wanted with no need to ever marry you.'

'I didn't give him *that*,' I say. 'We never—'

'It's done now.' He picks at the stray hairs on his narrow trousers, taking in my words. I need him to know that truth.

'I've never felt so miserable,' I say.

'No point dwelling, sister. You're here, in Paris, with me. Best enjoy your punishment instead.'

'My punishment?' I'm looking at his face, searching for clues; he's smiling.

'Pa *banishing* you from Amsterdam for the summer.'

I smile too. I close my eyes, listening to the clip-clop of the horses' hooves.

'You've always loved books and art,' Andries says and I open my eyes.

'*Women should be supporters of fine art and never artists*,' I say, mimicking Pa's stern voice.

Andries looks at me, and he lets out a laugh. His smile lingers. 'There are many female artists in Paris,' he says.

'And how many are making a living that way?' I ask. 'How many of them are allowed to exhibit their work in the salons?' I wait for my brother to respond; his features are set in concentration. I imagine he's searching through his acquaintances, trying to find an example to support his argument.

Art fascinates me – the making, the discovering, the dissecting too. It always has. I'm obsessed with understanding technique and how artists create. I'd once dreamed of studying in Paris, but

Pa wouldn't listen to my arguments. He'd never give my art his time or opinion; he wouldn't even look at my canvases and sketches. Piles and piles of them still stacked in the cellar, attempts at watercolours, charcoals, even some oils; all poor experiments in technique really. I never claimed I had instinctive talent or hidden creative genius, and when I decided the battle I wanted to fight was for an education, to be the first woman in our family to reject the expected roles and strive for something else – something better, something more – I knew that wouldn't be to study art. Instead, I chose English literature – novelists and poets – and my love of art was relegated to a pastime; secret and indulgent. Only Andries knew I remained fascinated with artistic technique. Pa would have told me it was a waste of both my time and money.

'I've a friend who's an emerging art dealer. Quite the man around town. I'll ask him about female artists, and for help with your art. But for now, you need to focus on forgetting *that* man,' Andries says. He waves his hand as if to dismiss Eduard with a magic trick. I nod. My eyes close again, the clip-clop offering rhythm to my thoughts.

I met that man, Eduard, at the beginning of my second year of teaching; both of us were employed at a boarding school for girls in Utrecht. He was smart, witty, with the palest, widest blue eyes I'd ever seen. Ten years older than me, he was wiser, he was full of experience: in literature, in the arts, in women. My love for him was instant and, in return, he quickly unravelled my very being. He told me he'd never loved anyone until me, that I was his muse, that if I left him, he'd never write another word. I justified us not being engaged for the three years we kept meeting, believing his words and wild notions. I tried not to listen when Cook mentioned Eduard Stumpff being engaged, or when he forgot to mention trips away, or when there were rumours around school about Eduard and the music teacher, Miss Blom. I accepted his sulks, accepted the discomfort of his silences and jumped when he decided he had an hour or two for me. I was ridiculous, a caricature, distorted into the worst possible version of me.

'It's only been two days. This,' Andries says and I open my eyes and see him flapping his hand in the direction of my face, 'will pass.' I hadn't even realised I was crying.

'He's the only man I'll ever love,' I say, but even as the words escape I know they're not truthful. He was the first man I loved. The wrong man to love. He wasn't ever mine to love. A thief in a schoolmaster's gown; three years of my life stolen and for what?

Andries laughs. 'You … *we* have a reputation. There are expectations. You know that.' He sits for a moment, his eyes looking at the passing buildings. 'There'll be another *love*, Mamma and Pa will see to that. They'll have you married before the end of the year.'

'I won't ever marry.'

He waves my words away with his hand. 'There are things you'll have to do, consequences for actions, Jo. But everything can be fixed. For now, you have a summer to read, sketch and paint. Montmartre will be your playground.'

'As long as I don't have to entertain men, and specifically not novelists,' I say. A pause as I look through the carriage's window. 'I still can't believe you chose to live in Montmartre.'

'Not quite in Montmartre,' Andries corrects. 'Mamma considers me living on the *right* side of Boulevard de Clichy, although I doubt she'll ever forgive my not choosing to live in the 8th arrondissement.' Andries laughs. 'I brought you a present.'

He reaches into the inside pocket of his frock coat and then hands me a sketchbook.

'Keep a diary of your time here. Fill the blank pages with words and sketches.'

Despite myself, a flicker of excitement stirs in my stomach at this unexpected opportunity to immerse myself in the Parisian art world as much as possible. I've longed to visit my brother in Paris and now my *punishme*nt seems to be this chance to see both him and his city.

'Let's enjoy this summer together, before you return to Amsterdam and whatever *solution* our parents have concocted for you,' he says.

I look out of the carriage's window. 'What are they building?' I ask. Construction has begun at the top of a small hill. It thrusts itself up from the earth, gleaming white stone amid a complicated wooden framework.

Andries leans forward, looking out of the carriage window.

'That? On butte Montmartre?' He points to the squat block of scaffolding that's been erected on the highest point in the city. 'A basilica, eventually. There's a chapel there already. You can just about see it behind the scaffolding. Everyone I know has donated at least enough for a brick, but they keep asking if I'll fund a column. God knows when it'll ever be finished.'

'The view will be stunning,' I say.

Andries nods. 'Paris is changing. Wait till you see what Eiffel's building down on Champ de Mars.' I can hear the excitement in his voice. 'We go there every week.'

'We?' I ask.

'Do you remember Sara Voort?'

I shake my head, turning back to my brother. 'Are you in love?'

He laughs from his belly. Apparently, the thought of him and Miss Voort together is comical. I wait.

'Pa's friend, Samuel Voort?' he says. 'She's his daughter. She came to Mamma's house a few times. Ugly. Face as round as a full moon, bulbous nose, mean, piggy eyes.'

'Such a kind description, brother,' I say, batting him with my sketchbook.

'She hounds a friend of mine daily. Theo van Gogh – have you heard of him?' I shake my head. 'He's the emerging art dealer I mentioned. Knows all the up-and-coming artists. We spend much time together. You'll like Theo. I'll get you an audience with him. Show him your art and—'

'I'm really not talented.'

'Then use this summer to perfect your artistic skills and learn from others. Let that be your focus, instead of that pompous idiot of a man who broke your heart and brought *disgrace to our family name*.' He mimics Mamma's voice, all squeaky and severe. I whack the sketchbook against his leg this time, before looping my arm through his and resting my head on his bony shoulder.

'Thank you,' I say.

'For what?' he asks, kissing the top of my head.

'For not locking me up in a stinking cellar.' I'm crying again, but this time my tears mix my sorrow with joy and relief.

Outskirts Of Paris Near Montmartre

'**B**y the way, we're going out tonight,' Andries says, as we step into his hallway and he places my leather trunk on the floor. I glance around: white walls, black and white tiled floor and a galleried back table with turned front legs. I can't help but run my finger over the intricate carvings. My brother has exquisite taste in furniture.

Andries picks his correspondence from the table, flapping it at me as he continues to talk. 'Your first taste of Parisian freedom, Jo.'

I've been distracted by his hallway; he's waiting for a response. 'Do I have to go? I'm really not in the mood for meeting people.' The journey was long and tiring and the thought of dressing up in my Amsterdam fashion and making small talk with strangers holds no appeal.

'It'll do you good. You can't be in Paris and hide,' he says. 'And it's in a windmill. It's the place to be seen. Students, artists and fortune-seekers flock there. Trust me, you'll love it.'

I shake my head. 'Maybe next week.'

'Jump straight in, Jo. Embrace Paris. These opportunities are for this summer only.'

I fold my arms across my chest. 'I can't go,' I say. Andries glares, waiting for my explanation. 'I've got one other dress with me and it's hardly suitable. I'll look like a dowdy schoolmistress.'

I'm hit with a sense of not fitting in, of not being refined enough for this city. I'm out of place – the way I've felt all my life.

A smile stretches across my brother's face. 'And that's the only reason not to go?' he asks. I nod. He laughs. 'My maid's already been out and acquired a new dress for you.'

'What?'

He nods, still smiling. 'It'll be on your bed.'

I turn and rush along the hallway, my heels click clacking over the tiles.

'Third door on the right,' he shouts after me.

And as I push open the door, I jump on the spot with joy at the sight of a gown so vivid in colour. Deep red satin with a contrasting peacock-blue velvet. A long-boned bodice, tight sleeves and high neck. There's nothing prudish about my new dress; my shape won't go unnoticed. I rush in and pick it up, twirling to watch it fan from all angles. The skirts are layered and draped, an apron front and a trained back, with pleating in both the skirt's construction and in the intricate trimming. There's a bustle, but it's less shelf-like and somehow more feminine. Bold, unapologetic. This dress is like nothing I've ever worn or owned.

'Do you like it?' he asks and I turn to see Andries in the open doorway to the bedroom.

'Mamma would never allow—'

'Well, you're in my house now,' he says, and I rush to him. I throw my arms, and the dress, around his neck.

'Thank you,' I say.

'Clara chose it,' he says. She's his maid and was our maid at home before that. She's known me since I was a baby and loves us both fiercely.

'Where is she?' I ask.

'Probably in the kitchen. Let's find her and eat, and then she'll help you dress for this evening.'

June, 1888.

Bonjour, Paris!

    My first ever entry in my sketchbook. I used to laugh at anyone who thought writing to themselves was a good thing, but Dries was right, and now I'm hit with a need to record my time here in words and sketches. I think it'll be good for me to reflect on everything I do, to consider all that I've already done, and to try to become better. I'm going to grow and learn in Paris this summer — that's my new and exciting aim. I'd hate to reach the end of my life and to never have achieved something that is great or even remarkable.

    And I'm free here. I'm lost. I'm without Eduard.

    I should like to tell all in Utrecht the truth to their faces, tell Pa what Eduard has been: a coward — a dissembler who never, never treated me fairly — oh, if only I could. And I should like to tell the world too. Everyone should know. I'd like to brand him — he who placed himself above everyone else, but is actually so far, far beneath us all.

    Yet what purpose would such vengeance serve?

    Instead, I'm truly grateful for my brother. I'm being swept along on a Dries-shaped wave; being distracted is definitely the best way through this. I can't spend every hour wishing that Eduard wasn't part of my story. That our names weren't being whispered by my family, by my pupils, by strangers, the shame travelling into my very being with each and every murmur.

    Tonight I must push that aside and put on my best Parisian face. Jump straight in. I can't disappoint Dries again, my biggest supporter and very best friend. Not when I've only just arrived in his city.

Le Moulin De La Galette

A rm in arm, Andries told me about Moulin de la Galette during our short walk. That on one Sunday each month, my brother and his many friends dressed up and met there to dance, drink and feast on pancakes. Andries talked about the many artists I'd be sure to meet, and about how countless had been inspired to create after their joyful Sunday gatherings. I couldn't help but feel excited.

'You might meet Camille Claudel,' he says. 'She's Rodin's lover.'

'Do you think I'm the same as Miss Claudel? That my experience with Eduard will give us a topic of conversation?' My fear tweaks my tone.

'You're a nightmare,' he says, but he's smiling. 'Camille's a sculptress. My friend Theo says she's the best in Paris, possibly even better than Rodin, but we're not to discuss that in front of him.' He laughs.

'Yet you define her in terms of a disreputable relationship with a man?' I ask and Andries shrugs.

'That's just how it is,' he says as we turn the corner. 'Take a right here.' I'm too busy glaring at Andries and not paying attention to where I'm stepping.

'*Pardon*,' I say, banging into two stationary men. They don't turn around. They're at the back of a slow-moving crowd, all stepping in the same direction along rue Lepic.

'Is this for Moulin de la Galette?' I ask and Andries nods as we join the queue and continue the slow stroll. Laughter and thick accents soon surround us. My brother places his arm around my shoulder as we walk another corner. The darkness of the Parisian night is lost; the wooden windmill looms tall and proud above us as we step under an entrance arch and into the courtyard's artificial light.

'Men already stare at you,' Andries says, nodding to those he recognises.

'I'm not trying to attract...' I start to say, worried my brother will think I need or want male attention.

'You've no idea how beautiful you are,' he says, kissing my head and removing his arm from my shoulder. 'Embrace the ambience and have fun. There's a terrace with a view of Paris and the Seine below.' He points to the right. Vibrant, brightly coloured men and women twirl and swerve around us.

I think about walking onto the terrace to admire the view, but Andries shouts to a friend. I follow him with my eyes as he weaves through the crowd and embraces the man warmly. I wonder if he hasn't seen him for years, but suspect it's only been days. My Parisian brother is wholly different to how he is around our Dutch parents. He's tactile, expressive, entirely confident in his own skin. I don't move. Instead, I stand in the entrance, people having to swerve around me to step inside, apologising to me as they knock my shoulder or bump into my slight bustle.

'Your dress, all of you, is stunning,' a woman says in rapid French. She's stopped beside me, the fingers of one hand caressing the deep red satin, the fingers of the other stroking the peacock blue velvet.

'*Merci*,' I say. The French word rolls from my tongue, my accent a little too amplified. She blows a kiss and laughs before heading into the throng. I smile, I nod. I nod and smile, keeping to the edge of the melee of dancers. The music is loud and joyful. I can't help but beam. I can't help but sway my hips in time. This place oozes happiness. It's buzzing like a beehive; Moulin de la Galette attracts joy.

I wish I'd brought my new sketchbook, to capture this moment in words and tiny sketches. Grinning, attractive couples stand in a line, kicking their legs high as they dance in time with each other, seemingly without a care in the world. There's a girl to my right, perhaps only a little younger than I am. Her straw bonnet has a wide pink ribbon, and her blue and pink striped dress moves as she twirls.

Two younger girls, clearly sisters and just taller than the tables dotted around, are chaperoned by an older woman who has to be their mamma. She stands within an arm's reach of her daughters. I see her foot tapping to a beat as the girls perform a lively jig. Further back, over the mother's shoulder and to the right, there's a man commanding the attention of those around him. He's exotic-looking, in striped trousers and without a tie, dancing to a polka with a stunning woman in an emerald-green dress. Perspiration sticks his long hair across his forehead, but soon he pirouettes to the back of the crowd.

I can't keep track of the many dancing couples as they step and twirl without uniformity, yet always with unexpected grace, to the polkas playing. It seems to me that each dancing couple performs a different step. They exist as individuals in a crowd; they're lost in each other, uninterested by what surrounds them. They interpret the music in their own way, not caring if others judge their unbridled joy.

Is this what it is to be Parisian? Could I ever belong in a place like this?

Those who don't dance stand talking, in groups, in couples, rarely anyone on their own. Others sit at small round tables, deep red wine from bottles being poured into glasses or being drunk straight from the bottle to the cheers of those around them. The air swirls with tobacco, laughter and song.

I see the composition. I laugh at the thought of carrying an easel and paints into this celebration – of painting badly in a room full of artists. If I were skilled, I'd use vibrant colours to capture the rich form and vitality with each stroke of my brush. I'd use soft pinks and purples for patches of light, with bolder shades of red, green, perhaps even blue for the figures. I'd want to capture movement in a brushstroke; I'd add depth to my piece with a flick of colour, use shadow and light too. I'd want and need to capture the energy of this scene.

I don't belong here, not yet. I have no role. Nothing creative to contribute to Montmartre. But can I already hope that one day I might?

Terrace And Observation Deck At The
Moulin De Blute-Fin

Ten minutes into my first visit to Moulin de la Galette and already I feel more alive than I have for the last three years, yet not quite bold enough to join in.

'Jo.' Andries' voice. 'Jo, come here.' I search the crowd of faces. Andries is a towering man – all of the men in our family are thin and tall – and I spot him across the makeshift dance floor.

Deep breath. *Smile.* I weave my way through the dancing crowd, unable to see who my brother's talking to. There's chatter, a man's voice, and a shrill woman's voice too, but I can't see beyond Andries. More laughter – one cackling, another low and hollow. Andries runs a palm over his short hair, parted slightly off-centre, flattening any strays into place. I mimic him, touching my hair, checking the fallen curls from my pompadour and resisting a desire to pull it free.

'Do you remember Sara Voort?' Andries asks and I draw to his side. His demeanour's stiff, formal, nodding for me to perform as he steps aside and Sara moves towards me. Her face isn't as round as a full moon, her nose isn't bulbous and her eyes aren't tiny. Rather, almond-shaped brown eyes, a slim small nose, full lips, a heart-shaped face; Sara is beautiful. I'm hoping she isn't as mean as my brother suggested.

'Sara, how wonderful to see you again. How are your parents?' I say, smiling and trying my best to appear confident.

'Darling Johanna, how are you?' she says, grasping my hands as she steps back and looks me up and down. 'They said you'd grown into your beauty.' A pause. Her unnaturally dark eyebrows crease together. 'I heard about that *terrible business* in Utrecht.'

I dart my eyes to my brother. *You told her?* He shakes his head. She's Dutch. Her parents will be like my parents: quick to pass on other people's misfortune. Gossip is carried by haters and spread by fools in the Netherlands.

'Mamma wrote to tell me the minute she heard,' she says. She's all sweet smiles, the gap in-between her teeth big enough to fit a franc, but her words aren't kind. She lets go of my hands and moves to pat my shoulder, as a mother might their least favourite child. Sara offers no comfort.

'My sister's here to study art for the summer,' Andries says, throwing his arm around me and pulling me into an embrace.

I rest my head on his shoulder and that's when movement catches my eye, a blur outside of my peripheral vision. I lift my head and turn to my right.

The man's rigid, he's entirely out of place in the swirl and rush of Moulin de la Galette. He looks as if he's been carved from wood. He's smart in a lounge coat, the front buttoned high, and carrying a bowler hat. He's delicate, feminine even, but with an expression that lacks any warmth. His complexion is reddish fair, but it's his light-blue eyes that tangle me up. Everything about him seems stiff and unyielding; yet as he stands alone among the cheeriness, I can't take my eyes from him. I'm almost frightened to blink in case he disappears.

He sees me. There's a linking. Something I don't quite recognise. Something unfamiliar but necessary. Something magnetic. Does he feel it too?

Andries pulls me in closer to him. 'Don't you think?' he asks, but I've no idea what he's talking about. I laugh, and that makes Andries laugh, then Sara too. Her laugh isn't real though and I've not taken my eyes off the stranger; he's still not removed his eyes from me either.

'Who is he?' I say. I think I'm asking the stranger rather than my brother.

'Who?' Andries asks, and I lift my hand, pointing at the red-haired man. The stranger looks to my finger and then turns away.

'That's him. My friend,' Andries says. 'That's Theo van Gogh.'

'We're to be married,' Sara says. I turn to her as she makes her apologies and hurries off in the direction of her fiancé.

June, 1888.

For the first four days of my stay in Paris, Andries sat beside me while I sketched different scenes en plein air around Montmartre and wrote descriptions of what I could see and hear. He listened to my stories about Eduard and then offered advice on how to stop my thoughts from replaying past conversations and snatched moments. He was patient and kind, and made just enough light of the situation to raise my spirits without dismissing the way I felt.

There's no one but my brother who I can speak to so openly about everything. Already each day with him, exploring Paris arm in arm, reminds me of our carefree childhood years. These are moments I never thought we'd capture again, not now that he's a fully-grown man. I might be his stupid little sister who knows so little of life and men, but no one could ever love him as much as I do.

My anxiety has eased slightly; that frenzied swirl whenever I think about the humiliation of my dismissal from teaching has lessened. Those stabs of Eduard's betrayal linger though — I still can't imagine ever trusting a suitor again. Distance, time, my brother, Paris, books and art: it seems that's all I currently need.

Perhaps I'd rather be entirely happy for one summer than have to spread it over my lifetime.

I haven't yet asked about Theo van Gogh.

Still Life With Paintbrushes In A Pot

We're standing outside Durand-Ruel Gallery on a *rue* just off Boulevard Haussman. I'd expected a stroll up a hill to sketch, but instead Andries points at a poster to the right of the gallery's door.

'Yes, a poster,' I say and my brother wiggles his index finger at it again.

'Use your words,' I say, batting his arm. 'I've no idea why it's of interest.'

He runs his finger underneath the large letters at the top, as if he's underlining them. 'The Anonymous Society of Painters, Sculptors, Engravers, etc.,' he says.

'I can read,' I say, exasperated. 'But who are they?'

'A group of artists. Monet, Degas and Pissarro were founding members,' he says. 'They joined together and exhibited independently.'

I raise my eyebrows at him to continue.

'It was radical back when they began. 1874, I think. They were self-promoted and away from the annual salon,' he explains.

'And that's a good thing?' I ask.

He nods. 'They weren't relying on a jury of artists from the Académie des Beaux-Arts to select artwork and award medals. Less about prestige, more about getting their art out there.'

Chapter One

I point to the date of the exhibition, not quite able to grasp what my brother's trying to say. 'But this poster's two years old.'

'These artists...' He waves at the poster. 'They tend to depict modern life.' A pause. 'And isn't that where your interest lies too?'

'Yes and no,' I say. 'It's more that attempts at copying what's in front of me will be the peak of my limited skill.'

He shakes his head. 'You'll learn,' he says.

'But if the poster's two years old ... doesn't that mean my taste's already outdated?'

He shakes his head again and then claps his hands together. 'You could start a new society with up-and-coming female artists.'

I begin to talk but he holds out his palm to stop me. 'When you're ready,' he says. 'And when you've *learned* whatever it is you need to learn, I know someone who can help.'

This time I shake my head. He's my biggest fan; he's refusing to see that my artistic skill will forever be inadequate.

I scan the names listed. 'Not one woman,' I say. I run my forefinger over each one and count. 'Sixteen men.'

'Marie Braquemond, Mary Cassatt, and Berthe Morisot were missing from the list,' Andries says and I turn to look at him. He's beaming. He's so very thrilled that he can educate me and I'm hit with gratitude. He's clearly discussed female artists with someone else since I've been here.

'Do you know any of them?' I ask.

'No, but I know a man who does,' Andries says. 'He's the one who told me Degas said it was "idiotic" that none of the women were listed. Said he even complained about it at the time.'

Andries' eagerness is contagious; excitement sweeps over me.

'Who told you—'

'I'm sure we could get you an audience with female artists, if that's something you'd be interested in?'

I nod enthusiastically. It is. I'd love that.

'I'll ask him to arrange a meeting. It'd be perfect for you, Jo,' he says. 'I was told we should come here. There's a Morisot inside. Let's...' He doesn't finish his sentence. My brother pushes the door to the gallery, a bell tinkling as it opens, and he strides inside.

27

Portrait Of A Man In A Top Hat

'That's the art dealer Paul Durand-Ruel,' Andries says, stopping and nodding towards the gallery's counter. 'He saved Monet's life.'

'What?' I ask, head flicking from Paul to my brother.

'Stopped him from jumping in the Seine twenty years ago,' Andries says, staring at the man for a little longer than acceptable.

'Do you know him personally?' I ask.

'Alas, no.' Andries gives a small sigh. My brother likes to collect good people: he believes surrounding himself with the worthy attracts more of that treasure to him. 'We don't walk in the same circles. But I've yet to hear a bad word spoken about him. Monet says all the Impressionists would have died from hunger without him. He's quite the man to have onside.'

I look at Paul. A small, beardless man, with the air of an old-fashioned clergyman I'd find in a novel. He's talking to a gentleman in a top hat; his voice is soft and slightly muffled from here. Paul looks up, catches my stare and tips his bowler hat. I smile; I like him instantly.

'A widower with five children, attends Mass every day and has steered clear of all scandal,' Andries says.

'A good man,' I say, still staring at the art dealer, but his eyes are locked on his patron.

'Just back from producing an exhibition of 289 Impressionist paintings at the American Art Galleries in New York.' A pause. 'There's talk of the organisers remounting it for a larger version in Manhattan. Can you imagine?

'No,' I say. I really can't but, one day, perhaps I will.

I turn my attention back to Andries and he's looking around the gallery. Something on the far wall grabs his attention, and his pace quickens towards it. I catch up with him as he stands behind two other men. Indistinguishable from behind, they're identical in top hats and sombre frock coats. They're looking at a painting of a mother next to a cradle.

'That's the Morisot,' Andries whispers. He nods at the painting and I shift to the side for an obstruction free view.

'This woman's work is exceptional,' one of the top-hat-wearing men says. I smile as I step a little closer. 'Too bad she's not a man,' he continues.

'Did you hear—' I say, moving back to Andries.

'Quiet,' he says. He whips his forefinger to my lips. I bat away his finger with my hand. 'This isn't the time or place to cause an argument, Jo,' he whispers.

I offer an angry glare at the men's backs; I must behave, I mustn't embarrass my brother. Not when he's going out of his way to encourage and support me. I know he doesn't feel the same as these men.

'She paints like Manet,' the same man continues.

I can't help myself. 'She paints like Morisot,' I say, my volume a little too loud for inside the gallery. Neither man turns to me, but I hear a tut. I definitely see their shoulders shifting as they side-glance at each other.

'I heard that the two artists respect each other,' Andries adds, in an attempt to placate us all.

'Some of us consider her an equal,' I say.

That causes the two men to laugh loudly.

'She knows her worth,' the same man says, still not turning to look at me, and before I can enquire as to what that might mean they walk away to view other paintings.

I watch them go, neither turning to look back at me, with my fist clenched by my side.

'You're going to have to learn which battles to fight,' Andries says, breaking my thoughts and my focus. 'Inhale. Exhale. Do what's needed to calm yourself, Jo.' He waves his hands in front of my face, wafting air towards me as if that'll cool my mood.

I swat his hands away but then I'm seeing the painting for the first time; it captures me. I can't speak. Minutes pass. I feel my brother's gaze on me. I know he's smiling.

I nod at the painting as I step closer. 'What do you know of her?'

'She juggles family life – a husband and a child – with her work as an artist.'

'The depth of feeling in the painting,' I say. 'It's beautiful. I'm surprised, with the subject of the piece, that it received critical attention.'

'It didn't,' Andries says. I still don't turn to him.

'But the mother's gentle gaze and the child's angelic face,' I say. I can't help but smile. I'm absorbing its beauty. 'It's perfect.'

'She's restricted to painting a domestic setting,' Andries says.

I nod, hoping he'll stop talking.

'You'll experience that eventually, but you're being afforded some freedom this summer.'

I nod again, over-enthusiastically. I need and want to focus entirely on the canvas.

'The locks of hair have been created with the lightest of touch,' I say. I bend in closer to the painting. 'So elegant. But the other brushwork is different. I wish I understood more about it.' I'm close enough that the tip of my nose touches the paint. I inhale the smell of oils on canvas. My favourite scent. 'Are you interested in buying it?'

'The subject of the painting isn't for me,' Andries says.

'I feel exactly like I did when I read Lewes' *Life of Goethe*,' I say. 'That I want to somehow express my enthusiasm, but instead I'm so very insignificant in this painting's presence.'

'I prefer my art to show women in various stages of undress.'

Chapter One

'You wish to gaze upon a fantasy,' I say. 'A woman cast in the role of a beautiful creature, sent to tempt and long for you.' I say the words but I'm not wanting that discussion. Not now. 'But Morisot's somehow captured the texture of the fabric.' I point at the trimmings on the mother's sleeve. 'How's that even possible, Dries?'

Andries laughs. 'And that, my dear sister, is what you'll learn this summer.'

But this painting's about so much more than just technique. This piece is a triumph. Berthe's skill is exceptional, but more than that she's shaking her angry fist at the restrictions that the Parisian art world have placed upon her. Upon every female artist. Her message is clear – she's a match for any male painter. And she'll continue to create exceptional works of art about whatever subjects she's able to access, and despite the expectations and restraints that angry men use to shackle her.

Courage in the face of adversity, that's what I want to learn, in abundance, this summer.

A thought arises. 'Who suggested we come here? Who's the man you've been talking to?'

'Theo, of course,' Andries says. 'Theo van Gogh.'

'Sara's fiancé?' I ask, failing to hide my interest. Andries doesn't answer. 'And he wanted me to see *this* painting?'

'Said it'd help direct your art,' Andries says.

A pause.

'Morisot's married to Manet's brother, Eugène. A painter too. But I heard a rumour that he's writing a novel,' Andries says.

A stab of grief, or perhaps it's fear: Eduard. But there's something else bubbling inside of me, drowning all thoughts of him – hope, possibility, joy.

I turn and throw my arms around Andries' waist. 'Thank you,' I whisper into his chest.

July, 1888.

Already I've been here six days and I've nothing new to tell Dries about disastrous relationship in Utrecht! Talking about Eduard made me furious today. I'm incensed that I believed his countless lies; the more I repeat myself, the more embarrassed I am too. How truly unoriginal of me to give my affections to a man who played with mine for three long years.

Perhaps my brother understood, perhaps he sought to distract my rage, because today he opened up and shared tales of his time in Paris.

He spoke about Montmartre being a space for him to escape and be entertained. He confessed that cabarets and café-concerts were his current favourite places to visit with friends. When that didn't shock me, he talked about renowned performers in romantic and hazy atmospheres. About snatched encounters. I giggled like a schoolgirl at the details of confused liaisons and mismatched relationships.

He described the city as brimming with colourful artists, composers, novelists, painters, poets, musicians, playwrights and sculptors. If Dries speaks the truth, then it seems that every type of creative flocks to exist in Paris. And perhaps, more than that, they all seem to be celebrating Montmartre in their work.

According to Dries, everyone who lives here is about to write an epic piece of prose or paint their masterpiece or compose a heroic symphony. Each individual is living a remarkable life. He said that Montmartre is a pocket of Paris where people don't fail; that they're simply yet to create their greatest piece and that being here sprinkles them all in creative magic.

I can't stop thinking about it. I want to become one of that significant flock; I need to stay here until that happens.

What's waiting for me in the Netherlands? Mamma, Pa, and constant conversation about the shame I've brought upon our precious family name.

I could move here, I could stay in Paris. Be remarkable. Live with my brother indefinitely. Be happy!

Still Life With Meat, Vegetables And Pottery

I n today's letter Mamma demanded that I describe where Andries lives. I've been sitting at the writing desk in my bedroom for the last ten minutes, deciding what to include. *It's in arrondissement 9*, I write. *Across Boulevard de Clichy, just past Pigalle.* I don't add that my brother's apartment is down the hill from Montmartre and only a stone's throw from *arrondissement 18*. Mamma doesn't need to know all the facts.

I add details that I know will please her. That will offer her currency to boast about when next in company. *Rue Victor is a quiet, narrow street, with the elegance of a ballerina and the refinement of a queen. They live horizontally here. What a peculiar observation to make! Yet our vertical living is entirely unknown to these modern Parisians. Still, the buildings are uniformed, with perfectly positioned balconies that offer symmetry to the tall, elegant façades. It's hard to ever imagine the crooked alleyways and disease-ridden slums that existed before Baron Haussmann worked his magic.*

We enter by a grand 'porte-cochère', which is always defended by the concierge. Indeed, the ground floor of this building is devoted to stables and to his quarters. He's a humourless man, close to Pa's age and I've yet to hear him speak. He guards the building twenty-four hours of each day. I'd be entirely dour too if I were woken, at all hours, just to

glide the bolt on an outer door whenever a resident returned! Dries says
that he offers frequent gratuities to appease the man.

A wide circular staircase leads up to the different apartments. Your
son occupies the first floor of the five-storey building – apartment
Number 1. It's said to be the very best in the erection – in terms of both
height and decoration – and thus, as you'd expect, the most costly too.

I look around my bedroom, the nib of my pen poised above its
ink. This room, one of the two on offer, is light and airy, with a
high ceiling and floor-length windows. It's grander and larger
than any room I've ever slept in, but Mamma would see that as a
criticism. She's skilled at bending a harmless comment into
something negative. A dip of the pen's nib into the ink and I write,
The spacious courtyard is for his use only, a fact he's told me at least
seven times during my ten-day stay.

That's ten days of sightseeing and as many visits to
Montmartre. In between his work and armed with my sketchbook,
Andries has walked with me daily to the village. Perched atop the
hill, at first Montmartre reminded me of the Netherlands, with its
old buildings, steep and narrow streets, and rustic windmills.
Quickly, I realised how entirely different it was.

'Jo,' Andries shouts from the hallway.

I put my pen on the writing desk, grab a novel from the bed
and hurry to the open doorway. Andries is bending down and
rubbing a finger over a black floor tile. As he straightens, he holds
the finger close to his eyes.

'Brother?'

'There you are,' he says. He's smiling. His company for the last
ten days has been the best punishment imaginable.

He wipes his finger on the sleeve of his jacket. A slim fit,
partially undone, with his high buttoning waistcoat and watch-
chain on show. His look is finished with a knotted necktie and
polished shoes. He's dressed to impress, but I'm not quite
sure why.

'We're expecting guests,' he says, perhaps reading the enquiry
in my expression.

'I thought I was free to read this afternoon.' I hold up the book to illustrate my point. 'Then you said we'd take a walk to Montmartre.'

Andries shakes a piece of paper in the air. Evidently whatever's on that paper outplays my book and our walk. 'I've arranged for Alexander Comte, a wealthy merchant, to join us for lunch. He'll be here at one o'clock.' He looks at the piece of paper. His index finger points to a list of names.

I lean in to follow his finger as it jumps over names and times. 'What—'

'Arthur Bouget, son of a wealthy shoemaker, at three o'clock. Possibly an unconfirmed at four. Guy Loti, my lawyer at five—'

'What are you up to?' I ask. I place my hand on his piece of paper. I need him to stop moving it around and to let me read what he's written. The paper is flimsy; he tries to pull it away. 'Why are all these men visiting today?'

'Word has spread of both my little sister being in Paris and of her beauty. My friends wish to meet with you.'

'Friends?' I ask. I don't believe him. 'In your *many* recent tales, I've never heard you mention any of these men.' I point at the piece of paper.

My brother shrugs his shoulders, avoiding eye contact, and returns to his list.

'Charles du Musset, newly wealthy, is calling at six-thirty, and Alfred Le Rouge, the banker, is calling for dinner at eight. He refused to come unless I fed him.'

'You're having to bribe people to meet with me?' I ask. There's a flush of heat to my cheeks; I'm not quite sure why. I don't really understand what's happening. 'There are no artists on your list. Shouldn't I meet some if I'm to spend more time on learning technique?'

Andries doesn't respond. Not in words anyway. His lips twist before he sucks them in, as if trying to swallow them away. He pushes the paper to the wall outside my bedroom. He takes a sharp pencil from his jacket's inside pocket and adds something to his list. Suddenly he seems more like Pa than himself. Stiff, single-minded and sombre. There's not a sniff of fun in the air. He's hiding something.

'What are you up to, brother?' No response and a suspicion arises, unbidden but fully formed. 'Are they married?'

A pause. I watch as Andries stops writing. He doesn't turn to face me. He considers my question a little too long. His lips reappear.

'I'm not sure,' he says, still not looking at me but a slight smile forming. He scribbles furiously again.

'You're not sure if your *friends* are married?'

'They're all eligible,' he says. He removes the piece of paper from the wall, folding it in half, and glances at the book I'm clutching to my chest.

'Have you read *Aurora Leigh*?' I ask and Andries shakes his head. 'It's resolving so many doubts and fears I've been struggling with.'

'Make sure it's not in the parlour when our visitors arrive,' he says. 'We don't want our guests thinking you're one of *those* women.'

I laugh. 'But I am one of *those* women.'

'And I love you for it,' he says, reaching for the book.

I twist it out of his grasp. 'You can read it after me.'

He chuckles, the sound making me smile, and consults his gold pocket watch; I study the decoration on the back of the case. An enamel scene of a lakeside with houses, a small portrait of a young woman too.

'Do you know her?' I ask, pointing at the case. He's not listening to me. His mind's elsewhere. He's plotting and planning and, because I know my brother, I know that I'm not being told an entire truth.

'You've fifty minutes to make yourself presentable,' he says, signalling me back into my bedroom with a wave of his hand.

'Are you ordering me to make myself pretty?' I say.

He nods his head, grinning though. 'I'll send Clara in to supervise.'

'But—' I haven't moved.

He turns and walks back towards his parlour, reading his list and muttering to himself with each step.

Still Life With Three Boots

I heard them first, laughter booming from the hallway, as Andries rushed to greet them.

I've been standing in front of an easel for the last half hour, trying to work out what's wrong with my painting. Today's focus was supposed to be an attempt at the new technique people are calling cloisonnism, but now I'm convinced I've chosen the wrong object to paint. I take a step backwards, squinting at the canvas through my eyelashes, trying to recognise Andries' bookcase within the bold form and thick black contours. It's really not very good at all. No matter how hard I squint, it's still unrecognisable. I select a paintbrush with a rounded tip and dip the bristles into black oil paint, ignoring the chatter of Andries and his guests from the hallway. Nine visitors in four days – all young men and not one artist among them. I really don't have the energy for another awkward afternoon of entertaining.

After visit number four – Andries' lawyer, Guy Loti – and suffering the dullest hour of him boasting about the amount he earned and how he'd expect a wife to give him at least ten children, I told my brother that I'd had enough. That I'd no interest in marrying a man who made me want to push my paintbrushes into my ears. Added to this, and much to Andries' frustration, I refused to meet with anyone else that day. I actually said that my heart was 'raw' and 'exposed', that it might 'never heal'. He laughed at that, loud and from his belly.

That was three days ago now and, despite enduring five more introductions to unexciting men, where I did speak the odd word and where I did make eye contact every now and then, not one of them interested me.

It's several minutes later when my brother appears in the doorway to his parlour. He coughs and I turn to the sound.

'We have company,' he says.

I nod pointedly at my canvas, telling Andries that I'd prefer an afternoon alone and hoping he'll entertain whoever it is in the drawing room instead. Andries looks over at my art. His features are set in concentration and I know he's struggling to figure out what it is I've painted. There's no way he can though, what with it being shockingly bad; I quickly decide that I'll agree with whatever he thinks it might be.

'You're too good to be hidden away,' he says.

'This...' I point at the canvas, 'fails to tell today's story. It's awful, at best.'

A slight hesitation. 'I like it,' he says, pushing his hands into his trouser pockets. Andries is a terrible liar. He has no idea what it is. He hates it.

'Only you believe in me,' I say.

'Isn't that all you need, for now?' he asks, he smiles. I nod; it is. 'And this visit's different.'

I raise my eyebrows, signalling for him to continue.

'Two men; one's requested an audience with you. He's even paid his brother, an artist, to come along and give you advice on painting technique. It'll be entertaining, I promise.'

Head Of A Young Man With A Pipe

There's chatter from in the hallway, men's voices, but I can't see beyond my tall brother. He's waiting for me in the doorway. Andries smiles, then runs a palm over his short hair; I've noticed he does this when he's nervous. There's something about all of these introductions that bothers me. My brother's sudden urgency to matchmake doesn't quite make sense. There's something he's not telling me, and, equally, there's something stopping me from asking him about it all.

'Jo,' he says. For fun, I twist my face, like a bad-tempered child, into the ugliest expression I can. 'May I formally introduce the almost renowned art dealer Theo van Gogh and his brother, Vincent.' He bows flamboyantly, his narrow trousers straining with the bend. 'Gentlemen, this is my favourite sister, Johanna Gezina Bonger.'

Andries pauses, clearly enjoying my now startled expression, before he steps aside to allow our guests entrance. 'She's visiting for the summer.'

Before I can adjust my face to neutral and before I can plan an escape to the kitchen for tea and wisdom with Clara, I see the guests. And it is him. It's the man from Moulin de la Galette, Sara's fiancé; it's Theo van Gogh.

With their matching red hair, there's no mistaking that they're

40

brothers, although they couldn't be dressed more differently. Theo, the art dealer, is stiff and smart in a lounge coat and carrying a bowler hat, while Vincent looks like he's been dragged through several hedges by a lame horse. His grey felt hat is askew and his blue smock is covered in a rainbow of paint smudges and streaks: yellow, blue, red, green. He puffs on a pipe, already looking bored.

I'm silent. I'm staring at the brothers. I'm smiling – probably like an idiot.

Over the last two weeks I've heard much about the Van Gogh brothers. They're the subject of gossip in Andries' circle and every person we encounter has an opinion or story about them. Every time they've been talked about, I've listened keenly. Theo, although younger, seems to be quite the emerging figure in the art world. Andries talks about him as if he's practically the King of Montmartre. Apparently, he's regarded as very eligible, but that makes no sense as Sara said they were engaged. *Outlandish Parisian ways*: that's my only conclusion. Perhaps men here are open about entertaining several female companions at once.

Vincent, the older brother, is mainly called 'a penniless artist'. I've overheard Andries and his friends talking about how Vincent enjoys visiting brothels and spending the monthly allowance that Theo gives him on the women who work there. Vincent's the butt of many people's jokes. That kind of comedy makes me itch; I wonder how many in Utrecht and Amsterdam joke about me now.

The Van Goghs walk further into the parlour and I step away from my canvas to greet them. *Oh, God! The canvas.* Today's creation isn't a piece of art I'd ever share with a stranger, never mind two strangers with links to the Parisian art world.

'I wasn't expecting company,' I say. 'Please, ignore *that*.' I gesture to the canvas. 'Really, don't even look at it. Ignore it,' I say, waving my hand in its direction and making sure everyone's attention is now on my rubbish art.

Silence, possibly for a hundred years; they all stare at the painting. I can't bring myself to look at Theo's face. I want the floor tiles to separate and for me and that terrible picture to be sucked down to the basement.

'I came dressed to paint,' Vincent says. I can't help but glance at him. He points his pipe at his smock. 'But it's clear that *she* requires more instruction than I could ever offer.' He nods at my canvas.

'I was trying out a technique. Pushing myself to—'

'She's rather small and underdeveloped,' Vincent says to Andries, interrupting my explanation and staring at my breasts.

I raise my eyebrows, unable to stop the surprise from splashing across my face. *You pompous little man.* I fold my arms across my chest and immediately understand why he'd have to pay women to spend intimate time with him. I need to not say that aloud. I need to perform as is expected, but my hand's already formed into a fist. I so want to please Andries, but one comment from this Van Gogh and I'm already pushed to my limit.

'Vincent.' Theo speaks his brother's name like the letters are burning coals in his mouth.

'Yet entirely ferocious,' Andries replies. 'Beware of my sister's punch.' He looks at my fist.

'And rather old to be without a mate,' Vincent continues, undeterred.

I'm standing right in front of him yet he's got the nerve to bend his neck and look me up and down as if negotiating a purchase.

'Already twenty-five,' Andries adds. I glare at my brother. His moustache bristles are tamed at the ends and they don't turn up or down as he smiles at me. Perhaps he wants to diffuse the situation. Perhaps I need to nod, to reassure my brother, to breathe through—

'I heard a salacious piece of gossip about you. About—'

'You, of all people,' Theo interrupts before his brother can continue, 'should know that gossip dies when it hits a wise man's ears.'

'Thank you,' I say. I allow myself the briefest of looks at Theo. His face offers no reaction or emotion: a blank canvas of a man. I flick my eyes back to Vincent. He's still looking at me, his gaze unnerving and so very unwelcome. The sleeves of my bodice suddenly feel too tight and my high collar strangles my breath.

'Mr Van Gogh, I'm not a painting, created for your pleasure. Do not stare at me like that.'

Andries laughs from his belly. 'Told you she was ferocious,' he says when he's recovered. For the last three days my brother's been stiff and cold during each of the visits from those eligible men. This is the first time he's laughed in his arranged company. Yesterday I'd wondered what he feared about displaying his true self, but that isn't the case today. He clearly enjoys the Van Gogh brothers' company, especially Theo's, and I love Andries best when he laughs from his belly: when he forgets himself in those briefest moments of joy.

'Indeed,' Vincent says. A pause. Like fools, we wait for him to continue speaking. Instead, he puffs on his pipe again and keeps us anticipating, in silence, holding our collective breaths as his eyes wander around the room. 'Do you have an artist that you favour, dear Johanna Bonger?'

'My brother recently introduced me to Gauguin's work. Have you heard of him?' I say.

Vincent's laughter booms around the room. 'Have *I* heard of *him*?'

'He's not that well known,' I continue tentatively, not sure what I've said but I'm evidently hilarious. 'His art's adventurous and different. It's almost primitive, with bold colours and exaggerated—'

'*You* know art?' Vincent says, stopping me short, his eyebrows raised. His eyes meet mine. I'm not sure if this Van Gogh is handsome, slightly odd or overly intense, but I do know that he's rude, irritating and not the kind of man I want to entertain.

'Never underestimate my sister,' Andries says, moving to me and throwing his arm around my shoulder. 'She's quite the artist.'

'I'm really not,' I say, blushing, embarrassed by my brother's overenthusiasm.

'She's a woman,' Vincent mutters, but before I can respond Andries says, 'Come, come, let's know each other better.'

Vincent steps towards me; reluctantly I stretch out my hand as etiquette dictates. I note that his whiskers are in need of a trim and that his gaze pierces from under his bulging auburn eyebrows. He bends to my outstretched hand and, rather than the expected handshake, offers a delicate kiss. I suppose he expects me to gasp or faint at his feet, but instead I grimace in an overly dramatic way and seek out Andries. My *helpful* brother avoids my gaze and sits down on his blue carpet chair instead, smoothing the fringe tassels with his palm. Mamma had declared that my brother *needed* elaborately upholstered chairs with expensive fabric. Like everything he does, Andries took 'elaborately upholstered' to a new level.

As Vincent moves aside, Theo takes my clammy hand and offers a firm shake.

'A pleasure to finally meet you,' he says. 'I've been trying to arrange a time with Bonger for two weeks now.'

'You have?' I ask. My eyes shoot over to my brother and then back to Theo. 'Will Sara be joining us?' I ask, meeting Theo's gaze in an attempt to appear confident and to detract from my moist palm. He looks away. I think his cheeks redden; have I embarrassed him?

Andries coughs, a nudge for me to engage.

'Gentlemen, where are my manners?' I smile at our two guests. 'I'm sure my *delightful* brother will arrange tea for us. We're *his* guests after all.'

Andries laughs, but he takes the hint as he jumps up from his chair and hurries from the room to find Clara.

Head Of A Man

Theo sits with me on Andries' *canapé à confidante*. He leaves space between us, doesn't unbutton his coat and places his hat on his knee. I sneak a glance at him and see his beauty: red-haired, red-moustached, alabaster skin, a constellation of freckles covering his long nose. Only a little older than me, but he has an air of confidence that's been acquired through success and Parisian living. He strokes a palm over the seat's carved gilt wood and then the pink damask silk upholstery. Perhaps he approves, perhaps not; his face remains passive. I stare at his hand a little longer than I should.

Vincent inspects the surroundings. My brother decorates his apartment as if he were a wealthy man. He plays within the circles of the famous, and the could-be famous, of bohemian Paris. He works in the insurance business, treasuring beautiful people and beautiful objects in his spare time. As a result, his parlour's a feast for collectors: the seventeenth-century slate table serving as a desk, the tapestry screen, a recent gift from Edward Burne-Jones, and the Empire Aubusson rug. Yet it's quickly clear that Vincent's unimpressed by the finer items. He walks around the room, passing spiteful comments, before removing a novel from Andries' bookshelf.

'Vincent,' Theo growls. 'Don't touch his things. You know how

Bonger hates that.' He's right, he knows my brother; they're truly friends. My lips twitch into a smile.

Vincent replaces the novel on the shelf, turns and moves towards us. 'Bonger is much like Bismarck.' I wait for further explanation but none is offered. 'Why must I sit though? Because Miss Bonger requested it?' he asks. Theo growls again. 'I feel my conversation will be better if I stand for a few moments and examine these *vulgar* objects that have excited our hosts.' He smiles at Theo, not bothering to look at me, before moving to sit on the blue carpet chair.

Theo begins a discussion about the weather and their recent activities, and Vincent mutters words that I can't quite understand. They might even be in a different language, not Dutch, not French, not English either.

'Have you something to say?' I ask before I even consider how rude I sound. He doesn't reply. Instead he smiles wolfishly and the bubbles of my anger pop in my throat. I'm annoyed with myself for reacting. Perhaps it's because I'm surprisingly keen to make a good impression on Theo.

'You're so lucky to be in the Parisian art world,' I say. I'm trying to ignore Vincent, instead addressing Theo to my right. 'Tell me, who are you all talking about?'

'Have you heard of Henri de Toulouse-Lautrec?' Theo asks. I shake my head. 'There was a recent exposition where he used the name "Tréclau"? He admires my brother.' I shake my head again. I know so very little about Parisian art. 'But clearly you're aware of Anquetin and Bernard's painting style.' He nods towards my canvas.

'My failed attempt at cloisonnism?' I ask, now shaking my head in dismay. 'I've made the black contour lines too thick and it's all feeling forced. I wish you hadn't seen it.'

'It has promise. I can see what you're trying to do,' Theo says, his eyes still on my canvas.

'You flatter me, but *I* can see how awful it is,' I say. I'm excited though; it bounces along my words. I'm both astonished and elated that he recognised the technique.

Chapter One

'Art is a process,' he says. 'These things take time. But tell me, Miss Bonger, what is it that you like in your art?'

I pause. 'I'm fascinated by how artists show movement,' I say. 'People dancing or walking. How do they capture a larger scene when people rarely stand still?'

'Degas...' Theo says the name and then pauses, seeking confirmation that I know who he's talking about; I do. I nod for him to continue. 'He recently told me about his passion for photography. Perhaps how some artists are using such images as reference for their paintings would be of interest? I know Bonger loves that camera box of his.'

I laugh at that suggestion. 'I'm forbidden from ever touching it, unless Eiffel's tower falls and I'm somehow able to capture it happening,' I say.

Theo laughs. It's a full body response: feet stomp, arms wave, torso rocks, the sound deep and loud. 'Your brother's obsessed,' he says.

I like everything about this conversation, about his reaction, about how, for the first time in days, I'm with a man who genuinely seems interested in me.

'I'm taking this summer to experiment,' I say. I nod towards the canvas again. 'To understand art.'

I hear a tut-tut, but don't turn to the sound. I wait for Theo to respond to what I've said, but his eyes are locked on Vincent.

'Have you tried impasto?' Theo asks, eyes still on his brother. 'Vincent's a pioneer in the technique.'

'I've no idea what that is.' Again, I'm embarrassed by my lack of knowledge.

'Thickly textured, undiluted paint, straight from the tube. It's applied with a palette knife and mixed on the canvas,' Theo says.

'I don't have a palette knife,' I say, mortified that all of my responses sound so very inexperienced. Of course I put in an order for basic supplies when I arrived in Paris – a mixed selection of tubes of paint, ten metres of canvas, paintbrushes, a palette – but I didn't even consider buying a palette knife.

Theo waves a hand in the air, blowing away my inadequacies. 'I'll send you one. It'll add dimension to movement and—'

'You make it sound easy, brother,' Vincent interrupts. 'It's not technique, it's emotion, and it's certainly not for the inexperienced.'

'Well, perhaps *you* could demonstrate the emotion,' Theo says, his tone sharp. 'After all, I am paying you to offer Miss Bonger instruction.'

'I don't want to cause any—'

'She doesn't have a palette knife,' Vincent says. He shakes his head and mutters something I can't quite hear. 'Bonger claimed she was an artist, yet she's without even the basic tools required.' He shakes his head again, more robustly this time, and throws in a couple of tuts too. Beads of perspiration trickle down the back of my neck. 'And I'm not convinced a woman with dainty wrists like yours could manage it.'

A pause. Theo glances at my wrists, another pause, and then to my face. I try to smile; it's no doubt weak and unconvincing. I've no idea how I should react. Should I pretend to be shocked that he's looked at my wrist? Is there a wrist-gazing etiquette I've yet to learn?

'Are there no emerging female artists?' I ask Theo. It's a clumsy attempt to shift the conversation away from my wrists and his brother, but it's all I can offer.

He smiles. 'Alas, not many so far this year. There's Berthe Morisot.' My grin hopefully shows my gratitude. That he pointed Andries in the direction of the Durand-Ruel Gallery has been a frequent thought over the past few days. 'She's established and continues to produce exquisite work.' A pause while he thinks. 'Virginie Demont-Breton continues to flourish; her parents are both well-known painters. She exhibited last year.'

Andries practically bounces into the room. 'What have I missed?' His smile is wide; he oozes excitement and mischief.

'Bonger, I've inspected her further and am angered that you never said she was a beauty,' Vincent says.

Chapter One

Why now, Vincent? Because your brother's paying me the attention that's usually reserved for you?

I bite my lip. I don't turn to him; I won't react. I'll show the Van Goghs that I'm mature and calm, even when provoked. Instead Theo catches my eye, his face awash with apology.

'I must say sorry for my brother,' he says in a low voice, his hands clasped together on his lap. 'Paint fumes have depleted his sensibilities.' A smile.

I hold his gaze longer than I should. I smile too.

'And I must apologise for *my* brother,' Vincent retorts. 'He's younger and has had more success than all of us could ever muster. I fear that some of it is even trapped in his protruding forehead.'

Andries' laughter roars around the room. He clearly finds the Van Gogh brothers an entertaining double act.

Clara comes into the parlour before I can respond. She was only fifteen when she started looking after baby me. Mamma knew Clara's mother; Clara never knew her father. She used to call him Othello, and spoke about plantations in Curaçao when I asked about him. Her thicker lips, her permanent suntan and her jet-black hair and eyes, all suggest that her mother fell for exotic charms. She's swaying slightly as she walks, clearly struggling to balance the weight of the heavy tea-urn on a tray. I start to stand, but my brother places a firm hand on my shoulder, pushing me down into the seat. When we have company, I'm not allowed to help her. Instead, I have to pretend that she's not one of the best, most loyal women I know. We remain silent, all eyes on poor Clara, as she places the tray on the walnut and burr table then pours drinks for us all. She keeps her head bowed, only addressing Andries before she leaves.

Vincent sighs, and we all turn to look at him. He waves what looks to be a rectangular sketchbook in the air – covered in a harsh brown hessian material – then places it in his lap.

'Why is it that you're not married?' Vincent asks. 'Miss Voort tells me that you often entertain men.'

'Vincent,' Theo shouts.

I send a silent prayer to stop the flush of heat travelling up my neck; it isn't heard. My guilt, my shame and my anger, they all decorate my face.

'Discussion of my sister's indiscretion in Utrecht is hardly a suitable topic,' Andries says, his tone snappy.

A deep breath in; we wait.

'Aren't we here to help Jo with her art?' Theo asks.

I'm a woman; I'm expected to let them talk about me as if I'm not in the room.

'And why are *you* not married?' I ask Vincent. I'm not yet fully trained in doing what's expected of me. I might even sound like a petulant child, yet still I continue. 'Have you failed to meet a woman who desires you? Are you an example of the single men that are on offer in Paris?'

Vincent laughs. I glare at him, not sure why he finds my insult amusing.

'I'm too busy fixing my brother's trail of broken hearts,' he says.

I look to Andries and raise my eyebrows. *What does that mean?* The *confidante* has a single outward-facing seat at each end, at right angles to the wide central section where I sit with Theo. My brother perches on the seat nearest me and places his hand on my arm. Comfort, not restraint. He'll explain later.

'Unlike our older sisters, who were committed to household duties, our parents allowed Jo to further her education in England,' Andries says. 'They've regretted their decision for several years now, but I love her fiercely and absolutely. She's the very best woman I know.'

'I've no desire for household duties. I was a teacher, in Utrecht,' I say.

'Until you were dismissed,' Vincent adds. His cheeks draw firmly to the bone as he sucks on his pipe.

'Honourable discharge on health grounds,' Andries says, his eyes willing Vincent to dare to argue, but the artist is already on his feet.

'Are we leaving now?' Vincent asks Theo.

50

'*You* can leave,' Theo says.

We watch as Vincent walks from the room, without saying goodbye. Andries laughs. Vincent's behaviour will be excused as eccentricity, but if I'd left in a similar way, my brother would be dragging me back in to the parlour by my skirts.

'Is he always so rude?' I ask.

'Give him time and you'll be the best of friends,' Theo says, but I shake my head in disbelief.

'Tell me, Johanna, how are you finding Paris?' Theo asks, offering a smile. I'm again hit with gratitude for the kindness he's already shown me.

'Stimulating, if a little too hot and containing one too many Van Gogh brother,' I say. Both Theo and my brother laugh.

'So you'll spend the summer here painting?' Theo asks and I nod.

'Reading, writing, painting,' I say. 'I'm hoping to discover more of my likes and dislikes.'

'A perfect summer,' he says, leaning in to me just slightly. 'I represent many artists. And if I can be of assistance… You should meet others and learn more about the Parisian art world. Perhaps I could introduce you to Degas?'

'That'd be wonderful,' I say. 'And I'm keen to meet female artists too.'

'Bonger knows where to reach me.' He waves at my brother. I turn to smile at Andries and he nods in agreement.

'Do you know much about cloisonnism?' I ask. I'm keen to continue our conversation. Hoping to keep his company a little longer. 'I clearly need to learn more.'

Theo glances at my canvas again. 'I'm almost reluctant to say this…' His cheeks flush the brightest red. 'I'm aware I've dropped many artists into our conversation, but they're in my every day. I'm truthfully not trying to impress you by saying, "Look at me and my artist friends!" … but only last week I was discussing that very movement with Dujardin.'

July, 1888.

That he's well connected and offered to introduce me to Parisian artists is both generous and kind of him.

So why do I want to delve deeper into his motivation? I trusted that Eduard spoke the truth; what a fool I was. Is that why I can't just accept that Theo's helping Dries by offering to assist me? That he's simply being polite, a good friend, a gentleman.

Sara Voort said that they were engaged. Theo isn't free to be attracted to others.

Yet here I am, tragically giddy.

Still Life With Mussels And Shrimps

I'm enjoying my first mouthful of shrimp, mussels and peas when the doorbell sounds.

Minutes later, Clara steps into the dining room. 'Miss Jo,' she says. 'Theo van Gogh's asked to talk with you. I've shown him into the parlour.'

I look longingly at the still hot bowl of food. 'But Dries is at work,' I say, unsure if I'm allowed to accept a guest when my brother's elsewhere.

'I'll remain in the room with you,' Clara says. 'Food can wait.' She smiles.

'Do I look acceptable?' I ask, as I stand and twirl.

'Lovely, Miss Jo.'

I hurry from the dining room but stop in the doorway to the parlour. A breath in to calm myself offers a second to admire his beauty, as Theo bends to Andries' *confidante* and flicks through my copy of *Aurora Leigh*. The pink upholstery complements his red hair; his red moustache is clearly oiled and brushed, and those freckles are exquisite.

'Mr Van Gogh.' Theo straightens quickly, his top hat tumbling to the floor. I smile. 'This is an unexpected treat,' I say, walking to him. Theo takes my outstretched hand; this time his palm's clammy, his shake less firm.

'Forgive my calling unannounced,' he says. He looks concerned, his expression set as if he's full of worry.

'Are you feeling fine? Is it Vincent?' I sit. 'Join me,' I say, patting the *confidante.*

I wait for a response as Theo unbuttons his coat and sits next to me. I watch as his fingers trace the cover of *Aurora Leigh*; its edges touch my skirts and Theo's trousers. Clara swoops in to lift his hat from the floor before shuffling back to near the doorway.

'I've never felt better,' he says. He looks up and smiles. His entire face alters; his joy is infectious.

'Have you read any Elizabeth Barrett Browning?' I ask, waving at my book. Theo shakes his head.

'I can't stop rereading this one,' I say. 'It makes sense of so many uncertainties and worries that I've kept in here recently.' I point at my head.

'Tell me more,' he says, leaning in slightly.

'Of course I'm simplifying.' I smile. 'I'm left with the feeling that art is truly wonderful, but that it can't ever replace the hollow where love should reside.'

I wait for Theo to respond, but instead of using words he looks directly into my eyes. His intensity catches me off-guard; I blink first.

'I've never met anyone quite like you,' he says. 'You have me wondering what thoughts of yours might inspire a conversation between us both, and if mine are worthy of inspiring the same with you.'

I'm not sure why I laugh. Perhaps it's a release of this weird energy that seems to have built up between us and into me.

'I'm really not that interesting,' I say, clasping my hands together on my lap and this time Theo chuckles. I like the sound. 'I lived mainly for my books and my study for years. Teaching became my world, then Eduard.' A pause; I can't stop the flush of heat to my cheeks.

'Johanna,' Theo says, leaning forward and placing a hand over mine. 'We all make mistakes.'

'I'm sorry, I'm talking far too much,' I say, looking at our hands and then up to his face. He shakes his head. 'But none of this.' I remove my hands from under his protection and sweep them around, drawing attention to my brother's parlour. 'Not art, not beautiful objects, not even a novel, nothing…' I stop, but Theo nods for me to continue. 'Nothing will take away the feeling of loneliness that sits within me alongside a renewed craving of being loved and to love entirely.'

'About that…' I watch as his cheeks turn the brightest of red.

'I'm sorry,' I say, wanting the *confidante* to swallow me whole. 'I didn't mean to make you feel awkward. I lost myself in *Aurora Leigh* for a moment and you had to bear my ramblings, when you're only here to see my brother. He'll return—'

'No, dear Johanna. Quite the opposite.' He reaches over and, this time, he takes my hand in his; our fingers entwine as if they've always known how. I don't resist. I can't help but think of Eduard and his—

'I think we should marry,' he says.

'What?' I pull my hand from his. I jump to my feet. I look at Clara, but she stands next to the open doorway with her eyes firmly fixed on the tiled floor.

'I want you to be my wife,' he says, getting to his feet and reaching for my hands again.

I take a step backwards. 'Your wife?' An echo.

'You'll make me happy,' he says, taking a step towards me.

'*I'll* make *you* happy?' I'm repeating the words to give myself time to process what's actually happening, to formulate a suitable response. 'Theo,' I say.

'Yes.' I hear the anticipation in that one word.

'You've met me once.' He waits. 'You can't possibly put all of your happiness into my hands.' I wave my palms in the air as if to illustrate the enormity of what he's saying. 'We know so little about each other.'

'I know I love you,' he says. His shoulders have dropped and I can see his confidence spilling off them and down to the tiled floor. 'There was an instant connection?' he says. 'Surely you felt it too?' He's doubting himself.

'That's entirely irrelevant,' I say. 'We know … we know too little about each other.'

'But I can promise you a rich life, filled with variety, one that stimulates your beautiful mind. We'd be surrounded by people who wished us well, who wanted to add to our happiness.'

I shake my head.

'We could work together, find a cause, do something worthwhile,' he says.

Why can't he hear just how ridiculous he's being? Why can't he see that his timing's entirely wrong?

'Do you feel nothing for me?' he asks and I watch his eyes searching my face for a clue: hope, reassurance, validation even.

'I don't know how I feel,' I say, my legs shaking as I move to sit back on the *confidante*.

He frowns and bends his head forward again. 'Are you still in love with *him*?'

'It's not even three weeks since I was caught with Eduard,' I say. 'I don't know if I still love him, but I do know—'

'You made me think you were interested.'

'I didn't *make* you think anything of the sort.' I glare up at him, daring him to look at me. 'It's too soon.'

I've come alive since joining my brother in Paris and I refuse to give that up for a man I've met once: a man who declares his love without a thought for what I might desire. I need time to both heal and to discover what I crave most for my life.

A sneer this time; he looks more like Vincent than himself.

'You're not listening to me,' I whisper.

'You said you required a man's love,' he says, as if that proves his point.

'You're only thinking about your own happiness.' Another whisper.

'Bonger agrees that I'll make you happy and—'

Enough. 'I won't marry you,' I say. I've found my voice again. Thoughts of Miss Voort jump into my head. 'And what of Sara? Aren't you already engaged?'

He pushes his hands into his trouser pockets. 'We

corresponded for a few months,' he says, his tone altered. I can hear anger, bitterness perhaps. 'I may have mentioned a future engagement,' he says. 'But that was right at the beginning. When things were new and—'

'Exactly like this?' I ask, refusing to take my stare from his face. He looks anywhere but down at me.

Are Eduard and Theo the same? Am I destined to be a plaything for deceitful men?

'Do you enjoy asking women to marry you?' I say. 'Is this a cruel game for you? To manipulate affections? To see how many broken hearts you can leave in a trail behind you?'

'Sara's moved on,' he says, the words snappy like a crocodile's bite. 'She and Vincent are—'

'I don't want to hear. Women aren't toys to be passed around and gossiped about.'

'I'm not him.' The words carry a familiar severity; he's a parent scolding his naughtiest child. 'I'm not Eduard Stumpff.'

I stand from the *confidante* again. 'I'd like you to leave now. I have shrimps, mussels and peas to eat.'

'My apologies, Miss Bonger.' His cheeks flush and his eyes remain on the tiles, as he hurries to the doorway. 'I misread your signals. I won't ever bother you again.'

July, 1888.

But I want him to bother me again.

Still Life With Red Cabbages And Onions

Barely nine o'clock and the morning's already warm. The drapes have been drawn, the shutters opened and the bay windows in the parlour are ajar. French conversations dance into the room as people stroll along rue Victor's cobbles. Tinkling laughter, someone singing upstairs, shouts for a *maman*; that sense of never being entirely alone in a city sends a flutter of joy into my stomach.

I sit sideways on the *confidante*. My heeled boots on the pink upholstery. The heavy material of my tiered skirts bunches up around my thighs, as I attempt a loose sketch of my legs from a reclined angle. Mamma still hasn't forwarded my luggage from Utrecht, but Andries has delighted in providing an entirely new Parisian wardrobe: flatter bustles (making my silhouette an S-curve shape), overskirts that swoop up (sometimes rather high, leaving the underskirt exposed and me amused at how horrified Mamma would be), tightly fitted bodices (with very narrow sleeves and high necklines). My new wardrobe bursts with rich blues, greens and reds, with contrasting trimmings and extravagant beadwork. Today an ornate chrysanthemum design decorates my skirts; every day I'm here, I feel and look that little bit more Parisian. Some days I am sure my glee bursts from every pore. My scent is happiness.

'You do realise that I'm not your maid,' Andries says as he enters the parlour. I look up and he's smiling; he's not at all cross with me.

Putting down my sketchbook and pencil, I pull down my skirts and attempt a graceful shuffle to sit upright. I fail; I'll never master grace. My brother flicks the correspondence at the fallen curls from my messy pompadour, before handing me the two envelopes.

'Told you he'd be in contact again,' he says.

'Theo?' I ask, unable to keep the excitement from my voice.

My brother grins and nods. 'Only three days of sulking. I believe his extravagant affections might actually be real.'

I raise my eyebrows, but I can't help but smile.

'Theo's not used to being turned down,' Andries says. 'He's the most eligible man I know. Women are practically queuing outside his apartment for a glimpse.'

I laugh and bat the envelopes at him.

Andries spoke to Theo the day after the encounter. Told him that I needed to heal from Eduard's cruelty and that 'patient support' would be the best approach. So, over the past three days, my brother has eased my anxiety about the unexpected proposal and enjoyed mocking me about Theo.

'I couldn't say yes to a declaration of love,' I say. 'Not after just one meeting.' The *and not when I still have feelings for Eduard*, is left unspoken.

Andries shrugs. 'Perhaps,' he says. 'Be a sightseer for the next week or so, and then we can reassess the proposition.'

'But—'

'And there's a letter from Vincent too.'

He hunches over the top of the *confidante*. I look at the yellow envelopes, seeing my name and Andries' address written on both. One envelope's large and pristine, the other with charcoal thumbprints and splashes of yellow.

'I made the mistake of mentioning the Van Gogh brothers to Mamma. Received quite the lecture about Vincent's loose ways in today's correspondence,' I say. 'How his reputation has travelled to Amsterdam...' I watch Andries for a reaction. I've no doubt he's been telling Mamma tales and I'm curious to know what he's been saying.

'And that's raised your interest in him?' he teases.

'Absolutely not,' I say, then fan myself with the correspondence.

I've no interest in the unpleasant Vincent and it would appear that the Van Gogh brothers are the least of my problems. Mamma's letter is worrying. She's ordered my return home at the end of August. She wrote that there was an 'exciting surprise' waiting for me and that thought already weighs down on my shoulders. Mamma's idea of something exciting would be news that I've been chosen to collect hymn cards after Mass. Throw in my being in charge of the collection basket and Mamma might actually combust from joy. A sad fact, but I don't think I've ever seen her happy about anything related to me. I'm trying to distract myself with the tiny hope that the surprise is a Grand Tour, possibly with a lavish stipend, but I know that's unlikely. Mamma blames the 'foreign water' I drank during my studies in England for my 'inappropriate liaison' with Eduard. On my second day here she even wrote that I was 'forbidden' from drinking any water during my stay. Without even trying, I seem to have perfected every single thing that Mamma hates about modern women. Some days I still wish she liked me.

I place Theo's letter next to me on the sofa and rip open the paint splattered correspondence.

Dearest Johanna,

I'm longing to see you again. I heard that you refused my brother's proposal of marriage. It is customary for all of my brother's former love interests to turn their attention to me, and I look forward to us being better acquainted.

Herewith, a small contribution of a sketch of you that I attempted. I have not yet perfected Gauguin's recall from memory and I can but assume that the likeness doesn't offend you.

I might look in on you today.

Tout à toi, Vincent

'What's he talking about?' I ask. My brother shrugs and looks away; he's a terrible liar.

'Dries…'

A sigh. 'When the relationship hit a rut, Theo wanted a short and sharp end to his association with Sara,' Andries says. 'But he was worried about her madness and how she'd react to his rejection.'

I frown. I don't like how this conversation is unravelling, but I nod at my brother.

'Vincent agreed to take her on.'

'He what?'

'The plan was for Vincent to distract her from Theo,' Andries says. 'It's what they do. Theo attracts many women, and when he decides that they're not for him, Vincent steps in. It's worked many times before, usually takes about a month—'

'It's barbaric,' I say.

'It was working this time, but Theo proposing…'

I shake my head – the Van Gogh brothers invite chaos – as I unfold the piece of paper that Vincent said was a sketch.

'Oh, Dries, look.'

A pen-and-ink drawing, an entire sheet filled with thousands of strokes of varying lengths and thickness, all forming into my portrait. A great deal of hatchwork shows the shape of my face, fine lines render shadows around and between my eyes. This is the first piece of Vincent van Gogh's artwork that I've seen. I'm caught off-guard; it's both beautiful and flattering. Nothing from Vincent since the visit – when he was rude and critical, dismissive too – and now this. Why has he observed me this closely? Has my rejecting Theo somehow made me desirable to him?

'He's quite the talent,' I say. I'm both captivated and distracted by his skill.

Andries leans over my shoulder. 'Look at the additional lines surrounding your nose.' He pokes his finger at the sketch and I pull it away from his reach. 'He's struggled with your overly spherical nose.'

My fingers quickly squeeze the tip of my nose and my brother laughs.

'It's wonderful,' I say. I fold both the sketch and the letter, place them back into the envelope, and push them into my sketchbook. I'll inspect them again later, with Clara, away from Andries' *unconstructiveness*. Perhaps she'll offer wisdom and explanation about this man's sudden interest in me.

'Do you think there's hope for Vincent's art?' I ask, turning to my brother. 'I'd love to see his paintings.'

'He's getting recognition. Theo has great faith in him. He's worked so hard to get Vincent's work into the hands of the right people.'

I laugh. 'Surely Vincent should receive some credit for his skill?' I ask.

'He's created some beautiful things; his flower pieces have *something* about them. I'm always honest with him,' Andries says. His mouth curls into a smile beneath his moustache.

I bat his arm with my sketchbook. 'You criticise Vincent, but you can't even draw a stickman.'

'Constructive criticism,' my brother says, giving his arm an exaggerated rub. He chuckles. 'Isn't that how we all learn? Isn't that how you wish to learn?'

It is, yet Andries never critiques my art. I wish that he would. Perhaps if he was critical I'd feel more like a developing artist and less like a little girl being praised by her favourite brother.

'Mamma would never let you keep that sketch,' Andries says, nodding towards my sketchbook. 'Scandalous association, she'd declare.'

'In her letter, she said that *any association with Vincent van Gogh would cause new shame and more unwanted attention on our family,*' I say, mimicking Mamma's voice. 'She said that I've already caused her *enough heartache to last a lifetime.*' I pause, this time observing Andries. He refuses to meet my gaze. 'I assume you've told her I turned down Theo?'

My brother nods and his eyes shift to meet mine. 'She's of the opinion that you should marry first and then see if it fits you.'

'Your sharing my romantic life with Mamma makes no sense. Tell me what's really going on?'

He shrugs. 'Mamma's fear is that you're becoming highly undesirable.'

I look to Andries; he doesn't offer further agreement or argument, and that's unlike him. There's more to be said. I wait as he moves to perch next to me on the *confidante*.

'Mamma has…' he begins, his voice deeper than usual. 'Now, you need to stay calm,' he says, which of course makes me panic.

Twilight, Before The Storm: Montmartre

I'm up on my feet and pacing a small circle on the Empire Aubusson rug.

'What? She's told you to—'

'She's burdened me with the task of finding you a husband before the end of the summer.'

'In seven weeks?' I ask and Andries nods.

'When was this arranged?' I ask.

'Just over two weeks ago.'

A pause and a quick calculation of recent events. 'When you started inviting every eligible man in Paris to your apartment?'

'Yes.'

He refuses to make eye contact with me. I want to shake him until all of the words and plans he's exchanged with Mamma fall out.

'And you agreed? Not feeling that my opinion on this matter was important?' I ask, my voice almost a shout. 'So, all those dull introductions were because of Mamma?'

'Who would you prefer to find you a match? Me or her?' he says. 'It was either that or they wanted you back in Amsterdam immediately.'

I guess that makes sense. I flop back down into the *confidante*.

'I honestly thought Theo was perfect for you,' he says. 'If he'd not been quite so … impatient.'

I reach over and grasp my brother's hand in mine. 'With your love, your support, with all this time for my books and art, thoughts of Eduard are being pushed away. I'm just starting to question who I am and who I could possibly become. Why would you want to rush me into marriage?'

He takes a moment to reply. 'Because … because Mamma's almost right,' he says. He holds up both his palms to stop me from jumping to my feet in anger again. 'Remaining unmarried, at your age, will make life difficult for you in the long run. You'll become ugly. It's inevitable, Jo. There's little choice.'

'There's always choice,' I say. I exhale through my nose; the sound resembles a snort.

'Mamma's keen to prevent you causing any more scandal. She believes that you've had *sufficient time to remove all notions of freedom from your system*. That the Stumpff debacle was proof of your inability to…' Another pause.

'Tell me.'

'Mamma's already found you a match.'

And now it all falls into place: I understand. 'Is that her surprise?' I ask. 'The reason why she wants me home in August?'

Andries nods. 'He's wealthy but…' His face twists in disgust. 'Really old.'

'Who is he?' I'm shaking from my thighs up to my jaw; the words rattle.

'Do you remember Pa's friend, Dr Janssen?'

'The old man with a face like a suckling pig and an engorged gut to match? Wasn't he married?' I ask. I'm unable to keep the panic from my voice. I rub my now clammy palms on my skirts. *This isn't happening*. I can't believe that my parents would consider *him* an ideal match.

'He's almost seventy, a widower. Mamma considers him a suitable companion and Pa's begun negotiation.'

'Begun negotiations.' An echo.

'There'll be an announcement of engagement by September.'

'I've a price on my head,' I say. I think it might be a whisper.

'That's why I stepped in. Initially, Mamma wanted you home straight away. She knows that I don't approve of the match and allowed until the end of summer to find an alternative,' Andries says. 'I can't bear the thought of you shackled to some ancient bore. I know you'll be miserable and you deserve better… That's why I've been trying to find you someone here, hoping you'd fall in love and be saved—'

'I don't need saving,' I say, but the words lack belief. I'm not convincing my brother or myself.

'I'm on your side, Jo,' he says, and we smile – weak smiles. I'm out of my depth. Fear already bubbles in my belly.

'Let me continue with my introductions here in Paris.' His tone's soothing; he's trying to calm my panic. 'And I said we could reassess Theo's proposal in a week or so.' I start to speak but Andries holds up his palm. 'There are a number of men who would make you a good husband. Many would even let you carry on with your art studies. At least until you have children.'

'But I don't want a husband. It's still too soon after Eduard; I'm not ready.'

Andries shuffles closer on the *confidante* and I lean into him.

'I've negotiated until the end of the summer to find someone suitable. If I fail…'

He doesn't need to finish his sentence.

I'm everything Mamma and my sisters would hate to be. There was a time when I tried harder, but my many failures have worn me down. Measured by Mamma's ridiculous standards, I'll never be good enough. And there's something about here, about Paris, that offers freedom to be whoever I need to be. I want to stay here; I want that with every ounce of my being. The longer I'm away from Mamma, the less likely I'll be to mimic her. I've never said that I won't marry; I simply need time to heal from Eduard's betrayal, time to stop missing him too. Opportunity to find and know who I really am, before becoming a wife, and then even a mother. Andries is older than me and no one's forcing him down an aisle and into a marital bed. Montmartre promises space to be bohemian, flamboyant, artistic. There isn't the rush to marry here.

Or that's what I thought. Until now. Today everything's shifted up a notch. Now everything goes faster than my steady pace.

I stand and walk to the open windows, leaning my head outside and letting the sun kiss my face. I look down to the *porte-cochère*. Clara's standing on the cobbles outside and talking to someone I can't see; it might be the concierge. I watch her pause, wiping perspiration from her forehead and adjusting her cap. A crisp white apron's worn over her black dress, ready to be cast aside if a visitor should appear.

I turn to my brother. 'Pass me Theo's letter,' I say.

Andries mumbles something about him still not being a maid, but delivers the letter to me again. He pulls me into an embrace and kisses my head before moving back to the *confidante*. I open the envelope, removing an object wrapped in brown paper. I rip the covering and see the shiny palette knife. I can't help but smile. I read the letter aloud.

Dear Miss Bonger,

Please forgive my assertiveness during our last meeting. I know that I said I'd not bother you again, but that was, clearly, a ludicrous claim. As promised and in lieu of an apology, find enclosed a palette knife so that you may sweep into impasto with ease.

Thanks to Bonger's extended explanation and finally hearing what you were trying to explain about Eduard Stumpff, I now understand your need to heal from that cruel relationship. I cannot apologise enough for my impatience.

Please, give me the opportunity to prove myself worthy of your love and affection. May I dare to consider that I do not live without hope? Let us become friends first, let us know each other entirely and allow matters of the heart to emerge naturally when yours is free from your past encounter.

If you do not find objections to responding to this note, please allow me to call on you again.

Time goes slowly when waiting!

Chapter One

'He's certainly ... wordy?' my brother says, raising his eyebrows in contemplation. 'But clearly he's still interested in marriage. And the longer you know him, the more you'll like him, Jo. His sense of family matches ours.'

'He listened to you,' I say and Andries nods. 'But he might quickly become bored of me and pass me on to his brother.'

Anxiety begins to flutter in my stomach; what if I start to want him? What if I allow myself to like Theo and he decides he's tired of me? Eduard devastated me, he betrayed me – how can I trust that Theo speaks the truth? At least Dr Janssen won't break my heart, and, right now, that seems more appealing than further despair.

I read the letter again. 'I don't have the space in my head and heart to know how I feel about Theo van Gogh.'

Andries sighs. 'I admit that he's a little...'

'Exhausting?' I say. My words dance along my brother's laughter as he walks towards me.

'I was thinking *keen*, but yes. The poor man's fallen for your charms, my favourite sister,' Andries says. 'And here I was thinking you had none.'

Geranium In A Flowerpot

I've been in my bedroom since my conversation with Andries, dwelling on Mamma's 'surprise', rereading Theo's letter and sending out a million wishes that Vincent won't call. I've decided that I'll fake an illness if he does, something contagious like smallpox or yellow fever. The floor-length windows are ajar, the shutters unfastened and I kneel on the window seat with my head poking out and over the courtyard. A gentle breeze carries traces of baked bread, tobacco and coffee from a neighbour's kitchen; my stomach grumbles, craving an early lunch.

Rue Victor is a gem of a street. It's unexpectedly quiet and there's rarely unknown footfall stepping over its cobbles. The *rue* curves off a busy boulevard and my brother's hidden courtyard, at the back of the building, adds an additional dash of privacy and solitude. Ivy grows up and over the courtyard's three walls, potted geraniums and lilac thrive in the suntrap. There's one entrance – a door that's accessed from a tiny alley between buildings. I've checked, several times, and that door's always locked. Andries fears both passing pedestrians and people he knows sneaking in to explore his secret area. Yesterday he told me that one of his upstairs neighbours, a Muriel Tomas from floor three, had offered him a substantial sum of francs for shared access. His face had beamed with joy when he spoke about how he'd declined her 'generous offer'. Andries explained that Paris concealed a city of hidden courtyards, each a cherished possession for its owner, and that his enclosure was a 'prized additional extra'. It isn't that he's a spoilt child, that isn't why my brother refuses to share. My brother simply accumulates the extravagance and beauty that was banned from our childhood; luxury is his pursuit, collecting beautiful things makes his heart sing. My days here are making me understand and love his purity even more.

Movement catches my eye and I twist to lean out of the window a little further. The door to the courtyard is unlocked. Clara grips the handrail and stares down at the seventeen stone steps. A wave of excitement that the door is finally open is brushed away and replaced by an instinct that something's not quite right. I don't grab my paints and canvas, I don't rush outside. Instead, I stay kneeling on the window seat and I watch her. The parlour's heavy drapes are wrapped around her shoulders and they drag down the steps as she walks. When she reaches the bottom, she pushes them off and they fall to the courtyard's uneven cobblestones. Clara kneels on the drapes, she bends over and clutches her stomach. A pause, but then I hear her sob.

Jumping from the window seat, I run from my room, out of Andries' apartment and out through the *porte-cochère*, along the tiny alley and to the unlocked door.

'Are you hurt?' I ask as I rush down the steps to the courtyard. I'm out of breath but Clara's no longer on her knees.

Church bells toll, calling some to Mass. From the third floor, Muriel Tomas sings a song I don't recognise, her honeyed voice escaping through the open window. Andries' parlour curtains now drape over the washing line in the courtyard and Clara hunches over, one hand on her plump stomach, the other clutching a bamboo beater. Something's wrong; I'm not sure if she's hurt, injured, heartbroken, or perhaps carrying the heavy drapes has exhausted her. The midday sun's far too hot for manual labour.

'Miss Jo,' she says. She straightens up too quickly and reaches for the ivy-covered wall to steady herself. She adjusts her cap to ensure it's straight, then fattens her white apron with her palms and pulls the shoulder straps back into place. I watch as the realisation hits that she's let her mask of perfection slip; she showed her true self.

'Can I get you a glass of water?' I ask and Clara laughs. The sound is fake; it fails to chase away my concern.

'That's my job, Miss Jo,' she says. Her eyes flick up to the open windows. She's searching to see who watches. A drip of perspiration travels down her nose, falling from the tip. She wipes it on the back of her hand and I can't help but spot the wet patches under her arms.

'I don't mind,' I say, but she's already shooing away my words with her beater.

Andries doesn't have other staff, so all the household tasks fall to Clara. She answers his front door, liaises with the concierge, cooks, waits on the dining table, washes dishes, makes beds, polishes my brother's boots, shines his silver and carries out a seemingly endless number of other chores. I told Andries that he needed to employ others, but he argued that Mamma had said Clara would be enough. It'd be clear to an idiot that the workload, especially with my staying, is too much for her. It'd be too much for two servants. I make a promise that I'll talk to him again.

Seconds have passed in my silent observation of Clara. 'Is there somethin' preyin' on your mind?' she asks, interrupting my thoughts.

'I wanted to sit out here...' I stop talking. Clara knows me better than I know myself. 'You're busy,' I say. I shuffle from one boot to the other.

'Never too busy to listen to you, Miss Jo,' she says. 'I'll do the beatin', you be forthright with your talkin'.'

On The Outskirts Of Paris

C lara first came to work for Mamma when I was a baby, only a teen herself and caring for me when Mamma wouldn't. A constant, Clara's helped me recover through every illness and stumble. I think Mamma underestimated Clara, believing she would be the perfect snoop when Andries moved to Paris two years ago. But Clara's refused to betray my brother, and I'm quite sure that Mamma will never welcome her back into her household in Amsterdam.

'I've spent the last hour blotting out all thoughts about him, but...'

She nods for me to continue.

'Do you remember Pa's friend, Dr Janssen?' I ask.

'The widower,' she says. A statement. She hits the drapes and sends dust flying into the air. I move out of its path.

'The old piggish man,' I say. 'Well, surprise,' I fling my hands into the air, 'I'm to marry him.'

Clara doesn't respond, instead she hits the drapes again, and then again. Her beats are weak.

'You knew?' I ask and she nods.

'Master Andries might have mentioned somethin'.'

'Why am I the last to know?' I ask. I want to throw myself onto the floor. I want to bang my fists and kick out at the row of potted

73

lilac by the wall. I don't though. 'The man's almost seventy and my parents will want to announce our engagement by September.' I pause and the silence is filled with another beat of the drapes. 'Why would they consider him a match?'

'He's rich,' she says, catching her breath. 'Your parents consider money to be all that matters.'

'Dries wants me to marry one of the eligible men on his list. It's all "Lie back and do what's expected" with him. Can you imagine?'

'I'd rather not,' Clara says. Her thick lips curl into a smile and I laugh. She returns to her work. 'Now best you stop soundin' like a brat.' She pauses. Her eyes flick up to the open windows again. 'Master Andries has been showin' you men who aren't fat and seventy. Has your best interests at heart, Miss Jo.'

'But I don't want to marry. Not this summer. Not until I stop loving Eduard,' I say. 'You understand that, don't you? You're almost forty and exist just fine without a husband.'

'Another person's perfect life isn't always as it appears. We rarely get what we might be dreamin' we deserve.' There's sadness in her tone. Romantic love isn't something we've ever really discussed. When I was in Amsterdam I never showed an interest in courting and Clara's not so much as hinted that she's found love.

'Have you ever been in love?' I ask.

'Once,' she says. Another beat. 'Was enough for me.'

'Who was he?' I ask, but she shakes her head. I don't know if the memory's too painful or if she somehow thinks it'd be improper to discuss her personal life with me. I wish she would though.

'I'd not kissed a man before Eduard,' I say, offering a little more of myself in the hope that she'll trust me with her secrets. 'And look where that got me.'

'He's the only one you've loved?' Clara asks, her eyebrows raised. She stops her beating. I smile and nod my head.

'I even thought about ... you know,' I say. Clara smiles.

'But you didn't?' she says and I nod again. 'I've had my fair share of romantic trysts,' Clara says.

'In Paris?' I ask. 'Since I've been here?'

Clara laughs. 'I barely have time to sleep these days, never mind gallivantin' around.' She returns to her beating.

'When then? Who with?' I ask. 'Tell me about them.' I'm desperate to know more about Clara's experience. I need to learn about being a woman.

She doesn't respond. I watch as the woven head of the beater creates a strong, flat surface, releasing dust without damaging the drapes. It's clever. Her strikes have a slow rhythm and little strength, but perspiration curls her black fringe and runs down her long nose.

'There's much you don't know about me, Miss Jo,' she says. 'Needed more money and even worked as a model for a sculptress until a few months back.'

'Was it Camille Claudel?' I ask.

Clara nods, her eyes wide. 'You know her?' she asks.

'I've heard so much about her,' I say. 'Is she wonderful? Do you think you could introduce me to her?'

She shakes her head. 'I liked modellin' for Miss Claudel, but it all got to be a bit too much. What with her wantin' me all hours and your brother needin' me here, and then me not feelin' too good. Exhaustion, I reckon,' Clara says. 'Too many fingers in too many Parisian pots.'

'What's she like?' I ask.

'Fiery and with more talent than that Mr Rodin.'

'Creating every day and being surrounded by other artists. She must wake each morning excited about the day ahead,' I say. 'I wish I had her life.' I offer the words in time with the beat. Clara stops, transferring the beater to her left hand and wiping her palm on her apron. She's tired, looks too old for her years, and there's something else: her skin's a shade too pale for her colouring, the whites of her eyes have an odd sparkle.

'Now,' she says, interrupting my inspection, 'don't go wishin' for things you know nothin' about.'

I try to imagine what I might not know but fail. Then, 'Are you happy, Clara?'

She hesitates. 'I've you and Master Andries, a good job and few needs. I'm lucky.'

'All I really want is to be happy,' I say.

Clara laughs and shakes her head. 'Miss Jo, I've known you since you were this small.' She rocks the beater as if it's a baby. 'And you've always been searchin' for more than your family could offer, and more than settlin' for just being happy.'

'I know,' I say. 'Theo said we could work together, find a cause, do something worthwhile. I can't stop thinking about that.' A pause. 'It excites me.'

She stands still, beater in hand and I wait. 'Do you think being without a husband will make you happy?'

'I don't think an arranged marriage to an old, piggish man will bring me joy…' I shudder. 'Look at Mamma and Pa.'

'Oh, you and your riddles. If that brother of yours can match you with the right man.'

'He thinks Theo's an ideal match for me.'

Another pause. Clara, the beater poised, nods for me to continue.

'You heard the proposal,' I say. 'But what if he just likes the idea of being in love. That he enjoys how it feels when women fall for him. Then, when that happens, he panics and wants to run away.' I sigh. 'What if he rewrites what's occurred between them, making himself a victim even, to ease his conscience after Vincent's stepped in to divert affections?'

'And you worry that's what he'll do with you?' she says.

'Sara Voort…' I shake my head. 'I've no idea what to believe.'

'Mr Theo isn't like that Eduard Stumpff.'

'How can I be sure of that?' I say and Clara shrugs her shoulder. 'But, aside from that, who proposes after one meeting?'

'And who says yes?' Clara says. She smiles.

'I hoped you'd tell me what to do next.'

'Isn't my place, Miss Jo,' she says. 'What do *you* want to happen next?'

There's no hesitation in my reply. 'I'd like to get to know Theo, as friends, to stay in Paris and know more of the art world. To never have to go back to Amsterdam and definitely not to be within touching distance of Dr Janssen.'

Clara stops beating. 'Then tell that to your brother and to Mr Theo.' She stands still and straight, the beater in her right hand by her side. She looks down at her apron and shakes her head. 'I'm filthy. I need to change into a clean cotton dress … apron and cap too. Master Andries will be expectin' his lunch on time.' She waits for me to turn back into the house. She knows not to leave me in my brother's courtyard.

'Be careful with that Vincent van Gogh.' I wait for Clara to elaborate, but instead she holds my gaze, expecting a response.

'If he calls today, can you tell him I'm desperately ill with a contagious disease? Say my skin is yellow and I'm covered in boils?' I ask and Clara laughs again. 'I worry I'll turn into my mother,' I say and Clara shakes her head.

'Won't ever happen, Miss Jo. There's too much good in that heart of yours.'

I throw my arms around her. She feels smaller than when I last hugged her, like there's somehow less of her soul. She's aged decades in just a few short years and there's a smell I don't recognise: sour with a tinge of damp. The force of my hug makes Clara stagger back a few steps. I mumble an apology, before releasing her and heading back up the steps to the tiny alley.

Hand With Bowl And A Cat

L e Chat Noir looks like a curious parlour and the owner, Rodolphe, who my brother described as 'a failed artist', has covered the walls with the finest artwork from his friends. It's impossible to look closely at the art though, as this place is jam-packed, so instead I'm falling a little in love with the display of ceramic cats that covers the huge open fireplace next to us. I couldn't miss the black cat on the zinc sign outside or that the stained-glass windows in here each feature a feline friend, and it's those unexpected details that thrill me: a large ceramic cat's head in the centre of a chandelier, a tapestry depicting a black cat's story on the wall nearest to me and I've spotted at least seven real cats too, in various states of attack and sleep, dotted around this room.

'I can't quite understand the urgency to be here,' I say. 'Is he dead or not?'

'Not,' Andries says, waving and nodding to the many people he recognises. He's laughing again. 'The man's a genius. It was a hoax to drum up more custom.'

He's talking about the funeral procession through Montmartre this afternoon. I'd told my brother that I needed fresh air, explaining how I'd briefly talked to Clara in his courtyard this morning. Andries had suggested a walk while the drapes were rehung in the parlour.

When we'd arrived on Boulevard de Clichy we'd caught the end of the funeral procession and when my brother learned who had 'died', there was at least five minutes of him sitting on the cobbles, lost in personal grief. It was Andries' dull lawyer, Guy, the man who'd fancied the idea of me popping out a million children for him, who'd broken cover from the procession and told my brother about the 'fake death'. The man who we'd believed had died, a Rodolphe Salis, had arranged the procession himself. Guy told Andries that Rodolphe was very much alive and the purpose of the 'trick' had been to attract new patrons to his cabaret club, Le Chat Noir. At that time I didn't ask how faking a death was good for business.

Now I can see first-hand how the man's a mastermind. Because after the procession Andries was desperate to visit Rodolphe's club, to check for himself that the man wasn't deceased. That's why we're here this evening and clearly many others had that same need. We managed to claim the last round wooden table and two chairs and, amidst a fog of tobacco smoke and raucous chatter, Andries succeeded in ordering us two mugs of Bavarian beer.

'Such frightful and vulgar types, these women who drink beer,' he says, he smiles, lifting his mug to mine.

'Santé. To the beauty of Parisian life and to those ugly women who enjoy this glorious boisson hygiénique.' Our mugs clink together.

'That's a Van Gogh,' Andries says. He points over my shoulder to the far wall. I turn and look, but can't really see where Vincent's art might hang.

'The master of ceremonies should announce the first act soon,' Andries says. He puts his mug on the table and consults his gold pocket watch, but then he's distracted and his eyes dart around the room. 'Look! Here he is,' he shouts as he stands. 'Not even slightly dead.' My brother's laughter booms out, attracting the attention of a passing man. He's tall with short reddish hair and pointed red whiskers and, on seeing Andries, the man's face beams with joy.

'Bonger,' he shouts.

My brother embraces him and, when he's finally stopped slapping his friend's back and is satisfied that he's not about to keel over and die, they turn to me. 'Salis, this is my sister, Johanna.'

I stand and knock the wooden table with my knee. I manage to swoop up Andries' mug of beer before it tumbles over. 'You gave my brother quite the shock,' I say.

I hold out my hand, the one that's still gripping a mug, beer sticking to my fingers, but Rodolphe bends slightly to embrace me. '*Je suis désolé.*' He kisses each cheek. 'So you're the lady Theo van Gogh's in love with,' Rodolphe says. He concludes his sentence with a dramatic wiggle of his eyebrows; I can't help but laugh.

'We've met twice now. It's ludicrous,' I say.

'Jo,' Andries says. I like that he won't have a word said against his King of Montmartre. I want to keep talking about Theo; I'm collecting opinions. I'm keen to know if Rodolphe thinks the man's one bad decision away from being admitted to an asylum.

'Come on, brother,' I say. I wave the beer mug in the air, sending drops in their direction. 'Even you agree that a proposal of marriage, after one meeting, smells of desperation. He *thinks* he loves me.'

Rodolphe laughs and Andries shrugs his shoulders. 'It's her first time in Paris,' he says to Rodolphe. 'She's still very Dutch.'

'Then I'll tell Theo to be gentle with her,' Rodolphe says and winks.

I can't help but laugh. He places a hand on Andries' shoulder and leans in to whisper. I watch as my brother chuckles, before turning his face from my sight and leaning in to Rodolphe's ear. Whatever words are exchanged, they're both amused. More mutual slaps to each other's back occur before the master of ceremonies turns to greet a different patron.

We both sit down and I hand Andries his mug of beer. 'It's a peculiar atmosphere,' I say.

'*Santé*.' We clink our mugs together again. Andries is smiling, still amused.

I glance around the room. 'Is it supposed to be a music hall or an ironic art salon?'

'Both. Salis' idea is to cater to painters, composers, poets,' Andries says. 'Everyone comes here. There's Toulouse-Lautrec, Signac, Debussy—' He points at people quickly and I can't quite keep up.

'Toulouse-Lautrec?' My eyes dart around. 'Theo mentioned him.'

'Over there. Shall I introduce you?' I shake my head. 'That's one of his too, I think.' He points to a wall on my right. I can see a number of canvases but the fog of tobacco and the dim lighting prevents a clear view.

I take a sip of beer.

'Salis said that Sara Voort told Theo that she was able and willing to accept a proposal,' Andries says. 'As if the one you declined is now somehow up for grabs.' He laughs.

'And what did Theo do?'

'Told her that there was only one woman he'd ever marry.' He winks at me and I smile. 'Theo's in love,' Andries says. He leans in closer, lowering his voice. 'And Sara's crazy.'

I shake my head. Society always blames its women. No one talks about the man's role in a once stable woman's decline to 'crazy'.

'She's telling anyone who'll listen that you've cast a spell over poor Theo.' He squeezes my hand; I hope he's joking. 'If you're concerned about Sara, Guy Loti's still top of my list.' He looks around again and then waves at someone.

'Is he here?' I ask and Andries nods.

'Not the most entertaining man, but he's wealthy and keen to start a family. His first wife died during childbirth last year. You could be quite the tonic.'

I shake my head. 'He requires ten children,' I say, gulping down the remains of my beer.

'We could come to an agreement where you're allowed to pursue art, at least until the first child's delivered safely.'

I turn and see that Guy's watching me. His expression's sturdy, unlike mine, which I'm sure is currently quaking. He's a very tall and a very tubby man, with a circular, spongy face. His whiskers – they frame his features – are grey and bushy. I'd consider his appearance strong, others might think him handsome. But there's something about his glance that unsettles me. A tiny voice inside my head screams for me to run away from him. My brother's plan to have a marriage of convenience with Guy is so very flawed; my body's shrieking in protest just sitting in the same room as him.

'So, with the end of summer fast-approaching, your only choices are either Loti.' He nods towards where Guy is sitting and I just know that the man's still staring at me. 'Or Theo...' Andries says. He looks up to the ceiling, as if praying for some kind of heavenly intervention. 'Mamma would approve of your association with Theo.'

I nod. 'I was going to talk to you about him on our walk earlier, but...' He leans in closer and bobs his head for me to continue. 'I'd like to know Theo more, to take him up on his offer of time and friendship,' I say and Andries claps his hands with excitement.

'That's wonderful news.'

I want to join in his enthusiasm, but instead my eyes remain fixed on my empty beer mug.

'There's a but?' he asks. I both hate and love that he knows me so very well.

'What if I commit to him and his infatuation ends?' I say and Andries sighs. 'Imagine if he passed me on for Vincent to distract. I'd be back in Amsterdam and married to that stinking, fat—'

'I genuinely doubt that would happen, but there's still the safer option.' He nods in Guy's direction.

I shake my head. There's no way I could trick my body and mind into pursuing the eligible but creepy lawyer.

'Women your age, especially those who refuse to marry, are always viewed with suspicion,' Andries says. He bobs his head in enthusiastic agreement with himself.

'But not men?' I ask, batting his arm with my hand.

'Loti said that if you marry he'll make sure you have all the...' His face is suddenly serious. I wait for my brother to continue. 'All the dresses you desire.'

Good God! 'I have all the dresses I require already, thank you very much,' I say.

His loud belly laugh surprises me; I can't help but giggle as he throws his arm around my shoulder.

'Your face,' he says. 'Are you ready?' he asks, pointing at the stage as the master of ceremonies looks to be preparing to announce the first act. 'The *théatre d'ombres* will begin in a few minutes.' He holds our empty beer mugs in the air and wiggles them in an attempt to attract the waiter's attention. 'There'll be songs and other surprises. You're going to love it, Jo. I promise.'

'Are women really charmed at the thought of a man buying them a dress?' I ask, shaking my head.

'*On peut avoir la même chose, s'il vous plaît?*' he shouts into the crowd.

July, 1888.

After how late we stayed at Le Chat Noir last night, and how many mugs of beer we consumed, today was supposed to be a lazy day. I'd fallen asleep on the confidante when Dries came rushing in and woke me. Vincent had written, proposing a wonderful day out with the Van Goghs tomorrow. Clearly, he's being supportive of his brother and wishes us all to get along! My favourite part is that I'm being allowed to walk to Montmartre on my own. Ten to twenty minutes alone, in Paris, before I rendezvous with Theo and Vincent outside Moulin de la Galette at eleven o'clock.

Next the brothers will accompany me to see several artists at work in their ateliers. Vincent said one of the workshops has two emerging female artists creating there and we're to lunch with them both. Dries was super excited for me. He even mentioned how this could be the very first meeting of the new society for up-and-coming female artists that he dreams of me founding. He's furious that he has work he can't miss, and was a little concerned about my walking alone for the short distance to Montmartre, but I convinced him that I'll be fine and he trusts the Van Gogh brothers (possibly Theo more than Vincent).

Dries also said that I need to make a list of art techniques that puzzle me before tomorrow and that Vincent has promised to demonstrate them all. He made no comment about my spending the day with Theo and I tried to keep my expression entirely neutral, but this will be the start of our friendship.

I've already made three lists of techniques and planned my route to Moulin de la Galette.

But now I'm too excited to sleep.

First Steps

R ue Victor might be a quiet, narrow street, but the same can't be said for Boulevard de Clichy. I'm about to cross the road when I hear the crack of a whip and a scream of, '*Hé, la-bas!*'

I jump backwards. '*Pardon, pardon,*' I say. I smile and wave at the coachman as the *fiacre* dashes past. Eyes darting left and right, I scurry across the boulevard and turn onto rue Lepic.

After only a couple of strides, I stop walking and someone bangs into me. '*Pardon,*' I say. I don't turn to look at them. There's a mumble and a grunt, but still I don't turn. Instead, I look ahead, bewitched by daytime Parisian life on rue Lepic, wishing I had my sketchbook and that it would be acceptable to sit down on this very spot, making notes and tiny drawings of what I can see.

There's a steady stream of merchants straining to push their little wooden hand carts over the cobblestones. The air is filled with their calls as they shout about the goods they're selling.

'*Voilà des beaux poissons!*'

'*Demandez des haricots!*'

'*Voilà des bons merlans.*'

They compete against each other to be heard. Hand bells, whistles, bellowing out their call – the vendors contend with each other for that all-important sale. An odd little man wanders alongside me, stopping and nodding for my attention. A large tin can is strapped to his back, looming over his head, with cups hanging from hooks off the sides. I shake my head. I'm not going to buy anything. He rings his handbell as he walks away.

A well-dressed man – pinstriped trousers, lounge coat, glossy boots – happens to be manoeuvring around me at that very moment. '*Excusez-moi*,' I say. 'What's he selling?' I point at the strange contraption on the odd little man's back, ignoring that my talking to an unknown gentleman is entirely improper.

The man stops, clearly shocked that I've spoken to him. He looks from me to where I'm pointing. He removes his well-brushed bowler hat and wipes his brow with a handkerchief, then he holds up his hand. 'Wait for it,' he says.

'*A la fraiche!*' the man sings, his voice hoarse from hours of calling.

'Sugared water,' he says. 'It's quite delicious, but there are too many vendors in Paris.' Hat back on head and with a slight tip of the brim, the gentleman continues along rue Lepic.

I walk again – my cheeks already aching from my constant smile – keen to be on time for my arranged meeting with the Van Goghs, when a different vendor bounces past. He skips with two black bags slung over his shoulders. I stand and watch as he stops in the middle of the street, dropping his bags. A coat, several hats, various household essentials, spill onto the stones. I'm horrified. *Fiacres* don't stop in Paris. They rule the cobbles. There'll be one rushing along here any moment, squashing the vendor and his goods until they're as flat as a crêpe.

'Move,' I shout, and then, '*Bougez-vous!*' I look left and right, straining to hear the sound of a distant whip, yet no one else seems concerned. Two maids now bend over the bags, one grabs a large copper nougat mould, the other inspects a silver candlestick. All the time they talk and, in less than a minute, francs are exchanged.

Bags back over his shoulders, the man skips away singing, '*Marchand d'habit. Marchand d'habit,*' with every bounce. I shake my head. Panic over. I can't help but smile again.

Parisians stroll along the cobblestones and around me. They

have places to go, people to see. They're insusceptible to the charm of the sellers. I'm not. The longer I stay here, the more I have the urge to buy every single thing they're selling: even the whiting.

Church bells ring. Eleven o'clock. I'm late. I scoop up the material from my skirts and run along the cobblestones. Mamma would be horrified; she'd have me arrested and sent back to Amsterdam immediately, but she's not here to see me run.

This is the freest I've ever felt. This is the most alive I've ever been.

I arrive outside Moulin de la Galette a few minutes late and out of breath. I slump over, hands on my knees, trying to suck in air. It takes me a couple of minutes to recover and to realise that neither Vincent nor Theo have arrived yet. I'm not sure what to do. Perhaps I've missed them. Surely they'd have waited a few minutes?

I stand under the entrance's arch, the wooden windmill tall behind me, chatter from its terrace a distant rumble. I look left and right, trying to spot the brothers through the stream of Parisians, *fiacres*, vendors and their carts, but there's not a Van Gogh in sight.

'Johanna Bonger,' I hear and I turn to face the windmill. Vincent's there, pipe in hand as he strolls over to me. 'So nice of you to turn up,' he says. He wears the same grey felt hat and the same blue artist's smock. The rainbow of paint seems brighter, the quantity of smudges, splotches and streaks increased. I look beyond him, but Theo isn't there.

'Is your brother—'

'Work that is far more important than you or me occupies him,' Vincent says. 'We shall walk until he graces us with his time.'

That Theo thinks more of work than me shouldn't stab into my belly, but it does. Of course I'm disappointed that he's not here, but it's more than that. It's a niggle and it's a fear that he's already passed me over for his brother to distract. Him not being here and my being alone with Vincent are neither what was promised nor what was arranged.

What to do? Stamp my feet and refuse to walk with Vincent? Demand that he runs off and brings back his brother?

Vincent coughs. Perhaps to get my attention. 'There are still artists to see,' he says.

I nod. There are, and techniques to be demonstrated – that remains unchanged. It's clear that Vincent's arrived dressed to paint and therefore willing to teach me. He's considered me before his own art today. I can't miss this opportunity to meet and learn from other artists. Andries would agree. Perhaps it's even fortuitous that I've this chance to form a friendship with Theo's brother and best friend.

'Lead the way,' I say.

View From Theo's Apartment

'S ince Theo sent the palette knife, I've been trying to find out more about your impasto,' I say. 'What is it about the technique that appeals?'

'Texture,' Vincent says. One word and then he shrugs his shoulders. His pace is quicker than mine, causing me to almost skip to keep up. Sharing his knowledge with someone as inexperienced as me is evidently beneath him.

'That's it?' I ask. I'm unable to hide my frustration.

He sighs. 'Sometimes the subject demands less paint, other times the material. They place their burdens on my impasto.'

'To make the brushwork more visible?' I ask. 'Once the paint has dried?'

He tuts. I've no idea which of my words have offended him, but his unwillingness to explain his technique is frustrating. We've been walking unaccompanied around Montmartre for over an hour, no doubt seen by all of Andries' friends, and there's still no sign of Theo.

'Have you any idea when your brother will join us?' I ask. 'Won't your artist friends be wondering where we are? What time do they expect us?'

Today isn't going to plan. So far all we've done is walk, and I can't shake the feeling that I'm being paraded like a prize-winning cow. What did Vincent hope would happen? I'm tired and I'm desperate for a drink; I'm even tempted to buy sugared water from the next vendor I see. He's not taken me to see artists at work in their ateliers, he's not even mentioned the two emerging female artists who want to meet me, and my stomach growls for food. Mainly Vincent's jumped from topic to topic. Is his unease because Theo isn't here? Am I merely a pawn in a game between two brothers?

He's flitted between talking about his family, about overbearing siblings, his art and not quite fitting in. He's spoken about Jean Richepin, Emile Zola and Edmond de Goncourt: novelists I've not read – much to his disgust. Vincent hasn't asked one single question about me, clearly doesn't consider me worthy of instruction. He has shown no interest in my views on art; yet why would he invest time and creativity in drawing my portrait, if this is how he feels about me? Why would he invite me to a day that promised so much, yet make me feel that my presence is inconvenient? Instead, he likes the sound of his own voice and I'm beginning to suspect that he consumed alcohol for his *petit-déjeuner*. Vincent van Gogh both demands and expects attention.

'He'll find us,' Vincent says, breaking my thoughts and dismissing my concerns. Could he be judging me? Was today a test? Has this Van Gogh already decided that I'm undeserving of his brother?

We continue to walk quickly, with the pace suiting him. I've no interest in taking his arm, and earlier, when our steps collided, our fingers brushed each other; his touch has left me feeling uncomfortable, unsettled too. I'm pushing aside my spiralling thoughts of what Andries will say about all of this. I made the wrong decision – I should have returned home the moment Theo didn't turn up.

I try to admire the summer sun and the scenery, hoping that Theo will arrive at any moment; if he does, I'll be creative in what I tell Andries about time spent alone with Vincent. The temperature has cooled slightly from the recent heatwave, but still exertion of any form, especially in these skirts, is tiring. I use my handkerchief to dab beads of perspiration from my face. We walk among courting couples and young chestnut trees, my head full of new beginnings and thoughts of the impossible love stories others might be having in Paris this summer. There are so many sights I'd love to stop and sketch or write about, but I'd never have the courage to draw anything in front of Vincent.

'Do you ever look at the beautiful sky, see the clouds sailing through it,' I say, stretching my neck back and looking at the blue overhead, 'and simply feel true gratitude for nature?'

Vincent wipes his nose on the back of his hand, looking to the sky briefly but offering no comment.

'So few observe what's around them,' I say. 'In Paris, I'm finally beginning to understand Wordsworth.'

Vincent snorts; I've clearly, and unwittingly, amused him. But why must he mock me? Didn't he manipulate the situation to spend this time with me? I want to admire his knowledge and intellectual skill, but instead my discomfort grows.

Still, from the highest part of the hill of Saint Denis, Vincent points to vineyards on its slopes, to windmills, to small cottages and to gardens. He waves towards where he once placed his easel and canvas, talks about where winds swept away his, where light wasn't favourable, where a dog chased him up a tree. He shows me vague snippets of his life as an artist and I take mental notes of where to visit later with my sketchbook. We hurry past raucous café-concerts and we peep into cabarets mocking bourgeois morality. Smoky atmospheres, artificial stage lighting, boisterous laughter: those sights and sounds excite me.

Vincent's almost skittish though; his eyes dart from sound to sound, as if he fears he's missing out. I watch as he waves excitedly to those who shout his name, at how he yells manically while sharing peculiar jokes with people I don't know. Artists, writers, musicians and radicals – they all know him. A tiny taste of an artist's daytime life and despite his rudeness I'm craving something similar but different – something that belongs to me, or somewhere I belong. Montmartre promises me most of all my desires – happiness, freedom, pleasure, entertainment, stimulation, creativity – yet still I'm constantly being reminded that I won't ever be permitted to live like a man. Is it too much to wish for women to have equal freedoms? It's not that I seek to be selfish and manipulate people, like so many men I've encountered, by pulling strings and expecting others to perform. Instead, I long to be free of the strings that others have attached.

But where are you, Theo?

'You said that you don't sketch from memory. Dries said it was "visible reality",' I say and Vincent nods. 'Then what if you're out and the urge to create overwhelms you?'

'All artists carry a sketchpad,' he says. He pats his coat pocket.

We walk another few steps in silence. 'We're learning much about each other,' Vincent says, pausing to turn and look at me. I refuse to make eye contact and continue walking.

'In some ways, yes,' I say, 'but I'm hoping for more.' I'm referring to the art techniques that I so wish to be taught, to the artists we were supposed to visit and the meeting with his brother that hasn't yet occurred.

'More?' Vincent says, still not moving.

'Is your brother at home? Should we call there?' I ask as I walk. If we can collect Theo in the next few minutes, then we'll just about have time to visit the ateliers and have lunch with the female artists. I've got three lists of techniques I'd like demonstrating.

We've arrived back on Boulevard de Clichy. We've walked a full circle. To the far right, rue Lepic begins again. We're strides away from Theo's apartment. I stop walking and turn to Vincent, waiting for a reply, waiting for some form of instruction. His eyes sparkle and his full lips curve into a smile. Something's shifted: *what did I say?*

'Are you seducing me?' he asks.

He strides towards me and I laugh nervously. 'No, Vincent,' I say, my palms up. 'I'm really not interested in anything other than your artistic technique.'

He steps too close to my side, his breath teasing my earlobe. 'What was the man like, the one who explored you?'

I shuffle backwards, creating distance between us. 'I've never been *explored*,' I say, the words rushing out. The shift in topic catches me off-guard. I search Vincent's face for clues, finding only a smile that stretches wide and I'm unable to stop the blush to my cheeks.

'Theo's apartment offers a magnificent view across the city.' He points in its direction.

A flutter in my belly. 'Is Theo there?' I ask.

'No, he's working,' Vincent says. 'Do you want to see his apartment?'

I gaze at him, allowing his words to settle. He's comparable to Eduard; he's using me for some purpose of his own, and he has no regard for my sense of self. Still, his request is blunt and my response is sudden, primal even. I shake my head; I don't want to be alone in Theo's apartment with Vincent van Gogh.

'You've been toying with me all day,' he says. 'Clear signals of your interest in—'

'The only man I'm *interested* in is your brother,' I say, clasping my hands behind my back to hide my shakes. 'Has he sent you here to distract me, like he did with Sara?'

Vincent laughs and I'm unsure if that's a confirmation. 'Since your rejection, my brother spends more time with me,' he says. 'He adopts my lifestyle or perhaps rather we share the same women.'

My tongue is fat within my mouth. My skin is hot, my bones are heavy. My knees quiver under my skirts; I can't move. So am I the prize in a competition between the brothers? Or is Vincent collecting evidence, seeking to prove that I'm unworthy of Theo's time?

'I've no desire to be a plaything for the Van Gogh brothers,' I say. 'And if that's what Theo wants, you can tell him that—'

A shout of, '*Hé, la-bas*!' A *fiacre* rushes past, the clip clops dancing along the boulevard, the whip swishing and swooshing. I want to call out for one, to be back with Andries right now, to be away from Vincent and the air between us that's as awkward as a cow on ice.

'Theo will probably be watching from his window and coveting a gun to shoot me,' Vincent says, breaking the silence that dances between us.

'He's there?' I ask. I look up at the buildings and then back to Vincent. 'You just said he was working. Why isn't he here?' He shrugs his shoulders. 'Did you invite him?' I ask.

Vincent shakes his head. 'And now he's jealous that you'd choose to spend time with me,' he says. This isn't a joke; his mouth doesn't form into a smile. 'And a little bewildered that you'd select me over him.'

'What?' I say. 'Take me to him right now and let me explain.'

I've no idea what's going on. I haven't and would never *select* Vincent. Today was supposed to be about art, about meeting other artists, about an arrangement with both of the Van Gogh brothers. I'm so very confused.

'I like your brother,' I say. 'Family matters and I hoped you, Theo, me, Dries – that we all could be friends.'

'You're just the latest in a queue of women desperate to know my brother,' he says. 'Mark my words, before long you'll be passed on to me.'

Vincent laughs from his belly as he waves and leaves me standing on Boulevard de Clichy.

July, 1888.

Dries was waiting in the hallway when I came home. I panicked. I enthused about how my day was wonderful and that I'd learned so much about technique and how to be an artist. I said I was now an expert in impasto. An expert! Then I told him that I had a hideous headache and needed to lie down, which somehow allowed me to swerve questions about the emerging female artists.

I've been hiding in my bedroom since. I hope that Clara comes in soon; I don't think I've ever felt this hungry.

What was I thinking? Why didn't I just tell him the truth?

If I'm honest, I've no idea how or why today happened. Please don't let it be that Theo thinks I've chosen to spend time with Vincent. If he does, then what must he think of me now? What lies has Vincent fed him about me?

Not even a month of knowing of the Van Gogh brothers and already they've filled my head with chaotic thoughts and confusion.

Vincent is so very important to Theo – they live together, they eat together, they socialise together. Theo adores his brother. To have Vincent like me, to respect me even, feels important. For him to see me as an equal matters, if I'm to consider a future with Theo.

Yet today Vincent treated me like a toy he'd stolen from his brother.

I don't know how to placate him; he's like no one I've ever met.

And what are these 'signals' I keep giving to men? First Eduard, then Theo, now Vincent: is it men or is it me? How can I prevent this from happening when I don't understand what I'm doing wrong?

Portrait Of Père Tanguy

O ur carriage dropped us at the Quai d'Orsay and now we're
walking over the sandy Champs de Mars. I say 'walking',
but my brother's practically bouncing. He points to the reason for
his excitement: a carcass of metal ladders that's waiting to be
fleshed out. Four iron legs thrust up from the ground. The beams
are grey and stark. Each reaches an abrupt halt: a skeleton waiting
skin.

'Eventually it'll be an impressive height,' Andries says.

I'm not really listening. I've spent most of this morning
worrying about the fact that Theo probably believes I chose to
spend time with Vincent and not with him. It's a messy situation,
made worse by the fact that Vincent said I'd been signalling my
interest all day. Part of me wants to write and ask for precise
examples, so I can understand what I did wrong. Instead, I'm
jumpy like a bucket of frogs, searching Champs de Mars for the
Van Gogh brothers. Why didn't I tell Andries everything last
night? A confession now and he'll think I've even more to hide, so
instead I'm trying to work out how to stop the Van Goghs from
telling Andries, here on the Champs de Mars, that there were no
visits to artist ateliers, that there were no demonstrations of artistic
techniques, and, mainly, that there was no Theo van Gogh.

'Jo?' Andries says. 'Where's your head today?'

'I'm tired, that's all,' I say. I lift a hand to my mouth, as if I'm stifling a yawn. 'I was up too late thinking, writing and reading.' I loop my arm with Andries as we walk. 'I wish I was more like Charlotte Brontë. That I could work into the night and not be utterly unfit for everything the next day. I'm honestly not sure there's a creative bone in my body.'

'Nonsense,' Andries says. 'You're just exhausted after a stimulating day. But what do you think?' It takes me a brief moment to realise that we're at the base and that he's talking about Eiffel's tower.

'But what's its purpose?' I ask. I don't really understand what I'm looking at.

'Eiffel has all the technical expertise and his ambition will set new records for height,' Andries says. 'It's difficult to imagine right now but it'll be the tallest building in the world. Right here. In Paris.'

He removes his hat, placing it near his forehead to offer shelter from the sun as he looks up at the construction. 'They've just begun the second floor,' he says.

I glance at the wooden scaffolds and small hoists directly fixed to the tower. Andries is right; I can't imagine how it'll finally look. I can't imagine anything that height. For now the metal uprights seem like they burst from the ground, as if ready for battle with the elements.

'I hate it,' I say. 'It lacks warmth and charm.'

'It's art,' Andries says. He's clearly offended by my opinion. 'Even Theo thinks the same.'

'Is he here?' I ask, hearing my own tinge of panic.

A pause. Andries observes my face with a curious expression on his own. 'No,' he says. 'A family gathering. Neither of the Van Goghs will grace Champs de Mars today.' He holds my gaze. 'Did they not mention it yesterday?' My brother's astute; *he smells a Dutch rat.*

A pause. A deep breath. A smile. 'It's not at all Parisian,' I say. I glance back at the construction, keen to remove my brother's eyes from my face.

Tomorrow I'll write to the Van Goghs separately and explain my concerns. For now, I focus on Eiffel's tower, in an attempt to understand how this metal monstrosity is art. It's already clear that my idea of art differs from Andries' and Theo's – it lacks education, experience, knowledge – but the longer I stare at the construction, the firmer I am in the belief that there's nothing beautiful about this erection. Is this actually what constitutes skill and beauty? What am I missing? I shrug my shoulders. My failure to appreciate my brother's taste matches my struggle to understand fully the complicated relationships that I seem to be developing with men.

'There are months of construction remaining and its shape isn't yet clear. Perhaps you'll hold back your criticism until completion.'

I shake my head and Andries bats his hat against my arm. My brother, an expert on engineering now, has collected strong opinions about the emerging tower. I wonder how many of them are his own and how many he's acquired from Theo. I love my brother dearly, but still, when I express opinion, when I try to be heard, I'm dismissed too often. Even here, among artists in Paris, women aren't permitted to occupy an equivalent space to men. We exist as objects – not equals with views. His hat back on his head, Andries grips his box camera and snaps a photograph of the evolving tower.

'One photograph each week,' he says. He turns the key at the top of the camera, winding the film onto the next frame. 'I'm capturing history right here.' He taps the mahogany box.

'Look at all of them,' I say. Hundreds of men scatter around the base legs, climbing ladders and dangling from scaffolding. They ignore the crowds of spectators – those men in top hats and those men in bowler hats watching them, with hands raised to protect their eyes from the sunlight – instead fully focused on their important tasks.

'Almost three hundred employed,' Andries says. 'We've been coming here every week since the foundations were being laid.

Eighteen months already and four of those months on the foundations.'

'We?' I ask.

'Theo, sometimes Vincent, but mainly other artist friends,' he says. 'I did ask you to join us.'

'Bonger,' we hear. 'Bonger. Is that you?'

I look around; the crowd's nothing but a sea of hats, bonnets and parasols. For a second my heart bolts; it might be Theo.

'Rodin, old man,' my brother says. He moves to embrace the gentleman. The man's older than us both, stockier too, with the longest and bushiest whiskers I've ever seen. Tiny round spectacles rest on the bridge of his nose and a too-large top hat balances on his head.

'Jo, this is Auguste Rodin,' Andries says.

Rodin holds out a hand for me. His fingers are fleshy, craggy and cracked; they're covered in a white dust. Delighted, I thrust out my hand for a shake.

'The finest sculptor in Paris, soon to be world renowned,' Andries says.

The woman next to him tuts then laughs. She captures my attention.

'He wishes,' she says and Rodin laughs.

She's about my age, my height too, and her beauty is as natural as daylight: faultless skin, a slightly upturned petite nose, eyes so brown they almost appear black. With a butter-lemon skirt, the bustle barely there, and a high-collared matching blouse, she's the picture of modern femininity and comfort. Her straw bonnet's yellow ribbon sails in the breeze and she's gripping it with both hands.

'Are you Camille Claudel?' I ask, bowing slightly. She observes me through her long eyelashes; *you are exquisite*.

'And already I'm at a disadvantage,' she says. 'You are?' But before I can tell her who I am, she reaches out a hand for me to shake it and the breeze whips her bonnet into the air. It dances along Champs de Mars.

'*Mon chapeau de paille*,' Camille shouts. She hitches up her skirts and runs after it. She chuckles with each step and I can't help but laugh. Rodin and my brother watch, smiling too.

'Perhaps she should have been a boy,' Andries says and I bat his arm with my hand.

'Nonsense,' Rodin replies. He laughs. 'She behaves as a female artist must.'

I don't understand what that means.

'Jo met with two emerging female artists yesterday,' Andries says, turning and nodding at me to talk about my art-filled day. 'Who were they? Rodin's sure to know them.'

Oh God! I hesitate. I don't know what to say. I can't just invent artists and imaginary ateliers on the spot. 'I think … erm. They…' I'm unable to keep the panic from my voice. All eyes are on me. I rub my now clammy palms on my skirts, knowing my brother will press for further details.

But then Camille returns, bonnet in one hand and her skirts bunched in the other.

'Johanna Bonger,' I say. 'His favourite sister.' I nod to my brother and hold out my clammy hand.

'Ah, *la soeur de Bonger*,' she exclaims. She throws her arms around me and pulls me into a tight embrace. 'I've been wanting to meet with you for weeks. You've been hiding yourself away. You're a painter, are you not?'

I shake my head. 'Not at all.'

'Nonsense,' Andries says. 'She's here to learn, and I'm hoping you can offer some guidance.'

'I don't know the first thing about sculpting,' I say quickly. 'But I'm keen to try everything.'

'Did you hear that I *assist* him with his commissions?' she asks, nodding at Rodin – he laughs from his belly in response – and I shake my head. I hadn't heard that. I'd heard she was his lover, a mistress, half his age, and that his almost-wife was called Rose. 'He's the genius sculptor and I exist in his shadow. Try not to look him in the eye though. His gaze will penetrate beneath what you'd like others to see and he'll know your truth before you've time to count to five.' She holds up her fingers as she counts to five in French, then she claps her hands together. 'And don't let my ferret's whiskers fool you,' she says, grabbing at Rodin's bush and tugging. 'He'll seduce you with a tickle and a smile.'

'Ignore Mademoiselle C,' Rodin says. 'I'm leaving for home in an hour and she's punishing me.'

'One day he'll leave that other woman for me,' Camille says. The words are almost whispered; I'm not sure the others hear.

Camille and Rodin smile at each other, holding hands now too, with not a hint of anger. I don't understand the playful tones of their relationship but I recognise her pain. I catch her eye and she nods. *I like you.*

'My sister wishes for your life,' Andries says.

'Damaged, neglected and invisible? You wish to be a female artist unfulfilled?' she asks. Camille laughs and Andries laughs too. I shake my head. Again, I don't understand. 'And you would miss the love and affection of your brother,' she adds.

I can't help but wonder what she's sacrificed. She appears uncomplicated, unapologetic, her smile contagious, but I see beyond her performance. I gave myself to a man who didn't want me for three years and she hides her pain as poorly as I did.

'*Allez, allez, allons-y.* We can find a café and a glass, then you can tell me all of your secrets and desires,' Camille says.

Self-Portrait

Two days since the disastrous Montmartre walk with no reply from Vincent, and I'd spent most of it anxious that Andries would discover I'd lied about the outing. I'd even convinced myself that I was about to be sent back to Amsterdam. But his letter arrived just now and, full of relief, I rush to the parlour.

My brother looks majestic sitting at his slate table, his surrounding furnishings all grand, and I can't help but smile. His papers are scattered in front of him, his eyes locked on a document.

'Vincent has requested—'

'Say no,' Andries says before I can explain Vincent's invite: an opportunity to demonstrate art techniques, a promise that Theo will definitely be there.

'What's wrong?' I ask

Eyes now locked on me, Andries holds up the piece of paper he was reading and waves it in the air.

'Theo's written. Did you really think I wouldn't find out?'

I snap my eyes away from Andries' glare, and lower my head. I don't answer.

'He's raised a concern about your desire to spend time alone with Vincent,' he says, his voice unnervingly calm. 'He's concluded that you're interested in his brother.'

'I'm really not,' I say. It's almost a whisper. I stare at the tiled floor.

'Yet you planned an outing with him, to ensure time alone?'

My eyes dart up and I'm shaking my head. 'Surely you don't believe that? I had no idea.'

Andries' face is set in concentration. I wait.

'I believe you,' he says and then I watch as his face softens. He smiles. 'But you've got to see how this looks, Jo.'

I nod; I do.

'If the events were innocent, why not tell me when you arrived home?' he asks. His argument's fair. 'Instead you lied to my *face*.' He points to his nose as he says 'face'. 'It wasn't as if your deceit was even convincing. On Champs de Mars, with Rodin, you couldn't even remember the two emerging female artists.' A pause. A sigh. 'If I hadn't written to ask Theo—'

'And would you have believed me if I'd told you that Vincent manipulated us both? That there were no female artists and no visits to ateliers?' I ask. 'And what about how he propositioned me to go to Theo's apartment with him?'

'Did you?' he asks, his voice raised for the first time.

'Of course not,' I say. 'What kind of woman do you think I am?'

Andries doesn't answer. *You think I'm that kind of woman.* We stare at each other, both unblinking, but I'm the first to look away.

'Is the woman always the guilty party?' I ask and my brother shrugs.

'Vincent's told Theo that you're in a relationship with him.'

'What?' The word's a shout. 'Why would he lie?'

Andries raises his eyebrows, as if my question is a ridiculous one, but I really do want an answer. I need to understand why this is happening.

'Then read his letter to me,' I say, stepping to his desk. I hand my brother the envelope and watch as he removes the letter and reads

Vincent's words. There's an apology for his behaviour and for failing to stick to the arranged schedule of meetings and art demonstrations and a tiny sketch of us walking around Montmartre together.

When Andries has finished, he shakes his head, folds the letter and places it back into the envelope. His movement is slow; he's considering his response.

'He's a one-off. I'll let Theo know,' he says. 'I doubt he'll be surprised, but it's best you stay away from Vincent.'

'But isn't he useful to know?' I say, running my hand along the edge of the slate desk. Andries said himself that Vincent's 'getting recognition', that Theo's getting Vincent's work into the hands of 'the right people'. It's more than that though. The Van Gogh brothers exist alongside each other. Won't 'staying away' from one mean I lose the other?

'I'm sure Theo has better contacts. But…'

I nod for him to continue.

'Apparently, during the walk, there was hand holding.'

'There was what?' I say, but I can see my brother's amusement. He's smiling while shaking his head.

'Vincent's hand brushed mine a couple of times. As hands do when people walk quickly next to each other.'

'Loti saw you together,' he says, picking up a different piece of paper and shaking it in the air – no doubt a letter from his unnerving lawyer. 'It's fair to say that he's no longer a consideration for marriage.'

'You know this is the opposite of *fair*, don't you?' I say. The words lack conviction. Am I concerned that he no longer considers me a suitable wife? No, I'm really not. I'm glad. My mouth curls into a light smile; Andries watches.

'When Theo didn't turn up, you should have returned here,' he says, and I know he's right.

'At the very least I should have told you everything when I returned,' I say. 'I'm sorry.'

Andries walks to me, pulling me into an embrace.

'I wanted to see the female artists,' I say and my brother kisses the top of my head.

'You're my responsibility and I'm struggling to quash all the rumours about your reputation. They're multiplying beyond my control.'

I pull out of the embrace. 'What rumours?' I ask.

'Sara Voort has informed many in my circle about your *relationship* with Stumpff. Now she's saying that you and Vincent—'

'But wasn't *she* involved with Vincent?' I say, immediately irritated.

'Only those close to Theo knew of that plan.'

A sigh. 'Will she not leave me alone? I can't believe I felt sorry for that woman.'

'She's telling everyone that you're Vincent's latest plaything. Do you fully understand the implications of that?' Andries says.

I shake my head; I don't.

'If it was proven correct...' A loud exhale of breath. 'You'd be abandoned by Mamma and Pa, and shunned by polite society.'

He takes my hand, brushing a kiss on it, his lips soft. 'I'm not attempting to control or frighten you, it's rather that I can't see a positive ending for you, if you're interested in pursuing Vincent.'

My eyes jump up to meet him. 'I'm not *pursuing* him,' I say. I shake my head and I pull my hand from his grasp. 'I thought I'd be safe with Vincent. Theo adores his brother and I hoped that, after time spent together, I'd gain Vincent's respect. That he'd see me as an equal, or even that Vincent's approval of me would matter to Theo. But I don't understand Vincent's mind. I can't make sense of his actions and reactions.' Another pause. 'He doesn't seem to care about Theo's happiness. He has zero respect for me. He's wild, untamed even, and that scares me. I've never met a man quite like him.'

I don't add that being challenged by Vincent stirs something new within me; that it feels as if the brothers already expect, even demand, more of me than just being a pretty wife and mother.

'Of late, Vincent's increasingly a burden for his brother to bear,' Andries says, nodding in agreement. 'He accuses Theo of extreme acts and Theo placates him, but it wasn't always like that. It takes time to understand their relationship.'

'Why can't I be like you?' I ask.

My brother gives me a curious look, a mix of concern and interest. 'Like me?'

'You have the luxury of time,' I say. 'You're a constant reminder that freedom is an illusion and that, at some point, I've got to give up all creative pursuits and fall back in line with society's expectations. Time is passing too quickly. The inevitability...' I stop my words; my eyes now fix on a stray red thread escaping from the Empire Aubusson rug. My instinct is to bend and push the thread underneath, hiding it from my brother's inspection. I'd quite like to climb under there too. I don't though. I don't move.

'Tell me,' Andries says.

'Look at Camille.'

'Claudel?' he asks, and I nod.

'She's said to be an amazing talent, a sculptress in her own right, yet people only ever refer to her as Rodin's lover.'

'*Difficult* women make problematic choices. She made hers and now she's fast becoming ugly.'

I shake my head. 'She fell in love,' I say. 'That doesn't take from her skill as a sculptress.'

'She fell in love with a man who isn't available,' Andries says. 'She knew that when they started their *arrangement*.' He's unable to grasp my argument. I'm not being heard.

'Vincent's free like you. Theo is too. Every man in Paris is free. You can take your time to fall into any embrace, have a different lover for each weekday, break hearts, leave emotional wrecks in your path, yet you'll still be defined by the career path you choose.'

'But you can't see that Vincent's freedom comes at a huge price?' my brother says, his tone gentle and open to communication. 'Even art must exist within the confines of humanity, if the artist is to operate in that society.'

'And Vincent doesn't?' I say, raising my eyes to explore Andries' expression.

'He isn't yet defined by his art. His reputation is deserved,' he says. He crinkles his nose in disgust. What I'd give to know what's caused that reaction. He pauses, clearly reluctant to explain further.

'I'll write to Theo and let him know what happened between you and Vincent,' Andries says.

I clasp my hands behind my back: frustration, anger, fear too. 'I'm more than capable of writing by myself,' I say.

'This needs fixing or you'll end up with the nauseating Dr Janssen.'

'And I'll fix it,' I say. I throw my arms wide with my words. 'I won't be made to marry that fat pig.' Andries walks back to his desk – he's clearly bored with this conversation – then turns to face me again.

'Honestly, Jo. I love you, but some days you're a nightmare.'

'Brother, you're being too kind.'

'You can't afford to be so…' He lifts the letters from the desk and waves them in the air. 'So dramatic and untrusting of me.' A big sigh. 'We're on the same side.'

'And you can't resist being a pompous idiot,' I say. I know I'm being a brat. I know my brother's on my side, that he only wants what's best for me. Andries shakes his head before flopping back onto his throne.

'Take a moment to consider the current and only other option,' he says. 'I'm trying to help you. Mamma's suitor of choice is quite despicable.' He pauses; I think about speaking but instead I shrug my shoulders. 'Have you considered all that you'll sacrifice when you marry Dr Janssen?'

'I want your life.' I'm a hair's breadth away from stamping my feet.

'That isn't an option and you're not listening. If Theo withdraws his interest, we'll have to go back to my list of suitors,' he says. 'Time is running out. Can't you see that I'm trying to find you someone who'll allow you to pursue your own path.'

'Allow?' I shout. 'Why do I need permission in a way a man never would?'

'What you need is to calm down,' he says. 'You're being a hysterical woman.'

'And you sound like Pa,' I shout. 'I won't be controlled by you or by—'

'Grow up, Jo.' He's suddenly angry. 'Act your age or I'll arrange for your return to Amsterdam at the earliest convenience.'

My heart thumps in my ears. Tears prick my eyes. He's never angry with me; the seriousness of the situation stabs into my belly.

'Where's Clara?' I ask, my volume loud enough for her to hear.

'Running an errand,' he says, and I turn to walk from the room.

'Where are you going?'

'To fix this,' I say. I'm not sure if he can hear, as I hurry along the hallway to the apartment's door. 'I assume that's allowed, or would you prefer I be your prisoner, shackled to your desk?'

Agostina Segatori Sitting In The Café Du Tambourin

I'm sitting next to him in Café du Tambourin, on Boulevard de Clichy, and he's proving to be a child that I can't coax out of a tantrum. I've tried everything I can think of – food, alcohol, his brother – and still he refuses to leave with me.

'It took me nearly an hour to find you,' I say. 'I'm out, without a chaperone, risking my reputation... Dries will be furious.'

I'd formulated my plan between leaving my brother's apartment and before reaching the end of rue Victor. I'd find Vincent and he would simply agree to confess his trickery to our brothers. I then retraced our route from the disastrous walk, convinced he'd be painting *en plein air*. He wasn't. Instead, I found him amidst a fog of tobacco smoke and raucous chatter in Le Tambourin.

'I really shouldn't be in here,' I say, my eyes jumping around, hoping not to find one of Andries' many acquaintances. 'If Mamma finds out...'

Vincent's not listening. His eyes are locked on one person and he tracks her movement around the room.

'I need you to return with me.' I've told him that already. 'Then for me to send Clara for Theo, and then for you to tell everyone the truth about our *relationship* and our walk around Montmartre.'

Vincent nods but it's clear he's not listening; his thoughts are elsewhere.

'Who is she?' I ask. I have to shout to be heard over the noise of the piano and the singing of sentimental lyrics that call for revenge. Some in the bar jeer at the pianist, others stand, arms around each other's shoulders, to sing along.

'She owns the bar,' he says. He leans forward in his seat, his eyes still on her. 'Gives artists a place to exhibit.'

In this bar, I'm Dutch. I'm plain and dowdy and she's exotic and interesting. A red scarf covers the top of her hair, loose curls slip from it and frame her pinched face. Her dress is vibrant, colourful, a patchwork pattern with no weighty bustle, and a silhouette showing her slim figure. Considerably older than me, she's striking and somehow both handsome and beautiful: a large nose, bulky lips and olive skin. But it's her remarkable eyes that hold my attention. They're the deepest and bravest eyes I've ever seen. She's bold, like a successful man. She walks with her head held high, with not a grain of doubt about who she is.

'Agostina Segatori.' His eyes are still on her. I look around the café and everyone's eyes watch Agostina's movement. There's singing, there's laughter, there's chatter, but all gazes follow the host. 'I remain fond of her,' he says.

'Is she French?' I ask.

'Italian.'

She lights a cigarette and is given a glass of beer, as she stops and leans her back against the bar.

I bend forward to be heard, speaking close to his ear. 'I want a cigarette,' I say. I still don't take my eyes off Agostina.

He laughs. He flicks his left earlobe. 'You don't smoke,' he says, but doesn't turn to look at me.

'I want a glass of beer,' I say. *To be like her.* Vincent clicks his fingers and I watch as her eyes flick to him.

There's a moment, a slight twitch of recognition in the corner of her mouth. Agostina walks to us. Her hips sway under Vincent's gaze. She glides with the café's music, never stepping out of beat. She stares at him, never blinking. Her dark eyes seem to burrow into his very soul with each step. There's a current of excitement between Vincent and this woman, so intense that it leaps and tangos around them both. I sink back into my chair. I'm invisible; I've never felt so out of place and time. I'm a female artist who's colour-blind, a writer who's never read a book, an actor unable to learn his lines. I don't belong in this world, yet now, in this very moment, I'd sell my left arm to be her. I want to be Agostina Segatori.

'*Una birra e una sigaretta per la signora,*' Vincent says. He gestures for a beer and cigarette with his hands. Agostina's eyes flick over me, her facial expression unaltered, then she turns her glance back to Vincent. She clicks her teeth and tips her head upwards. Vincent laughs. The sound travels from deep within his belly as Agostina walks back to her bar.

'She said no,' Vincent says. 'She considers you a decent lady.'

They're laughing at me. 'I'm done with your games,' I say. I stand to leave, but he reaches out and grips my hand. I shake it loose and take a deep breath.

'Come back with me to Andries' apartment,' I say.

Vincent raises his eyebrows. 'Isn't this how our last *misunderstanding* began?' He laughs again.

The man thinks he's hilarious. 'Tell both of our brothers that nothing has occurred between us. Tell Theo that I spent our *outing* waiting for him to arrive.'

'Many seek to tame me, to dumb down my eccentricities. I fear passion is seen as weakness by lots,' Vincent says. He presses tobacco into the bowl of his pipe. He strikes a match, letting it burn for a few seconds, then moves it in a circular motion over his tobacco.

'I'm interested in Theo and you matter to him. That's why I'm here, that's why I'm *trying* to like you.' I stare at him, but he refuses to look at me. I don't even know if he hears what I'm saying.

A shift, his fear instantaneous; as if he sees something or

someone that I can't. Vincent's eyes are wild, they jump from person to person. The noise of glasses clinking, of matches being struck, of singing, of laughter – each sound seems to sting his very being.

'You don't want to know me,' he says. His voice is almost a whisper, but I read the shape of his lips. He puffs on his pipe.

'Your knowledge of art technique and of the art world fascinates me. I'd love to know more—'

'I love entirely, I commit entirely, or not at all. I fear it's the same with how others feel about me. They adore me or loathe me with gusto. There doesn't seem to be a stable ground,' he says. I've no idea what he means; we're speaking the same language yet his words are entirely foreign.

I reach out and touch his arm. He jumps, his knee banging on the tambourine-topped table. I steady it before everything tumbles to the floor. 'Can we cut this nonsense and have a proper conversation?' I ask before I even consider how rude I sound. 'Just this once?' I add, my tone softer. 'Will you talk to me about your brother?' Vincent doesn't reply, perhaps he doesn't hear. Perhaps he chooses not to hear. He strikes another match and holds it over the bowl of tobacco again.

'The expression in trees is quite remarkable,' Vincent says.

'What?'

His eyes fix on a painting on the wall, he puffs on his pipe at the same time. I follow his gaze to a *sous-bois*.

'You admire that painting?' I ask tentatively; perhaps we'll find common ground in talking about art. 'The step away from the traditional painting of landscapes and instead being immersed within the forest that's being painted … that must be exciting for the artist,' I say. I don't know how to pull Vincent into conversation, because I've never spoken with anyone quite like him.

'It could be that when I'm failing to create, I'm actually destroying myself. Through art, through creating, I stop my decline into darkness. Art and novels excite me,' he says. 'But I'm a meagre financier.'

'Shall I ask for the bill?' I say. I hold up my hand, clicking my fingers for attention, but Agostina doesn't turn in my direction. Women don't demand of other women, not even in Le Tambourin. Vincent doesn't respond either. 'How do you exist?' I ask. 'In terms of money.'

'Theo exists for both of us.'

I exhale through my nose. He's infuriating. The conversation's like pulling teeth from a horse. 'That makes little sense.'

'And yet you understand every word.' He holds his pipe close to his eyes, inspecting its bowl.

'But what of your future prospects?'

'Oh, the illicit future. It's all that others seek to meet. Vincent in the future. What will he be? What funds will he have procured? Could he be the most famous man in the history of art?' He pulls in air through his nose and then exhales through his mouth. He puts his pipe on the tambourine-topped table. He stretches his arms in front and then he waves them both, as if shaking away my question.

'No,' I say, 'that's not what I mean. I want to—'

'Yet what of present Vincent? Is he not worthy of your time and attention, Miss Bonger? Will you always tease me to anticipation and then feign knowledge of your seductive skills?' He's shouting over the singing in Le Tambourin, his eyes wide as he glares at me. 'I spent a lifetime too timid to introduce myself to those who interest me. I admired from afar, always feeling the inferiority of being in the company of greatness.'

'I'm not great. So far from it. Miss Segatori is greatness,' I say, my tongue a little too sharp as her name rolls from it.

'Would you like to know my greatest fear?' he says, and I nod.

He takes a sip from his glass of beer. He leans in close. His lips are inches from my right ear. His whiskers tickle my skin. I pull back from their touch; it's instinctive. *No, Vincent.* I don't want him close to me. It's fair to say that this conversation isn't going quite the way I planned it would; I'm out of my depth again.

'That I'll never serve any purpose. That I'll never be good

enough. A master of nothing,' he says. Each word is anchored with sadness.

I pause. Caught by this sudden shift in Vincent; I wish I could understand his longing. I need to get back to my plan. Andries will be out searching for me if I don't return soon. A thought about how furious he'll be spurs me on. 'I must insist that you come with me to see Andries—'

'One day, under the sulphur sun, I'll found an artists' colony. A place artists can be, and paint.'

Vincent pauses. Two tables to our right a lady laughs. Vincent jumps. His leg kicks our table, this time knocking the empty glasses and his pipe to the floor. The glasses shatter. The musicians stop. There's a moment of silence as everyone turns to our noise. Vincent bends to the floor. He scoops up the glass with his bare hands.

'Stop,' I say. I grab his wrists and see his blood spotting from tiny cuts. Vincent's eyes meet mine; they secrete sorrow.

'Dries said Theo believes your art will be celebrated. He ranks you with the masters,' I say.

'He's blinded by sibling duty.'

Noise returns around us. I loosen my grip on Vincent's wrists. He picks up his pipe. 'Oh, to smoke my pipe and drink in peace.' We straighten back into our seats.

'Dries says that colour and paint thickness is altering your art. I'd like to see that. I'd love you to show me how.'

'Theo believes I'm mastering my craft. Says it comes from the stability of us living together.' Vincent stares at his palms. He picks out tiny shards of glass from his skin and places them on the table.

'Do you feel the same?' I ask. I'm on guard, alert, fearful of his next move.

'You're my last obsession.' He speaks with a firmness that suggests he has knowledge of this to be fact, and that unsettles me again.

'I need your help,' I say. The words sound harsh because I'm shouting. 'I need Theo to know that we,' I indicate to us both, 'that we're not in a relationship. That there's nothing between us. Please, Vincent. Please tell him the truth.'

Vincent stands. He's no longer interested in our conversation. He waves at Agostina Segatori and she nods in response. His steps crunch over the broken glass as he walks away, leaving me alone in Le Tambourin.

My brother had been informed about my 'secret meeting with Vincent' by the time I arrived home. I told him all about the conversation and how Vincent unnerves me because his actions and reactions make no sense. I've no capacity to predict what he'll do or say next.

I doubt there's a woman in Paris who could placate Vincent van Gogh.

Dries had no choice but to explain why Vincent's reputation was justly deserved. He outlined the (very) intimate details of Vincent's obsession with his relative, and of his once living in sin with a pregnant prostitute.

I'd hoped myself to be more bohemian since arriving in Paris, but the details were sickening. My stomach flipped with every sordid fact and every suspected disease. The thought of others believing I'd been intimate with the man sent me into a cold sweat – no wonder Guy Loti retracted his interest.

But what do I do? He's Theo's brother and if I'm allowing Theo into my life, then won't that mean that I'll have to learn to bear his brother too?

Of course Theo will now know about my meeting Vincent in Le Tambourin and, given the 'evidence', he'll probably conclude that I'm obsessed with his brother. I doubt I'll even hear from him again.

How do I always seem to make things worse?

Two Women In The Woods

F or the third time in the last ten minutes, I ask, 'And you're sure they said to visit today?'

It's not even ten o'clock and we've already arrived outside.

'Perhaps sculpting will be your weapon,' Andries says. He pulls the cord, sounding the doorbell outside Rodin's atelier.

Minutes later and we watch Camille inside, running towards the large door, a white artist's smock over her clothes. Her fingers are outstretched, covered in wet clay. Her energy is infectious despite the door still separating us; Andries laughs and I can't help but smile.

'Johanna, mon amie.' We hear her through the glass panelling as she fumbles to unlock the door using her palms to turn the key. 'Je suis si contente que tu sois là.' Then, arms wide and attempting to keep her clay-smothered hands from my clothes, she pulls me into a tight embrace with both elbows.

'Bonger, you're always a delight,' she says. She shifts her energetic hug to my brother. 'My ferret is in there.' She waves her hand to the right. Tiny beads of clay sink to the floor. I watch them fall, resisting the urge to catch them in my palms. 'Go see him, and let me have Johanna to myself.'

I can't help but smile. Too often in the past, I've worried I like other women more than they like me; Camille doesn't make me feel that way. This artist's pleasure in my visiting covers me in joy. Here, I'm not invisible, my interest in art is being taken seriously.

'The welcome you've just offered is more than my parents muster when I visit,' I say. I follow Camille through the entrance room. 'Thank you for being so kind.' She stops, waiting for my step to reach her, then links her arm through mine, only transferring a drop or two of clay onto my dress. I like that; here, I'm an artist too.

'And does your mother like you?' she asks. The bold directness infects me. She's interested in me – in Johanna Bonger, not in Andries' younger sister. I can't help but smile as I shake my head. A no. Mamma has never hidden her dislike of me.

'My mother detests me. She'd wished I was born a man and believes my art obscene,' Camille says. She laughs. 'When I was told that I was the wrong sex to attend Ecole des Beaux Arts, I thought myself cursed being born a woman.'

I nod. 'I've wished to be a man this past week.'

'But a woman's body and form are wondrous gifts,' Camille says, she smiles. 'Change is coming and Paris is going to be at the centre of it all.'

'Really?' I ask.

'Absolutely.' There's not a fragment of doubt in her word.

We step into a vast banquet hall, the floor patterned with white sheets and pails of water. Statues, in varying sizes, shapes and states of completion, are positioned around the room.

'This is your atelier?' I ask.

'Rodin's, but we share. Most are yet to be completed,' she says, as we walk in. A fine layer of white dust floats in the air and rests on every surface. Lumps of marble and blocks of stone breathe on wooden wedges and crates. 'Point chisels, rasps and tooth chisels.' Camille points to the tools in a neat line next to the stone as she strides towards a muddy pile of wet clay. She picks up a soaked cloth and rubs at her fingers vigorously.

I point to the piles of sculpted body parts. 'Why are there so many feet and hands?' I ask. They're scattered around the great room as if a bloodless battle has recently concluded.

'I make them for Rodin,' she says. 'He finds them difficult.'

'He uses them in his sculptures?' I ask, and Camille nods. 'And you're given credit for your contribution?'

She shakes her head. 'Sometimes he even signs them as his own.'

'But—'

'I'd rather be part of something than nothing,' Camille says without even a hint of bitterness.

'But that's so unfair. Why—'

Her laughter interrupts my outburst. She shakes her head again. 'I arrived in Paris aged eighteen, to study under Alfred Boucher.' She looks at me for confirmation but I don't know him. 'When Alfred left for Florence, he asked Rodin to take over my teachings but instead my ferret invited me to be one of his assistants. I've been his model, lover, inspiration and artistic equal since. Yet to others I'll only ever be acknowledged as his lover.'

'For how long?' I ask. I walk around the statues, resisting the urge to reach out and stroke the smooth form.

'Four years,' she says. My face betrays my shock. *Four stolen years*. 'He's not a bad man,' she says, her response quick. 'He loves two women, each of us providing what the other can't. Insecurity or too large a hunger, I'm yet to know fully.'

I stop and turn to her. She's staring at a clay statue. 'Are you happy?' I ask.

'No,' she says, without hesitation. 'My sadness infects my soul. This,' she throws her arms out, showing her vast atelier, 'keeps me sane. I think my mind would implode if I didn't have my art.' A pause. 'And I couldn't bear life without him. He's helped make me the artist that I am, but...'

'He destroys you.' I walk to her.

'I want him for myself. He chooses to live with her,' she says, her deathly quiet.

'His wife?'

'They're not married, but they have a son together. He's promised he'll leave her...'

I'm about to respond, but then I see the statue beside her. I'm caught off-guard; its beauty silences me.

'I started this one the year I met Rodin,' she says. 'I call it *La Valse*.'

'The Waltz. Your creation of movement … I mean, in this solid form – it's breath-taking.' I take a step closer. 'How is that even possible?'

I walk around the statue, breathing in the many intricacies. It alters when seen from even the slightest shift in angle. A couple are depicted as they dance together. They're attentive to each other's body and to the movement of the dance they perform.

'That they're entirely in love is without question,' I say. 'The incline of their lean, the pausing in that very moment … it cries vulnerability.' I'm thrown by the fragility of love exposed; of being offered this glimpse of Camille's affection. The piece is utterly joyous and tender.

'It's truly stunning. It's magnificent,' I say. 'I think you might be the most talented artist I've ever met.'

She laughs as if to dismiss my praise. 'I exhibited it and people were appalled,' she says. She doesn't hide her sorrow from the words.

'What?' I ask, bending closer to the art. 'How could anyone not be moved by its beauty?'

'Because of my sex and my reputation as Rodin's lover,' she says. 'As a sculptress it's difficult to gain access to nude models and, if it occurs, only a modest nude would be acceptable. I refused to play by the rules.'

'What happened?'

'It was considered obscene and I've been told it has no place in a public gallery.'

'Yet male artists can study the naked form and their art is celebrated?' I ask, and Camille nods.

'I long to have it cast in bronze, but the Société Nationale des Beaux-Arts won't support this nudity.' She points at the statue and we remain in silence for two or three minutes, both observing and contemplating her creation.

'I know it's not ideal,' I say, 'but have you considered adding a skirt to her?'

No response in words, but I watch as Camille walks around the sculpture. 'Just to this part.' I point from the naked derriere to the base of the statue.

'The loss of self,' she says. Her fingers run over the clay. 'It could cling without a bustle, allowing the body's outline to emerge.'

'A flowing shape would work,' I add. 'As if the earth is swallowing her very being.'

'Such as it is to love Rodin,' Camille says.

I try to be discreet as I flick away a tear with my finger. The vulnerability and truth she displays is unlike any art I've ever encountered. Her talent is unconceivable. This conversation, living this life; I am more like me than ever before.

'Who was he?' she asks. She moves to me and places an arm around my shoulders.

'A writer, older, wiser, still employed at the school that dismissed me,' I say. 'In Amsterdam, I'll always be defined by my indiscretion. But soon my past will be wiped away and I'll become a wife.'

'I'm detecting not a hint of joy,' she says.

'A widower, nearly seventy. My parents have arranged it all. I agree or they'll wipe their hands of me.'

She twists out of the embrace, positioning me in front of her, her hands on my shoulders. There'll be clay prints there long after her hands aren't. 'Let them,' she says.

'I've no means to support myself,' I say. I'm unable to match her stare. Suddenly, I'm inadequate: no longer her equal. 'Dries is trying to find me a suitable husband in Paris, but that's already complicated. Theo proposed.'

'Van Gogh?'

I nod. 'I like him but I loved Eduard for three years. I'm still not ready to commit to someone else…'

'They lie, they cheat, yet we carry the weight of the scandal on our shoulders,' she says. 'That you were moved by my art will connect us forever.'

July, 1888.

I read about the life of Beethoven once and it made me appreciate and enjoy his music so much more.

And now that I've met Camille, I'll forever seek to hear her story within each sculpture.

Nude Woman Reclining, Seen From The Back

I hear Vincent's shouts in the hallway but don't have time to adjust my skirts or hair, as he barges past Clara and into the parlour. My latest canvas is drying – an experiment in still life: a china plate, a napkin, a crystal glass, a lace tablecloth, violets in a small vase, a spoon, a knife, and a fork – and I've just started reading the first volume of *Les Misérables* with my boots up on my brother's pouffe. I wasn't expecting Vincent and I don't want to see him. He must have been outside, loitering in the shadows of rue Victor and waiting for his moment.

Clara's close behind him. Her face far too pale for her complexion; it's a picture of concern and sickness. Andries will blame her, not the concierge, for letting Vincent into the apartment. I nod to her, *I'll deal with him*, knowing that I have to keep this meeting short and that I'll need to be firm with my *guest*.

I stand to greet him. I wobble slightly as I adjust to the weight of my skirts, holding out my hand to him, but he refuses the expected shake; Vincent's clearly not in the mood for sticking to the rules of etiquette. His eyes are volcanic and he's nearly running on the spot. Clara remains in the room, waiting for instruction, as I lower my arm back to my side. I'm sure she's already considered the quickest way to get help.

I correct my bodice, take a deep breath and then turn to Clara. 'Allow me a few minutes with Mr Van Gogh,' I say.

She bows slightly before taking steps backwards and standing in the doorway.

'You can't stay, Dries will be back any min—' My tone is stern.

'Bonger's meeting with Theo.' His volume is close to a shout, his words slurred. 'At Le Tambourin, to talk about *us*. We have time.'

'Lower your voice,' I say. I pray that my face is expressionless, that my tone sounds sour. 'There is no *us* for them to discuss. Why are you here?'

'You didn't respond to my letter and it's been four days since I saw you at Le Tambourin,' he says. 'You left me with no choice but to come.'

He acts like a wounded lover, as if I'm somehow to blame; that catches me off-guard.

'It been two days since I received your correspondence, and I've been busy with my art.' I nod to my canvas but he doesn't turn to look. Instead, he maintains his stare. I nod for Clara to leave, and watch her step away from the doorway. 'And *I* am not responsible for *your* choices.'

'You're avoiding me,' he says. His tone is sulky like a child, but he stares with an intensity that makes me desperate to bite my fingernails down to their root.

I blink. I exhale through my nose. Not even the sullenest of children in Utrecht is quite like Vincent van Gogh.

'I demand you tell me what I've done to offend you,' he says, swaying slightly as he struggles to stand still.

A quick consideration of what I could actually say in response: that I didn't write because I was stalling for time to formulate a suitable response. That I can't forget what Andries told me about the sexual diseases that Vincent's said to have collected in and on his intimate parts. That it isn't about being a prude or proper, that it's about valuing myself and worrying about people thinking I've been intimate with him. That it's been three days since I wrote to Theo and that I'm desperate to hear from him again.

The thought that Theo might no longer be interested makes my stomach flip. Dries is talking to him about it all right now and my plan was to reply to Vincent's correspondence after I was back on track with Theo. I'd write something that left him with a 'we both know I'm being polite, and this is my way to let you know that I'm not interested in you in a romantic way. This correspondence is simply because I am interested in your brother' type message. I hadn't expected a confrontation today; I'd underestimated Vincent's reaction to rejection.

He claps his hands together. 'Are you listening?' My eyes jump to him, but his eyes jolt from my face and around the parlour's whitewashed walls, resting on an oil painting of two sisters that hangs close to the windows.

His face scrunches in disgust. 'A monstrosity,' he says.

'It's a Renoir,' I say.

'I had thought Bonger to be a man of fine taste. I must—'

'Why are you here?' I ask again.

There's a pause, Vincent's eyes still observe the oil painting, but there's a shift. 'A request,' he says.

'And?'

'I want to draw you,' he says. He studies me closely for reaction.

'Another ink portrait?'

'I heard that you admire Claudel?' he asks, and I nod. 'She's a nude model for Rodin.'

'She's a sculptress in her own right,' I say. 'Too often fighting upstream. I've never seen such emotion and depth in art.'

'Horse shit,' he says. He laughs as if I've made a hilarious joke. 'Let me draw you now. Naked, from behind.'

His words are both desperate and pathetic. If he intends to shock, he's failed.

'I've seen many naked bodies,' he says. His hands wave in the air as if attempting to outline a shape.

I clap my hands. 'Well done,' I say. 'You're lucky. I can only learn to draw anatomy from casts.'

Vincent snorts and shakes his head. 'I'm an artist. I study human form and shape.'

'You're a privileged male artist,' I say. 'Society supports that you paint nude models, while it's considered improper and dangerous for female artists to study the same. Take Camille and her—'

'I want to paint you naked,' he says. He glares at me, daring my response. He considers me a pathetic woman, and embarrassing me is a game; women are objects for men's pleasure – submissive and ready to conform. I hold his stare. He blinks and looks away. A brief victory.

'Have you been drinking?' I ask. Vincent shrugs his shoulders.

'Go sleep it off,' I say, pointing to the door.

'Oh to sleep, perchance to dream of guilt or things that scare me. The Devil wants his contract paid in full, this failed pastor proves to be quite the prize.' He glances at my canvas, offering no comment on my art, then looks to the books that are piled on the *confidante*. 'You've had a profitable morning,' he says. He nods at *Les Misérables*, and this time I shrug my shoulders. He's a mess of a man – a drunk, a desperate egotist – and I've had enough of his drama.

'I want you to leave before my brother—'

'Brothels no longer satisfy me.'

Vincent steps back. He looks me up and down. He's incapable of seeing me as a woman, never mind as an artist or as his equal. Instead he thinks I exist solely for his pleasure. He values me for my beauty and sexual availability, just as he would a model.

'I've told you before and I'll tell you again – I'm not a painting, created for your pleasure. Do not stare at me in that manner.'

'With honesty?' he says. He clicks his fingers as if he's reached a conclusion. 'I'm not sure why I'm here. I doubt you could satisfy me either. But when you breathed into this ear at Le Tambourin…' He pulls at his left earlobe.

'What?' This conversation is just beyond my grasp

'Did you lie about having little experience?'

I shake my head, my cheeks reddening and instantly betraying my desire to hide all emotion. 'But I'm not easily shocked, Vincent. Now ... I'd like you to leave.'

'No,' he says. 'I want to fling you onto the rug below me.' He points to Andries' Empire Aubusson.

I can't help but laugh. A nervous reaction. He wants to possess me, for me to exist to satisfy his ridiculous fantasy. This situation is ridiculous; the man's a few apples short of a bushel.

'I'll flip you onto that rounded belly of yours and rip your skirts and under garments from you.' His voice has an irritated spike, the words slur together. My laughter's angered him or it could be that it's aroused him, but either way there's been a change.

I'm prey.

I wrap my arms around my torso, taking a slight step backwards. 'Vincent, stop,' I say.

He glares at me; he's a wild animal ready to pounce. 'I'll do as I wish.'

I take another step backwards.

'I'll take you from behind, like a dog riding a bitch, basking in the majestic reek and wetness from your round buttocks.'

'Mr Van Gogh—'

He holds up his palm, stepping towards me. 'I'll flip you over and feel your fingers caressing my testicles before your mouth encloses around the tip of—'

'Enough,' I shout. I turn away from him, hurrying towards the doorway.

'But first, pull up your clothes and come sit on—'

I hear a bang. I turn to find a lamp on the floor. But he's there too, kneeling on the rug, in front of the open fireplace. He's fiddling with the buttons on his trousers, too intoxicated to function.

I'm going to vomit. This isn't what I want. Not here, not ever with Vincent van Gogh.

Vincent pushes his trousers over his hips, revealing his grey undergarments. 'Enough?' He smiles. He's mocking me.

'Leave,' I say. The tremble in my voice betrays me. Vincent

hears my fear. I don't want to see his diseased manhood. I can't have this happen.

'We've not even started yet. Come here.' He rolls onto his side, his elbow bent and his head bobbing in failed attempts to rest it on his palm. 'And here's me thinking you wanted help with my brother.'

He cups his manhood through his undergarments. I can't help but stare at the bulge. There's a wet circle where the tip must be.

'Keep your *diseased penis* away from me.' I jab a finger in the air when I say 'diseased penis'.

This is the third time I've been alone with Vincent – even Andries will struggle to believe this wasn't planned. And Theo – what will he think of me? Could he believe Vincent lied three times?

Vincent's laughing. He's on his feet and staggering towards either me or the doorway. I move to the right, allowing clear passage, but as he totters by his arm snakes around my waist and he pulls me to him. His other arm grips the open waistband of his trousers.

We're in sight of the large bay windows, anyone passing will see this intimacy and possibly Vincent van Gogh's undergarments

'Get off,' I scream. I slap him. His hand shoots up to his stinging cheek, his trousers fall to the floor. 'Get out. Get out. Get out.' I scream out the words, each repeat increasing in volume.

'Be quiet, Johanna,' he says, his words no longer bold. His eyes dart to the parlour door. 'The maid will hear you. Bonger will—'

'Get out, get out, get out.' It's a continuous scream. The words merge together. I sound deranged. Clara rushes into the room.

'Miss Jo?' she says. Her voice is stern, breathy too. Her face is somehow as white as chalk. 'I've requested assistance,' she says. Her eyes search my face and clothes. She sees Vincent's trousers bunched around my ankles. I shake my head, *nothing happened*. I'm embarrassed.

Vincent scrambles for his waistband and almost trips over his own feet in a hurry to escape my screeches and Clara's anger.

'And don't be comin' back,' Clara shouts after him. 'I'm tellin' Mr Theo about this.' Clara coughs, a fit that fills the room.

I turn back to the window. My entire body trembles. I watch the front door slam and Vincent jump down the stoop. It's then that he bangs into another woman, almost knocking her from her feet. I watch as she staggers to find her footing before she looks up to the window and her eyes lock with mine. Vincent puts his hand on her coat sleeve and grasps her arm. She looks at him. She looks at his trousers; they're back around his ankles. She looks at me again; those almond-shaped brown eyes, that slim small nose, those full lips, that heart-shaped face. Her eyebrows crease inwards. Sara and her perfect timing.

Am I expected to believe that she just happened to be strolling along the cobbles of this quiet rue Victor? Vincent's talking, but I can't hear his words; Sara's responding, smiling, a hand touching Vincent's arm, his hand still grasping her arm to steady himself. He bends and wobbles to pull his trousers back to his waist. He fumbles with the buttons, smiling or even laughing with Miss Voort.

July, 1888.

This is becoming repetitive; of course Dries was told that Vincent was here.

He arrived home like a storm. I'd no choice but to relay the sordid details of my encounter. Thankfully Clara offered support and gave an account from her viewpoint too. Dries paced the parlour as he listened, neither shocked by the particulars of the meeting nor angry with me. He did suggest that I reconsider my impulsive need to act — that I pause and think before rushing into tempests.

Is this the life of an artist though? Dramatic, full of emotions and struggle; do I still wish to be one?

I asked how he knew Vincent had called here, and of course he was with Theo when Sara accosted them both. Apparently she was 'distraught' to have witnessed a wild, 'naked' Vincent running from Dries' apartment.

After being reassured I was safe and well, my brother left immediately. He returned an hour later, telling me that Theo sent his kind regards and that he would call on me in a day or two.

Is there no calm weather in Paris?

Three Novels

My brother stands as straight as an arrow as he reads his correspondence, his camera box on his slate desk next to him. He's not even removed his frock coat yet; whatever's contained in those letters has captured his attention.

'There's another dance, tonight, at Moulin de la Galette,' he says, without an ounce of excitement.

'And that's bad?' I ask from the *confidante*.

'Not exactly,' he says with his eyes still fixed on the letter.

'It'll give me the perfect opportunity to speak to Theo again,' I say. I can't help but wonder if he likes to dance. The thought of him secretly enjoying exotic polkas makes me grin. 'Did you take your photograph of Eiffel's structure?'

Andries looks up and smiles. 'Much progress this week; they're securing the second floor already,' he says. 'But about tonight...'

'All women are welcome,' I say.

Andries nods. 'Usually, yes,' Andries says. 'Those occasions are so very full of cheer, quite the place to be with a glass of Muscat. But tonight's different,' he says. 'A private dance, one that won't be welcoming all women, and definitely not those considered to have *loose morals*. It's invitation only.' He mimics a voice when he says 'loose morals' but I'm not sure who he's imitating.

'Will Sara be there?' I ask. Andries nods again. Perhaps it'll give me a chance to talk to her, and for her to realise that she can't intimidate me. 'What should I wear? There's that new satin dress, the green and peacock blue—' I stop as a flush of red sweeps across Andries' face. 'What?' I ask, not sure what I've said to embarrass him.

'Sara,' he says.

'She'll be there. You said.' I stand and walk to him. 'And you'd like me to behave appropriately with Theo when in front of her?' I assume that my brother's concerned I'll cause mischief. No canoodling on the tables, no flashing of my ankles on the dance floor.

Andries shakes his head. 'Worse,' he says. He looks towards his fireplace and then down to the rug. 'She's...'

'Out with it,' I say.

'Sara has been updated on your relationship with Theo.'

'I don't yet have a relationship,' I say.

'After my chat with Theo and my informing him just how keen you'd been for Vincent to state that nothing had happened between you both,' he says, 'Theo's realised that you're serious about him.'

'I'm serious about him?' An echo. 'Am I?'

'I may have exaggerated a *little*,' Andries says, but then he holds up his palm before I can reply.

'And this was when you met with him in Le Tambourin?' I ask and Andries bobs his head.

'And then again when I returned to tell him what Vincent tried to do...'

'Was Sara still with him the second time?' I ask.

'No but we saw her today on Champs de Mars.'

'And?'

'And Theo was vocal about the possibility of you and him...' Andries pauses, but I nod for my brother to continue. 'He told

Sara that you and him ... that you'll be engaged soon.' The last part of his statement escapes in a gush.

'He's said what?' I move closer to my brother and bat his arm with my hand.

'Sara provoked him,' he says, palms up in defence. 'She declared, standing on Champs de Mars and in front of our friends, that she'd told tonight's organiser she'd not attend if you were invited. Said that the social status of the event would be diminished if you were there.'

'And that was Theo's response?' I say, attempting to process the rush of details. 'To declare we'd be engaged soon?'

Andries nods. 'It certainly quietened her nonsense.' He's grinning; Theo and my brother are cut from that same protective cloth.

'She needs to be put in her place.'

'She was today.' Andries' smile is contagious. 'The organiser won't upset Sara though and now I've been told,' he shakes the letter in the air, 'that my invitation doesn't extend to you.'

'So she got her own way?' I say. 'A woman controlling men.'

'Hardly,' Andries says. He laughs. 'Not when you consider her obsession with Theo.'

'Why do they jump at her beck and call then?' I ask, taking the letter from him and reading the words about me.

'Her father has sway and substantial wealth.'

'Does she have influence over everyone she meets?'

Andries sniggers. 'Of course not. She's a woman and her reputation declines daily,' he says. 'She's fast becoming the butt of my friends' jokes.'

'And you have no problem with that?'

My brother shrugs his shoulders and I shake my head. He can't understand why this angers me. I have my own concerns about Sara, but we both exist in a society that dismisses women. Her desires were only heard because of her powerful father. She won't even know that the event organiser was far from thrilled to bend to a woman's tantrum; that he only supported her scheme to court Mr Voort's influence. Why would I want to attend such an event?

'Then tonight I'll be alone with my canvas, oils and Charlotte Brontë, or maybe you'll allow me to read one of the novels you keep trapped in your bookcase.' I nod towards his shelves, the unread books standing to attention, no doubt longing to one day be held and read.

'That reminds me.' His tone's altered. 'A parcel of novels arrived for you earlier.'

'I haven't placed an order.'

'Vincent,' Andries says. His eyes search over my shoulder. I turn, expecting to catch a glimpse of the man. That name's fast becoming a ghoul in my brother's apartment. 'They're in the hallway.'

I turn on the spot and hurry out of the parlour. In the hallway, sitting atop the galleried back table, a pile of books tied with string. I bend to read the spines. Three authors. Three novels. All already loved and read by Vincent. *Braves Gens* by Jean Richepin, *Au Bonheur des Dames* by Emile Zola and *La Fille Elisa* by Edmond de Goncourt. And a note.

My dear Johanna,
    These artists capture life as we bear it ourselves.
    Tout à toi, Vincent

I don't move, I don't untie the string connecting them.

'He's delusional.' I jump at Andries' voice and then I nod.

'We should return them to him,' I say.

'Won't that make him keener?'

'I want the novels, but I don't want anything to do with Vincent.' If I keep them, am I placating him? Am I excusing his behaviour? I read his note again. 'Not a hint of an apology for what he did.' I run my finger over their spines. 'But is it insulting to Theo if I return a gift from his brother?'

I focus on the black and white floor tiles as I try to figure out the best response to Vincent. But how can I second-guess the reactions of a man I don't understand? The tiles are already dirty and in need of another clean. I think about poor Clara, about how impossible it is to keep on top of the housework, but soon my eyes are back on the books.

They're novels he mentioned during our walk. Works that stimulated his creativity. But already I know they're so much more than that. They're words that moulded his stance as an artist. From any other painter, it'd be the perfect gift: the most generous gift. I want to turn the pages that so enthralled Vincent, I want to consume every word that motivated him to create and to see if those words stir me too. I want that creativity to jump into my very being. I want to know his craft better. To acquire a sharper sense of the artist and how they view the world.

But I'm fast learning that everything Vincent offers comes with a price.

'Keep them,' Andries says. 'Vincent likes the chase. He'll tire of you when his next woman is found.'

I shake my head; I don't agree. 'This isn't an apology. Vincent's marking his territory.' This is as much a message for Theo as it is for me.

Andries shrugs his shoulders. 'The latest rumour is that you're Vincent's newest model, and that yesterday he sketched you without clothes,' he says.

I look at my brother and he raises an eyebrow, inviting a response. 'Seriously?' I ask and my brother laughs. 'I honestly don't know what else I can say about Vincent van Gogh. I'll never have the words to comprehend him.'

Andries pulls me into an embrace, planting a kiss on my forehead. 'Anyway, you haven't asked about my plans for this evening,' he says.

I pull back and look up at him. 'The party at Moulin de la Galette?' My anger towards Sara simmers in a pot with my Vincent frustrations.

'Wrong,' Andries says. His smile is playful. 'Theo's written too.' I start talking but he holds up a palm to stop me. 'And we've decided that if you're banished from the party, then we'll not attend either. Instead, Theo will be dining here with us.'

I can't help but laugh. Sara didn't win.

'See, he's already quite the entertaining *friend*,' Andries says.

'Sara will have earmarked him as her special guest.'

'He was,' Andries says. 'He's successful, he's well-connected. She'll be furious.' He laughs from his belly; the sound is contagious. 'And Theo refuses to send word that he'll not be attending. I imagine she'll spend her entire evening waiting for his arrival.'

I still smile, but unease simmers in my stomach. Sara loves a man who'll never return that love. She longs for his time and for him to want her entirely. She's a plaything, at the mercy of the Van Goghs; her love for Theo is a half-love. Her path twists towards the insanity that Camille fears, that I once feared – that too many women endure.

July, 1888.

Waiting for Theo to arrive for dinner but the more I observe the female condition, the more I'm struck with the realisation that I wilfully spurned my own happiness for Eduard. Already I question if I was ever in love with him; I even wonder if I was obsessed with its notion, rather than truly experiencing love's depth.

Sara is on my mind too. For her, insanity and the perception of love dance hand in hand. I wonder if she's already as despondent as I became – if she fears she'll die from longing, if she worries herself unable to live without Theo.

Why do too many women endure? Are we made to by the men who control everything about our lives?

Italian Woman

D inner was delightful, full of laughter, full of tales of what my brother's been up to in Paris. Theo and Andries bounced their playful stories off each other, and when they laughed their whole bodies responded: feet stomps, arm waves, bodies rocking. Now Theo helps Clara clear the table. I like that he does. She refused my help but was too polite to reject our guest.

My brother excused himself, claiming he had important correspondence that needed to be addressed in his bedroom, that very minute, and after several glasses of Muscat. His unsubtle method of leaving me alone with Theo amuses me. That he's encouraging an unchaperoned moment is unexpected. I stand and watch Theo being kind-hearted and respectful to Clara, before excusing myself and moving into the parlour.

Rain clouds have burst outside. The parlour's drapes remain open, the shutters not yet closed. The fall of rain against the windowpanes offer beat to the silence of the room. The rhythm soothes me; summer rain is full of magic. Tonight has been my best yet in Paris. I'm hit with joy that I've been given this second chance to enjoy Theo's company, but also that it was void of Van Gogh drama. Unsurprisingly Theo's knowledge of pointillism offered insight into the technique when conversation shifted in that direction. He even knows Paul Signac, and spoke of his 'loose painting techniques'. He advised against the methods currently being suggested, even outlining them all so I'd know what to avoid, then he offered numerous reasons why I wasn't to adapt that style of brushwork when applying the paint to my canvas. I can't quite grasp how or why, but all the advice offered seemed to burst with kindness and genuine interest. Theo's as keen to help me understand new artistic skills as I am to learn them. Excitement fizzes within me; there's so much that this man can teach me.

'Johanna.'

I can't help but smile. He speaks my name as if it were sugar on his lips and suddenly I'm a cliché of my former self. I turn to see Theo in the open doorway. His red moustache is well-maintained; his expression is steady.

'I should go,' he says.

I stand still, my back to the parlour windows, the raindrops dance outside. Theo glances at me, then to the window. I watch his expression alter.

'Stay,' I say. 'Until the rain breaks?'

His entire face changes again, becoming even kinder, as he maintains eye contact. He smiles, entering the room and moving to stand next to me. I can't help but smile too.

'Johanna,' he repeats. He picks up my right hand, turns it over as he lifts it to his mouth and then holds his lips on my palm. His eyes are closed. I think about Vincent, about his lack of refinement. Theo's movements are graceful in comparison; his every act is governed by a sense of propriety. Yet there's a hint of something else. It's just beyond what he's showing me, and that suggestion of what he holds back makes me grin. It's enticing, he's enticing; if I'm not careful, I'll soon be lost in a fog of Muscat and desire.

'Do you ever wish to be free?' I ask. Alcohol fuels words and Theo opens his eyes.

'I don't think any of us can ever be free. Not even my brother. Although he fails to realise this,' he says.

'Society dictates our path,' I say.

'And we may wander from it when the occasion arises.' A

pause. 'Yet I truly believe that we thrive when boundaries are in place. My brother exists within chaos; he's causing trouble again with—' He stops talking and swallows.

'Are you trying to gulp away unsaid words?' I ask. He strokes my palm with his thumb. It's a surprising gesture; he's already performing outside of my expectations of him. 'I'm not a delicate petal, terrified at the mention of his name. You can talk about Vincent.'

Theo scans my face. He's capturing my expression, reading it and deciding if what I've spoken is truthful. He nods.

'Vincent's much more cheerful now that he lives with me. Not a day goes by when he isn't invited to ateliers of major painters.'

'You're telling me what you feel I want to hear, aren't you?'

A pause. 'Yes.' He exhales. 'My brother has no manners at all. Of late, he seems to like being at loggerheads with everyone. And his provocative conduct…'

I nod; I know that behaviour.

'I don't have enough apologies,' he says.

'And yet he's your brother and your love for him absolute,' I say.

'You know Agostina Segatori,' he says.

The mention of her name makes my cheeks flush, but I try to hide that reaction. 'I met her in Le Tambourin. Her hatred of me was instant,' I say.

'Vincent believes that she recently aborted his child.'

I'm sure my expression is frozen, that my eyes are open too wide. This is outside of my general knowledge and alien to my experience.

'They're still a couple?' I say.

'It's hard to explain. Vincent's relationships are never … well … let's say *traditional*. And Vincent knows of many who have danced in her boudoir.'

'So the child might not have been Vincent's?' I say.

Theo frowns, his head bent slightly. 'Vincent believes she'll recover in two months,' he says, his tone seeping sadness.

'They exist within a world I can't quite grasp,' I say. The words are caught in a whisper.

'Yet one you wish to enter?'

I pause to consider his question. Seconds later, I shake my head. I don't know how to function within that world. I don't want to exist within the sordid corners of society, but still I seek a normality that's different from anything my parents know. I seek remarkable, yet fear falling into the chaos, into the abyss, into the madness and turbulence that seems to accompany its acquisition. It's hard to find the words to explain what I want, but I'm quickly learning that straddling two worlds can never be secure.

'Do you want to know more about my brother, the artist?' Theo says.

'I do,' I say, hoping that's the correct response.

'He's finished four paintings this last month and is currently working on something that's overly large, in the hope that I'll find him a buyer. The big canvases are difficult to sell though.'

'Do you like your work?' I ask.

'Dealing art fills my day. Monet and Degas keep me busy,' Theo says. 'You should come to my office. I'll show you what interests collectors and I still owe you that introduction with Degas.'

I smile. 'I'd love that,' I say. 'Are people beginning to admire Vincent's art more?'

'There's much to cheer in my brother's work, and his larger canvases make fine decoration for a dining room,' Theo says.

I'm still grinning like a fool, but there's a pause in our conversation. There's a question I need to voice. I remove my hand from his touch and let it fall back to my side.

'What do you want from me?' I ask.

'I've loved you since our first encounter.' No hesitation. Theo sees my grimace. 'What?'

'The concept of love at first sight,' I say.

Theo laughs from his belly. 'Did you not feel something for me during that first meeting in Moulin de la Galette?' I did, and I'm sure he knows that already. 'The first time I laid eyes on you, I saw mething that I'd sought in others in vain. You were never a stranger,' he says.

'I felt that too.' A whisper.

'Perhaps it's simply that my heart was free to love,' he says. 'I've never met anyone who excites me in the way—'

'Do I remind you of your brother?' I ask and Theo's expression changes.

'Miss Bonger, do you consider me *debauched*?'

I laugh. 'But finding out about my … my *thing* with Eduard shocked you?'

'My brother's Vincent van Gogh. There's little you could achieve that would shock me,' he says and I find myself wanting to embrace the man. He keeps his humour underneath his tightly buttoned coat. I want to hear more, everything; I doubt I'll ever tire of him.

Perhaps he's finally relaxing and trusting me with his true self. Perhaps Clara was right that I've always been searching for more than my family can offer. That thought about Clara brings with it sadness.

'What is it?' Theo says. My expression must have altered.

'I'm worried about Clara,' I say. 'She could be mistaken for someone who's eighty, but she's barely forty years old.'

He nods. 'It looks like consumption.'

'I love my brother, but he's not even noticed she's ill. You realised and helped her clear the table within a few hours of being here.'

'She means a lot to you?'

'I've known her forever,' I say. 'But she's proud and keeps refusing my offers of help.'

'Let me talk to her.'

'Dries can't know,' I say and Theo nods his agreement.

Seconds pass. Neither of us talk. The sound of rain on the pane fills our silence. There's no awkwardness. And I recognise, in that moment, that there's something remarkable about my connection with Theo van Gogh.

'You didn't answer my question,' I say. I watch as he looks

confused, perhaps rewinding our conversation to remember what I'd asked.

'What do I wish from you?' He pauses only for a moment. 'I've the means to allow you the freedom to be yourself. I can hold my own in conversation on a range of topics. Financial security would be a given, I can free you from your mother.' I laugh at that and he smiles. 'I'd never expect you to perform the role of a wife that demeaned your intelligence. I'd encourage you to pursue art, I'd help you develop your standing in the art world. Romantic love, in this instant, isn't a priority but I hope our love will be equal one day. You already know how I feel about you...' Another pause. I can't stop the dread that bubbles in my stomach. 'That marrying you adds to my standing within society is an added bonus. You'd be my equal, my Parisian partner.'

I hold up my palm to stop his words. 'But that's what you *think* I want to hear,' I say. 'Are you simply making promises in order to get what you want? When the reality might be different and—'

'You think I'm tricking you?' he says.

I nod. I can't live an 'ordinary' life; I'll become my mother. I won't be swept in her direction on a flurry of rash promises.

'That I'll take what I want and then abandon you?'

I've offended him. I study my hands; but what if he merely wishes to possess me? 'I've heard similar words before,' I say.

'My feelings are sincere,' he says.

'But nothing you've spoken is about what *you* desire. Are you so blinded by a ridiculous notion of love at first sight that you ignore your fundamental needs?'

A sigh. 'You wish for honesty?' A nod. 'I'd quite like a peaceful life. Recently Vincent's been ... *challenging*. He's also a drain on my bank account. I want laughter, intelligent conversation and, if I'm being entirely candid...' Another nod for him to continue. 'Would it help if I said I needed exotic sexual acts? Lots of them.'

'What?' I ask, raising my eyebrows so much that I think my eyes might pop out. I laugh from deep within. That wasn't the request I was expecting. I've no idea if he's joking.

'I don't want to disappoint you,' I say.

'Then try not to underestimate me,' he says. 'Time will tell, but, for now, a reminder … I'm not Stumpff.'

I smile so wide that there's a twinge of pain in my cheeks. 'I've seen you for the very first time this evening, haven't I?' I say. 'This is what my soul—' His eyebrows raise, and he smiles. 'No,' I say, holding up my palm, 'not love at first sight, but recognition. It felt I knew you already, that night at Moulin de la Galette.'

'I'm winning you over,' he says.

I'm still smiling a wide and full beam. He is, but so much more than that too; he's easing my fear.

Theo reaches for my hand again. From the corner of my eye I spy movement beside the open doorway. A shadow, a cap perched on a head. Clara listens.

'Come, let's sit together,' I say, walking across the room.

July, 1888.

I can't stop thinking about the unhappy, wretched life of Charlotte Brontë. How she suffered in that cold and comfortless parsonage in Haworth. All those years of monotony and torment. I keep considering the opportunities I've been given, here, in Paris with Dries, and now with Theo. I mustn't ever complain about this life I'm living.

It worries me how many others suffer like Charlotte, but worse they've not the skill to write Jane Eyre. *Instead they'll exist and die alone, and without the world ever knowing they lived.*

Why does that scare me so very much?

Undergrowth

They've left the doorway to the parlour open and I've crept downstairs. Theo's presence hasn't been announced and so I need to sneak; clearly, he's something to discuss with Andries that isn't intended for my ears.

I tiptoe along the hallway, stepping as close to the doorway as possible but still concealing my presence. The light from the parlour's large windows spills through the open entrance and across the hallway's tiles. Clara isn't near. I haven't seen her for hours.

'Sara is saying that your sister has feelings for my brother,' Theo says. 'I've had three other visitors today, all suggesting I'm being a fool.'

What the hell?

'We both know of Miss Voort's infatuation. Why are you letting this bother you so much?' Andries says. 'Jo tolerates Vincent because he's your brother and she cares for you. If he wasn't, she'd have refused conversation with him weeks ago. Surely you've—'

'Vincent implies they've been intimate. That day they walked around Montmartre together, in a bush, and again in here. On that rug,' Theo says.

In a bush?

'And you believe him?' Andries asks. 'He actually said they'd had intercourse?'

There's no spoken response. He believes Vincent.

'The only other man in Jo's life was Stumpff,' Andries says. There's a mumbled response that I can't quite hear. 'And she didn't have intercourse with him.'

My fingers form into a fist; I'm furious. My secrets are being discussed without my permission.

'I've seen a huge shift in her affection towards you,' Andries says. 'You've been a visitor here every day this week. Surely you've noted the difference?'

'And you feel that's genuine?'

'You don't?' Andries says. There's no disguising the irritation in his voice.

I wonder if Theo shrugs or nods or shakes away the consideration. Fury bubbles in my stomach; he doesn't believe my interest in him is honest, he can't feel my growing love, he believes Vincent over me.

'Aside from vulgar comments about Johanna, Vincent's withdrawn from me entirely. He spirals into depression and I've heard...'

'What?' Andries says. 'Is it Jo? Have you evidence of further contact?'

'No, Bonger, nothing like that. Your sister's maintained her promise to you and, much to my brother's anger, has refused all contact from him.'

'Are you wanting to retract your interest in my sister?'

'Far from it,' Theo says, the words rushing out. 'It's just that ... I've heard the women he pays to spend time with all resemble Johanna.'

My gut twists.

'Vincent has a taste, and my sister's a beauty,' Andries says.

'She is, but I've been told—'

'Who's fuelling this anxiety?' my brother says. I hear the concern in his tone; I wonder if Theo hears it too.

'Sara.'

Always that woman. When did I become her enemy?

'I can't get rid of her,' Theo says; I hear that he's defeated. 'She's everywhere I turn. Always, something to tell me. Something dire that needs attention. Some juicy piece of gossip that I simply must know. Vincent's behaviour, Johanna's reputation, what she might be doing with Vincent, what Sara might do to herself if I won't listen.'

'You're too polite,' Andries says and I hear Theo's strained laugh.

Sara Voort is as cunning as a fox. She's entirely delusional if she thinks Theo's in love with her, but she's astute. She knows exactly what she's doing. Her topics pull at Theo's heart and link to matters he can't, in good conscience, ignore.

'She said that Vincent calls each of his women by Johanna's name.'

'How could she possibly know such an intimate detail?' my brother asks.

'Unless she was there…'

I hear my brother's laughter. This is infuriating. Why am I hiding out here? I should be in there and—

'Even if it were true, so what?' Andries asks.

'So what?' Theo says. It's an echo. He's clearly taking a moment to consider the question.

'I've seen Vincent with Agostina every day this week. Apparently, she's recovering well,' Andries says.

'So I've heard,' Theo says, then I hear a loud sigh. 'But why would Vincent imply that…'

'Sara's a woman scorned, Vincent a man rejected,' my brother says. 'That's quite a combination. I imagine Sara's been pecking at Vincent's ear.'

What I don't understand is why Theo's listening to her. Why he won't stand up to her. What grasp does she have on him? I'm hit with a wave of emotion that's unfamiliar. It takes me a moment to realise: I'm jealous.

'Could his recent spiral be because of Miss Segatori's abortion?

Vincent's fond of her, and has often said how he'd like to be a father.'

Silence. I wish I could see Theo's expression. I bend in closer to the gap between the door and its frame, but the angle's wrong. I can't see anything new and instead I cast my shadow across the hallway tiles. I jump back.

'How could I engage in a proper marriage, when my brother, my best friend in the world, lusts after my wife?' Theo says, interrupting my thoughts. I hold my breath.

'Would he still be living in Paris when you're married? Please don't say you'd consider Vincent living with you both?'

'Of course not,' Theo says. A small laugh tinkles the end of the sentence.

'Vincent's spoken about founding an artists' colony in the country,' Andries says. 'I have the financial means to assist.' What? What does that mean? I wish I could see Theo's reaction. 'Arles was mentioned. It would be an ideal destination. Far enough to ensure Jo is free of his unwanted attention and without Vincent realising that he's being removed. It'd also give him space from Agostina. She's cast quite the spell over him, and several others too. And a removal of Sara from his ear would be good. Did you know that—'

'I've lost count of the amount of times he's said that he's most himself when among nature. It's where he's happiest,' Theo interrupts. 'Just yesterday he spoke of longing for the unspoiled countryside... The woodland in Asnieres was a favoured location for him; his ability to capture the play of light and shadow on foliage remarkable, but recently he's refused to walk there. If his current spiral continues, I worry what will become of him.'

'Then consider the arrangement for the better good,' Andries says. 'He's weary of Paris and in Arles he'll discover both sunshine and harmony. Him going to the country might be the best solution for everyone.'

'I'll miss my brother though.' Sorrow covers his words. Theo's sense of family matches mine: the love of and for our brothers matters most.

Guilt punches into my stomach and whirls around with my rage. I'm not sure if I need to storm in there or vomit onto the floor tiles. If Andries fell in love and his wife thought it best to send me away, my heart would break. Siblings love each other and then hate each other in equal measure – back and forth, back and forth – yet to let a new relationship break that bond... What would allowing that say about me?

'If Johanna finds out that we sent Vincent away because of her...' Theo says.

'The more space we can put between Vincent, Sara and my sister, the better. He's destroying—'

Enough.

'Is this your plan?' I ask, marching into the room. I jab my finger towards Theo. The words are almost a shout. 'To remove any man who happens to look at me? Do you have such little faith in my affections that you fear me falling in love with someone who isn't you?'

'Johanna,' Theo says. Distress splatters like paint across his face.

'I heard everything,' I say, hands on my hips. 'Is this arrangement in lieu of a marriage proposal?'

'You heard a private conversation,' Andries says. He's smiling as if to dismiss me.

I point my index finger at my brother. 'And you're a pompous idiot.'

'Mamma would disapprove of your lack of decorum,' Andries says and I growl like a dog.

'Whenever Sara Voort comes to you with a piece of gossip, I'm to be punished. Is that our future?' I ask. 'What did you tell Vincent? That gossip dies when it hits a wise man's ears?'

'She drills into me every single day,' Theo says.

I roll my eyes and shake my head in an exaggerated manner; I possibly appear deranged. 'Poor you,' I say. 'Are you so weak a man that you can't ignore that desperate woman?' Theo doesn't respond. 'And you think I've been intimate with Vincent in a *bush*?' I shout the word 'bush' and I hear Andries stifling his laughter.

'Not really, of course not,' Theo says and I glare at him.

'Sending Vincent away from his beloved Paris, because of me,' I say. My eyes flick between them both. Theo refuses my eye contact now. 'That's your great plan? To keep you from your brother, your very best friend, for the rest of your life? How exactly do you see that working for *our* future? Am I supposed to feel grateful every time I see your pain? Am I to carry the guilt of breaking both the Van Gogh brothers' hearts?'

'It won't be like that—' Theo begins.

'You're monsters. Domineering, arrogant... I'll tell him.' I'm shouting again, my face contorting with my rage. 'And then he'll tell you the truth – that nothing has ever happened between us. Not even in a *bush*. And then you'll stop with this nonsense.'

'You think you know Vincent, but you're mistaken. You've got this entirely wrong, Johanna. Vincent despises Paris,' Theo says. His cheeks flush red and he can't hold my eye contact. I'm not sure if my outbursts, or him being embarrassed at being overheard, are the cause. But that's almost irrelevant; what hurts more is that Theo's failed to accept and embrace the depth of emotion I have for him. He's entertained the idea that I might have feelings for Vincent. He doesn't trust me.

'I love you,' I say. I see his shock, I see his delight. I can't allow my confession to distract from this moment. 'Where's your compassion?' I say, my voice high-pitched and squeaking.

'Clearly off dancing along Boulevard de Clichy with your sanity,' Andries says. He chuckles.

I turn and run from the parlour.

'Where are you going?' I hear my brother shout.

'To find Vincent,' I say.

'Congratulations on being in love,' he shouts after me.

I don't turn back.

Still Life With Glass Of Absinthe And A Carafe

'They plot to send you to Arles,' I shout, rushing into Le Tambourin. 'Because of me, because of us. But there's no us. And Theo's heart will break if you don't...' I stop, catching my breath. I see Agostina sitting so close to Vincent she's practically in his lap.

'I ran here to tell you,' I say, my shoulders slumped and my confidence already gliding down them. 'I need you to stop playing whatever game this is.' I wave my arms in the air. 'Tell Theo the truth about us. Let's all be friends instead.'

Nausea swirls in my stomach: I hate even being in the same room as this filthy man. But if I can make Vincent tell the truth, then I'll save Theo's heart and I'll put an end to this Van Gogh madness. All the clientele turn to me. The smoky air whirls and no doubt sticks to my clothes and hair. Today there's no noise from the piano, today there's no singing of sentimental lyrics that call for revenge. I'm steps away from their table, perhaps Agostina thinks I want her to move away. I don't and she's marked her territory. He belongs to her; the thought of him being mine turns my stomach again. Instead, she lifts a cigarette to her lips, her motion slow, striking a match and lighting the tip. I'm close enough to see the finer details of her ensemble: that her jacket and dress have different patterns, that her parasol sits on the stool to her left, that her fashionable blue hat's held in place with hatpins. She oozes bohemian style and detail. I let my worst emotions and insecurities surface. I'm still Dutch, plain and dowdy; she's still everything that I'm not. I appreciate that's far from her responsibility, and knowing that makes disgust for myself whirl alongside the nausea.

'I pursue the self-assurance that makes a person glad,' Vincent says. His voice breaks my interest in the café's owner. Everything he says carries a tone that mocks me.

'That makes no sense,' I say. I sound rude, but I owe him no respect. 'Didn't you hear what I said? My brother and Theo are plotting to send you away. To keep you away from me, despite my telling them that I've no interest in you and that we weren't intimate in a bush. God, the thought of you and me—'

He laughs. 'And yet here you are.'

I scowl. 'I'm here out to protect Theo's heart. You're his brother and he loves you dearly,' I say. 'And Theo matters to me. If I'm to be in his future—'

Vincent laughs again. 'You're his latest woman.'

I clasp my hands behind my back. 'You've no idea—'

'When I'm in the country, gladness will materialise much more freely in my being. In this Parisian *hell*, I'm surrounded by rumour, judgement and the stifling glares of those who seek to own me. Here I'm only ever relaxed with those who ecclesiastics seek to condemn.' He's waving his hands about as he speaks. He's slurring his words and his tone's dismissive. He wants me to leave; he doesn't give a donkey's derriere about what I'm telling him.

'More riddles. Is your sole aim in life to make others feel stupid?' I ask. 'Come back to Dries' apartment with me. Your brother's there,' I say. 'Let's talk this through like adults.'

Agostina looks me up and down as if I'm a goose in need of plucking. I place my hands on my hips and thrust out my bosom. *Stop looking at me.* It seems that the desire to intimidate other women is an essential part of being a strong female. I'm trying desperately to mask my body's nervous trembles. I'm perspiring like a hog. I'm uncomfortable in my clothes; possibly she gains pleasure from my squirms.

Vincent places a sugar cube on a spoon, over a glass of water. He dribbles absinthe from a carafe onto the sugar cube. I watch as the clear water turns into a cloudy green in his glass. He repeats this for the second glass on the tambourine-top of the table. His sketchpad is there too. I wait for him to offer me a drink. He doesn't. They clink glasses. They drink the shots in single gulps. Agostina's eyes speak to Vincent in a language I've no interest in mastering.

'Too many Parisian painters repulse me as men,' he says. 'Theo entertains them all, but none interest me.'

'Don't you even care that they want to send you to Arles? That you'll be without Theo?' I ask, attempting to sound confident and bold.

'Answer me this, Miss Bonger. Do you seek to own me too?'

I laugh. It's fake. 'I'm trying my hardest to bear you,' I say. 'I won't come between the Van Gogh brothers. Won't be why you're sent away.'

He sniggers. 'You already place too much importance upon yourself,' he says. 'Soon, when my brother grows bored of his latest obsession, you'll be passed on for me to play with.'

I shake my head. 'You're wrong, Vincent.'

He smirks, then nods. 'You seek an escape from your suffocating family. You play with my affections and are ashamed of any association with me,' he says. He pours more absinthe, through a new sugar cube on a spoon, into the same two glasses. He stares at the liquid. His calmness disturbs me. He considers himself a victim and has cast me as the villain in his story. 'Is it not true that you seek a marriage of convenience with my brother?'

'I love him,' I say, my voice sounding shrill.

Agostina laughs. I turn to her and she clicks her teeth and tips her head upwards. Vincent watches, clapping with delight; he's enjoying our performances.

I point at her. 'You had an abortion.' I'm not being the best version of myself. 'And you don't even know who the father was.'

Unkindness bounces along the words; it makes me want to shrink to the floor. Vincent's laughter booms. He presses tobacco into the bowl of his pipe.

'Our business is not your business,' she says. She's unfazed. She rests her head on Vincent's shoulder and places a protective hand over her stomach. 'Who are you to judge me? Worry about your own sins, you will not be asked about mine.'

Heat rushes to my cheeks, I lower my eyes for a moment. Who am I becoming?

I look at Agostina again; she has risen. She has both the control of her reactions and a self-confidence that I lack. Even without kindness, she's beautiful. How is that possible? If all is stripped from you in Paris, do you only have two choices? To crumble into pity or to fight with conviction? Camille has risen too; her rebirth is with compassion and her depth of beauty overwhelming. Yet here I am – my first confrontation – and I've somehow managed to both react with cruelty and to sound like Mamma. I'm standing here, sneering at what it means to be a woman. I'm unsure I could like myself less than I do now.

I've much to learn about how women rise. Courage and kindness in the face of adversity: that's who I need to be. Inhale, exhale. I switch my attention back to Vincent. 'Why do you both gain such pleasure from mocking me?' I ask.

'I have three failed marriage proposals attached to my name, all higher beings than you,' he says. He strikes a match, letting it burn for a few seconds, then moves the match in a circular motion over the tobacco. 'Yet you've failed to acknowledge my letters and even that I gifted you three novels. You decided that I wasn't worthy of your time.'

'Your sense of family matches mine. Our brothers mean everything to us...' I sway on the spot; all eyes are on me. I'm aware that the other customers listen and judge. This encounter will be reported to Andries. No doubt word for hideous word.

'You think we're the same?' Vincent laughs. 'We're completely different, Miss Bonger. You're shackled to society and I'm not. I seek neither love, stability nor money. I chase passion, excitement, lust and chaos. One day I'll marry and my children will be a product of pure joy. What do you pursue?' Vincent asks. 'You claim to be a female artist, yet have failed to create a single piece worthy of an audience.' A pause.

I have no words. I've never made that claim.

'What could ever satisfy your hollow heart?' He laughs – a cruel sound. 'You're an immature and inexperienced imp.'

'You've no idea what I'm capable of, Vincent van Gogh. If you did, you'd not be this cruel,' I say. I'm crying: frustration, sadness, loss. My fingers smear my tears over my cheeks. 'I'll make Theo happy.'

'Why are you even here? You hound me.' He puffs on his pipe, and Agostina nods in agreement.

'I came here to stop them sending you away. To help Theo, to help you too,' I say, wiping my nose on the back of my hand. 'In spite of what you tried to do to me.'

He waves his hand as if to bat away my words. 'You think yourself better than me, but what can *you* offer a man?' he asks. 'What is it that you think you can give my brother?' He gulps down the first green shot, and then the second. 'He is blinded by his infatuation. He thinks you special, your connection extraordinary, but you're just another tourist in Paris.' A pause. Agostina smirks as she lights another cigarette. 'You don't know me, Miss Bonger. If you did, then you'd know that I'd jump at the chance to escape to Arles.'

'Is Paris not enough for you? Is *she* not enough?' I ask and Agostina laughs from her belly. The sound rumbles into Vincent and he echoes her mirth.

'You want to save me,' he says.

'I want to prevent Theo's heartache.'

'You think you want my life. But have you not realised that it's Theo who affords me that luxury? You think I'm free? You consider Agostina free?' They laugh again. 'You fail to see that we've been stripped to nil, that we've no choice but to behave in this way. Have you never asked why I numb myself by drinking a good glass and smoking a lot? It's you who we envy.'

'Me?' I let my tears zigzag down to my chin.

'Yes, Miss Bonger. You have choice, wealth, an education and opportunity. You're the one who is truly free,' he says. 'I offer a life in poverty and a *diseased penis*,' he says. 'Why are you *really* here? Surely not a marriage of convenience with me?' He laughs.

'I'd rather have intercourse with an oversized bull than with you,' I say. 'I want us to fix this mess before you become my brother.' I look at Vincent but his eyes are locked on Agostina. She consumes him in a way I can't yet grasp. How did I ever consider myself skilled enough to end this Van Gogh madness?

'I dance to my brother's generosity. He funds my every step, down to which paints I purchase and if I can afford another canvas. I'm his slave.'

Vincent drapes his arm around Agostina's shoulders, before pulling her to him and kissing her mouth. He's all tongues and slurps. A hand gropes her left breast. I watch their display of affection: it's desperate, it's depraved, it's the saddest thing I've ever seen. I understand him for the first time – Vincent is lost and alone. He constantly seeks approval and acceptance as an artist and a man, yet instead he faces rejection after rejection.

'Is the thought of Theo being happy with me too much for you to stand?'

Vincent snaps his eyes to me, glaring with an intensity that shoots fear. 'Go, run to our brothers, Johanna.' He kisses Agostina's neck as she moans out her pleasure. 'Are you even aware of what Theo does for Bonger's housemaid?'

'Clara?' I ask, dread sparking in my stomach. What have I missed?

'That's why he went to Bonger's today.'

'You're an embarrassment to women,' Agostina Segatori says, clicking her teeth. 'You mimic us. Ashamed of who you are, desperate to be like us, yet you quiver at our feet. Run, little girl.' She waves her cigarette towards the open doorway. 'Run to your men. You're not welcome here.'

I turn, head bent forward. I scuttle from Le Tambourin, knocking over one of their tambourine-topped tables. The glasses and bottles fly to the ground. They smash on impact. Raised voices, '*Attention*!', scraping chair leg on tile, laughter, singing. I keep scuttling. My arms flail. Tears and snot gush down my face; all decorum has vanished. I stop only when I'm outside.

People nod to me, some look inquiringly as I pass them. '*Vous vous sentez bien, Mademoiselle*?' someone asks.

I scoop up the material from my skirts and run along the cobblestones. Over Boulevard de Clichy, looking neither left nor right for *fiacres*, I run to Andries' apartment.

I need Clara. I need to know that she's safe. I need to know what Theo has done for her.

Head Of A Peasant Woman With White Cap

I stop running when I'm in Andries' hallway. I slump over, hands on my knees, trying to suck in air.

'Where is she? Is she dead?' I stutter out words between gasps. No reply. A pause. Deep breaths. Someone steps towards me. I straighten up: a girl.

'Who the hell are you?' I shout at the poor girl. She jumps at the volume and aggression in my words, panic sweeping across her face. A teen, overly thin, not quite grown into her long limbs: she's pristine in her maid's dress, apron and hat, but she's not my Clara. I don't allow her the chance to reply.

'Clara!' I shout. I pace the hallway, peering into rooms and waiting for her to come rushing to my aid. 'Clara!' Louder this time. With each second of silence my stomach twists and turns. *Please don't be dead.* I head towards the kitchen.

A squeak of a sound behind me. 'She's not...'

I stop. I turn.

'*What*?' I shout. I move closer to the girl. She quivers, she melts. I'm terrifying. I must appear ready for a fight: all aggression and fury. '*Waar is Clara*?' I'm speaking Dutch and she doesn't understand. 'Where's Clara?' I ask again, this time in French.

'Germany, Miss Johanna. Arranged this morning,' she says, her voice a whisper. She seems to curtsey with every word she says to me. Her eyes remain glued to the tiles as she bobs up and down.

'Germany?' My echo's a shout. The girl hunches her shoulders, still not daring to meet my eyes. She might even be crying. I know how she feels. 'Where's my brother?' I ask.

'In there, Miss Johanna.' She points to the closed parlour door mid-bob and I hurry towards it.

The door slams off the wall with the force of my entry. Andries is waiting. He's standing in front of his slate desk, hands on his hips: his facial expression confused, his stance ready for combat. He has all the answers, I have none.

'Jo, come here and sit—'

'You dismissed her?' I shout, my feet glued to the floor.

'Clara's ill,' Andries says. The words are firm, conclusive even.

'So you threw her onto the streets?' I say, my fingers forming into a fist.

He shakes his head. 'No, she's safe. I promise,' he says. 'Come here. Deep breath.' Arms spread wide, he invites me into an embrace.

'She was exhausted,' I say, looking down to the floor. I don't move. This is my fault. I should have focused on her, made sure Andries employed others. 'She needs this job. We're all the family she has. We're all she's ever known,' I say. I can't stop the tears tracking from my eyes to my chin.

'Theo's arranged everything,' Andries says. 'That's why he was here earlier.'

My eyes snap to meet my brother's. 'But Vincent—'

'You caught the end of our conversation,' he says, he smiles; it isn't convincing. There's sadness. 'I should have noticed. She wasn't Theo's responsibility.'

'What's Theo done?'

'He asked his doctor to evaluate Clara's symptoms, and then ordered a physical examination of her chest. Her pulse was counted, her temperature taken, she was weighed...'

'And?' I ask.

'*Mal du siècle*,' he says.

'Consumption,' I say.

A pause. I feel sick. My knees wobble. I step over to the *confidante*, placing a hand on the carved back to steady myself. I've heard too much about the disease. There have been whispers, coming down to us from the educated, of it being contagious. A single cough or sneeze is said to carry the disease. The chances of my having caught it are high enough to place a bet.

'I read that it's infectious,' I say. I try recalling the symptoms that others discussed. 'Have you coughed? Your voice sounds hoarse. Is my skin paler than usual?' The words rush together; I'm full of panic.

'I've been examined.' He pauses. A spark of dread shoots through me and covers my face. He must see my fear. 'Healthy as an ox,' he says, but there's no celebration to be found in his tone.

Mal du siècle has been the talk of polite society for years now. The message we're being given is clear – stay away from people with consumption. Yet we've been living with poor Clara. She's been preparing our food, washing our clothes, touching our cutlery, drying our cups and glassware. But then I'm hit with guilt. It punches into my stomach. All this concern for myself and Andries, when the most loyal, best servant I know is dangerously unwell.

'She's an outcast now,' I say. That's what happened to a neighbour's maid, back home in Amsterdam. The family discovered she was ill and cast her out. No home, shunned by all who encountered her, no one offering a shred of kindness: she was said to have died on the street.

'Theo wouldn't allow that,' Andries says. His tone conveys two facts: one, that he considers Theo courageous. Two, that he wishes he were more like Theo.

'Is she in Germany with Theo?' I ask. I'm overwhelmed, I'm alarmed. 'He'll catch the deadly—'

'She's on her way to a sanatorium there.'

'They're prisons,' I say, perching on the edge of the *confidante*. 'They force the poor there to die. Why have you let—'

'Do you know of Peter Dettweiler?' he says. I shake my head.

My entire body trembles. I've lost control of my emotions, of myself. I'm not sure how to react next.

'Theo knows him. His facility isn't where people of Clara's class...' He pauses. Perhaps he notices the shift in my expression. 'Theo's arranged passage to Falkenstein Sanatórium in the Taunus Mountains, near Frankfurt. There she'll follow a strict regimen of diet and exercise. She'll be given three meals every day, and a glass of milk every four hours. Few will ever know.'

'And then she'll have a speedy death?' I say.

The need to know that someone's caring for Clara, that she won't have a prolonged and lonely passing overwhelms me. I should have forced her to rest. I meant to talk to Andries about employing more staff. I should have sought help for her. I should have forced and ordered so much more than I did.

'Theo's doctor has predicted a full recovery.' But his shoulders drop.

'What is it?' I ask.

A sigh. 'He reprimanded me. Said Clara lived the life of a slave and that I should be ashamed of myself.'

'Theo did?'

Andries moves to the *confidante* and slumps down next to me. 'No, his physician.' I rest my head on his shoulder.

'A full recovery.' I echo the words and their meaning hits me, but still I'm full of sadness.

'The stay there is to include mental rest, with protection from visitors and from talkative neighbours.'

'So we can't visit,' I say and I feel his head shake.

'It's an infectious disease, Jo. Who in their right mind would travel to Germany to visit a servant with a contagious ailment?' A tinkle of a laugh escapes and I can't help but smile. I bat his knee with my hand. 'Mamma and Pa won't ever allow her back in their house.'

'Will you?' I say, shifting on the *confidante* to sit up and face him.

'I've been given Anaïs in exchange.'

'Like cattle,' I say. The words are a whisper. I bite down on my lip.

'Not at all. Clara's our family. She can return when she's well.' He places his arm around my shoulder and pulls me close to him. 'Anaïs,' he says. She rushes into the room. 'Can you bring us tea?' I don't look up to see her; I can't bear that she isn't Clara.

'Yes, sir. Tea, sir,' she says.

Theo, that kind, generous man, has taken care of my brother's housemaid. She's served Bongers all my life and now Theo's written himself into her new chapter.

'I'm worried that you're looking pale,' my brother says.

July, 1888.

Dries stood in the doorway while Theo's doctor examined me. My brother offered no words when my lack of consumption was declared.

I saw him wipe his eyes as he left the room.

From: Hermine Bonger
To: Johanna Bonger

Come to Amsterdam immediately. Urgent. Come today.

Summer 1888

AMSTERDAM

A few hours ago, exhausted from travel, I'd not even removed my mantelet when Mamma declared that I was dressing like a Parisian whore and that my attire wouldn't be suitable for a first meeting with my fiancé. A fat, old man that I detest already.

She then felt the need to inform me that I'm never to return to Paris; that my engagement to that horrid pig is to be announced within a week. I won't ever marry him. I've written to Dries and asked him to come here immediately. They always listen to my brother, and I can't offer words without anger and tears.

Why didn't I accept Theo's proposal right away? Why do all of those motives now seem both immature and irrelevant? Being able to marry the man of my choice, having the kind of marriage that I want, that matters more than I can voice.

When I was younger, I'd have sworn that Mamma would have been the single constant in my aging but recently I've wanted more and more distance between her and myself. I see her differently, or possibly I see her truly... I like her less and I detest her more.

We're told that our parents are everything, forgetting that being born into that unit is accidental.

Dear Theo,

Dries promised he'd visit and tell you about Mamma's demand that I return to Amsterdam immediately. I hadn't the chance as I rushed to catch the only train, not pausing to question why the demand was made of me and not of my brother.

I wish I still didn't understand what was happening. Yet tomorrow Dr Janssen will arrive at my parents' home and there's an expectation. One I can't quite commit to paper, yet am desperate that you'll somehow understand.

Leaving Paris has caused my soul to ache. I've left behind my canvas and paints, and I've left behind you – the man I love. My stay with Dries changed me. I think I've aged a million years and had as much wisdom showered upon me in the last few weeks of knowing the Van Gogh brothers. All I now know for sure is that I think of you too much. Barely an hour passes without you climbing into a thought. That my parents insist I be engaged to someone, who is not you, makes that entirely inappropriate, yet my mind is as wilful as I am suddenly lost again.

Last night while travelling I considered how we can exist in different countries yet share the same sky. And that sky held my focus; it still does. That sense of there being so much more than the drama and commotion existing in the Bonger household today. I counted eleven stars and noted their various colours. Lemon, pink, silver and snow-white in the rich violet and blue of a night sky. Do you ever look to the skies and wonder if we see the same stars? Time and travel allow for consideration.

Those colours disappeared and the glory of God's morning star rose into the bluest of skies.

Nothing is permanent; I see that now.

Your, Jo

Starry Night

I can't bear to be near my parents. Their relentless talk of the numerous desirable qualities that Dr Janssen holds makes me want to vomit onto my boots. Mamma just said how he was likely to pop his clogs soon, what with him being elderly, and that my lying back and 'doing my duty' would reap financial rewards.

'I refuse,' I say, my voice too high and too squeaky. I'm ignoring the stench of cabbage.

'You cannot,' Mamma says. The candles around the ground-floor dining room dance with the draft. They flicker eerie shadows across her long face. Straight-backed and emaciated by religious fasting, she's dressed from her high collar to ankle in black. Her eyes are icicles, her mouth's solemn and grey; Mamma never slouches or relaxes, Mamma rarely smiles and never embraces. She personifies gloomy. Tonight, she's a storm.

'We will announce your engagement within the week,' she says.

'I'm in love with someone else.' I want to throw things around the room, but I don't. I'm trying to be an adult. This is me being courageous. I take a moment. I inhale, I exhale. 'What monsters you are,' I say, lowering my volume slightly.

'So dramatic,' Mamma says, nodding pointedly at Pa. 'A foul-mouthed wretch. How is she my child?' She sighs, then lifts her glass of water and takes several sips. I wait. 'You have met Dr Janssen. Numerous times. You were *in love* with Stumpff. We have yet to meet this Theo van Gogh.' She places her glass on the large wooden dining table, next to her neatly folded napkin. She looks at Pa, her face thunder. She's signalling that I'm tiresome, and that the short conversation already bores her. She wants Pa's agreement and support. I'm outnumbered. There's no help for me in this room.

'I've met the doctor as your daughter, not as my...' I can't finish the sentence. Queasiness swirls and threatens from my stomach. My parents wait. 'I'm educated and more than capable of choosing my own husband,' I say. 'Let me return to Paris and continue courting Theo. Dries will tell you that Theo wants to marry me.'

'In Utrecht, you behaved like a whore and hounded a poor man. In Paris, you chased after a penniless artist with a reputation to match,' Mamma says, her voice measured and firm. 'You had your chance to find a suitable husband, but it proved a task beyond you. Now the artist's brother has stepped in—'

'It wasn't like that. Theo is—'

'All that foreign water changed you. It poisoned your mind and filled you with sin. I told your father not to allow—'

I hammer my fists on the wooden table. 'Strap Dr Janssen naked at this table and push an apple in his mouth. He's a stinking hog,' I say. The glasses and plates rattle in response. I'm full of frustration and know this isn't the way to win over my parents. I should show self-restraint. I should breathe more, react less, but their refusal to listen is exasperating.

'With all respect, Johanna,' Pa responds in the calmest of tones. He ignores my anger and takes a moment to sip from a glass of beer. 'You're being unnecessarily *difficult*. Both you and Andries have failed to find a suitable match in Paris.'

'Dries found Theo. I want to marry Theo.'

'You do, you do not, you do again ... and then there's the hand holding with his brother. Your ugly actions mean that we have few options. I cannot risk your bringing more shame to our family,' he says. 'This matter will not be discussed further.' He takes another sip, not placing the glass on the table. His left hand hovers near a half-full pitcher. 'Come, join us for a toast.' He points with his glass to an empty chair to his right: a table setting already prepared for me.

'Will it always be this way?' I ask and Pa raises an eyebrow. He's curious yet he'll be braced for my next outburst.

'A life governed by expectation and cruelty. I'm being silenced and ignored,' I say. The words have a snap. 'First your mercilessness regarding Eduard and then Dr Janssen's—'

'I forbid further conversation about Stumpff,' Pa yells.

'Frederick is a good man and a suitable match. You will want for nothing,' Mamma says.

'I'll want Theo,' I say.

Mamma laughs. 'Frederick has ill-health and wants only an heir,' she says. 'Why you're making such a fuss is beyond me. Upon his death, you'll never want for a thing.'

'But the man's a pompous oaf. I won't have him ride me like the animal he is. I refuse,' I say.

'Enough,' Pa roars. He shakes his glass. Drops of beer jump onto the dining table. 'This discussion is tiresome and immaterial. This is not a choice for you to make. Your engagement will be announced within the next seven days.'

My stomach growls its protest. Food, comfort, kindness – I need it all. Mamma folds her arms across her chest, sadness and anger cover her face in patches. She's all bones and negativity. Pa drains his glass of beer. He reaches for the pitcher to quench his thirst and disappointment.

'Come, Johanna, eat something,' Mamma says. Her stern expression remains but her voice is softer. *No, Mamma, I won't stop making a fuss and accept my fate.*

'I can't stomach anything, knowing he expects—'

'Your future *husband* will visit tomorrow morning and you will greet him with Bonger grace and dignity,' Mamma says, making her expectation clear.

'I will do no such thing,' I say.

'Go to your room,' Pa shouts. 'You'll be woken with time to prepare for your appointment with Frederick.' I look at my mother, forever desperate for her support, but her lips are pinched together as if to prevent a kind word escaping.

I scurry out of the dining room. Disappointment causes a shiver and makes me pull my shawl even tighter around my shoulders. I long for Andries. I long for Theo. I long for Clara. I even long for Camille Claudel. I long for an ally, for a supporter, for anyone to help with my escape.

Is acceptance of a life full of sadness what it means to be courageous?

I hear the slam of the dining room's heavy door and raised voices that I strain to catch but can't. They're arguing. I'm not sure which parent would reason a case for the marriage not to happen. I suspect neither. I imagine their voices are raised as each blames the other for my improper ways.

August, 1888.

Dread covers me.
　That piggish old man will visit today.

Vase With Daisies And Anemones

His death was entirely unexpected.

We were informed late afternoon. I'd spent the day dressed in my best clothes but refusing to leave my bedroom, my stomach growling in complaint. My parents spent the day awaiting the visit that would occur 'at any moment'. Eventually and possibly because she was tired of hearing Pa's complaints, Mamma sent her maid to Dr Janssen's home on Herengracht, to enquire about the delay in his visit.

The maid returned, out of breath and shouting the death announcement as she ran through the house. Mamma was torn between fury at her maid's inappropriate behaviour – a reverend should have been the one to inform us – and despair that the man's death had occurred before we were even engaged. Andries later suggested that I may have wished, on the stars the night before, for it to happen.

'As the coffin was lowered into its hole, I felt a million eyes on me,' he says.

'Was it awful?' I ask and my brother nods. I was forbidden from attending. My mother feared I would find it too difficult to restrain my weeping and would bring additional embarrassment to our family.

'Mamma declared Dr Janssen was a man of reputation, he

saved many lives with early detection of disease,' I say. 'She even suggested that he was kind in allowing hopeless cases to pass away.'

Andries stands beside me: tall, thin, persistent. I shiver and he leans closer, his shoulder touching mine. He arrived in Amsterdam twenty minutes after we'd learned of Dr Janssen's death and was faced with Mamma's hysterical sobbing. That he rushed to Amsterdam upon receiving my letter made me wail with relief. Indeed, this summer I am continuously grateful for our bond and for his desire to protect me. He's so much better at all things proper and social than I am. Now we stand on the opposite side of the canal to Dr Janssen's home. We watch as people enter. We watch as the black front door closes again. Visits of condolences can occur now that the funeral's over.

'Put your face on,' he says quietly, and I adjust my expression as we walk over the cobbles and to the bridge, crossing to Herengracht 247. Today's not the day to show my relief regarding Dr Janssen's death. Today calls for grief to be etched around my eyes. I need to play the part of a grieving almost-fiancée, of a woman who has had her loved one stolen cruelly from her, before they could consummate their union. Mamma has demanded that this piece of gossip replaces the lingering slice about me and Eduard.

The only grief I actually feel is for my uncertain future and the fear that my parents will sell me to the next highest bidder. I call on those emotions with each step towards the house. I consider how it would feel to never see Theo again.

'I almost lived there,' I say. 'All seven floors of it.'

'Far grander than our family home,' Andries says. His arm reaches around my shoulder and his embrace keeps me safe.

'I never wanted to marry him.' My brother squeezes my arm.

'That's why I rushed here,' he says.

'But I never wished him…'

'We'll tackle Mamma and Pa together. Tomorrow.'

I hold the posy of daisies and anemones that Mamma insisted I bring to Dr Janssen's former home. Eyes will be on me. People will be searching for reaction, for emotion and for a hint that I might want to rush back to the grave and throw myself on the coffin to be buried with my one true love. Behind me I hear a sob, but I don't dare turn to look. The fear of not performing quite right and the relief of escaping the hog have combined and threaten to escape in an inappropriate sound.

'Head down. Avoid eye contact,' Andries whispers as he puts his arm back by his side. We stand on the stoop in front of the house. Black crepe tied with black ribbon has been placed upon the door knocker. 'Amsterdam is entirely medieval,' he says.

'Do we use that?' I ask. I point my posy at the wrapped knocker and Andries shrugs. We wait a few seconds, neither of us daring to be the one to interfere with the formalities of mourning, but then I nod at my brother for him to do the honours. Andries lifts and releases the brass knocker. It thuds. The black crepe rips slightly. We wait, but no one comes.

'Can I leave the posy on the stoop? We can tell Mamma that we tried,' I say.

'She'll be inside. You've a role to play,' he says, more a whisper really. His eyes are fixed on the door knocker. 'If you could force a tear or two out of those too joyful eyes of yours...'

'And then Mamma will let me return to Theo in Paris,' I say.

Andries reaches out and lifts the brass door knocker again, and then again. Thud, thud. We wait.

'Such a shame.' The words are spoken behind us.

'Taken in his prime,' a Dutch woman replies.

I don't turn. I keep my eyes on the crepe covered door knocker. I need to perform. I need to be the expected version of Johanna Bonger: grief-ridden, distraught at having her future snatched away by cruel Death, longing for her true love, and not wanting to skip, dance, laugh and rejoice in the glory of God's goodness.

The door begins to open. It creaks and stutters with slow movement. We keep waiting. There's no one there to greet us.

'That door knocker should never have been touched,' someone says behind us. 'You'll have woken the dead. Will have jarred the nerves of everyone inside.'

Chapter One

'Move aside,' someone says and we do. We take a step backwards and the mourners behind hurry past, bouncing the front door off the hallway's wall.

'Face on,' Andries repeats. His expression switches to neutral and he removes his hat. I draw in a breath as I step into Dr Janssen's hallway. It smells of damp and cloves.

It's the first time that I've visited his house. Mamma had spoken of his magnificent home, but had planned that my first visit would be on the wedding night. That would have been next month, had my future husband not died in our wedding bed, of heart failure, naked on his back while a prostitute bounced on top of him. Mamma hadn't told me such details. She'd only spoken of heart failure. Thankfully Andries had felt my *sensibilities* could cope.

I look to the ceiling and offer a tiny prayer to Dr Janssen, thanking him for sparing me. *I'm glad you died happy.*

'My dear child, you must be devastated,' a woman says, as she rushes along the hallway towards me. Her attire gives the immediate impression that she's in deepest mourning. A black dress made from bombazine and trimmed with crepe hangs from her neck to toes. Black gloves cover her hands and her face is obscured by a heavy black veil. I struggle to find a fragment of flesh. She's somehow formless and entirely rotund: a solid egg-shaped woman, with tiny black boots click-clacking as she scurries across the tiled floor.

'Look at you,' she says. She might look me up and down from under her veil. I think I see a slight movement of her head. 'My brother was right – you would have birthed many beautiful children.' I turn to Andries, hoping for a hint of recognition or introduction, but he raises his eyebrows instead. 'I have attended the deceased, for a lack of loved ones or friends volunteered for the honour. I had hoped—'

'My sister's pain and grief made her bed-ridden,' Andries says. I look to the tiled flooring, to show her my deep dismay and sorrow.

'I am all too familiar with the grief and loneliness that death mutters. Indeed, this house has been entirely oppressive since—'

'I'm sorry,' I say. I curtsey, as if she's royalty and not an equal. 'I don't think we've met.'

'My brother spoke of you often and fondly. He longed for an heir.' She lifts a lace handkerchief under her veil. I assume that she dabs at her tears. 'I'm truly sorry, dear *Miss* Bonger, this must be a difficult time for you. Your entire future is gone.'

'I'm sorry for your loss,' Andries says. He reaches out a hand to Miss Janssen. 'I am Andries Bonger. Johanna's brother.' Dr Janssen's sister appears to refuse his hand. Andries keeps his arm outstretched, suspended for some time, before I push it back to his side. I watch him frown. Andries runs a palm over his hair, flattening any strays into place. He's thinking about his next move.

I imagine that Miss Janssen is Mamma's age. She carries the impression of being confident, unregretful, and is entirely pompous like her brother.

'This is for you,' I say. I thrust the posy of flowers forward, in an attempt to comply with Mamma's instructions.

'Oh, my dear *almost*-sister,' Miss Janssen says. Her voice echoes around the silent hallway. 'Come, let me show you around my brother's home. To think that all of Herengracht 247 would have been yours ... but now it is entirely mine.' She throws her arms out wide. 'If only the good Lord had spared my brother but a few more weeks.' She places her arm around my shoulders and guides me down the dark hallway.

'Will you be buried in what would have been the attire for your wedding night? Your mother said that it was already bought in anticipation.' She pauses. She's waiting for a positive reply. 'It's usually worn once on the wedding night and finally when you are buried...' She thinks my lack of response reflects my understanding. It doesn't. I can't formulate a suitable reply. I'm trying not to blurt out how I actually feel about her beloved brother.

I look over my shoulder, wordlessly pleading for Andries to help me, but he remains next to the open front door, laughing. The forbidden sound bounces off the walls, then he waves. I'm being ushered into a room as I catch a glimpse of my brother, his hat back on his head, closing the front door on his way out of Dr Janssen's home.

Vase With Honesty

He's there when I return to my parents' house. He's sitting on the stoop, with a wooden box at his feet and his hat on his knee.

'Theo,' I shriek, running to him. 'You're here.'

Theo remains sitting. His grin is wide but he shakes his head as he points to the window above him; it is a warning of sorts. I look up at my parents' house – tall, thin, five storeys, many windows. Mamma will be watching and I'm expected to behave with Bonger decorum.

I hold out my hand and Theo lifts it to his lips as he stands from the stoop. I'm almost too scared to blink unless he disappears; part of me even wonders if I've somehow wished him here. The sun's beating on him and I'm sure he's melting under all of his layers of outer garments.

'So, I received your letter,' he says. 'I thought I'd reply in person. Hand deliver these.' He gestures to the box.

'For me?' I ask and Theo nods as he sits down again. I'm shaking under my bustle; I can't believe he's here. I bend to look inside – a mixed selection of tubes of paint, metres of canvas, paint brushes, a palette and, of course, a palette knife. I place a hand on the concrete step to steady myself: heat, the shock, the surge of love.

'An artist needs her tools,' he says.

It's taking all of my restraint not to throw my arms around him. 'Thank you,' I murmur, overwhelmed and just about keeping my emotion under control. I'm either about to sob or laugh hysterically.

'Your mother's been a delight.' He's smiling. *Oh God.* I'd not hurried home after my encounter with Dr Janssen's sister; I felt I required a little time alone to consider the last few days.

'To the point where you prefer being outside in this heat?' I ask.

'Needed some fresh air, and to take in that view.' He nods at the new Rijksmuseum. 'Maybe they'll exhibit a Van Gogh one day.'

It's not been a week since I last saw Theo, but still I'm staggered by just how striking he is: his alabaster skin, that constellation of freckles dancing down his long nose, his perfect lips. I'm staring; he coughs to get my attention and my cheeks flush red.

'You know about Dr Janssen's death?' I ask, moving my Dutch bustle to sit on the stoop, with an acceptable space between us.

'In detail, thanks to Mamma Bonger,' he says, leaning over and nudging me playfully with his elbow.

'I planned on writing to you later today.' I'm whispering my words, aware that my mother is no doubt straining to hear from one of our open windows.

'She's furious that her plans have been *inconvenienced*. Quite at a loss as to what to do next, what with you being such an *ugly child*.'

I shake my head. 'Did she cry?' I ask and Theo nods.

'Uncontrollably.' His lips twitch as he tries not to smile. 'She has a *hopeless case* for a daughter and is convinced no man would ever be able to put up with your *difficult personality*.'

'I'm sorry,' I say, wishing the stoop would split apart and swallow me whole.

'And she asked if I'd ever seen you drink Parisian water.'

He pauses, waiting for further explanation, but all I can offer is a shrug. I've heard worse. Last night Mamma blamed the Devil, Pa's bad blood and a foreign disease for my hideous character, and all within one wail. My current goal is to stay out of her way as much as possible.

'There's no demand on me to be perfect, is there?' I ask.

'I'd rather you be truthful,' he says.

Theo continues to stare with a look that I can't quite recognise; a wave of dread hits and I stand up a little too quickly.

'Are you here with bad news about Clara?' I wobble, unsteady under the heavy bustle.

Theo shakes his head, reaching out a hand to help steady me. 'No, not at all. She's already afebrile and the doctor is satisfied with her early progress.'

Relief. Today's been the strangest of days.

'I rushed here to stop the woman I love from marrying the wrong man,' Theo says.

'Oh, your rescue's a little late…'

Theo laughs. The sound's unexpected, the timing and location inappropriate. It's contagious though; I giggle despite myself. He reaches out his hand to take mine.

I shake my head. 'Mamma will see.' My eyes search each window for her disapproving face.

'I've spoken to Dries,' Theo says. 'We're going to get you back to Paris.'

August, 1888.

Instead of sleep, I finished reading Anna Karenina *and it's awakened all of my emotions. I have such compassion for poor Anna that I won't criticise her at all. Instead, I think I'm actually enlightened from devouring such a precious book. What depth of truth it contains!*

I'm sure that the reading has left me better prepared to scrutinise my future emotions closely, and to hold myself accountable for every decision I now make. I'll even pause and assess each sensation felt; perhaps that understanding of self will help me appreciate what triggers my sadness, my hot-headedness, my happiness too. Perhaps, with that awareness, I'll even grasp those fleeting moments of gladness that pass oh so quickly.

Like now, right now, too excited to sleep. A grin so very wide that my cheeks ache. What has caused such joy? A spoken promise of freedom and happiness.

I can't even contemplate sleep yet. I keep thinking about how Theo travelled here to stop me marrying a pig. Would Camille or Agostina understand my gratitude? Theo's coming here has caused Mamma to declare, before it was even a topic to be discussed, that after Dr Janssen's sudden death it would be improper to announce a new engagement until the winter.

Mamma cares too much about what others think of her, but I'm left delighted that my brother has negotiated both my return to Paris next week and that no alternative suitors are to be considered.

Somehow, and I can't quite believe these words to be truthful, I have been gifted time to know Theo deeply before we commit the rest of our lives to each other. His grand passion ridicules the notion that I was ever in love with that Stumpff man.

Autumn 1888

PARIS

Dear Johanna,

At long last, and with my brother's reassurance that you'll be accepting of this letter, I write to apologise: I am truly sorry. In his letters, Theo talks of you often and I have wanted to write for the past month. How I long to hear that you'll forgive my bygone behaviour. How happy Theo will be; indeed a new sun will rise in him when he discovers that we are friends again.

Here in Arles, this morning the weather has become milder. The sky has been a hard blue with an abundant bright sun since my arrival. Today the wind blew cold and dry, and I have become cloaked with goose-pimples. There is much that is beautiful here, much that inspires my art: a tumbledown abbey on the top of a hill, pines that touch the sky, grey olive trees that I'd never before considered. I look forward to my daily hikes and discovering something new each day.

Did you know that Gauguin lives here with me? Of course Theo will have told you, yet I remember that you were a fan of his art. The poor man claims to be sick and has currently taken to his bed. Exhaustion hits him daily, and he lacks energy for even the simplest of tasks. He's broke and desperate for Theo to sell one of his many pieces. With illness and his fatigue there's additional pressure to earn money to live. He's decided to decrease the price of his paintings still further and that might be of interest to you, if his style is still to your liking.

In terms of my art, I've been pleasantly surprised that I can get any art supply I require, more or less at Paris prices. Lately I've been using a perspective frame. Of course you'll know it as a tool for ancient German and Italian painters, but modern artists will use them differently. It will be only a matter of time before more painters create with them. Or perhaps it's more that I am being forced to use it contrarily because I paint with oils. These new studies with the frame excite me though. I would be happy to instruct you further if this is at all of interest to you.

Here in Arles, I am seeing so much that is new. I am learning greatly about myself and others, and in return I am both being and being offered *unexpected gentleness. I myself feel healthier and stronger than I ever did in Paris. Abstinence suits me. With this newfound condition, I do worry about the current Parisian generation of artists and fear for their unhealthy bodies.*

Perhaps if I could invite more from Paris to this Yellow House I could inspire a new generation of more fortunate and healthier artists. Some days I even dream of opening a pied-à-terre, for the exhausted and downtrodden to escape here to heal. A place to rest in the country for my neglecting friends.

Other days I'm entirely furious with myself, as I used to judge being less ill or less intoxicated than other artists as acceptable. Here, my body breathes, lives, and suffers from regrets that often haunt me. My disregard for you was unforgivable, and yet still I seek your compassion.

I won't write more as I remain unsure if you welcome my correspondence. Perhaps you would offer a reply through Theo.

Tout à toi, Vincent

The Yellow House

Theo's presence this close on the *confidante*, our shoulders touching, excites me. He's enjoyed playing with me these last two months. He's aroused my desire again, that taste of unknown pleasure with him, and he seems to relish in the torment it causes. The promise of our first kiss and of intimate touching hangs in the air. Two months since I returned from Amsterdam and Theo's restraint has been remarkable. He laughs at my sighs of frustration. He whispers his desires so quietly that I wonder if I hear them correctly: each word tantalisingly inappropriate. I long for our wedding night.

'And now that you've received an apology?' he asks.

I shift myself, our shoulders no longer touch. 'My thoughts on Vincent remain unchanged.'

'He's apologised,' Theo says. I hear the implication; that I'm somehow now at fault for not jumping to Vincent's agenda.

'I've taught children to apologise from an early age,' I say. 'That they can do something impolite or truly unacceptable and a simple *sorry* will make it well again.'

'My brother's being sincere,' Theo says, his hands now clasped together on his lap. 'He's abstemious and keen to know you.'

'Perhaps, but an apology in a letter... How does that fix my relationship with him? Does he think his *sorry* a magic word to wipe away the pain and fear he's caused?'

'You shouldn't have gotten him so—'

'No,' I say, holding my palm up to stop his words. 'Don't take from his apology by making me responsible for Vincent's actions. A true *sorry* won't end with his letter.' I place my hands on Theo's, and our fingers shift as our palms connect. 'Even after what he tried to do to me … I rushed to him, hoping to save him from exile, to protect him from being punished for my sake.'

'And he ridiculed you.'

I nod. 'Perhaps we'll rebuild trust, but that'll take time. And he's not currently my priority.'

A sigh. 'What should I tell him?' Theo asks. I can hear that he's exasperated, but I won't withdraw and alter who I am. This strength is me; disagreeing with the man I love brings me no fear.

'Thank him for his apology and say I'll correspond with him when and if that ever feels appropriate.'

A frown this time. That isn't the response he wants from me. 'In some ways…' I nod for him to continue. 'I'm glad that I've not had to explain my brother to you. His actions speak far louder than my words ever could.'

I rest my head on Theo's shoulder, then lift our hands to my lips: a gentle kiss. There's a peacefulness in this parlour, a calmness in my life since Vincent left for Arles. His latest sketches and paintings of the Yellow House sit atop my brother's pouffe. They capture perfectly a two-up, two-down house, painted the colour of butter with wonderful green shutters. The inside appears whitewashed and with a red bricked flooring. I may not yet admire him as a man, but his ability to capture form often leaves me breathless. In today's letter to Theo, Vincent mentioned his apology to me alongside other sketches and details of a pink restaurant where he eats all of his meals. He said it was run by Widow Venissac; I live in hope that the artist will find someone who can tease out that best version of him.

Vincent's life appears idyllic and the perfect setting for him to achieve his dream of founding an artists' colony. He wrote to Theo about his new intention of showing his friends' paintings in the Yellow House, attracting art buyers and supporters, and that later the artists would want to stay and paint for their already established audience. That's how he anticipates his artists' colony to grow and develop; it somehow both contrasts and complements that wish for a new generation of healthier artists that he spoke of in his letter to me. Dare I hope for this new version of Vincent? For him, for Theo, for me too. Would that letting down of my guard bring chaos back into my life again?

'You and me are already stronger together than alone,' Theo says, breaking my thoughts and kissing the top of my head.

'We made a promise to accept each other's faults, opinions and flaws,' I say.

He laughs. 'I seek your wisdom and truth. Especially in the larger life lessons,' he says. A deep breath in. 'Your response to Vincent is fair.'

'I want to know and understand him, not to simply bear him,' I say. 'He'll forever be in our lives.'

'These difficult conversations are necessary,' Theo says.

'And because he's your brother, I'm sure he would appreciate the news from you, face to face, rather than receiving the engagement announcement by mail.' I sit forward on the *confidante* and turn to look at him. 'Now that she's decided enough time has passed since the dear doctor's death, Mamma won't allow the delay in announcement much longer.'

'I'm quite the catch,' he says. He smiles, before leaning forward and kissing my cheek.

Theo's gained a boldness in my presence. He's secure, knows that what we share is mutual. He brushes his finger over my wrist and I close my eyes. Another lingering kiss to my cheek, his lips just too far out of reach of my own. The sour smell of his breath is appealing. The sleeves of my bodice feel too tight, my neckline strangles my breath. I wish to remove them and have Theo explore my body here on Andries' *confidante*. I won't, of course. His confidence speaks of experience, but I don't want to know where he's existed before me. I'll be a virgin on our wedding night, Theo will be the first to know me entirely. My neck and face flush with thoughts of what's to come.

I send a daily prayer to the heavens to show my gratitude for this new chance at life. Theo and I walk freely together, but news of our engagement won't be made public until January. I want Theo to tell Vincent, before gossip reaches him from someone here.

'Word of our engagement will reach Sara with speed,' I say. So far, we've avoided any contact with Miss Voort; she was travelling but returned a few days ago.

'She's Dutch,' Theo says. That's enough explanation. As Mamma has made her decision, news will be spreading through the Netherlands imminently.

'Sara will discover Vincent's address before long. She'll be sure to tell him herself,' I say. 'She hated me passionately when we were merely stepping out. I imagine there's a price on my head now.'

'Gauguin struggles,' Theo says, the shift in topic somehow giving his words extra weight.

'With his illness?'

'He's not ill; Vincent's still difficult to live with.' He pauses. 'Gauguin wrote that he's not sure if he'll last the month.' Theo's left leg is restless, sending tiny judders through his body and into mine.

'He's only been there six weeks,' I say.

Of course Vincent has no idea that it was Theo who convinced Paul Gauguin to move there six weeks ago. He seemed the perfect partner for Vincent and now Theo's the financial crutch for them both.

'And already writing to tell me that Vincent's entirely impossible.'

I place my hand on his left leg to calm the tiny jolts. A pattern's developing: Vincent or Gauguin write with details of their latest woe – no paint, no food, illness, no money for stamps – and Theo replies instantly with money. I can't help but wonder if Theo believes giving them money is the only way to keep Vincent in Arles.

'Gauguin's ability to paint from memory still impresses me,' I say.

Theo's body stiffens next to me.

'What?' I ask, but he shakes his head.

'My brother wrote that he only works from memory on bad days, knowing that Gauguin is near.'

'He struggles to be alone,' I say, sadness apparent in my tone, and Theo nods. I'm hit with a now familiar wave of guilt; I'm keeping the Van Gogh brothers apart. 'Do you want to go to him? You could tell him about our engagement while...' I stop mid-sentence.

'Before knowing you, I dedicated my life to my brother.'

I nudge his shoulder for him to continue.

'He's demanded a lot of me these last few years, but things have shifted... My place is here, close to you,' Theo says. He pushes his shoulder onto mine and I can't help but smile.

'Why does he sign his paintings with only Vincent? Why never Vincent van Gogh?' I ask.

'He claims it's because no French person can say Van Gogh.'

'But?'

'He feels a disconnect with our parents, and now even with me.' Theo doesn't hide his sadness from me; I wish I knew how to react, I wish I liked Vincent more.

'I've only ever known your brother in his storms,' I say. 'It's hard to imagine how he exists when at peace.'

'I'm already beginning to forget that version of him,' he says. 'But look at all that my brother's painting.' He bends forward, takes a letter from an envelope on the pouffe and hands it to me. I read the words quickly. Theo leans back and points to a section of text. 'Two canvases dedicated to fallen leaves and another to a vineyard since his last letter. Arles inspires him.'

'He seems to be favouring unmixed Prussian blue of late,' I say. 'And he's sketching a brothel?' I point to a line near the bottom of the letter. 'Bright patches of contrasting colour, thickly applied paint and odd perspectives. His style is altering.'

Theo nods. 'Yes, but here.' He points at the final lines of the letter. I read them. Vincent fears that Gauguin's dismayed with Arles, with the Yellow House and with him; the positivity found in my apology letter is lacking from these words. He seems to believe the only artist in his colony might leave him.

'My brother's being perceptive.'

'What will you do?' I ask.

'He won't return to Paris,' Theo says. *I'll keep him away from you*: they're words unspoken. 'I'll write to Gauguin again and see what he requires to stay with my brother.'

October, 1888.

I'm unsettled. It isn't that I'm unhappy or wanting, it's more that I'm restless. Waiting for my life to begin, yet entirely uncertain how that will look.

Theo's spoken about the freedom our marriage will gift me – about the adventures we'll have in the future, about travel that fits around his work, about how he'll help me find a position in the art world that best fits with my skills. He enables Vincent, he'll enable my love of art too – in whatever form that takes. For I have persisted with a paintbrush, but my attempts all end up so imperfectly on the canvas; I clearly have no real skill with oils.

Theo was full of excitement earlier though: 'I've arranged instruction in clay from Camille.'

Yet the more I hear about poor artists and their relentless torment to reproduce what they see, the more I look at art differently: for each piece tells the story of the creator's fleeting moments of joyful making before returning to their everlasting torture.

Perhaps I'm finally acknowledging that I have no artistic aptitude? Be that temperament or ability.

Yet still I so want to find my place in that world. Later I spoke to Theo about how the observing of art and artists pleases me: how the offering of opinion and comment is something I adore.

'Perhaps you're destined to be an art dealer,' he said.

Prisoners Exercising

'Many use life drawings of models as the first stage of sculpting. Here.' She hands me a piece of paper with a sketch of a naked man on it. I turn the paper over in my hands, the sketch pointing to the floor; I am uncomfortable with both my awkwardness and my need to hide that from Camille. A fine layer of white dust covers the paper and now my fingers.

'Rodin prefers to consider his models from many different profiles and even to sketch from different heights.'

We're in front of two wooden sculpting stands: a rag-covered lump of wet clay, tools and a glass bowl full of a murky liquid sits on each. Camille looks delightful in a too-large artist's smock from neck to toe, her loose curls pinned in place. I'd thought myself bold to be wearing a pale pink tea-gown; its light corseting and bustle offering freedom to move and create. Unlike me, Camille looks ready to sculpt.

'And you're sure this isn't an inconvenient time for you?' I ask, because I'm absolutely convinced it is. Today's arrangements were all relayed from Rodin to Theo, and then to me. Now I'm challenged with her monotonous voice, her lack of warmth, her inability to match my eyes; it's as if I've offended her without knowing how or when.

Camille pulls the rag from the clay and throws it to the floor. I do the same.

'You must start by considering form, to capture the general pose. Don't expect it to look anything like the end product, rather rudimentary shapes at this stage.' She demonstrates quickly by moulding lumps of clay into a sphere, two cylinders, two triangles, a rectangular slab too. 'This is the body.' She picks up the rectangle. 'I'll add the other limbs to it, yes?'

I nod, hastily sketching the shapes in my sketchbook. Desperate to remember her instruction.

'Break the figure into smaller parts.' She points at the shapes. 'It's an easy way for a beginner to start.'

I have questions but somehow lack the courage to ask. Yes, she's going through the motion of instructing, but the lack of enthusiasm is in contrast with how Camille has been during our previous encounters. This artist shows no pleasure in my visiting today; I feel that I like her more than she likes me.

'If you simply join two of the separate pieces together they'll fall apart – especially when the clay dries out.' She demonstrates with the rectangle and triangle. 'So you need slip. This.' She places her fingers into a bowl, then reaches over and runs the liquid down my nose. I stand perfectly still. 'A baptism by clay and water.' There's no humour in her words or actions, rather a melancholic welcome to her world.

'But why do you use that?' I point to the bowl of murky liquid.

'The slip's a liquid clay. It works like glue.' She yawns: tiredness or boredom?

I'm scribbling away in my sketchbook – a drip of slip falling from my nose and hitting the page – words, fragments of sentences, tiny diagrams to remember the steps.

'When you're looking to join the separate shapes together, create little hatch marks on all of the pieces, like this.' She lifts the cylinder and cuts little scores and grooves into its base. 'Apply the slip with your finger and *voila*.' She mashes the cylinder to the rectangle and I watch as they stick.

'And how does it feel?' I ask.

She looks at me for a moment, before flicking her eyes back to the clay and shaking her head. 'I sometimes feel the clay is happiest when joined back with its parts. Like only then does it feel whole again.'

I write what she's said, word for word.

'Then you build up, refine and focus on the joins first, add the little details – the outlines, textures. Smooth out the flesh parts.'

As she talks she builds and manipulates the clay with an ease that makes it appear almost as if the statue has always existed and she's simply reassembling it. She points at the wooden modelling tools and I sketch them, but I'm not brave enough to ask for their names. 'They'll help with the finer details.' She's talking quickly, building hastily, and all the time jumping at distant sounds as her eyes flick to the atelier's closed doors.

'Before being fired, the clay has to be hollowed,' she says.

I shake my head. She's going too fast. This process makes little sense to me: perfecting a shape to destroy it?

'Now you try.'

I look from my pile of clay to my sketchbook, then back to the pile of wet earth. The pages are a mess of scribbled notes and sketches in my desperate attempt to keep up with Camille's rapid instruction. I glance at her and she's staring at me, dissecting me even, perhaps considering whether I could cope with whatever troubles her.

'Camille,' I say, 'tell me.'

'It's nothing.' Her eyes carry a thousand secrets. I wish she'd trust me.

The smell of clay connects us: earthy, fresh, lush. It somehow smells like rain, but I'd never considered rain's odour before. I push a hand into the wet pile. It feels heavy around my fingers, a drowning of sorts. I pull out quickly, hating the change from heavy to light. I look to Camille's fingers. Clay sticks. Her hands wear the clay as if it's meant to be part of her. I rub my fingers on my tea-gown and Camille bats my hand from the silk.

'Come, let's find you an artist's smock.'

She strides ahead and I hurry to catch up in this vast banquet hall. I step around the statues, in varying sizes, shapes and states of completion, fearing my foot will tangle with a white sheet and cause them to tumble one by one

'Are you quite yourself today?' I ask.

She stops, turns, and looks at me wordlessly before taking a cigarette from the table beside her. She lights it and I wait.

'Camille?' I ask.

'Sickness this morning,' she says, sucking on the cigarette, her inexperience betraying her. 'And just before your arrival Rodin spoke of a critic who believed me to be an *artiste maudit*.'

'I've no idea what that means.'

Camille shrugs her shoulders, turning and walking again. 'That my work gives evidence of the drama I live. Clearly a comment on the relationship with my ferret.'

'Must you always be defined by him?' I ask and I watch the back of Camille's head as she nods.

'The critic hinted that it's caused a madness that infects my creativity.'

'Like Vincent.' A whisper. I've been trying to arrange time with Camille since my return to Paris; I had hoped to share what had happened with Vincent in Andries' apartment. Letters written without response from Camille, and now Theo arranged today with Rodin. I doubt her opinion was sought.

She stops next to a table with two complete pieces on it, the cigarette burning without her lifting it back to her lips. 'I've had an interest in clay and modelling for as long as I can remember. Have you?'

'I'd honestly never considered it before. Not until Dries talked about your work.'

She shakes her head: wrong response. 'I was eight when I first sculpted my heroes: Bismarck, Napoleon.'

'Strong men.'

'They inspired such powerful thoughts within. Brought me out of the shell I'd used as an escape, as a way to protect me from my mother.'

'Camille.' I move to her, placing my hand on her arm, but she pushes my touch away.

'Not today, Johanna,' she says. 'No kindness, please. Let today be about art.'

I nod, trying to accept the distance between us, mentally, and physically too.

'I completed this two years ago. I call her *Jeune Fille à la Gerbe*.'

'*Young Girl with a Sheaf*,' I say. I run my fingers over the terracotta statue. A seated young woman leans against a sheaf of wheat. An expression of beautiful melancholy.

'Look at the firmness of the girl's flesh against the way I've only roughly modelled the background,' she says.

'As if that location is unimportant?' I ask and Camille nods. The woman's head twists to the right, her knees are crossed. 'There's both modesty and an awkwardness in the pose,' I say. 'A denial of her sexuality.' I turn the statue on the table, considering its exquisiteness from different angles. 'The girl's position is compelling from all viewpoints,' I say. 'You've truly captured the tension that underlies her difficult stance.'

She stares, smiles, nods: a silent thank you. She stubs her cigarette on the edge of the table, then tosses it to the floor.

'Some consider women are not strong enough to carve into the material.' She shakes her head; I wish I had the words to express my outrage. 'So, unlike Rodin, I must *specialise* in small-scale sculpture and appeal to private collectors mainly. I've created multiple versions of her.' She strokes the girl's face, leaving tiny pieces of wet clay. 'Soon there will be a series cast in bronze.'

'It's stunning,' I say. Camille smiles again, but it lacks her usual joy and happiness. Today she is less than half of her former self. I wish she trusted me with her truth.

'Now consider this one that Rodin completed this week. He calls it *Galatea*,' Camille says. There's a pause as I walk around the table to study the second statue from all perspectives. It's the same young girl, in the same pose, in marble. 'I think it's fair of me to say that the sensibility is *similar*.'

'He's copied you?' I say and Camille nods. 'And your skill is mistaken for that of Rodin's?'

'But never the reverse.'

I point at the twin statues. 'But surely you can show them side by side?'

'I'll always be his follower or his whore. I exist in his shadow,' she says. She picks up a discarded cloth from the table and rubs at her fingers vigorously. The clay is soon removed, but still she wipes, her eyes locked on *Galatea*. 'Some days I want to destroy all of my art.'

'No, Camille,' I say, moving to her. My arms reach out but she staggers backwards as if my touch will burn.

'I emerge, I become, I rise, I persist,' she says. 'But still he steals my ideas.'

November, 1888.

Before Paris, whenever I read, I was being gifted time to experience everything that the author had worked through, thought about and agonised over. It was a privilege to read. But there was always distance between us. That glimpse of Shelley's deepest self, of Byron's loving and complex heart, the meandering walks with Wordsworth over hills and by streams. I escaped in the pages because I lacked that stimulation and experience in my own life. I longed to be anyone or anywhere else.

Now Paris has taught me so much more about myself and that need to escape from my thoughts wanes. A shift in why I love literature. No more distraction in other people's dreams and fantasies, but instead the chance to piece together what it is to be this emerging Johanna Bonger.

It seems that all of the ingredients I had stolen from fiction, and once thought necessary to be a strong woman, were partly wrong. Being strong isn't about being alone, being fiercely independent or rejecting love. It isn't about rushing to act, to shout loudly, before considering what is best for any given situation or storm. Rather, I've realised that being strong is allowing love despite fear. It lives in the gaps and silences. It pauses to consider. It speaks with integrity and truth. It embraces flaws. It increases after errors. It rises.

I am rising.

I've accepted that I'm truly full of flaws, and out of them my strength continues its ascent.

How I cringe at the many mistakes made during that first stay in Paris! The impetuous acts. Those times I shouted, I rushed, certain I'd be able to drag Vincent back to my brother. Naively believing, when given choice, that all would choose decency; daring to trust that Vincent would prefer to act with my measure of decorum.

Paris broke Vincent, it heals me. More than that, here I'm growing despite my inadequacies and now my desires are changing. I'm not a painter, I'm not a sculptor – my yearning to be a female artist has been defeated.

The more time I spend with Theo, the more I wish to learn about art and the selling of art.

Portrait Of An Old Man With Beard

We walk over the sandy Champs de Mars. One hand grips my straw bonnet as an icy wind whips at my cheeks and my cloak billows around me. I link my arm through Theo's and I lean into him, desperate for protection from the chilly gusts. My brother's on my other side but he's striding ahead.

'Clara's health continues to improve,' Theo says. 'She's being encouraged to spend much time outdoors, sitting on the sanatorium's veranda.'

'I miss her far more than I'll ever miss Mamma or Pa,' I say but then I stop walking and look up at the construction. 'I still don't understand its purpose.'

'For a brief time it'll be the tallest building in the world. Right here. In Paris,' Andries says. He's obsessed. He's still not missed a weekly visit since work on the foundations began.

'But it's useless and … well, I still think it's ugly,' I say. Theo laughs next to me. 'Do you consider it art, Mr Van Gogh? I fear I'm entirely missing the point.'

'Why must everything have a point?' Theo asks. I shrug as I grip his arm closer to me. I wish that I'd thought to bring my gloves. 'Not everyone's a fan at first,' Theo says, 'but Eiffel's tower grows both up and on people. Look, they're already past the middle floor.'

I stare up at the tower, gripping my bonnet a little tighter to stop the wind from whipping it away. My fingers are numb with cold. The clouds are plump and full; snow is expected this afternoon. The four metal legs have continued their push up to the sky. The weight has moved them closer together. The grey skeleton has begun the crescendo towards its point. It's already too tall, destined to continue its growth, but this tower isn't increasing in my affections.

'Look at the workmen,' I say. I point up to a ledge that teeters out from the highest point. Wind lashes at them. Black figures are suspended, perched or dangling on a ledge just a few centimetres wide. Their tools hammer out rhythm as they strike the iron structure.

'How are they not terrified? Look how it's swaying in the wind.'

Andries positions his box camera and snaps the tower.

'Still only one photograph each week?' Theo says. My brother nods as he turns the key at the top of the camera, winding the film onto the next frame. 'Go on, throw caution to this autumn breeze and take an extra one,' Theo says, but before Andries can reply we hear his name being bellowed. We look around.

'Bonger,' we hear again. The sound moving nearer. 'Bonger!' We all turn to the shouts, searching the sea of raised parasols that attempt to shelter bonnets from the gusts and cold. Today people favour moving with pace over standing in huddles talking.

'Rodin, old man,' Andries says. '*Bonjour*.'

He moves to embrace Rodin. I'd not seen him at the atelier two weeks ago and now I barely recognise him. He's a poor sketch of the man I met in the summer. He looks stockier, misshapen even. His whiskers are matted slightly, the lines on his face more pronounced. He embodies neglect. I want to ask what the last four months have done to him, but I'd never be that brave. He grips his round spectacles with his forefinger and thumb, rubbing at the lens as if distracted by something. I unlink my arm from Theo's and look around; I can't see Camille.

'*Bonjour*, Rodin,' I say. 'Is Camille not with you today?' His eyes jump to mine. I see the anger and then recognition as his face softens. I'm not quite sure how to behave around an artist who steals from another.

'Mademoiselle Bonger,' Rodin says. He leans in and offers a brush of his lips on each of my cheeks. His whiskers scratch my skin.

'The unfamiliar French,' Theo says, and Rodin laughs before they embrace each other.

'I'd heard a rumour,' Rodin says. He looks at me and then nods to Theo. We're both smiling, both entirely useless at keeping our joy to ourselves.

'Marvellous news,' Rodin says. He claps his hands together. 'And how is your art?'

'It isn't,' I say. 'Every second person I meet dreams of being an artist one day. I, unfortunately, am accepting that I have inadequate skills. My time with Camille proved—'

'You're your own worst critic,' Theo interrupts.

I look to him, curious, then continue, 'I've been meaning to write to Camille. To thank her for the instruction and to comment again on her wonderful *Jeune Fille à la Gerbe*...'

A pause. They all watch me.

'But I worried that she seemed—'

'I'm not that girl's keeper,' Rodin says. His words are spiky and harsh. He turns and walks away without a goodbye. His shoulders slumped, no urgency in his steps yet he doesn't want to be near me. Andries runs after him, throwing an arm around Rodin's shoulders.

'Did you know that he steals her ideas?' I ask.

'It's Camille,' Theo says. A wave of dread whirls in my stomach. I nod: *tell me*. 'She's no longer pregnant.'

'What?' It's a shout. 'What does that even mean? I was there. She didn't tell me she was pregnant. She'd been sick that morning. That's all.'

'I don't gossip,' Theo says. 'She'd tell you herself, if she wanted others to know.' It takes me a moment to realise that I'm annoyed; I'm angry at Theo for being a good man and at myself for not hearing what she was trying to say.

'Will Rodin leave Rose and—'

'Camille had an abortion a few days ago,' Theo says. 'Rodin knew nothing about the pregnancy.'

'But—'

'Their love affair's too intense, it consumes both professional and personal parts. And...'

'And?'

'She relies on him in financial ways. She struggles to get funding. Some consider her art daring, so she depends on Rodin and his collaborations.'

A chilly gust threatens to lift my straw hat from my head. I remove it, tightening my grip of Theo's arm. I don't want to be on Champs de Mars anymore. I turn, Theo moves with me as we begin our walk back in the direction we came. We stride in silence, nodding to those we recognise.

'Will her family not help?' I ask, but I know the answer. Camille couldn't comprehend why I didn't reject my family when that hideous marriage was arranged. She saw me as weak. She'd rejected them in favour of her art and her scandalous love of Rodin. I'd seen her as brave.

'They'd happily have her a beggar on the streets.'

'And so society views Camille through the lens of Rodin's splendour. Can you help her?' I ask.

'Rodin will continue his financial support, but their relationship is doomed now.' Theo rubs at his temples. 'She said it was her sacrifice for love. That this was Rodin's moment to leave Rose for her.'

'And now Camille knows he never will,' I say and Theo nods. I link my arm back through his. I lean in. 'I'll visit.'

'She's refusing all company,' Theo says.

'She's not my friend, is she?' I say.

'She's an artist seeking to connect with others who fight the same battle,' Theo says.

'And I don't fight that battle anymore,' I whisper.

Camille Claudel is more like Agostina Segatori than like myself.

November, 1888.

I'd woken covered in sadness, thoughts of Camille, of the too many artiste maudit in Paris, when Theo arrived unexpectedly. A bouquet of roses and an entire day planned.

We spent the afternoon walking and laughing, strolling under young chestnut trees and pausing to sit along winding paths. With our engagement fast approaching, I voiced the question of how realistic our expectations are. We talked about fulfilling each other's needs. I expressed my own desire to live a remarkable life alongside a deep longing for social acceptance: something Vincent, Camille and Agostina have rejected. Theo even spoke about his concern that he'd not come up to scratch, and I countered with my fear of not having it within me to be a home-loving wife.

I asked if long-suffering and creative genius had to dance together. If the achievement of something great required suffering too. Decisions and conclusions were neither needed nor reached, instead our honesty and forthright conversation leaves me with hope.

Later, as we walked a route back to Dries' apartment, when it was very quiet and almost dark, we paused on the bridge at Courbevoie. Focusing on the reflections in the water, our hands found each other. It was truly enchanting; the lights of the city were mirrored in the water. A silent longing connected us.

If ever I'm asked what it is to be happy, I can describe this day and night.

Winter 1888

PARIS

Winter 1668

PARIS

December 22, 1888.
Paris.

ENGAGEMENT ANNOUNCEMENT OF

THEODORUS VAN GOGH
AND
JOHANNA GEZINA BONGER

JANUARY 1889

PARIS

AMSTERDAM

Dear Vincent,

I am aware that my news might have been better received in person, yet I hope that it finds you well and that you will share our joy.

Mamma knows and you are next in our family to be notified. I am to be engaged to Johanna Bonger next month. We plan for a reception for family on January 9, in Amsterdam, and I enclose notification for your consideration.

On behalf of Johanna, as well as myself, a sincere handshake to you.

Ever yours, Theo

213

Portrait Of Postman Roulin

I stand next to my brother in his hallway. The scent of violets fills the room; elsewhere Anaïs sings 'Weihnachts glocken'. I'm out of breath, and without doubt pale and stricken. Andries had shouted my name several times, his voice full of urgency, and I'd run from my bedroom immediately. Theo's here. He's soaked through; raindrops fall from him onto the tiled floor. He stands still, in silence, his eyes plead. He looks smaller. He seems lost. He clutches a piece of paper and it trembles in his grip. My stomach swirls.

'Is it Clara?' I ask.

No reply.

'What is it?' Andries persists. He takes a couple of steps towards Theo and removes the piece of paper from his clutches. I watch as he reads, taking steps to me, and then he hands over the correspondence. No words are spoken. Theo's eyes remain locked on me.

I look at the paper. A telegram, with today's date. December 24.

FROM: PAUL GAUGUIN
TO: MONSIEUR THEO VAN GOGH

Chapter One

COME STRAIGHT AWAY. VINCENT ADMITTED TO THE HOSPITAL
TODAY AS A MATTER OF URGENCY.

'Is he ill?' I ask.

'An accident?' Andries asks.

'You know the same as me,' Theo says. He licks his lips and
rubs at his throat. 'I'll catch the night train to Arles this afternoon.'

'Can I get you a glass of water?' I ask, but he shakes his head.

'No time, I must leave immediately. I've left the gallery staff to
finalise travel arrangements and have to pack a small case. Can we
postpone our first Christmas Day meal?'

'Don't give that another thought,' I say. '*Sinterklaas* visited
weeks ago. Go, be with your brother and send word when you
know more.'

'Gauguin would only send a telegram if the situation were
grave,' Andries says. I bat his arm. 'What?' he says, his eyebrows
raised and his eyes wide.

I glare at him. 'That was a given, dear brother.' I ask. I turn my
attention back to Theo. 'Do you want to postpone our
engagement?'

'Let's not speculate,' Theo says. He moves to me and takes
back the telegram. He kisses my cheek before replacing his hat
and turning to leave.

'Do you want me to travel with you?' I ask and Theo turns
to me.

He shakes his head, not looking me in the eye. 'I think it best
you remain here.'

'To support you,' I explain. I move my arms across my torso.

'I'm not sure what I'll find when I get there,' Theo says. 'And I
don't know when I'll be back. That'll depend on ... the
circumstances.'

'He would have received our engagement announcement and
your note yesterday,' I say. The words are barely loud enough to
be a whisper. The tremor in my voice is clear despite the lowered
volume. Theo hears. Theo nods.

Christmas Day, 1888.
Paris.

Dearest Theo,

A brief letter to wish you a merry Christmas, to say hello and to let you know that my thoughts were constantly with you on your journey to Vincent. Now all I can think about is what you may have discovered upon your arrival. I'm terrified that you've faced something horrendous: that your brother might no longer be with us.

Please know that we'll help each other with whatever has been thrown into our path. Together we are stronger; tell me what you need, allow me to support you in every way that I can.

Please give my regards to Vincent. I can but hope that you know I'd never wish illness or despair on him.

Peace and goodwill to you.

Please write soon.

Your, Jo

Dearest Johanna,

I hope it goes without saying that you have been in my thoughts these last few days. Indeed, thinking about you has brightened the darkness that I met in Arles. Face to face and without reprieve, I have spent the days since my arrival fearing that my brother will lose his battle with life.

There's much to tell you, much that I need and want to share, but I cannot commit to paper the horror that I've witnessed here. The sentiment that shrouds me is despair.

For I'm hit with the realisation that my brother is much a part of me. If he were no longer in my life, there would be an emptiness that no other could fill. I mean that not as an insult to you, my dearest Johanna, but just as I'm certain you cannot contemplate a life without Andries, when I consider my future I see my brother by my side.

Now, with Vincent in hospital, showing symptoms of madness and a high fever, I contemplate what I need from you. My wish, if I could dare to voice it, would be for him to be in our future too. That you and he could be friends again. My brother has moments where he's lucid: he suffers, he fights. His anguish is so very deep within him and I cannot bear to describe how he has mutilated himself. Had he just had someone to talk to, someone to trust with his dark thoughts and despair.

The way that you look at me and our promise to bring out the very best in each other, to fulfil our deepest needs gives me faith in this path I step; it covers me in hope. Had we not shared that faith with Vincent, had we not pulled him into our positivity, would he have done to himself what he has?

I've let him down.

In the next few days a decision will be made about a transfer, perhaps to a special institution. Your love is my beacon of light in this latest storm.

Your loving, Theo

My dearest Theo,

I've just this second received your letter. Since you left I've been praying that Vincent is still alive – thank God he is.

I've endeavoured to read into the gaps, but am failing to grasp how Vincent might have harmed himself. I'm grateful that you've mentioned moments of lucidity though – both Dries and I are hopeful that Vincent will return to us fully. Of course, I'll assist with any recovery; I want and need to support you both.

I so wish I were there with you – to bring you comfort, but also to speak to Vincent. I should have been kinder to him, Theo.

How can we ever truly know how another suffers? How many other silenced yet tortured souls hide within the darker bends of this society?

Please keep writing and sharing, so that I can support you from a distance. Today I've decided to learn housekeeping, for when we eventually live together, but even writing that feels too trivial when there is much still to learn about Vincent.

I long to hear from you again. Give your brother my regards.

Your loving, Jo

Dearest Johanna,

A quick note to thank you for your letter, for your sincere offer of support, and for you to know that you persist in my thoughts.

The news remains dire here.

They still talk about where and when Vincent can be committed to an institution, and each morning I fear news that he's passed during the night. I'm torn between a loss that stabs into me and relief that my brother will no longer suffer; still I know that to lose him would break my heart. Though it's fair to say that the life I'm proposing for us may not be untroubled, I'll forever seek light for us in these storms.

I'm running out of time as another appointment with his doctor approaches, but I look forward to a new year – the year that you'll become Mrs Van Gogh.

Your loving, Theo

Sunflowers

No word from Theo, in any form, since his last letter two days ago. Vincent has Theo's attention, and lack of communication could be because of a change in his condition. Still, the fact that more days could slip by, before he has a moment to write, overwhelms me.

The week between Christmas Day and New Year's Day passed in a quiet whirl of anxiety. A day later and Andries has spent this evening trying to lift my spirits with parlour games; I've turned down each suggestion. I've no interest in playing blind man's bluff with him and Anaïs, and a game of charades feels tedious. I don't have the energy to fake enthusiasm. Instead I carry the weight of the world on my shoulders; I've tried to read, I've considered sketching, I've learned how to polish silver, I can't eat, I've struggled to sit still for these two days. But now, during one of my circuits of pacing the parlour with the shutters not yet closed, I happen to look outside into the darkness. In that very moment, two figures walk past the only gaslight at the end of rue Victor.

I recognise his shape immediately. Theo trudges through the rain, his head down. He's with another man who strides close to his side. I don't recognise him.

'Is that Vincent with Theo?' I whisper, but my brother hears.

'Where?' Andries says. He jumps from his seat at his slate desk and rushes to the window beside me. 'Perhaps things weren't as dire as Theo wrote,' he begins, but stops when he sees the two figures moving closer to the apartment. It's late and it's too dark to see clearly. Both men stoop forward, hats upon their heads, with the winter rain thrashing down upon them.

'Definitely Theo. I'm not sure who he's with,' I say. I'm trying to identify the stranger's gait. 'I don't think it's Vincent; he's possibly too short.'

Andries turns and rushes to his apartment's front door. I stay. I watch them stop at the *porte-cochère*. They'll be waiting for the concierge to glide the bolt on the door; neither turn to look up to the parlour window. The door must swing open door, as I see them step inside.

'This is most unexpected but very welcomed,' I hear Andries say, as I rush into the hallway.

'Apologies for the late hour,' Theo says. 'I expected you'd both appreciate news of my brother.'

The man with Theo isn't Vincent. He's a short man, smaller than me, with a strong jawline and a narrow forehead. His lips are too thin and his eyes bulge a little too much. I watch as Theo removes his hat. He places it on the hallway table, rain dripping a path to the floor tiles, before looking up and seeing me. His face is so swollen it's almost disappeared. His eyes are red: puffy from tears, exhausted from Vincent. I see his relief. His joy. I see his pain too. I rush across the tiled floor and fling myself into his arms. He embraces with a tightness that pinches an exhalation from me. I hear my brother and the other man laughing.

'I'm glad you missed me,' Theo says into my hair, before pulling out of the embrace and planting a gentle kiss on my forehead. He smiles but his eyes are downcast.

'Vincent?' I ask.

'Still alive. He has been transferred ... as he displays symptoms of insanity.' Our eyes lock. We offer each other silent reassurance, then he turns to Andries and to the strange man. 'My apologies. Paul Gauguin, may I introduce my almost-fiancée

Johanna, and her brother Andries Bonger.' His tone is flat, joyless and entirely unlike Theo. *He doesn't like Gauguin.*

'*Enchanté de vous rencontrer,*' Andries says with a little too much delight. 'Absolutely thrilled.' He holds out his hand and a boisterous handshake occurs. 'Jo's an admirer of your work. Come in, let me arrange food and tea. The fire is lit.' He rushes off to find his housemaid and Gauguin takes off his overcoat. He drapes it over his arm as it drips onto the hallway tiles.

'Johanna's an artist,' Theo says.

'A female artist?' Gauguin scowls. My artistic ability has been dismissed. 'You're a fan of my work?' he says, his voice husky like there's a bread roll lodged in his throat. He tilts his head and stares a little too long.

'Artists create art, just as writers write, regardless of their sex,' I say, not quite sure if my bold statement even makes sense. I hold out a hand.

'*Enchanté,*' Gauguin says and then he laughs. He dismisses my hand with a wave of his own. I'm not sure what's amused him, but his refusal to stop staring at me leaves me uncomfortable.

I look to Theo and he shakes his head. His brow is furrowed.

'He thinks the pursuit of all women a competition,' Theo says. He kisses my cheek again and then places his arm around my shoulders. A surge of warmth rushes through me. A red flush travels up my neck and onto my cheeks. I can still feel Gauguin's eyes. I try to mask my grimace by turning my attention to Theo.

'How could I have missed you so much when you've only been gone from the city for eight days? I've become one of those women,' I say. Theo's lips tremble. 'What is it?'

'Alas I like my women younger than you,' Gauguin says, making us both turn to look at him. He clearly wants our attention to be on him and his peculiar sentence catches me off-guard. I bite my lips to prevent words that may embarrass Theo.

'Although he has a wife and five children,' Theo says. He pulls me closer to him. 'Come, Johanna, let us warm our bones. There's much to discuss.' His tone remains flat. Moving his hand to my lower back, he guides me.

Chapter One

As we step into Andries' parlour, Gauguin releases an overly dramatic sigh. He paces the room, observing the lavish furnishings.

'The tasteless sophistications of civilization usually bore me, but Bonger has...' His forehead wrinkles and his eyebrows tilt towards the centre of his face. He squints and he glares. 'How can I have been here but five minutes and already feel savage?'

I look at Theo and raise my eyebrows, showing my lack of understanding. He shrugs to display his confusion too and moves to stand beside the windows. Gauguin's clearly annoying Theo and that makes me love my almost-fiancé a little bit more.

'Will you not sit?' I ask, but Theo shakes his head.

'My brother has had an acute episode,' he says. I hear the tremors in his voice. 'He cut off part of his ear then delivered it to the maid in his local brothel. Gauguin alerted the police and they admitted Vincent to hospital.'

'Oh my, his ear?' Andries asks. I'd not noticed him in the parlour's doorway. He moves beside me and I sit on the *confidante*.

'He did what?' I ask, hoping I've misunderstood.

'He's crazed with disease,' Gauguin says. He stands by Andries' slate desk and fiddles with the private papers upon it. 'He's lost control of his mental functions. He chooses women who are riddled.'

'Riddled,' I say, only an echo really.

'With disease,' Gauguin says, turning to look at me. His lips are slightly parted, his head tilting to the right and I watch as his tongue pokes out slightly.

I can't stop my nostrils from flaring. I'm sure my face twists into a sneer. I look to Andries for explanation and he nods; he'll tell me later. I turn my attention to Theo. His eyes meet mine. I don't know which reaction to show. I'm horrified that someone would injure themselves in such a brutal way, I'm bothered by Gauguin's glare, I'm alarmed by what new disease might riddle Vincent, but mainly I'm full of love for Theo. He looks broken; I need to ease his pain.

'Will he still hear?' Andries says. No one answers him. I nod for Theo to continue.

'By the time I got to Arles, Vincent was already in hospital and—'

'This act wasn't out of the blue,' Gauguin interrupts. We all turn our attention to him. 'He'd been showing symptoms of madness for the days leading up. Then he received notice of your engagement and that very day he…' His words lack emotion. They feel rehearsed, as if each word has been selected to fit with the tale he wants to tell.

'But how?' Andries asks. He points to his ear.

'With a razor,' Gauguin says. 'The fellow attacked me with it first, before turning it on himself.'

'Will he remain insane?' I ask, again diverting attention away from Gauguin.

'No doctor was willing to commit to an answer. There seems to be a high possibility that he will…' Theo pauses. He's unable to look at me. His entire being droops, his eyes are fixed on his sodden shoes. I watch a raindrop travel the length of his nose and drip to the floor. 'I'm to wait a few days. When he's settled, they'll have a better understanding of his condition.'

'Did you see him before he was moved?' Andries asks and Theo nods. 'Was he lucid?' Andries asks. Theo nods again. He refuses to look up to meet my brother's eyes.

'He was fine for a few moments. He enquired about our engagement…' He stops. He looks up at me then, the tremble in his lips no longer hidden.

'Tell me,' I say.

'It was terribly sad.' He clasps his hands in front of him but his fingers fidget to escape. He's fighting to withhold his own emotion. He's trying to control himself, to fight his own tears. 'One moment he was talking to me about art and his last painting, the next he was full of grief… He's drowning in an anguish that I don't quite understand.'

I'm hit with the most terrible punch of sorrow. Tears escape. I try to wipe them before the others notice. I fail. Gauguin stares, but I refuse to look at him.

'What caused this?' I ask. I'm unable to hide the quiver in my voice. 'The engagement?'

'He'd been descending for days,' Theo says, not denying that our engagement has added to the madness, yet I'm hit with a tiny sense of relief that we're not the entire cause of the breakdown. 'If only he'd had someone to talk to, this—'

'He's been quite unbearable,' Gauguin interrupts. He bangs his fist on the slate desk. He's overly keen for his innocence to be noted. 'He requires medical help.'

'And that's what he's receiving,' Theo says, his tone calm. He bites his bottom lip. I think he might have learned that trick from me. 'I'll put my own plans on hold.' He looks at me and again I nod, offering a smile but knowing that my downcast eyes will show my sadness. Theo's struggling to stay in control of his emotions. My responses are wholly inadequate; I'm at a loss for words. I've stepped into a world where madness and art seem to hold hands to dance. I'm not sure I know how to exist here.

January, 1889.

An ear!

    Vincent cut off part of his ear? How must he look now? How hideous will he be? Society will recognise him instantly – and not for his art. Must he forever be the earless painter?

    Oh, Vincent, what have you done?

    Four months of calm behind me; here I am back in Vincent's madness. How will we save him?

Head Of A Woman With Her Hair Loose

The heavens have been angry all of today: they've mirrored my mood. The sky is black and thunderous. Rain pelted the cobbles in protest. I prepared an image with charcoal on my new canvas, my first attempt in weeks, but my head and heart were elsewhere and I immediately struggled with perspective. Theo arrived a few minutes ago; perhaps I even summoned him to me.

I told him to sit on the *confidante* in Andries' parlour while I scrubbed at the black on my fingers. He's barely been here during the four days since his return from Vincent. Hardly a conversation had. It's added to my anxiety and doubt. Now I stand in front of him, balled fists on my hips and trying to be braver than I feel.

'Talk to me,' I say, nodding at him.

'There's been a change in Vincent,' he says. There's no smile; I fear the worst. 'A chance he'll recover fully.'

'And that troubles you?'

'I must take responsibility for Vincent's...' He pauses, incapable of finishing the sentence and saying the words aloud. His tone's flat. His body droops in the seat as if trying to escape through a gap between cushions.

I waggle my finger at him. 'Did you attack him with a razor?' I ask, my voice a little too jagged. There's a slight pause before he shakes his head. 'Then I'm not sure why you think you're responsible.' Another pause. 'You look more like Vincent than yourself today.'

'Is that a compliment?' he asks, a tinge of anger in his words.

'So far from it,' I say. My voice is low and stern. The corners of his mouth twitch under his moustache. I laugh, a short laugh, convincing neither of us that there's any joy in this room.

'You said it would have been kinder to visit him with news of our engagement.' He refuses to allow his eyes to meet mine.

'I did,' I say. 'And you ignored me. Scold yourself about your poor delivery of the news, but not for what happened next. You can't hold yourself responsible for Vincent's reaction.'

There's silence. It's uncomfortable. An awkwardness that's vaguely familiar and too full of unsaid words. Theo looks towards my canvas, tilting his head to the left, and then to the right.

'I've written to Vincent,' I say and Theo's unable to conceal his surprise. 'Wondered if you could look at it.' I hand him the letter.

Dear Vincent,

I hope you don't mind my brief note, but I realised earlier that we – you, Theo and I – face the same battles as those who came before us and as those who'll walk this earth a hundred years from now. Those battles remain unchanged and at the moment, for reasons unknown, we each seem determined to fight alone.

Yet, isn't it obvious that together we'd be a hundred times stronger? Are you already nodding your head in agreement? Doesn't it make perfect sense for us to embrace, to love and to support each other in this combat?

Because that's why I reach out to you, dear Vincent. In the hope that, from this day forward, you'll allow Theo and me to step into battle alongside you.

We are family now.

Believe me.

Your loving, Jo

I watch Theo read my words. 'Thank you,' is all he says, wiping a tear from his check.

'It's our duty to help him,' I say. 'I know I once flinched at the thought of Vincent in our lives, but I no longer feel that way. I realise now how very ill he was. That he needs our help.'

He nods. 'We'll support each other,' Theo says.

I wait, but then rush out my words. 'Mamma has asked if we'll have the reception this weekend. She thinks the engagement won't now go ahead and is panicking.' I stop. I look at my almost-fiancé, his face pale as he gazes at Andries' rug. 'Do you wish to call it off?' I ask with faked boldness; I dread his response.

Theo lifts his gaze from the rug. His lips smile in tandem with the creases at the corner of his eyes. I notice more tears too.

'Because if you wish to postpone...' I hesitate. 'If you regret your decision and wish to cancel the—'

'Knowing you'll marry me is the happiest I've ever felt. I'll never regret that.'

'But?'

'I'm not sure how to proceed,' he says. 'Vincent once told me that marriage shouldn't be the main goal in life.'

'And you feel calling off our engagement might be the solution?'

'No.' He shakes his head. 'Entirely not that. We should announce our wedding date at the reception.'

'But—'

'But nothing, Jo. I love my brother entirely; you know how I fear a future without him. But I've lived my life in the shadow of Vincent's moods for too long. Living feels overly short of late. I worry you'll think me harsh and unkind, but his need to have my full attention, all of the time, exhausts me.'

'But your sadness,' I say.

'I've lost too much happiness at the hands of my brother. I live with a constant fear of news of his death. And now the thought of losing you...' He stops. He wipes his eyes on his shirt sleeve. 'I wasn't sure I could love entirely... I wasn't even convinced I was a full being, until I met you.'

I take a few steps forward.

'You make me happier than I ever wished to be,' I say. I remove my lace handkerchief from my sleeve. I hand it to him.

'What must you think of me?' he says. He blows his nose.

'Only that I'll do everything in my power to love you till the day I die,' I say.

'Will you do something for me right now?' he asks and I nod. 'Release your hair.'

I don't hesitate. I remove the pins and ties, before shaking my head and letting my hair fall to my shoulders. Brown and full of frizz, my hair has always refused to be tamed. Mamma used to blame the Devil. She said he'd touched the hair follicles and given them an unruly kink. Theo watches me, the look unrecognisable: animalistic perhaps.

I sit next to him in the centre of the *confidante*. I adjust my skirts in an attempt to find a comfortable position. He remains silent, watching me, always consuming my lack of grace but never passing comment. He leans closer. He fingers my round cameo brooch; it offers a feminine touch, decorating the military collar of my bodice. The high neck seems to pull tighter with the closeness of his touch. I move to rest my head on his shoulder. I look up at him; my eyes move to his mouth.

'Johanna,' he says, his lips forming my name.

I lift a hand to the back of his neck. My fingers play with his hair. It's wet and clammy. This room's suddenly too hot. He leans down. His eyes lock with mine. His lips brush across my cheek until they're too close. The bristles of his moustache tickle my skin.

'Please,' I say. A whisper.

His lips find mine. Soft at first, tentative; he's not sure it's what I want. My fingers pull the red curls at the base of his neck. *More.* Theo groans in response: a low, almost inaudible sound. I close my eyes. My heart's beat hammers out the message in my ears – *I need you closer.* My back arches as the tip of his tongue probes the open space between my lips. This time I groan. It might be a whimper. Or even a purr. Theo pulls away. My breath judders. My eyes jump open. I smell his breath; sour and bitter. One kiss isn't enough. I want more. I need more.

The giggles start in my belly and I can't stop their escape.

'What is it?' Theo asks. My laugh is contagious, he laughs too. The sound is wonderful. It's infectious and silly. It's far too loud.

'What you do to me,' he says. He moves in to nuzzle my neck. I squeal. I squirm on the spot. His hands clutch my waist, moving with my wriggle and finding the outline of my breasts; only thin material protecting my decency. Our laughter stops. Our eyes engage. His pupils dilate.

'Oh, Miss,' Anaïs says. The tea tray clatters to the floor.

Theo and I jump away from each other on the *confidante*, adjusting our clothes as we move. We sit upright, our backs perfectly straight. Neither of us turn to look at the housemaid. Neither of us stop our cackles of joy.

January, 1889.

Gauguin sent a portrait of Vincent painting sunflowers during the last few days that he spent with him in the Yellow House. He captured it from memory, and offered it to Theo as an engagement 'gift'. Is it wrong of me to imagine money was still exchanged?

Our engagement goes ahead – one hundred and twenty-five announcements already sent out. The family reception will happen tomorrow. What a lot of friends and family write with kind wishes. Already we've been given much for our future home: a majolica fish vase, twelve silver teaspoons, a hideous Japanese vase, a pair of sugar tongs too.

So much passes as if in a dream; tomorrow I'll wear a ring on my finger.

Spring 1889

PARIS

March, 1889.

But to think only yesterday I asked Theo about Vincent's ear. He knew little more than that Vincent still wore a white bandage covering the place where his complete ear had once been. We were celebrating better news – that Vincent was painting again!

Yet today a letter from a Widow Venissac, who owns the pink restaurant where Vincent eats all of his meals, and Theo offers news of how his brother is suddenly known as 'fou-rou' in Arles. Crazy redhead! The townspeople are wearied of Vincent, of his constant drama and chaos. Already there are too many echoes of how he was towards the end of his time in Paris: friends finding him difficult, models refusing to pose for him, drunken outbursts, women fearing being alone with him, Vincent too volatile to sit and paint in the street.

What should we do?

Still Life Drawing Board Pipe Onions And Sealing-Wax

I open the front door to the apartment and he struggles to juggle a canvas and letters while wiggling arms from his coat.

'Did the concierge not offer to assist you?' I ask and Theo shakes his head. I help, pulling his arm free from a sleeve and handing his lounge coat to Anaïs.

'I'm receiving too many letters and updates about Vincent and his acts of madness. I don't even know where to begin,' Theo says. I remove his bowler hat from his head and place it on the table.

'Is he still in the Yellow House?' I ask. He shakes his head again. 'Let's go and sit in the parlour,' I say. 'Anaïs will bring some tea.' I nod to my brother's housemaid and she smiles as she rushes to the kitchen.

Theo waits until we're sitting on the *confidante*. The canvas, wrapped in brown paper, rests beside the sofa. The smell of oil paint wafts across us, as if Vincent is here, running laps around the room.

'He's been readmitted to hospital. I received this from Dr Urpar this morning.' He unfolds a piece of paper and passes it to me.

'A certificate of his condition?' I say. Theo nods.

'It was sent to the Mayor of Arles too. It seems the Yellow House's neighbours aren't so happy about having a crazy man staying near them. His behaviour has been spiralling.' A pause and I nod for him to continue. 'Some claim they fear for their lives.'

'But surely he's only of danger to himself?' I ask. I can't mask the tremor in my voice. I search Theo's face for clues.

'They requested that he's moved to a special asylum or back here.'

'Will you—'

'I don't know what to do. Should he live with us?' Theo says and I shrug my shoulders. Fear whirls in my stomach. 'He was allowed to write.' He hands me the letter and I skim the contents.

'He's to stay in hospital a few days and asks that you don't worry,' I say, to myself really, as Theo already knows the contents of his letter. 'He's worried about Gauguin?' I point to the words.

'Gauguin isn't replying to any of our letters.'

'He's a pompous idiot, only interested in financial gain,' I say. The words escape on a breath. My fiancé nods. 'But this bit.' I point to where Vincent's written about how when I live with Theo everything will change and that Theo won't be alone anymore. 'I can't tell if he considers that positive or negative.'

'I hoped positive,' Theo says, but the words betray his doubt.

'But it could be that he considers me an irritation? That our marriage prevents his return?' I say. I sigh. 'He might even think there'd be no room for him or his paintings.'

Theo shrugs. 'Should we tell him that nothing's changed?'

I bob my head enthusiastically. 'And make sure he knows he's welcome. That everything can be as before...' But Vincent is right – life is changing and everything feels just outside of my control. I hand the letter back. 'Why do his words leave me with an overwhelming desire to do something kind for someone?'

'Of late my brother leaves sorrow in all who encounter him,' Theo says. 'And Clara...' he begins.

'Is she well? I sent her our engagement announcement, hoping that a doctor would read the words to her, but haven't had a reply.'

'She's wonderful. Her doctors are thrilled with her progress.

She's exercising outside for eight to ten hours each day,' he says. 'Regardless of the weather.'

I smile. 'Any news of when she'll be able to return?' I ask. Theo shakes his head.

I pick my copy of *Le Livre d'Or* from the *confidante*. Theo had it delivered this morning. I open it, smiling at the *Febr.'89* he has scribbled inside. Questions and answers about life and love are contained within: important considerations and discussions as we step towards our marriage.

'Thank you,' I say, nodding to the book. Theo grins. I flick to one of the pages where I've folded the top corner. 'This one asks, "What do you think of marriage?"'

Theo raises an eyebrow, awaiting my response.

'Comtesse Diane offers, "If you look for happiness together, that is where you will find it." And I like that a lot.'

Theo nods. 'And perhaps you'll like this too.' He lifts the package as he stands and walks over to Andries' slate desk. I hurry behind. 'Vincent has sent us an engagement gift.' I move my brother's papers into an untidy pile as Theo unwraps the canvas.

'A still life,' he says. 'The first painting since his self-mutilation.' He places the canvas onto the desk and we both take a step back to admire Vincent's art.

'Four onions. A medical self-help book. A candle.' Theo points at all of the inclusions as he names them. 'His pipe, his tobacco. A teapot. A large bottle of absinthe.'

'Emptied,' I say and Theo laughs.

'The colours are more tempered than his other art. Less penetrating,' Theo says.

We stand in silence, feasting on the art, smiling at Vincent's skill. 'These are the items that ground your brother,' I say.

'He's clinging to any semblance of normality in this first piece since his mental collapse. He'll be quelling his inner—'

'What's that?' I point to the bottom right of the painting.

'A letter.'

'An envelope? Why?' I step closer. I bend to focus on the details Vincent has included. This is his first, his only painting for months. Every inclusion will have significance. The brushwork is fiery: thick impasto mixed with bare canvas.

'My brother reveals his soul in each painting.' A pause. 'I think this is his apology to us. For taking from the glory of our announcement.'

I'm not really listening. My focus is entirely on the envelope.

'The post office number on the envelope,' I say. 'It's 67.'

'The post office I use,' Theo says. He bends close to me and stares at the envelope.

'The stamp shows it was sent around Christmas,' I say. 'And we know that Vincent cut his ear on the day that he received your letter about our engagement … and this is his first painting since his mental collapse.'

'What are you saying, Jo?' Theo stands upright. He's suddenly as stiff as a pillar; he knows exactly what I'm saying.

'That perhaps rather than an apology, your brother is making a statement,' I say. I still bend close to the painting. The smell of Vincent van Gogh wafts up my nose and into my very being. 'I think that those fiery strokes warn of Vincent's continued mental decline.'

'And there's more,' he says. 'Vincent doesn't know yet, but twenty of his neighbours want him to leave.' He places a piece of paper onto the slate desk. The words '*La Pétition*' title the document.

March, 1889.

Theo's been kept busy preparing his Monet exhibition. His role is to get sales and, as no other place in town currently sells Monet, he expects it to be a success. I refer to it as the Monet exhibition, but there are also a few pastels from Degas and Rodin's marble sculpture of John the Baptist's head on a platter. Theo said that when he first saw Rodin's piece he was convinced that Vincent stared back at him.

Tonight I braved a snowstorm to visit. Upstairs in the gallery all of the other paintings had been removed, allowing Theo's display full focus. He was so very thrilled to see me; attendance, because of the weather, was lower than expected and only a few journalists and Theo's acquaintances had arrived.

I spent most of the evening wandering alone, overhearing snippets of conversation and braving the odd handshake when Theo was able to introduce me.

But then I encountered Rodin's head and was shaken entirely. The face held such a look of suffering – with its furrowed brow portraying a life of anguish and self-denial. I stared and all I could see was my dear Theo; an exact replica of the man I love, with his mouth slightly open, with the shape of the nose so entirely Theo and even the head's form was identical too.

Theo said that Rodin's piece complimented and contrasted with Monet's paintings (that celebrate life and light; leaves glisten, wind rustles, water sparkles – the colours are rich, the lines elegant), because Rodin made him consider death. I stood in front of Rodin's head with tears streaming from my eyes. Thoughts of Theo suffering, of his death, of my grief. A life half-lived, a marriage not yet consummated and already I fear my husband's death.

Monet's Antibes, Vue de Salis *sold to a Mr Taconet for fr 3,000. Theo had to play cashier as the bookkeeper was ill and in the morning* Figaro *will publish an article about my fiancé's successful exhibition.*

Tomorrow people will flock to the gallery; Monet an overnight success, as if he only emerged today.

Self-Portrait With Bandaged Ear

I met him at his work and we've been strolling the *petits boulevards* around Montmartre for nearly an hour. Mainly we've been talking about Mamma's plans, the travel arrangements back to the Netherlands for our wedding next month and the dances that have been arranged for the summer. Theo and I walk slowly, and the pace suits us both. I take his arm and we laugh. I had considered him a little distracted though, or possibly a little nervous.

We stop walking along rue Houdon. 'Hold out your hand and close your eyes,' he says. It seems I was right; something occupies his mind.

'Right here. In the middle of the cobbles?' I ask.

'*Hé, la-bas!*' is shouted.

We both turn and see a *fiacre* lurching towards us. Theo jumps, taking my hand and pulling me from the carriage's path as we just escape the horse's hooves. I close my parasol and shuffle closer to the wall.

A door is pushed ajar to the right of us. A tall, dishevelled woman, dressed only in her undergarments, steps barefooted onto the narrow street. Her chestnut hair is loose and tangled. Her front teeth are decayed stumps and her skin carries a yellow tinge.

Drawing on her cigarette she looks left and then right. She spots Theo, but his eyes are on me.

'*Bonjour, Monsieur Van Gogh*,' she says. '*Comment vas-tu?*' The cigarette balances on her bottom lip as she slurs her words. Theo looks up and she winks at him. She pulls at the misshapen neck of her chemise. 'Got any jobs for me today? Or maybe you'd like me for yourself.'

I'm unable to keep the surprise from my face. 'You know her?' I ask.

'One of Manet's models,' he says. '*Non, pas aujourd'hui, Victorine.*'

'She doesn't look well,' I say. 'Should we help?' Theo shakes his head as we watch Victorine stagger around people and along the narrow street towards a huddle of men. I shift my focus back to my fiancé. 'You wanted to tell me something?'

'Hold out your hand and close your eyes,' he repeats.

I hold out my hand. A pause and then I feel the cold metal in my palm. Opening my eyes I see a key.

'It's time to start building a nest,' he says. 'I've found us a new home.'

'In town?' I ask.

'Of course! Being out-of-town hermits wouldn't suit us at all.' He laughs. 'Eight cité Pigalle, on the third floor left.'

'A new apartment?' I say. Theo nods. I throw my arms around him, embracing him, not caring for the wicked tones and judgement from passing strangers. This close to our wedding, my reputation is less likely to be the subject of gossip.

We'd talked about where we'd live after our wedding. We'd talked about the apartment on rue Lepic being too small, both of us agreeing that somewhere new and entirely ours was important.

'I've endured countless viewings of too many unsuitable places.'

'Without me? Why didn't you say? I'd have—'

'And where would the surprise be in that?' he says. 'It'll be ready for when we return from our wedding.'

I note the slight raising of his eyebrows, the small widening of his eyes; I hold eye contact, smiling. Two can play at his game. My desires are equal to his.

'Bonger went with me to view this one and was quick to highlight its many shortcomings: an ugly entrance, dark kitchen too,' he says, mimicking my brother's voice and his need for perfection.

'We won't be living on the staircase or in the kitchen,' I say. I laugh. 'Can we afford it?'

'Eight hundred and twenty francs a month, and we'll pay for all urgent repairs,' he says. 'I can start taking things there immediately.'

'Immediately?' I say and he bobs his head enthusiastically.

'And my Aunt Cornelie has gifted us her piano.'

I shake my head in disbelief. My fiancé and his grand passion. 'How have you managed all of this without my having even the slightest inclination?'

Theo taps the side of his nose with his finger, before rubbing his moustache and smiling. I stand on my tiptoes to kiss his cheek, lingering a little too long.

'I've drawn you a floor plan,' he says. He fumbles in his pockets. 'I've viewed this one twice alone and once with Bonger.' He hands me the floor plan. I've no idea why we're having this discussion at the side of the road. Clearly Theo was unable to wait any longer.

'See how the dining room has two windows,' he says.

'It's long, rather than wide?' I say and Theo nods. 'And a balcony? Tell me about the view.'

'It's off our bedroom and looks out onto the backs of other buildings. One is full of artists' studios. We'll be able to sit there and gaze into other people's lives.'

'How very Dutch,' I say and Theo laughs.

'I'm going to start furnishing it this week,' he says.

'Don't I get a say?' I ask, feigning upset.

I see his expression alter; he searches my face for reassurance. I smile, and reach out my hand to his; this is the best surprise.

'Of course, and I welcome your opinion. But let me prepare

this as a gift for you.' He moves to me and brushes his fingers over my cheek. He leans in and I close my eyes, inhaling a breath of him. The bristles of his moustache tickle my skin. His lips are millimetres from mine. He brushes my lips; it's a whisper.

'Mamma will be pleased with this development,' I say. 'In letters of late, she's been unrelenting in her demand for details of our plans for after the wedding.'

'Shall we stroll again?' he says. I take his arm. 'It's within walking distance of the Montmartre neighbourhood, not far from Boussod, Valadon & Cie too.'

'You can escape work to eat lunch with me each day,' I say.

'There's something else I needed to share with you,' he says. 'Vincent knows about the petition.'

A cold wind appears to swirl around us. I shiver, leaning towards Theo a little bit more. The change in the direction of our conversation catches my breath.

'Go on,' I say. My pace quickens slightly.

'Nearly thirty of his neighbours have signed the document now. The mayor has written to me; a police investigation is happening. They have five witnesses giving evidence.'

'And the choices remain for him to return to you in Paris or to be committed to an asylum? Is that why you've arranged a new home for us? Is it large enough for Vincent too?'

'This'll be our home,' Theo says. He waves the floor plan in the air as we walk. 'The police commissioner, Joseph d'Ornano, has recommended that Vincent be confined in the local hospital. You were right.'

'About his continued decline?'

Theo nods. 'The bandage he wears hides all that is horrific beneath.'

'Must madness and creativity dance hand in hand?' I ask.

'Aristotle noted some creative types to be depressives. The connection persists. Vincent, Camille—'

'Camille Claudel?' I ask.

'She ended the affair with Rodin, but now they're saying she bends into madness too.'

Chapter One

'I must—'
'No, Johanna, you really mustn't.'
Reluctantly, I nod.

March, 1889.

François Lafon asked us to dejeuner with him and his wife. Theo had described him as a 'mediocre' history painter and his wife a keen pianist, but said that François' brother was a remarkable Dominican monk. Theo liked him immensely; considered him kind.

Alas the brother wasn't there and conversation over lunch left me sad. She asked how many maids would live with us when we married. I replied, 'None,' before Theo could speak, adding that I would require only a housemaid for a few hours each day. They discussed literature: how they'd like their daughters to read Paul de Kock's book one day and about Zola's greatness. In spite of permanently being keen to discuss literature and perhaps because I was suddenly reminded of Vincent sending me Zola's novel (why haven't I read it yet?), I remained silent. Theo said that Zola was the writer he appreciated most: that he loved his writing as much as he loved Degas' painting. How did I not know that already?

From Zola they talked about an exhibition of des peintres-graveurs. How good and mediocre exhibited together, and how the only Dutch artist shown was Thijs Maris – stating his three etchings to be among the best there. Again I remained quiet, regarding their enthusiasm and knowledge, unable to contribute. I considered telling them about an etching I'd liked in an exhibition in Amsterdam but didn't. In some company, it feels that there is a 'right opinion' on every topic, and that those who have any other must hold their tongues.

And later I considered that the only thing Theo could do to make me happy would be to love me exactly as I am – with all of my faults, shortcomings, silences and uncertainties. Sometimes I prefer to observe and collect people, rather than contribute and pretend... Perhaps I can wish that Theo won't ever want to change me.

Because I have already considered how much I'll have to change about myself before we marry. Today offered a reminder of how unlike other wives I am. Perhaps I even wished myself more like her – so cheery, full of energy, always knowing exactly what to do and say.

The Novel Reader

Reminiscent of last December, he rushed here with two letters gripped in his trembling hand. I read the letter from Vincent: manic, scribbled and at times almost illegible, with a hurried sketch of a bottle. He believed someone wanted to poison him. He ranted about increasing numbers of cowardly people joining together to destroy him, about being armed with a razor at all times, about how impossible it was for him to work or even to function. Not knowing which of his neighbours had signed the petition was clearly increasing his paranoia. Some boys had even bombarded him with cabbage stalks, other adults had gathered to peer in his window daily; he feared the provocation and worried he'd be unable to control himself.

'Is he hallucinating again?' I ask

'They say he's mentally deranged.' Theo points to a second letter; this one is from Vincent's doctor. 'His moments of lucidity have decreased daily,' Theo says. 'They say he's diseased. The doctor talks of a rash and mouth lesions too. And...'

I pick *La Fille Elisa* from the *confidante* next to me, anxiously turning it in my hands as I avoid eye contact with Theo. 'And?'

'A foul-smelling discharge.'

I take a moment; where would the discharge leak from? I scrunch my face in disgust. Theo's been here only ten minutes, pacing and clearly avoiding the urgent paperwork that was included with the doctor's letter. Anaïs enters the parlour with a tray, placing it on the tea table next to me. I nod for her to leave and pour a cup for Theo as he sits down beside me.

'Can we talk about something else?' I say. I hand him the tea. The cup looks a little too small and dainty: his palm too large, his fingers too long and thin.

'Johanna Bonger,' he says. I can't help but smile as he takes a sip. I like how he says my full name as if it were covered in honey, knowing that soon I'll become someone else: *Mrs Van Gogh*. Theo's expression is steady. Both his red whiskers and moustache are a little less well-maintained, but few would notice. The strain of Vincent exhausts him; he'd never admit it to anyone but me.

'His neighbours claim to be terrified, that his bandaged head is a constant reminder of his fit of madness in December.' He places the cup and saucer onto the tea table. 'I need to write letters, send payments…' He nods to Andries' desk as if he might write them there. A pause. 'Yet in his letter to me a few days ago he appeared to be the calm and charming brother I once knew. He wasn't a madman, he isn't a madman.' A pause.

'But if all of the witnesses are truthful?' I say.

Theo pulls his lips into his mouth, their thinness only just visible under his moustache. He nods. His eyes cast down. I place my hand on his thigh and he covers it with his own.

'There's nothing I can do. The police have already shut down the Yellow House.'

'Have they locked him away?' I say and Theo nods.

'Like a prisoner.'

'They must have considered it the best solution,' I say.

'They've incarcerated *fou-rou* in an asylum, but he needs his art, he needs to create. Without that outlet, he'll spiral deeper.'

'Can you send him paint and canvas?' I say.

Theo shrugs. 'He's one of the most progressive painters alive. He has to keep painting,' he says. 'He forces us to surrender conventional ideas when viewing his art. But Jo… Can I hope that one day he'll be understood?'

'He will. I promise.' I long to ease Theo's pain. He carries Vincent's weight on his shoulders. Removing his hand from mine, he reaches to lift the cup and saucer. There's a slight tremor in his fingers. 'His head's too full of hallucinations and nightmares.'

'What can we do to help?' I ask. I nod towards the paperwork.

'Sara Voort's been to visit him,' Theo says. His voice is almost a whisper into the teacup.

'What? Is she still interested in your brother?' It's the first time Theo's mentioned her in weeks, months maybe. I asked Andries about her just last week but he had nothing new to report. We both concluded that she'd given up on the Van Gogh brothers.

Theo sips at his tea. 'She considers him a friend,' he says.

'They were much more than friends.' Theo laughs at my remark. But there's something in the sound that's not quite right, that doesn't reach the required *ting*. 'Have you seen her?'

'She called into my work before I left today.'

'And you didn't think to tell me?' I say, folding my arms across my torso. 'Was that the first visit in months?' I ask.

'She's irrelevant,' he says, dismissing my question, dismissing the woman. 'Whereas Vincent...' He waits and I nod for him to continue, pushing my own insecurities aside. 'He told me to focus on you, and on our marriage. He asked for details and dates,' Theo says.

I lick my lips. My mouth is suddenly a little too dry.

'He even asked if he could attend as my groomsman. Said it would give him something to aim for.'

'I hope you agreed,' I say.

He nods. He's unable to make eye contact; he doesn't want me to see his sorrow. 'Vincent's badly shaken, but he's sober, not even allowed his pipe. He needs hope.'

April, 1889.

Today I had my first cooking lesson, arranged by Dries with Madame Sethe. Tomorrow she'll visit again and we'll spend another entire day in the kitchen. Dries is delighted that he can taste all that's being made; myself less so as I already and passionately hate all things culinary.

When I shared today's activities with Theo, he said, 'I do appreciate the trouble you're taking,' and that somehow made me worry even more. There's an expectation that I'll be good at cooking and today has provided much evidence to counter that.

Already I worry that even the simplest of instructions and expectations of being a wife are beyond my grasp. I can't even confess to my almost-husband that conversation about whether I'd prefer to be given a silver soup spoon or a water kettle bores me.

Added to that, Madame Sethe talks continuously about her unhappy marriage and about how a husband does everything to please his wife when newly married, but that that quickly alters. I told Theo and he replied that marriage was to be viewed as if each of us were 'spinning our own thread', but that if a knot were to appear then the expectation would not be that we'd untangle it alone.

I loved his attempt at soothing my worry, but now, with my weariness, it's created even more. How does he always know the correct response? How has he already perfected his approach to marriage?

How can I ever hope to be the wife Theo deserves and needs?

View Of Paris

The elevators aren't yet completed, but Gustave Eiffel and a few resilient companions currently ascend the 1,710 steps to the top of the tower. Monsieur Eiffel began the climb to cheers, clutching an enormous French Tricolour to fly on the summit's flagpole. When they unfurl the French flag, a twenty-one-gun salute will sound and history will be made. But for now, we all wait at the base, cloaks billowing, hats being swept from heads, as we strain our necks watching the black figures climb; the Champs de Mars is a wind tunnel, yet no one complains.

'Oh my, I still can't believe Theo didn't want this invite,' Andries says. His eyes are wide, jumping about the other guests and the hundreds of construction workers waiting at the base of the tower.

My soon-to-be husband did indeed obtain two tickets to the Eiffel Tower's official inauguration ceremony. The tickets were largely given to famous personalities, but Edgar Degas, not wanting to support the monstrous construction, had gifted the tickets to Theo. Andries is beside himself. He's practically bouncing on the spot. I think he's taken more photographs in the last ten minutes than he has since work began on the tower, two years, two months and five days ago.

'Look there,' Andries says. He moves his box camera to the right. Seconds later he's winding on the frame. 'Did you see? Prime Minister Pierre Tirard.' I shake my head. 'Nine hundred and eighty-four feet tall. Iron framework supported on four masonry piers. Elevators that will ascend the piers on a curve.' He points his box camera in the tower's direction as the facts and figures gush from him, all covered in a tinge of pride and awe. 'Platforms, each with an observation deck, at three levels. A skeletal support system with a copper skin affixed to it. *Magnifique*.' With the word '*magnifique*' he brings the fingers and thumb of his right hand together and he moves them to his lips. After kissing them lightly, he tosses his fingers and thumb into the air. My brother is full of joy today.

'And to think it won't open to the public until May,' I say. 'But you'll climb it before any of them.'

'I can't ever thank Theo enough.' Andries pulls me into an embrace, knocking my bonnet to the floor.

'Can't say I'm excited about the 1,710 steps.' I angle my head to see the tip of the tower as I pick up my hat. 'With these skirts.'

Andries laughs. 'Our last adventure before you marry and it's history in the making.' He turns away, his camera capturing the crowd.

'Look at the pinnacle,' someone shouts in French. I look up as the Tricolour unfolds and the gun salute begins.

We all stand, stiff and proud. We mimic the phallic statue.

'No woman would have designed that,' I say but my words are unnoticed in the cheers.

Today Paris is majestic, this tower imposing but honest; and in this moment, I see how it connects. The ugliest building in Paris is both art and male. It has something to say. It commemorates the centennial of the French Revolution, it shouts France's industrial competence to the world, it speaks of man's expertise. The women of France are irrelevant and Eiffel's tower is unapologetic about that.

Fireworks explode from the second platform and the

privileged invited guests applaud and shout. Andries bounces on the spot; he's a small boy in a man's body, packed with gladness and wonder.

April, 1889.

Earlier today we were given a tea set from Mr and Mrs Hove. Immediately I wondered where it would be stored in our new apartment.

I truly don't recognise myself of late.

I've been so very excited by our discussions about furniture and the decoration in our rooms: whether there should be a cupboard or a modern buffet in the dining room, if the best use of the box room would be to fill it with cupboards for now or to prepare it for guests etc. etc. etc. We've discussed material for curtains, wallpaper, paint, parquet flooring – and I've loved each and every conversation in this building of our nest. That I've not yet visited, that I'll only see it after we're married, that Theo's so truly excited about this gift to me – how did I get to be this blessed?

And when did I gain such opinions on domestic life? Have my many lessons with Madame Sethe these last weeks altered my entire being? Might I even be excited to be a wife?

There's still much that we discuss about Vincent, about his health, about other tortured artists, but increasingly I distract myself with domesticity: unexpectedly, its bonds gift me power. Perhaps I seek diversion from the bad things that weigh us down, to stay grounded in this moment, to stay happy with this present; yet my almost-brother, Vincent, is always in our thoughts. That he remains too ill and can't attend our wedding is unspoken.

For tomorrow I'm travelling back to Amsterdam and there I'll cease to be Johanna Bonger – that person erased and replaced. Miss Bonger will be no more.

Ten months after knowing Theo and Vincent and already I'll be Mrs Van Gogh.

But one final surprise from my fiancé – Clara is well. She's returning to Paris.

~

MARRIED.

Miss Johanna Gezina Bonger,
of this city, and Mr Theodorus
van Gogh of Paris, were
married on April 17 1889. A
number of family members of
the contracting parties were
present, who, in conjunction with
several acquaintances, wished the
newly wedded pair all the joys
of felicity.

~

Chapter Two

BECOME

Summer 1889

PARIS

June, 1889.

Vincent still stays in Saint-Rémy. Today's letter offered more details of the asylum and was written to give Theo peace of mind. Indeed he writes daily with pages of costs and requirements, never not expecting his brother to pay and, for his part, Theo welcomes any chance to stay connected with Vincent.

Without his brother's chaos, already my husband and I have fallen into a routine that suits us both.

Up at eight and Theo is quick to turn on the gas to boil the water. By the time our tea has brewed, we're both dressed. Theo leaves around nine each morning and Madame Joseph arrives at ten. We employ her for only five hours a day and she's such a help; I'm learning much from her. She makes our bed, does sweeping, makes lunch, and then she goes off. Some days she comes back in the afternoon to do or to help with the cooking – this seems to be increasing of late and is perhaps due to Theo wanting food that's edible! Already we leave the washing of our plates and pots until the next day.

Because, yes, Madame Joseph helps – but there is still so much to do. Our apartment's cosy but it's also cluttered with ornaments and too many bits and bobs that require polishing and dusting. I understand why acquaintances scoffed when I said we'd not have staff living with us, but still that decision feels right and Clara's keen to instruct and help. I still can't believe that she's back in Paris. She adores the lodgings that Theo arranged for her and she's looking better than ever before. She visits daily – perhaps she feels the need to offer help with the housekeeping in lieu of all that Theo has done for her.

I enjoy shopping alone though, silent among the bustle and activity of people, fiacres and omnibuses. I love that the streets slope downwards around here, that I already know the best and easiest route back, that people are beginning to nod and to say, 'Bonjour,' when I walk to and from our home. Is it even odd to admit that I love that bread and milk are left in front of our door and that I'm the person who collects it each morning?

But mainly ... is it selfish that I simply want to pause and stay 'learning how to be a wife' for a little longer? I'm not even yet used to being Mrs Van Gogh.

I can't bear the thought of each or any conversation being about what grows inside me.

How on earth will I ever learn to be a mother?

June 08, 1889.
Paris.

Dearest Brother,

I've been meaning to write to you, aware that since our wedding it's always been Theo sending my regards. Now that I'm your little sister, it feels important that you know me that bit more. Indeed, I'm even hopeful that you might grow to love me as you do your brother.

Both Theo and I carried sadness that you weren't with us on our wedding day, but already we've been living together in our apartment for seven weeks and there are so many reminders of you here. If Theo has a fine vase or jug, I can always predict that you were the one who encouraged its purchase. Not a day goes by that you're not in our thoughts or conversations.

That my mother agreed to the wedding not being in a church, and my avoidance of saying how much of a farce that would have been, guaranteed that it went without hitch. The day itself was sunny and lovely, although both Theo and I had wished it over, and we stayed in Brussels for only one night, by way of a honeymoon. Mainly, I was so very excited to get back to Paris and to our new apartment and then the surprise, on return, was that Dries had made it even more homely – putting flowers in rooms, making beds etc.

Of course, reading about Dries being here might evoke a sadness in you and so what follows is a brief tour; so that you can imagine yourself a visitor already.

We enter the cité through a fence that separates it from the street. There are houses on the right and on the left, and ours has a little garden in front with trees and a couple of lilacs, which are flowering beautifully. As we enter the building, we look up and see the horses of the Parthenon carved into the arch above the entrance. We're on the third floor, on the left. When opening the door and entering our apartment, the corridor is decorated with white and blue paper – same in the box room. The salon is the first room we enter. Its walls are white with grey floral patterns. The new chiffonier is rosewood – a square cabinet with five drawers and a folding panel to write on. That's where I am now, writing this to you.

There's already a drawer that we call the 'Vincent drawer'; it's stuffed full of your letters. Your familiar yellow envelopes, distinctive handwriting – we always look forward to your news. The piano sits next to the chiffonier: a gift from your Aunt Cornelie and I enjoy playing – although I'll never be any good. This room is already quite full with that furniture, and armchairs, two small rugs too; we like it though. The parquet floors are truly beautiful. The dining room is next to the salon and it's also full, but neither Theo nor I are happy with how we've arranged it all. Of course Dries considers our furnishings vulgar and he's not at all impressed with where we live, but it's enough for Theo and me. The cabinet de debarras is full of wardrobes at the moment. One day we hope to welcome you here as our guest and so that box room awaits its transformation into a space for the great Vincent van Gogh.

Your Small Pear Tree in Blossom *hangs in our bedroom. It's the first thing I see when I wake and brings a smile to my face each and every time.* The Harvest *hangs above the piano,* La Berceuse *in the box room,* The Potato Eaters *in the dining room above the fireplace. We host our very own Vincent van Gogh exhibition for each visitor. Already, one of my most favourite things in the world, is to watch the awe, the amazement and the purity in reaction when others gaze on your paintings for the first time.*

Today is Sunday and Theo is home all day, which pleases me as he's been so very tired of late. Indeed it only hit me yesterday that I now live in Paris. Some days I worry I'll stop loving it, just as you did. Increasingly, I understand more how you viewed the chaos and busyness, how you craved the silence. We live in a quiet quarter now and I think that might suit me better. Silence and peace feel so very important these days; perhaps you'll understand that more than I do.

I worry often: about you, about me, about Theo too. I've been reading Heine and I don't think I've ever encountered a more profound writer, but he steals my peace of mind; my thoughts refuse to stay quiet after I've spent time with him. It's clear that he has suffered terribly and again I'm reminded of the many tortured souls that exist. Some days my only wish is that I could scoop them all up into my arms.

That said, and in case you feel I'm trying too hard to appear praiseworthy, my housekeeping skills leave much to be desired. The rice *has been burned twice this week already, our plums once. Poor Theo still eats it all, attempting to hide his squirms of displeasure about the taste! I'm sure Theo's employing our housemaid, Madame Joseph, for additional hours, in the hope that I'll let her cook for us both.*

But we get along so very well together; I love him more than I ever imagined I could.

I hope my ramblings haven't bored you, dear Vincent. I'm sure my letter writing skills will improve with time. I send you warm regards.

Your loving little sister, Jo

July, 1889.

My husband has a rash. Small reddish-brown lumps decorate his palms.

I have no rash. I've a fever though, a constant headache, fatigue, my appetite is gone. I've not spoken a word about my condition to Theo and he's not asked that I seek medical help.

When I spoke to Clara earlier, about the rash, she already knew; she even said that Theo was seeking treatment. Apparently, the doctor has promised that, if Theo endures his course of mercurial treatment for three years, he'll be cured entirely. She talked about how Theo and I could go on to produce healthy children. Theo had confided in Clara; they are firm friends now and my husband hides his shame from me.

So I'm being told, second-hand, that we're being gifted three years of liberty, three years before we seek to bring a child into the world.

If only I wasn't with child when Theo's rash appeared.

My head spins with possibilities and problems.

How can I tell my husband that the disease he carries could already have been passed to his child?

View Of The Roofs Of Paris

I'm standing on the balcony in my nightgown and cap, in silk hose, wool stockings, and drawers; I'm clutching the wrought iron railing and the rain is lashing down on me. I could be an asylum patient, locked up with Vincent. I wouldn't actually be surprised if Theo's sent Madame Joseph off searching for a doctor.

A mix of towering and squat structures surround this apartment building, but somehow our home's in the tallest and proudest of them all. During the days following our wedding, I'd spend hours being Dutch and peering into other households and artists' lives – curious about how they spent their days and what creations were coming into being – but today my Parisian skyline blends into the sky's gloom. The roofs and apartments are covered with a mist, and that means that they're greyer, duller too; they match my mood. Other balconies are empty. Other shutters are closed. I don't spot another manic woman standing in the morning rain. I shiver. Eiffel's tower will still be tall and erect in the distance, over there; I wish my brother were here. Right now, I'd happily rewind to when I lived with him.

'What is it, Jo?' Theo says. 'Is my company so bad that you'd prefer to be here in the rain?' He laughs, possibly hoping my behaviour to be an elaborate joke.

I turn to his voice. I bet he's already had enough of me. I wouldn't blame him.

'Is it your tooth again?' he asks but I don't respond. 'We have chloroform...'

'Have you read Thackeray's *The Newcomes*? It's a book that leaves you much changed than before reading it. And the description of Miss Honeyman's boarding house at Brighton must be based on a real place. I long to visit there.'

The rain's soaked through my clothes. I'd like to curl onto the wet floor and sleep forever; I want to ignore what grows inside. Theo takes a step outside then stops. He loses his nerve or perhaps the rain stops him.

'A trip to England sounds wonderful. Come indoors and we'll discuss it,' he says. He's trying to placate me – to lure me inside. I wonder if he perfected that tone with Vincent.

'Leave me alone,' I say.

Theo flares his nostrils, sucks in his cheeks, then turns to walk back into our apartment. He leaves me to the rain.

He'll expect an explanation later, yet what can I tell him?

'Miss Jo,' Clara says. 'What is it?' Her tone's flat. I turn to look at her. Her thicker lips, her permanent suntan, her jet-black hair and her eyes – they all seem more luscious than ever before. 'You'll catch your death standin' out here in just your undergarments.'

I shrug my shoulders. I don't think I even care.

'Shall I fetch Master Andries?' Her tone fails to hide that she's irritated. The rain thrashes down on her and I know she'll be uncertain what to do next. She's still recovering.

'Go back inside, Clara. You shouldn't be out here in this.' I turn back to the railing.

'Not without you,' she says. 'So are you wantin' us both to catch our deaths?' I hear the tap of her walking stick as she moves to me.

'I love Theo,' I say. 'My kind and gentle husband. He's the best man I know.'

'That isn't in question, is it Miss Jo? Has somethin' else

happened?'

Tears stream down my face. My body droops. My lips tremble.

'I've started being sick in the mornings,' I say. The words float around us. 'Sickness each morning, corset a little snugger.'

'You're with child,' she says.

She's next to me, she grabs my hand. 'Oh Miss Jo, that's wonder—' I turn to her; her face is bright with joy, but then I watch as she pauses, as her face twists. The rain defeats us both. She looks away from me, but together we stand, still holding hands, staring out over misty Paris.

'Why aren't you happy?'

'Theo's caught Vincent's disease, and that must mean he's a lover elsewhere. It's the only explanation.' My voice is raised to a shout. 'He's being intimate with someone else.'

'Calm yourself,' Clara says. 'Theo caught that illness long before you and him were intimate. You know there were others before you? Some of them shared with his brother.'

I nod and wipe my nose on the back of my hand.

'From the day you met, that man's only had eyes for you.'

'I was already pregnant when his rash appeared,' I say. 'He must have known he was ill and—'

'What's done is done,' she says. 'That child in your belly's already the luckiest in the world.'

'What if I've caught Theo's disease? What if the baby already has it too,' I whisper.

'Have you any symptoms?' she asks and I shake my head. *Not yet*, is left unspoken. 'I'll arrange for a doctor to call tomorrow.'

I don't move.

'Is there more?' Clara says.

'What will Vincent do this time?' I say. 'It almost feels inevitable.' The words are still barely louder than a whisper. He's Theo's brother, *our* brother. He'll have to be told. 'Agostina aborted his child. Look how he's reacted to our happiness so far. What if this news causes him to…'

Rain beats away the seconds. 'What matters most is the child,

Miss Jo. You're goin' to be a mamma and that growin' child in your belly should be your focus.'

'A mamma,' I say. An echo. 'I'm not even used to being a wife. I can't even cook rice without burning it.'

Clara laughs. 'I can help with the rice makin',' she says. 'And any mother who declares herself an expert the day their little one pops out is a lyin' idiot. Takes time, and a mountain or two of patience.'

I can't help but sob. I'm going to be a mamma.

'Let's go inside, dry ourselves off,' she says.

July, 1889.

The doctor examined me at length. He's confident that both mamma and baby are healthy, for now. He's advised that I'm not intimate with Theo.
  I've yet to share any of this news with my husband.

Blossoming Almond Branch In A Glass With A Book

Theo's avoiding me.

He'd gone out by the time I dried off from my rainy protest, he didn't arrive home before I fell asleep and, judging by the still-made portion of our bed, he must have slept on an armchair in the parlour last night.

Still alone but propped up by cushions in our bed, I sketch. The faint lines jump around the page and none will settle in place. My head's spinning, full of anxious thoughts: *what if my husband's already given up on me? What if the doctor was wrong and my baby's already ill?*

I close my sketchbook. I lean to place it and my pencils on the floor, but my stomach flips and my vision blurs at the edges: like I've just finished off an entire bottle of quinine wine. My queasiness is insistent. It stirs then shoots from my stomach to my throat. I swing my body from under the bedspread and lean over, vomiting into and over the edges of the chamber pot. It brings little relief, but I wipe my mouth on the back of my hand and try to lie down again. The movement makes the nausea worse; I'm retching far too loudly and my vomiting's uncontrollable. I miss the chamber pot. It splatters over the parquet floor.

I groan. My entire body aches.

Madame Joseph walks in, a jug of water in one hand and a

glass in the other. She places them on the floor next to the armoire, before pulling open the curtains; I try to focus on their pink and red flowers, but they begin dancing across the cream background. I look to the floor instead.

Clara hobbles into the room. She uses her stick as she walks and carries a plate with her other hand. 'Here Miss Jo,' she says. 'Try and nibble at this bread. Best get somethin' in your belly.'

She hangs her walking stick off the raised footboard and steps around the vomit. I watch as she breaks off a piece of bread. She hands it to me but I shake my head. My stomach flips. I'm not sure if it's hunger or nausea that's causing the protest.

'Little one needs it,' she says.

Madame Joseph gasps, then she echoes, 'Little one,' in a shout.

'Be quiet,' Clara says. She glares at her. 'Not a word. Mr Theo don't know yet.'

'Mr Theo doesn't know what?' he says. The words boom and bounce as he walks into our bedroom. He's undoing his lounge coat and he places his bowler hat on the unmade bed, next to Clara's walking stick.

'Apologies, Mr Theo,' Madame Joseph mutters. She bends to the floor and picks up the chamber pot. She scurries out before any of us speak another word. I watch as Theo takes in the scene: vomit on the floor, wife in bed, water, bread, a smiling housemaid.

'You're not ill,' he says. It's a statement. He's playing detective, deciphering the clues. 'And Clara wants you to eat,' he says, and then he pauses. His face is pale and he fidgets, drumming the rosewood posts as he stands at the bottom of the bed.

'Are you leaving me?' he asks. His eyes are fixed on the crumpled bed sheets. 'Is being married to me making you desperately unhappy and now ill?'

I look at Clara and she nods for me to speak, but my stomach groans. I daren't move. I might vomit again if I open my mouth.

'Miss Jo has wonderful news, Mr Theo,' Clara says. 'She's fearful of your reaction, what with it bein' so soon after your marriage. You had plans.'

'Plans? Wonderful news?' he repeats. I can see how he's

feeling, I can read his expressions with ease. Hope rushes across his face. He radiates joy. My husband's eyes glimmer with delight, his smile beams like a shooting star. He looks at me and I hold his gaze, then he flicks his eyes to my stomach.

'Are you?' he says and I nod.

Tears pour down my face as he rushes to me, springing onto his side of the bed and clasping my body to his. The sudden movement sends the nausea shooting through my body, but I try to gulp it away.

'This is the best news, the absolute greatest news.' I hear his heart thumping. The warmth of his body seeps through my thin nightgown; it's the safest I've felt for days.

He pulls away from me. 'But why the sadness?' he says.

'It's…' I begin.

Theo holds me at arm's length, the movement a rocking too many. I lean away from him, but the chamber pot's not there. Madame Joseph hasn't returned with a new one. I can't stop myself; I vomit.

'Miss Jo's concerned about Mr Vincent's madness,' Clara says. My body has its own agenda. I vomit onto the floor again.

'She fears for the baby?' Theo says. His tone's a little too high. I hear his anxiety in the rise of his question.

'We all should, Mr Theo.' A pause. 'But with the engagement and the weddin', and all your brother's episodes… He puts strain on the two of you, and with Miss Jo sufferin' with sickness and all the complications that women can have durin' confinement…' She pauses again.

I imagine she signals to Theo about his own illness and the complications this could cause an unborn. My husband carries his secrets. I imagine he's holding his breath and waiting for Clara's solution.

'Have you seen a doctor?' Theo asks.

'All fine, for now,' I say, trying not to move my head at all.

Theo exhales loudly.

'Miss Jo wondered if you could keep this news from your

brother for a few months. Just until she's over the worst of it all. She's worried about what he might do to himself this time...'

Another pause, then Theo's near me, pulling my loose hair back into a bundle. 'Is this what's been upsetting you? Vincent?' he asks. I nod my head ever so slightly. 'And here's me thinking you regretted marrying me.'

'I don't want this child making our brother ill again. Or worse... He's been calm for a little while now,' I say. I stare at the vomit-splattered parquet flooring.

'Vincent's tainted all of our good news with his drama,' Theo says. 'And you don't want him taking from our joy. We've no idea how he'll react.'

'I'm selfish,' I say. The words are a little too quiet, but Theo hears.

'No, darling Johanna, you're right.' he says. 'Let this be our secret for a few months longer.'

'But not as selfish as you,' I say.

A pause. Is he wondering if he heard me correctly?

'I won't let anything endanger you, our child or our brother,' he says.

'Yet you were intimate with me when you knew you carried disease,' I say.

'Jo, it wasn't like that,' he begins. I hear the uncertainty in his tone.

I vomit onto the flooring again.

July, 1889.

Theo thought I wanted to end our marriage. That thought matched with what he felt he deserved. He knew I'd seen the rash; he'd been avoiding me so that I'd not have that conversation with him.

We talked for hours, once I'd stopped vomiting. He explained how he caught the disease long before we were together. He didn't say where. How there'd been no others since me. Why we'd not been intimate since he was diagnosed.

He's adamant his doctor must call every day, until we're confident that I've escaped infection.

Later, he told me how the joy of the news that he was going to be a father mixed with the grief of not being able to share that happiness with his brother and the guilt of his illness. Theo said that his head was full of cork. I didn't understand what that meant or how I could help.

'When my head's full of cork and when I'm feeling empty, just be patient with me,' he said.

'What should I do?' I asked.

'Simply sit by me in silence,' he said.

'I fear you'll become bored of me if I do,' I said.

'Your silence will never be boredom,' was his reply.

Autumn 1889

PARIS

Portrait Of A Woman With Red Ribbon

I t was Rodin who advised Theo that I take regular, slow walks during pregnancy. Rose, the mother of his only son, had an uncomplicated pregnancy and birth and Rodin claimed that was all down to her daily exercise. When Theo passed on this advice, I couldn't help but ask about Camille.

'Her path is to the asylum,' he said and I sobbed, helpless, until Theo promised he'd try to find a way to assist her.

Still, Theo comes home from Boussod, Valadon & Cie every day for lunch, but instead of eating we walk around Montmartre. I'm not sure who is responsible for me living on a horse's diet of largely grass and water, but I'm a carrot away from pulling a *fiacre* behind us as we walk. A diet of fruits and vegetables is keeping me regular and healthy, but now that my morning sickness has faded I'm craving rich foods and extravagant ways. Poor Theo's been hearing my complaints since we stepped onto rue Lepic and now that we've turned onto Boulevard de Clichy, even I'm sick of the sound of my own whinnying. My husband's put himself on the same food restrictions, but he's not muttered a single word of complaint.

'Two days until your confinement begins,' Theo says, changing topic.

'I'll miss these lunchtime walks,' I say.

'And these views,' he says. I want to tut, but instead I stop walking as he spreads his arms out wide and in an overly dramatic way. 'Suck the smells and sounds into your memory, Johanna.'

I laugh. 'You make it seem like I'm being punished,' I say.

'It'll be months before you're *permitted* to venture out again.'

I take a moment to watch the hustle and bustle that decorates this busy street. Cracks of whips and screams of, '*Hé, la-bas!*' dance around. Men and women dodge carriages, horse-drawn omnibuses and manure, some stand chatting in doorways, others stumble from cabarets bent in laughter and joy. Their joy, Paris's bliss, is infectious.

'I'll miss all of this,' I say, smiling at passing strangers.

'You'll have time to paint,' he says.

The clip clop of horses fills the silence.

I shake my head. 'Being your wife and having this child has changed everything,' I say.

'For the better?' Theo asks and I shrug my shoulders. I think so, but time will tell. I'm only just used to being his wife, and the thought of having a tiny being dependent on me, for his or her every need, doesn't yet seem like a possibility. I do know that I've no desire to start a society with up-and-coming female artists and that I've no desire to learn painting techniques, yet unexpectedly I'm happier now than I've ever been. This new life with Theo fills me with contentment and joy.

'It'll all be good,' Theo says. His tone's calm; he's entirely convinced. I nod because I believe him wholeheartedly.

'I'm already torn though,' I say. 'On one hand there's physical and mental confinement, with a bout of loneliness until our baby arrives.' I smile, holding out my left palm. 'And on the other hand there's the chance to hide away and not have to wear this too-tight corset.' I hold out my right palm. I move each up and down, as if weighing the two sides of my current predicament. I raise the right palm up high. It wins. 'Being without a corset will be a luxury. I can't hide this bump much longer.'

'And just think of all those sour and salty foods you'll eat when the child is born,' Theo says, nudging my shoulder and linking his arm through mine. We resume walking.

'When I'm finally not being held responsible for every single thing I eat? The pressure on mammas,' I say. 'That I would carry complete responsibility for creating a sour disposition in our child.' I place a hand over my stomach.

That's when I hear her voice.

'*Bonjour*, Mr Van Gogh.' She's in front of us, just to the left. She stands in the open doorway to Café du Tambourin, a cigarette in one hand and a glass of beer in the other. How long has she been watching us? We stop walking as we reach her.

'Miss Voort,' Theo says, tipping his hat. Sara smiles, her full lips glisten, her almond-shaped brown eyes twinkle. Her beauty is arresting. Her eyes lock on my husband.

'*Bonjour*, Sara,' I say.

She flicks her eyes to me and the warmth that she exhibited for Theo disappears in that flick. 'Miss *Bonger*,' she says.

I smile. I don't correct her. Instead I watch as her eyes rest on my hand that's still over my stomach. I don't move it away. I smile. I refuse to feel pity for someone who persists in undermining my relationship. She gulps, rapid blinking, a deep breath too. A pause. *She knows.*

'You're looking very … *well*,' she says. Her unnaturally dark eyebrows crease together in mock concern.

'Never felt happier.' I hear my voice and the exaggerated enthusiasm that decorates 'happier'. 'Married life agrees with us.' I see her squirm; I feel no remorse.

Theo places his arm around my shoulder. 'Good day,' he says, nudging us past the open doorway to Le Tambourin. He's as keen to be away from her as I am.

'I'll see you soon, Theo,' she calls out, but neither of us turn to her.

'Have you an arrangement to meet with her?' I ask and Theo laughs.

'She sees me everywhere,' he says, and I don't push for further explanation.

October, 1889.

Confinement begins and conversation with Theo over lunch today included our collective wish for Vincent to somehow find a woman who loves him enough that she's willing to take him on. Theo even suggested that he'd be best matched with another who has experienced a depth of hopelessness equal to Vincent; that notion that the saddest often offer the greatest companionship.

I don't know if I agree though. I'd worry they'd fuel each other's sorrow.

Conversation shifted to how the stepping into insanity and the producing of 'true art' seem to dance alongside each other.

Theo said that Vincent considers himself like Monticelli – Theo owns several of his works for that very reason. That painter died for his art and Vincent admires that, perhaps even identifying with the artist's deranged behaviour. Again I'm reminded that genius brings with it a fragility and the smallest of snaps can cause its walls to fold inward.

I've considered my own breakability of late – Theo's, Vincent's, Camille's, Agostina's, Rodin's, Sara's too. Are we all not the same? Do we all not cling to our precious sanity as we navigate this life?

My need to understand the concept of 'true art' warrants further consideration. I haven't painted since our marriage and my sketches are infrequent too – and yet until now I'd not paused to ask myself why. Perhaps I've become all that Camille and Agostina hate, but only now am I pausing to question if this change in me deserves to be considered negatively. I've abandoned my pursuit of art, favouring instead this time to be both a wife and then a mother. I've travelled too quickly from unattached, to wife, to pregnant and I'm only just clinging to my sense of self.

Could it be that, for me, being a strong woman is about choice? Indeed, I'm selecting these roles (albeit at a heightened pace) and embracing them, rather than jumping to a demand that I must conform. Camille and Sara lack that luxury; absence of choice destroys their minds.

So why does that make me a disgrace to their womankind?

Chapter Two

Why do women seek to judge and condemn those who are merely trying their very best to stay intact?

Flowering Garden With Path

A week into my confinement and the thought of not having to go out for months now thrills me. The doctor has assured me that I'm well, that I've still not caught Theo's illness. My child is safe. I'm no longer bound in a corset. This is heaven.

We lie on the bedspread, me on my side. I rest my head on a pillow and Theo curls close to my swollen stomach. He's been telling our unborn child about the latest deal he has completed for Monet.

'You talk about Monet as if he's the personification of the movement,' I say. I laugh.

'And it's fair to say that your father conquered Durant-Ruel and Georges Petit today,' he says to my stomach.

'Hardly conquered.' I laugh and my stomach jiggles with me. 'You're making it sound like you're a great warrior.' I place a hand on my belly, rubbing circles over my nightgown. 'Your father's a pussy cat,' I say and the baby responds with a gentle kick.

'Put your hand here,' I say and Theo does. We wait. The baby kicks again. Theo's eyes widen and his smile beams.

'He's disagreeing with you,' Theo says. He laughs deeply.

I raise my eyebrows. 'He?'

'I know these things and Clara agrees.' He touches the side of his nose with his finger, as if the two of them share something undisclosed. 'Is another Van Gogh man a terrible thought?' Theo asks.

I shake my head. 'A wonderful thought,' I say. I smile. 'I like that you came home early tonight. An extra two hours with you.'

The corner of his eyes crinkle with his joy. 'I almost didn't return to work after our midday lunch. It's harder leaving you both these days.'

'Yet had you not, what news would you bring our unborn child?'

Our smiles match, as Theo claps his hands, causing another kick.

'Tinker,' I say, rubbing my rounded stomach again. 'Are you feeling well?' I ask. Theo's face is a little too pale and he looks to have lost even more weight.

'Overworked, that's all.'

He no longer hides his disease from me. He seeks much reassurance from the doctor about our unborn child. Sometimes my mind creates lists of who might have infected him. Occasionally I wonder if Sara carries the same ailment – if that's what bonds her with the Van Gogh brothers.

'Are you hungry?' I say, chasing that thought away. 'We could eat something a little bit more substantial than only greens tonight.'

Theo smiles and shifts his attention back to my bump. 'Today I sold my seventieth Monet painting. Others are talking about my technique, about how highlighting a single artist has ensured Monet's success. Of course, your uncle…'

He pauses and I watch as his eyes become locked on the red bedspread. We haven't talked about Vincent much these last few weeks. Instead, since Theo learned about the pregnancy, we've both been avoiding our brother's name, both feeling guilty that Vincent isn't sharing our joy. Instead his name's a patch of damp in the corner of our room – we both know he's there but we avoid that area.

'I can't bear that we haven't told him,' I whisper.

'Really?' he asks. I nod and Theo's entire face brightens. 'Let's not hide our wonderful news any longer. Dries knows and it's only right that the rest of our family are informed.'

'I'm sure Sara figured it out in an instant,' I say. 'I'll be surprised if it's not already the talk of the Netherlands.' Silence. Theo doesn't raise his eyes to mine. 'What?' I ask, before yawning.

'Nothing, she...' A pause. I nod for him to continue. 'Let's just share our joy with Vincent,' he says, catching the yawn himself. 'And he's been so very calm of late. His days have been spent painting.' Another nod from me. 'I didn't show you the finished *Starry Night* that he sent. A village in the moonlight. Swirls dominate the upper centre portion.'

I yawn again.

Theo moves off the bedspread, folding his side over my body and kissing my forehead. The bristles of his moustache tickle my skin. 'Rest now,' he says, moving towards the door.

'I'll write to Vincent first,' I say.

'I'll wake you in an hour so that you can prepare.'

'For?' I ask, shuffling into a comfortable position.

'Mr Pissarro and his son. They're dining with us this evening. We were talking about it only—'

'The baby,' I say, pointing to my enlarged stomach. Theo smiles.

Increasingly I'm forgetful, I'm tired, I'm tearful; I always blame our unborn child. I give my abdominal another little rub. *I'm sorry, my heart.*

My dear brother,

I've a splendid piece of news to share with you, one that we can keep secret no longer. Theo and I are to become parents within the next few months.

We are hoping for a boy, one that I'd love to name Vincent after you, his godfather, should you consent to the honour? We hope to hear no excuses about lack of funds, for your godfatherly duties will never be financial. I like to tease Theo that the baby could be a girl but, in my heart, I can only imagine him being a father to a son.

To tell the truth, when I first discovered I was with child I wasn't entirely pleased. It isn't that I dislike babies but still I struggled to accept the thought of becoming a mother. I'm only just learning all that it takes to be a good wife to your brother. Indeed, I worried so very much that we postponed the announcement out of fear that our baby might become ill or weak, or that he'd even not quite develop as he should. There is vast weight placed on a mother's shoulders, to produce a healthy child and to survive the ordeal. Some days I honestly can't bear to consider all that could go wrong. Yet we have a good doctor, who has assured me that wholesome food and much rest can work wonders.

Of late I've been thinking about the Roulin baby portrait that you painted. Is it wrong that we long for a healthy, strong baby, with plump cheeks and handsome eyes, just like the one you captured? He really seemed to be a bundle of health! We do hope that you'll agree to paint your nephew one day.

Theo will reply to your other letter, about the canvas and to send the required amount, tomorrow. He is still fatigued, and looking not at all well, but Mr Pissarro and his son are soon to arrive. I'd forgotten that they're dining with us this evening and now they'll have the misfortune of sampling my cooking.

I must bid you goodnight, but I welcome your words about our happy news.

Your sister, Jo

Dear Sister,

What a wonderful letter to receive this morning. My warm congratulations on your news. I received correspondence from the delightful Sara Voort, in which she claimed she had seen your swollen belly and wondered if I had more details to give her.

I wasn't convinced where she might have witnessed this, with all the materials Parisian women carry in their skirts, and I dismissed her gossip. You're newly married, there is an expectancy on news, is there not? We both know that Miss Voort enjoys stirring relations between us. I fear it seems she considers us forever united in both being rejected by Mr and Mrs Van Gogh. I didn't entertain her with a reply, confident that if you were about to have a child, I'd be the first person you'd tell.

So, this news is welcomed, and I look forward to meeting my nephew in the coming months. God allowing, I would accept the honour of godfather duties, but only if both of you are entirely convinced. If there is another more fitting for the role, I won't be offended.

The same can be said about naming the child after me. Is it not better to name the child after his father or after our father? That feels reasonable and I'm positive that Theo will have an opinion on the matter. Discuss further and do let me know your response. That said, I deliver my kind regards to you both and do know that you are all in my thoughts.

To ease your anxiety regarding Theo's wellbeing, let me reassure you that I've seen how changeable my brother's health can be. He sometimes appears both weak and uneven, but always recovers. I am convinced that he possesses a power to restore himself; just as I know, from my own vast experience, that Theo's love and care will ensure that a safe delivery of the child occurs. Good health is so vital – to be of sound mind and body for your unborn – and I'm sure that you are receiving the best attention, dear sister. Nature will take its course, and I'm already convinced that your patience will lead to you welcoming a bouncing baby boy.

What joy to have a child of your own! Oh, to experience fatherhood. I envy you both.

Chapter Two

I met with my doctor earlier today. Forgive my sharing of your news with him, but I wished to speak about that envy. He talked about my recovery, about the smallest of steps that I continue to take daily. He has said that only when I've gone a year without attack can I consider myself cured. Still, he fears the next assault could occur any day, and that although I continue to improve I still have a distance to travel. The doctor claimed the minutest of events or news could cause another breakdown, but your update has not harmed me in any way.

I still await news of the financial matters, but will post another canvas to Theo tomorrow. His last package of colours and ten metres of canvas have already been used.

Although I'm now sober, I find that I still spend a vast amount more than we first considered. How is this possible? Perhaps I relied on others buying my beer! The asylum proves to be even more expensive than my previous lodgings. I long to produce more, but the costs of materials soar and I'm attempting to live within my means. My sobriety offers my mind space and clarity that I welcome; some would consider allowing my thoughts to roam a negative, but I embrace the exploration. I feel good. Indeed, dear sister, you'll hardly recognise me when you see me next.

When will you both visit?

Tell Theo I'll write soon, when I receive his reply regarding financial matters. I couldn't wait to send this response, wanting to write my heartfelt congratulations immediately.

Tout à toi, Vincent

Winter 1890

PARIS

January, 1890.

*Each. And. Every. Morning. For the past month, Theo has greeted me
with a, 'I wonder if he'll arrive today?'*

At first it amused me. Now my patience grows thinner each day.

*I'm going to scream in my husband's face if he says those words again
tomorrow.*

*Aside from his impatience, his absolute conviction that I'm carrying a
boy fills me with angst. What if a 'she' arrives? Will he be disappointed?
Will he wish to push the poor thing back within me?*

*But it's a different fear that consumes me. Persistent, all-consuming
dread: what if the doctor was wrong and my child has caught his father's
disease?*

*Please let me deliver a healthy baby boy for Theo. Let that be the first
sign that everything will be fine and that I'll not be a terrible mamma.*

Portrait Of Marcelle Roulin

I'm convinced that my husband's now told everyone in Paris about the pregnancy, but only Andries and Clara ever visit. This close to delivery society expects me to hide away from the public eye. In the past, I'd have sought to rebel against any ridiculous rule that demanded I should be confined, but the liberation from all corsets continues to conquer everything else. My huge bump is free beneath my loose bedgown. Sometimes I watch my child squirm for space within me. Other times I'm convinced my insides will be bruised from the baby's daily attempts to kick his way out.

Theo rushes in to the room, his lounge coat and bowler hat not yet removed, placing a huge canvas at the foot of my bed. A layer of fine snow melts into the brim of his hat. A dusting of white decorates his shoulders. He glances at my stomach.

Yes, I'm still pregnant. Yes, the baby still isn't here. Go on, ask. I dare you.

He reads my expression and smiles knowingly. 'Time for lunch?' Theo says. 'What grass delight do we have today?'

'I've missed you,' I say.

'I'll consider our marriage a successful one if, after fifteen years, you feel the same when we've not seen each other for a few hours.' He places his hat and a wrapped canvas on the bed. 'Did Bonger not visit today?'

'Briefly. He had news,' I say and Theo waits for me to continue. 'He's fallen in love.'

'What? He said that?'

I can't help but laugh. 'I'm not sure he's even realised himself yet, but when he spoke of Annie van der Linden his entire face transformed into joyfulness. We've known her since childhood, but he met up with her again two weeks ago.'

'And he came to tell you?' Theo asks and I nod.

'Three unaccompanied outings with her and he's entirely smitten. He said he liked how she spoke "not a word too many and not a word too few". Apparently she's aloof, sophisticated – everything Mamma dislikes.'

'I assume he doesn't want your mother to know yet,' Theo asks and I smile an affirmative: *obviously*. 'Why was his visit brief?' Theo asks.

'He was rushing to visit the Exposition Universelle. The fact that Annie had never been made my brother jump on the spot with excitement,' I say.

'Was he armed with his camera box?'

'And the enthusiasm of twenty men,' I say. Theo laughs. 'How's the snow?' I ask. My husband rubs his hands together, desperate to warm himself before moving to place them on my engorged stomach.

'Hey, little one,' he says. He's smiling. The same daily routine: bump first, then time for me. Theo defines joy and excitement; it shines from his skin despite a continued exhaustion that he can't seem to shake. Each day that passes brings his baby closer to him. 'Filthy weather. It's practically rain and won't quite settle on the cobbles. I've slipped my way home. I dread to think how awful it'll be for Bonger down Champs de Mars.' He stands up straight, demonstrating how he glided, flapping his arms around and then chuckling from his belly. I can't help but laugh with him.

Last week the doctor explained that I needed to stay in bed. My unborn child requires I rest, but being alone with my worries about the delivery is torture. I've still no interest in painting, I've no desire to sketch either, and even the thought of reading a novel makes me yawn. I'm restless; I'm waiting for my child to arrive. Clara spends as much time as she possibly can with me, but she still has her own schedule of treatment and rest in the morning to follow. Theo, under Mamma's instruction, as she was 'far too busy' to help, has hired Madame Joseph for additional hours. Some days she reminds me a little too much of Mamma and I don't care for her overbearing ways. She lacks emotion, refuses to hide her astonishment at my absence of domestic capability, and speaks with a tone that often leaves me feeling like I've already failed as a mother.

'How's your new home?' Theo says. He nods to the delivery bed that Madame Joseph insisted we needed. As a result, I now exist in the *cabinet de debarras*. The room's still full of wardrobes but the new bed's presence has made me a guest in my own home.

'Lightweight, portable, a bit like sleeping on a cliff edge,' I say.

'That wonderful?' he asks. I throw one of my pillows towards him, but it falls short and lands on my legs.

'What did you bring me?' I ask, nodding towards the canvas. I'm expecting a new Monet but, when he unwraps and holds up the painting, its artist is easy to identify.

'He sent it for you,' Theo says. He moves to the head of the bed and hands me a note. He kisses my cheek; the bristles of his moustache prickle.

> *Dear Sister,*
>
> *I'd like to think that the next Van Gogh baby will be as healthy as this child. I look forward to painting him one day soon. I often think about you, Johanna, and hope that both you and your unborn son remain strong.*
>
> *I can but pray that we will visit each other again.*
>
> *Tout à toi, Vincent*

'He sounds lonely,' I say, looking at Theo for reassurance. 'And there's a fear whenever we receive a letter. Do you think we'll ever stop being scared of what he might do…' I pull in a large breath. My mouth's dry. I lick my lips before reaching to the nightstand for a glass of water.

'Let me help you,' Theo says. He rushes to the glass. He places the painting near to me. I look at it. It's the Roulin baby again.

'I think he's preparing for his nephew's portrait.' Theo lifts the glass to my lips and I take a sip. 'This is the fifth painting of that child and I can't recall another infant that he's studied as closely.'

I take another sip.

'Enough?' he asks and I nod.

'It's rather ugly,' I say. Theo mumbles, I'm not sure what he says; instead my eyes remain locked on the painting. Something unnerves me yet still I don't look away. 'The contrasting colour in the background intensifies the baby's impact.'

'I'll make an art dealer out of you yet,' Theo says and I can't help but smile.

I shuffle onto my side, facing my husband, and the bed creaks under my giant weight. 'I still don't understand why we had to buy this monstrosity.'

'Madame Joseph claims it would be a sin to give birth on the bed where he was conceived,' Theo says. He winks.

'Sounds like something Mamma would preach,' I say. I look to the open doorway, fearing the housemaid is listening. 'Can you stay here this afternoon?'

'I have to return. I'm expecting a delivery of frames.' He pauses, he smiles; whatever he considers brings him joy.

'What?' I ask.

'For Vincent's *Sunflowers*. The fourth version. There's a little wooden edge that I'll leave, but I think a white frame around that will be splendid. Do you remember Père Tanguy?' he asks and I nod.

'You said he discovers today's unknowns.'

'Yes, and he wants to exhibit Vincent in 14 rue Clauzel, but lacks a central piece to show my brother's talent.'

I clap my hands together. Theo's excitement is contagious. 'And you think *Sunflowers* to be the missing link?'

Theo nods. 'Sunflowers are my brother's symbol and this one's my favourite of all his paintings. There's a swell of interest.' Theo's passion spreads over me like a rash. I can't help but scratch my stomach over the bedspread. He's invested in Vincent for so many years already, funded every aspect, with his belief never faltering. My husband's a loyal man, but he would have backed Vincent even if they weren't related. Our brother has a remarkable talent.

'There's talk of him being invited to exhibit in Brussels next year. I think success will save Vincent.' He speaks quickly, each word blending into the next, barely stopping to breathe. 'If he avoids suffering further mental collapse, he might even move closer to us.'

As he mutters the last three words I see his body droop. I watch the excitement tumble down his sloped shoulders. Theo sits on the bed.

'You're worried about him being here and everything being too different for him,' I say.

He pulls me to him and holds me tight. His movements are quick. I place my ear to his chest; his heart thumps. Those beats offer me comfort and I'm safe in this moment.

'Never die,' I say. Tears spill from my eyes.

Theo releases the smallest giggle and he jiggles under me. 'I've no intention of ever leaving you.'

'I'd miss the sound of your heart too much,' I say. '

'What's gotten into you, Jo?' Theo asks.

'I need the doctor to be right about the baby not catching…'

He tries to pull away, but I cling closer, tighter.

'He's checked a million times. You're both healthy.'

'And being back in Vincent's world scares me,' I say. 'He's so far from being cured, not even close to a year without an attack… Theo, he chopped off his ear.'

'Part of it.' A pause. I hear his sigh; it escapes from deep within him. He agrees. I'm simply saying aloud what my husband's already considered.

'I want us to be able to live, a happy little family… I know that makes me a selfish sister, but we're not doctors. We're not what Vincent needs,' I say.

'I know,' he says. His voice a whisper. 'I think I put too much of myself onto my brother. I want him to have opportunities, to be the best version of himself, to be part of our family. He was my priority for too many years.'

'Is it time to put our little family first?' I say. Theo doesn't reply. He might nod, he might shake his head. He strokes my hair. Tiny movements at first, then his fingers create swirls on my scalp.

I place a hand on my magnificent stomach and close my eyes.

January, 1890.

Madame Joseph sleeps next to my bed.
  Doctor's orders.
  They feel the baby must arrive at any moment.
  There's urgency.
  Must arrive.
  And now,
  because of those words,
  because of their serious voices.
  I can't.
  I won't.
  I'm gripped with fear.
  Crossing my legs.
  Trying to ignore the waves of pain in my stomach.
  What if the child dies on his journey from me?
  The pain comes.

Again.

Mother By A Cradle

I never imagined myself as someone who could fall in love at first sight. I used to scoff at the silliness of new mothers, who cooed and looked at their ugly babies as if they were works of art.

And then my son was born.

Lying on my back, knees up, Clara stood at the base of the bed, chloroform and forceps ready. Madame Joseph crouched beside her. Neither expected the urgency. He wanted to escape, to live, to meet his parents. My boy was done waiting for me to be ready; he rushed to take his first breath.

I saw their fear. It decorated their faces as my boy catapulted onto the delivery bed with the third push. My entire body repelled him, the doctor arriving far too late. I lost all control. The violence of his escape left me torn and in shock.

And now, in the quiet, Theo sits straight-backed and awkward in a chair by my bed. He's stiff, everything unfamiliar: as if he's somehow forgotten how to be himself. Our boy is swaddled in my husband's arms; I can't stop looking at them both. Only hours old, I recognise so little about him. Our son is tiny. A swaddled bundle of possibility. Theo's palms look too large, his fingers too long. Our boy is miraculous. Wisps of blond hair. His fingers curled into a tiny fist. His nose squashed. There's a birthmark; a tiny red splodge at the crease of his right wrist. He's perfect. How can something so tiny alter every aspect of a life?

My husband bends closer to our baby and I watch as his eyes absorb his son. This is happiness.

'What are you thinking?' I ask, when minutes have passed in silence.

'I'm committing the boy to memory,' he says. 'Making sure I can describe him to every person who asks, and especially those who don't.'

'I don't think I've ever seen a more beautiful child,' I say.

'Far more handsome than that Roulin infant,' he says.

I look at Theo. His eyes are full. I watch as a single tear trickles from the corner.

'My boy,' he says. It's a whisper that I hear, as his tear lands on the baby's face. I watch as our tiny being squirms, his mouth wriggling. Theo laughs and the noise startles our son. His fingers unclench, stretching straight, his blue eyes open wide.

'I've got high hopes for you,' Theo says, his tone gentle. He strokes a finger over the baby's face. 'I'm going to teach you everything I know.' The child relaxes: his fingers curl back into a fist, his eyes shut. 'But first, his name. I know we considered...' He looks at me. He's expecting discussion. His eyes and lips smile in tandem. He nods for me to speak.

'We could still call him Theodorus, after your father and a clear celebration of you too,' I say, smiling at my son's tiny fist. 'I'd kill for you, my boy,' I say.

'And you worried you'd never feel maternal,' Theo says. 'But not Theodorus.'

My head bobs in agreement; I understand.

'I want to name him Vincent Willem,' Theo says. 'We'll be blessed with other children. Many, many more children. One of them will carry my name.'

I laugh, wagging a finger at him. 'Too soon,' I say. 'Far too soon, husband.'

'I'm already hoping for six or seven,' he says, but then his face switches. A serious thought pops into his head. 'Think of the honour we're gifting Vincent. His name will live on.'

'Do you think it'll offend Dries?' I ask.

He shrugs. 'He'll no doubt marry Annie, they'll have their own children.'

'Vincent could still marry, have a baby of his own,' I say, but my tone lacks conviction. I look to Theo; we both know that's unlikely. Perhaps this is the first time we're accepting that hope of Vincent being cured has faded with the news of each attack.

'Are we in agreement?' Theo says.

～

BORN.

JANUARY 31, 1890,

TO MR AND MRS

THEO VAN GOGH,

A BOY.

VINCENT WILLEM.

～

February, 1890.

Dries' face when seeing his nephew for the first time! An uncle's adoration. Utter delight and actual tears. My heart sang; his love for baby Vincent was instant.

Then, he told me to close my eyes. I did. I heard his footsteps leaving the room, heard him return. Nervous laughter and then, 'Open your eyes.'

And there, in front of me, my brother held Berthe Morisot's The Cradle.

'For me?' I asked and Dries nodded.

He told me how he'd bought it in the weeks after it captured me in Durand-Ruel Gallery, just days after I first arrived in Paris. I sobbed so loudly that Madame Joseph came rushing into the room. My utter delight; my brother's kind and glorious heart.

Dries' words: 'I believed this day would come.'

Self-Portrait As A Painter

Theo's eyes are downcast as he places the envelope next to me on the bed, before glancing at our son in the cradle. Baby Vincent's only nine days old, but already his father appears devoid of joy.

'Dr Peyron writes,' Theo says.

'About our brother?' I say and Theo nods sluggishly. Dread punches into my stomach. 'Is he alive?' I ask and Theo's eyes jump to meet mine. His head bobs again.

I open the letter and read as quickly as I can. Another attack of madness. It occurred just after the birth announcement, explaining why we hadn't received a reply or congratulations.

'Dr Peyron requests that we keep our happy news to a minimum,' Theo says.

'I know he won't mean to steal our joy,' I say and Theo sighs.

'I don't know if he means to or if that's merely a consequence. We shine a light on all that he lacks and wants.'

I turn to look at the baby's cradle: purity, joy, contentment.

'Peyron says he's unable to paint and incapable of conversation…' Theo says. 'What's to become of my brother?'

Theo's tone makes me ache. His words rattle around the box room. This kind man feels everything with such depth. I watch as he bends over baby Vincent's cradle, running a forefinger over his son's cheek. Tears track from Theo's eyes into his red whiskers.

'Let's do as the doctor suggests.'

'I've got so much and Vincent so little,' he says. His lips tremble out the words. 'Is the world cruel?'

'I wish I could wipe away your guilt for being successful and happy,' I say. I swing my legs from the bed and stand to join Theo. He places an arm around me and I lean my head onto his shoulder. We stand in silence. We're both spellbound, watching our sleeping son. Baby Vincent releases tiny hiccups, his entire body jumps with each. I lean forward and place my hand on his swaddled chest. *I'm here, you're not alone, I'll never leave you.*

'He had every opportunity given to him. More than you,' I say. The sound of my voice causes baby Vincent to stir. I lift the swaddled bundle. Holding him up to my neck. I feel his little mouth against my cheek, searching for food, ready to scream in protest.

'Dr Peyron requests more funds,' he says.

'You spend more on Vincent's upkeep than on the three of us.'

'He has no one else,' Theo says. His voice is almost a whisper. The truth in his words adds to their weight.

I rock from side to side in an attempt to soothe the baby. 'Perhaps he could try a different profession? Perhaps we could persuade him that the life of a penniless painter is no longer suited to his temperament.'

Theo shakes his head. Each movement he makes feels listless; my husband's exhausted. 'His success is just around his corner,' he says. 'And on that topic…'

I nod for him to continue.

'Degas wishes to offer you instruction. A gift for Vincent's birth. Perhaps together you could paint—'

Baby Vincent hiccups. The tiny sound grounds me: a reminder of all that matters.

'Send my apologies to Degas,' I say, 'but I've still no interest in being an artist. All that I require is in this room.'

February, 1890.

Theo talked about his brother's torment earlier and the discussion turned to how Vincent's greatest art was born from his suffering. He was quick to defend himself when I accused him of perpetuating that every artist must be a tortured soul to achieve success. Instead he explained that when an artist rises with honesty and no fear of their truth, then they have something significant to say.

Theo will forever argue that the truest expression comes directly from the heart. That the artist only ever shows us what the world reveals to him. My husband talks openly about painters and the impact of their pain. But still, is the unspoken that a person can only ever be remarkable when they've truly suffered? And is Theo saying that only after that anguish, that only then will their actions be seen, their opinions considered valid and their voice finally heard?

So ... I can have a content life or a remarkable life?

Never both.

The Man Is At Sea

'Milk leaks from me again,' I say. 'Is he not eating enough?'
'The baby takes what the baby wants, Miss Jo,' Clara says. 'We can change that nightgown of yours again.'

Baby Vincent is three weeks old. He sleeps in his cradle, but my breasts are solid and full. My ability to provide milk is firmly established; it leaks from my nipples and I try to push them inwards to stop the tingle.

'My body seems to think it's feeding time,' I say.

Clara glances at the clock on the mantle. 'Another thirty minutes. Theo will string us alive if we don't keep to that feedin' schedule of his.'

I sit on the nursing chair in the *cabinet de debarras*, fingers still on my nipples. I watch out the window, looking down to the fence that separates cité Pigalle from the street. Boys chase each other up and down the cobbles, two girls sit together on a neighbouring stoop plaiting each other's hair. Their clothes are ragged, ill-fitting and inadequate for a Parisian winter: no jacket or cape in sight. There's another girl, not much older than the playing children. She might be their sister. She's the one I watch, as she walks up and down. She tries too hard to look older, bolder and braver. Her hair's loose, she hobbles in too big shoes, she's uncomfortable in her own skin; watching her makes me anxious. She's scared but she tries to be fearless and confident in front of her brother and sisters. She steps into a doorway, I watch as a man follows her.

I stand, moving to open the window. I want to see more, I want to shout down to the children. The nursery door creaks open slowly.

'Apologies, Mistress,' Madame Joseph says. 'A Miss Voort is quite insistent that she sees you. She said that it would be "in your best interests not to ignore her".'

I look at Clara, who raises her eyebrows and then nods her head. She's right; I must allow the woman into this box room.

'For one who fancies herself a lady...' Clara says. 'The babe's only three weeks born. She knows better than to visit when you're lyin' in chambers.'

But then she's here, in the nursery, all swishes and bounds of material in her bustle. Sara's eyes scan the room, before spotting the cradle and scurrying to it. She unties her mantelet and removes her gloves as she walks. Her ornate bustle bops with each step. She scrunches her nose, sniffing whatever scent lingers in the room. By her crunched up face, I'm reasoning that it's an unpleasant aroma: probably a mix of my perspiration and my son's excrement.

Sara is poised though, prepared and flawless. I'm none of those things. I can't remember the last time I brushed my hair. I'm haggard, a sore new mamma in a milk-stained bedgown. I smell of baby sick and dampness. If this is a competition, she's winning already. I wait for her to reveal why she's in our apartment, but Sara bends over the cradle. Baby Vincent's eyes are open, his tiny fists are clenched to his cheek.

'What a chubby little boy,' she says. 'And how nice of you to name him after Vincent and not his father.' She turns to me and scans my face. She's searching for something. She smiles, showing the gap between her front teeth, then turns back to the cradle.

'What fat cheeks he has and such blue eyes.' Another pause. She turns to glare at me again. For someone with such beauty, today she both looks and sounds ugly. 'Have you heard from Vincent?'

I can't control my body's reaction. Her tone causes heat to travel up my neck and to my cheeks. This woman hates me. She hates my baby. She hates that I have her life. There's an urgency to her speech: it verges on hysteria.

'Yes, he writes ... when he can,' I say. My words are controlled and chosen carefully.

'He told me that you only ever write to boast,' Sara says. She flicks her hair; she's acting.

'I'm sure my husband would be saddened to hear that,' I say. I note that she grimaces when I say 'my husband'. *A small victory.*

'Bet he's a troublemaker, like his pa,' she says.

'Who?'

'Vincent,' she replies, then nods to the cradle. Her words carry implications. She has something that she wishes to say, and my patience is too thin to play her games. Clara lifts a swaddled baby Vincent. I remain unmoved, sitting in my nursing chair by the fire. She places the boy in my lap.

'I'm sure there's a reason for your visit,' I say.

Another pause. Sara looks me up and down. Her eyes find the wet milk stains at my breasts and stay there a little too long.

'Am I the only person to note that your baby is a tiny replica of Uncle Vincent?'

'My son's a Van Gogh, Miss Voort, and for that reason I'd expect him to resemble his kin,' I say. I pull my swaddled son to my chest. My nipples prickle. Milk squirts from the right one.

Sara places her hands on hips, and laughs aloud; she sounds unhinged. 'The truth will out. One way or another,' she says. 'We both know how the Van Gogh brothers like to share.' Then she turns and saunters from the room, swinging her hips as if in time to music. She slams the door behind her and the noise startles my son. He squawks his protest at being woken.

'That one's evil to the core,' Clara says.

'Did she really just suggest the baby's father was Vincent?' I ask.

'That woman's got the Devil in her. She's hell-bent on causin' mischief.'

My body starts to shake. 'But I haven't…' I say.

'I know,' Clara says.

'But what if she tells Theo…'

Starry Night Over The Rhone

Since his son's birth, Theo's arrived home from work promptly on the final chime of four o'clock each day. Today I jump as I hear the front door close.

'I had a most *interesting* visit at work,' Theo says as he walks into the box room. He places his bowler hat on the delivery bed and takes baby Vincent from my arms. 'Hello, boy,' he says. We both look weary these days. He lifts our swaddled son to kiss his forehead.

As I wait for him to tell me, anxiety bubbles.

'Miss Voort.'

'Won't she leave us alone?' I say. My words rush out, they're almost a shout. 'The crazy woman came here today. Who calls on a new mother, uninvited, during the lying-in period?'

'She came to me with a theory.' I nod for him to continue. 'That you chose to name our child Vincent after his father.' There's a pause. His eyes examine my face and I attempt to prevent any flash of emotion. Then he laughs, a laugh from his belly. 'I've told her to seek medical help. She's crazier than my brother.'

'I'm not sure why you ever loved her.'

Theo's expression snaps to serious. 'I've only ever loved you,' he says. 'She spoke about Vincent visiting you the day before our wedding. Of an encounter.'

'She lies,' I say. 'I was with family in Amsterdam all day.' My volume's too loud. I jump from the bed, startling the poor baby. He squawks in protest, but I don't rush to him. He'll feed on my anxiety, become as unsettled as me.

'Johanna,' Theo whispers. He lifts our swaddled bundle to his shoulder and rocks him slightly. I watch my husband. His eyes are widened. He absorbs my reaction, not sure what to think. 'Why are you pacing the room?'

I hadn't realised I was. 'She angers me. She brings you lies that I then have to disprove,' I say. The words wobble like jelly.

'But I don't believe a word she speaks,' Theo says, his tone soothing, but there's something else. I'm covered in fear, hyperalert, ready to pounce. A pause.

'Tell me,' I say.

'I'm worried about her hysteria.'

'What?' I ask. 'What are you not telling me?'

'She's obsessed. Said she'd still be my wife,' he says. 'Declared she'd be happy to take over as baby Vincent's mother.' His eyes are downcast, unable to meet with mine.

'Why would she say that? That's hardly something she'd bring up out of the blue.' I'm hit with fear. 'What aren't you telling me?'

'Johanna, please,' he says. The words are barely audible. He still rocks our unsettled child. 'I accept that I must have encouraged her without realising.'

'She has no respect for your wife,' I say.

Silence. 'And for that I'm truly sorry.'

'I thought she'd gone away. That she'd left us alone. Have you been meeting her behind my back?'

'She turns up at work, feigns interest in art.' A pause.

'How often?' I'm suddenly cold; my jaw chatters.

Another pause.

'How often?' I repeat, expanding the syllables of each word.

'Every day, for months.'

'Why didn't you…' I can't finish my sentence. My entire body shakes.

'I was controlling the situation,' he says.

'Badly.' It's a shout, and baby Vincent protests.

'I never meant to bring her madness into our home. Please climb back into bed.' He nods to the delivery bed. 'You're too pale.'

My knees tremble. Perspiration collects under my full breasts; my nipples ache and my head pounds.

'And what if she spreads those rumours within society,' I say. I sit on the edge of the bed and swing my legs up to lie down. 'My reputation—'

'When did you begin to care about such matters?'

'I care about you and your standing. I care about injustice. We need to protect our son,' I say. I'm unable to stop tears. 'She seeks to destroy us.' A squeaky sob escapes.

'And she'll never succeed,' Theo says. He puts baby Vincent next to me on the bed and perches close to place his arm around me. 'There's nothing on this earth that could break our little family.'

'Why do you entertain the woman?'

'Politeness, guilt over how I once treated her, pity even, but that ended today,' he says. 'I've made it quite clear that I'm going to talk to her father.'

'But—'

'No but. It ends today,' he says. I lean into his shoulder and minutes pass in silence. 'The woman chooses insanity.'

'I wish I felt better in myself,' I say. 'This continuous exhaustion and earlier I started bleeding again.'

'I'll ask the doctor to visit,' he says and I stroke his arm as a reply.

'Do you think I feign interest in art too?' I ask. 'That I'm a fake like Sara.'

'Your priorities have shifted,' he says. 'But I've no doubt art will wheedle its way back into your days soon.' Another pause and I prod him with my elbow.

'In better and astonishing news, Vincent wrote to say that he'd completed a painting for his nephew. It seems that the boy aids his uncle's recovery,' Theo says, and I feel his body relax. 'He's called it *Almond Blossom* and will send it as soon as the paint has dried. His first piece since his latest breakdown, his first outing with nature again, and every stroke had his nephew in mind.'

I smile. Family is everything. 'Did he offer a hint of what we're to expect?'

'His letter was entirely enthusiastic, joyful even. He spoke of using broken strokes of impressionism and dabs of divisionism. He said it sparkled and that it was a celebration of new life.'

'How kind,' I say.

'Perhaps this time…' I hear his smile.

'Perhaps this will be the start of his recovery,' I say.

'A painting to hang in our boy's bedroom, so that his uncle is never far from his thoughts,' Theo says.

Spring 1890

PARIS

March, 1890.

The heavy bleeding continues. Week two of bedrest and I'm increasingly feeling inadequate as a mother. Clara and Madame Joseph are doing everything for the boy and bringing him to me only when he requires feeding. Theo continues to bring home new art each day, possibly to stimulate my creativity. I referred to today's painting as ugly and said I'd hate to have it hanging in our home. Perhaps I used the word out of personal frustration, but what followed was a debate that lasted far more than an hour and stimulated my mind to consider art and to understand myself as I never had before.

Theo said I do it often. That I said the same word when describing Eiffel's tower. That I'd once referred to Vincent's Roulin baby as ugly too.

'Did I?' I asked. I thought about that painting often – possibly even considering it unforgettable. I was horrified that I'd referred to a child in that way.

Theo asked me to reflect on the painting in front of us again – it was by one of the moderns.

He asked, 'But why is it ugly?'

I commented that the artist had deliberately chosen his model and painted her into a setting and a costume that heightened the ugliness.

Theo replied, 'Or has the artist simply presented what was there, in front of his eyes, with honesty? That what you consider ugly, a painter would claim to be the truth.'

That threw me and I stayed silent for a good minute or two before asking him to explain a little more.

Theo then told me how his work and his experience in the art world allowed his appreciation of the 'ugly' painting, because it forced him to think about and to face his own discomfort. He said that although I rejected the ugly piece, that still my eyes were drawn there; that still I was lost in its sadness and unpleasantness, because it held a promise of something I feared.

'And that,' Theo declared with such enthusiasm, 'is true art.'

Finally – the explanation I've been seeking!

He described that what I considered distasteful or vulgar had in fact spoken to my soul, and that I couldn't allow myself to verbalise a connection with that painting for fear of what that would reveal about myself.

'When we look upon art our brains search for familiarity, for clarity too,' he said. 'Connection exposes truth, and who would be brave enough to voice that they have such ugliness within themselves?'

Almond Blossom

Theo walks into the box room, a dressing gown wrapped around him, and I watch as his entire face alters when he sees me. The delivery bed was taken away a month ago; baby Vincent's cradle rests in here. This room was never given a chance to be a guest room, and now it's a nursery.

'I woke and you weren't there,' he says. I know he'll have panicked. A month of bedrest and the heavy bleeding has eased. Now I'm being pushed to stop breastfeeding. I know I'm overtired, that giving the boy cow's milk will allow for additional rest, but it's the only time I truly feel like his mamma.

'I thought you'd gone.'

'Gone where?' I ask. 'I've not stepped outside for weeks now.'

'Have you slept?' Theo asks and I nod.

I can't tell him that I woke from a nightmare, convinced that Sara was hatching plans to steal my child and husband from me. I still exist in that space between slumber and reality, not quite forgiving Theo for the behaviour I imagined.

I stand in front of the windows. Theo places an arm around my shoulder. I've opened the curtains. The sun is awake, but the view's cloaked in a thin mist. The edges of buildings are blurred; I can't quite make out where one structure ends and another begins.

'Paris always puts on a good face, don't you think?' I say, but

Theo remains silent. 'Grandiose monuments, vast open spaces, enough apartment blocks for the rich to live wealthy, luxurious lives, when all the time...'

'What, Johanna?'

'When you open your eyes you see the truth, don't you?' I ask. Theo takes a moment, but then he nods. 'Like ugliness and art. The moneyed Parisians can lock themselves within their delectable apartments, they can hide behind their gated entrances and their thick drapes, they can escape to the coast during the summer. But the secrets and lies remain, don't they? The truth finds its way to the surface.'

'What are you trying to say?'

I shrug. I really don't know.

'There are rich, homeless, lost, loved and lonely people in every city,' he says.

'And in every home,' I whisper, but my husband doesn't probe my words. I want to ask him about Sara, about what happened when he spoke to her father. I even want to know if he caught the disease from her. Life has been too insular recently; the walls shrink inwards.

'Will you step outside with me tomorrow?' he asks. 'The doctor's said you're well enough now.'

I lean into him. 'It's been too hot,' I say. 'For me anyway, and others take our baby for walks.' The weather has given a taste of the summer before us.

I look to the wall. His uncle's painting hangs above baby Vincent's cradle, alongside a Rembrandt engraving in a gold frame. In daylight, Vincent's tree blossom holds the boy's gaze. The blue sky painted around the branches so very precisely, several variations in that blue to make the sky appear real. I sometimes wonder if there's a message within it, one that only kin can see. Now the baby sleeps. He sucks on his own thumb.

'And I thought I heard baby Vincent,' I say. Theo looks down at his sleeping son.

'He's thriving,' he says. 'His personality emerging a little more each day.'

'The boy's a thinker,' I say. 'I imagine he'll be the greatest philosopher.' I wipe the sleeve of my nightgown across my forehead.

'You prefer winter,' Theo says and I nod.

'The approaching vastness of summer unsettles me. I might still be trapped in here.' Baby Vincent releases a tiny sound, as if his dream has shocked him. We stand in silence, watching as our boy settles back into sleep.

'I wonder what he dreams of,' I say.

'Your breasts, most likely,' Theo says. He spins me on the spot and pulls me into an embrace. His lips brush across mine, then over my cheek. 'I know they're a frequent feature in my slumber,' he whispers. His warm breath tickles my earlobe.

We've had no sexual contact for months. Doctor's orders – my heavy bleeding and while Theo concludes his treatment. We've been married for not quite one year and still I worry that his interest in me has dwindled, that his curiosities will soon lie elsewhere. Sara climbs in my head too often still. I want him though; I long for him.

His lips meet mine, soft, wet but not quite committed. 'What is it?' I ask. I pull from our embrace and try to read Theo's expression.

'My brother,' he mutters. 'A letter.' His eyes cast down to the tiled floor.

'What has he said?' I ask. I hold my breath and tense every muscle in my body.

'He's...' Still no eye contact.

Panic swirls within my belly. *Dead?* 'Tell me,' I say. My words escape with unexpected volume. Theo flicks his eyes to meet mine. They're red and swollen. They're full of sadness; I'd been too immersed in myself to notice earlier.

'He attempted to poison himself by consuming paint,' he says, again casting his eyes from me. I step away. I pace the nursery.

'Now paint is a weapon,' I say; it's a whisper. I can't make sense of what I'm being told. 'Did he say why?' I ask and Theo shakes his head.

'He's ill, Johanna,' Theo says. His entire body droops. He's defeated, deflated, even possibly both.

'What should we do to help him?' I ask.

'We can invite him to live here,' Theo says. Heat rushes through me, a shake begins in my jaw.

'I ... we...'

'Say it,' Theo urges.

'We can't have him near our son.' My words squeak together. 'You understand that, don't you?' Theo doesn't respond. 'We don't know what he'll do next.' I cross my arms across my torso. My nose twitches, my eyes itch.

'He considers himself cured. He was talking about leaving Saint-Rémy.'

'But how? We were told he had to be one year incident-free,' I say. 'And now he's eating paint, that's hardly the behaviour of someone—'

'He said that when consuming the paint all he could think about was meeting his nephew and now that's his sole purpose. Even Dr Peyron seems convinced.'

'Is Dr Peyron trying to offload an ill man?' Shaking travels from my thighs to my jar; I rattle.

'It's for the best.'

'The best? For whom?' I ask.

I flick my tears away with my fingers, frustration and anger in each drop. Then, hands on my hips, I glare at my husband, daring him to continue this arrangement. I'm uncompromising, I'm tired, lost, scared; I want Theo to match my overwhelming need to protect our son. That he doesn't bubbles and boils inside my stomach.

'As long as my brother remains my blood, I'll do everything in my power to help him.'

'He's not my blood, but he's still my brother,' I say and Theo shakes his head; he's telling me that I don't understand how he feels.

I point a shaking finger to our baby, asleep in his cradle. 'You're a father before anything else. Protecting our son should be your priority. Have you invited Vincent to stay here with us?' I ask.

Silence.

'Theo?' I shout. Baby Vincent squawks. We pause, both watching as the boy wriggles and falls back into his sleep.

'I've written to him…' It's a whisper.

'And?' It's almost a hiss through teeth. That he's not just telling me, that I'm having to drag every word from him, is covering me with a fine layer of perspiration.

'It is best if he moves closer to us,' he says. 'But not here. Not in this apartment.'

'Where?'

'Auvers-sur-Oise. North-western Paris,' he says.

'When?'

'Soon,' he says, and I walk from the room, the door slamming behind me. I hear baby Vincent shriek his response. But I can't let Theo see my relief that our brother won't be living in our home.

I hate that I can't, that I won't, be a better sister.

May 03, 1890.
Paris.

Dear Johanna,

Apologies but I'm unable to make lunch today. Monet has requested a meeting with me at one o'clock and Gachet is expected at two.

A thousand kisses for you and to our boy.

Theo

Portrait Of Dr. Gachet

I'm surprised when I hear him enter. Monday to Thursday he didn't make it home for lunch: meetings and demanding artists, he'd said. He's working too hard and carries a look of exhaustion with him at all times. He reads a letter as he walks in to the nursery, not looking up to me or to the baby perched on my lap.

'It's done,' Theo says. His eyes remain glued to the piece of paper.

'What is?' Something in his tone makes me sit rigid on the chair, goosebumps erupting along my arms.

'Vincent has been discharged from the asylum in Saint-Rémy. He's moved to Auvers-sur-Oise,' he says, rubbing at his tired eyes with his hand. 'He looks forward to seeing us often.'

'Where's he living?' I ask. I attempt to keep my tone neutral.

'On his own, but under a doctor's supervision.' He's reading more of the letter. 'Dr Gachet.' He pushes his hand to his mouth as if trying to catch the many coughs. 'He considers Auvers beautiful. Thatched roofs, picturesque, heart of the country.' His voice sounds breathy and strained.

Theo looks up from the letter, his eyes search my face. He wants a response. I give nothing; I'm waiting to hear more before I pass comment. He flicks his eyes back to the letter.

'Dr Gachet's quite a character. An aspiring artist. I met him last week. Told you.' I shake my head and he laughs away my confusion: a rasping sound. 'Vincent's found accommodation for three and a half francs a day.'

Theo looks up again, his eyes search my face.

'What?' I ask.

'Do you hate him again?'

I release a sound: guttural, animal-like. The noise comes from my core. I don't hate Vincent, but I might be starting to hate myself. How can I tell my husband that stepping back into Vincent's world panics me? That his brother already threatens our peace. That I'm terrified how Theo will cope if Vincent harms himself. We connect eyes, but I don't offer explanation. This is the first discussion we've had about Vincent for two weeks. I'd no idea that the move would happen so quickly. Perhaps I'd even thought our not talking about it meant it was no longer proceeding.

Theo returns to his letter, saying requested items aloud. 'Ten metres of canvas, twenty sheets of Ingres paper—'

'List upon list of demands,' I say. My words are mumbled and sly.

'An artist requires tools,' Theo says. 'As you must remember.'

Cruel man. I can't remember the last time I picked up a paintbrush.

'He writes to you with tales of financial demands but can't be told anything about your life,' I say. 'Surely to call yourself an artist you must be feeding yourself from the profits of your work?'

'So a writer is only so if published, a mother ceases to be when her child leaves home, a chair is no longer a chair when a leg breaks.'

I wait for his coughing to stop. 'You're the bank of Vincent van Idiot Gogh,' I say. My volume's too high; it startles baby Vincent.

Theo laughs. It's a nervous, a hoarse sound that comes from the bottom of his throat and causes more coughing. 'Idiot Gogh?' he says. He smiles. His eyes don't smile though. His eyes are wide and full of fear.

'Shush, shush,' I say to Vincent, glaring at Theo. He reads his letter again.

'The doctor suggested a more expensive inn, at six francs a day, but Vincent favoured the cheaper one,' he says, then pauses as if waiting for me to retract my claim and praise Vincent for being thrifty.

'He takes the food from your baby's mouth,' I say and Theo laughs again.

'You nurse the boy.'

I stand. I juggle the baby up to my shoulder. I'm unable to fling anything or to throw my arms out in protest.

'You're a pompous idiot,' I say. 'Just like your brother.'

Theo's eyes jump to mine. They're wide and demanding. He holds his palms out to me, as if to bounce my words back.

'What the hell's wrong with you, Johanna?' he asks. 'When did this ugliness begin? When did you stop being grateful for this life we share? I hardly recognise you.'

'So now you demand I have an interest in what *your* brother's doing?' I ask. 'But you didn't share any of these plans with me?'

'He's *our* brother,' Theo says. His tone's gentle. He attempts to reason with me. 'He asks that I send you his deepest affection.'

'Why aren't you desperate to protect our son from his uncle's madness?' I shout and the baby squeaks. He's frightened, like me. I rock from side-to-side, my rhythm manic and too fast. Baby Vincent giggles. He brings my attention back to him, making me smile at his joy. I jiggle him a little more and he laughs again.

'Vincent writes asking when he can visit,' Theo says, the words breathy, 'or if we can visit him one Sunday.'

I don't respond. I walk towards the doorway, baby Vincent at my shoulder. I turn away from my husband as we pass, blocking our child from his father's eyesight, and then I'm out of the room.

'Johanna.' He follows me.

I don't turn around; I can't let him see my tears. His hand touches my shoulder. I shrug it away despite wishing he'd pull me into an embrace and hating myself for needing his comfort.

'We should talk,' he says. It's almost a whisper.

I turn to look at him.

'I love you because you live to help whoever you can in the world,' he says. 'You give love to whoever you can.'

My tears break free. Theo takes the baby, kissing his forehead before lifting him to his shoulder. I wipe away tear after tear, focusing on the gentleness of father with son.

'I know you're scared, but I promise that I'll never put you or our boy in danger,' he says. I look at his face and see his truth. 'But our brother needs us.'

I nod. I know he does. It's our duty to help Vincent.

'What if we're not strong enough to survive what he brings with him?' I say.

'Fearing storms won't prevent their arrival,' Theo says, moving to place a hand around my shoulder and pulling me closer. The three of us: our family.

May, 1890.

A new remedy from the doctor for his cough and Theo, worn out, already sleeps. I've settled a fretful Vincent but my mind keeps going back to a question my husband asked me. 'When did this ugliness begin? When did you stop being grateful for this life we share?'

And now I'm wide awake and I'm thinking about how 'ugly' and 'difficult' are so often used together when talking about women. A difficult woman is one with opinions. She follows a path that men tread with ease. If women accept their positions and fate, then they can be beautiful; if they've a voice or desires, they're ugly. It's engrained – I'm guilty of using those words too.

How am I only now realising that women are controlled by a fear of being branded with either of these words? To be marked 'ugly' or 'difficult' brings judgement, discomfort, rejection too – and so what do we do? We women step in accordance with male expectations and demands. Those words forever whispered: a threat, to shoot fear into our actions and decisions.

But why is 'ugly' seen as bad? Why is being 'difficult' considered wicked? Are those words not merely concepts that are entirely indefinable? Perceptions even. Still those words are used as weapons.

Power, power, power.

Have I answered my own question about why women judge each other? Are we not all seeking to find our place within a world of men? Imagine if all of us womenfolk joined together and demanded that our roles in their success be acknowledged and heard!

Camille, Agostina, Sara, Clara, Mother – I'm drawn to them all, then lost in their sadness, their ugliness, their unpleasantness too.

Summer 1890

PARIS

Portrait Of Adeline Ravoux (Half-Figure)

We meet him in Ravoux Inn. Vincent's lodging above the restaurant. He stands outside, dressed in a blue drill jacket and a fisherman's straw hat when we arrive.

'Theo, Johanna,' Vincent says, an embrace for his brother and a kiss on both of my cheeks. He smells of stale tobacco and vinegar. He looks taller, sturdier, his shoulders broader even. Perhaps also I'm seeing, for the first time, how slender and unhealthy Theo looks in comparison. Vincent fluffs the thin wisps of hair on my napping son's head. 'Come. Let's have a glass.' I note that his shoulder, the one below his wounded ear, slants down. He removes his hat and opens the door to Ravoux Inn; we walk inside.

I hadn't expected the inside to be quite so quaint. I count ten waxed oak tables, only three of them occupied. Murmurs of conversations dance around the room, in-between their mouthfuls of coq au vin. It smells delicious. Vincent walks to the table at the back of the room, furthest from the main door, and we sit on the three chairs.

'Let me look at my nephew,' he says, before leaning over and seeing Vincent for the first time. I watch for a change in expression, but he offers neither reaction nor comment.

'He's asleep for now, so we can chat without distraction,' Theo says. Vincent snaps his eyes from the baby to his brother and smiles.

'How I've missed seeing your face,' Vincent says. His cheeriness is contagious and Theo laughs. 'But why do you look so very thin and pale?'

'He works too hard. Dead tired in the evenings,' I say. 'Doesn't stop this little one squawking and waking his pa in the night though. His first tooth, I think.'

'But I have the appetite of a fox,' Theo says. He laughs again, but the sound is rasping and incomplete.

'True. He's taken to drinking raw egg in cognac each morning and demanding double portions of meat in the evening.' I stroke Theo's arm.

'That cough—' Vincent begins.

'Comes and goes,' Theo says. The brothers don't think I notice their silent communication: eye contact and a bob of their heads.

A pretty blonde girl in a blue dress, a matching ribbon in her loose hair, comes to our table. She pours two glasses of wine and smiles at Vincent. She waits, as if wanting introduction, but after a minute of silence she leaves.

'A friend of yours?' I say, watching as the petite figure walks away. 'What is she, fifteen?'

'Thirteen,' he says, his eyes following her. 'She's modelling for me next week.'

I raise an eyebrow at Theo, urging comment.

'You must send the painting to me,' my husband says.

Really? I shake my head and Theo shrugs.

'I'll do it in one sitting,' Vincent says, lighting his pipe. He looks over to her at the counter and waves. 'I sketched her but the family didn't see the resemblance.' He shakes his head. 'I'm hoping they'll like the painting better.'

'Shall we eat?' Theo says, looking over to the other customers, watching as they devour spoonfuls of stew.

'Are you hungry?' I ask Vincent. He's burlier, healthy of complexion, happier than I expected.

'Miss Voort wrote to me,' Vincent says. 'Did you know that she's been disowned, lives in lodgings in Paris?'

'I think she's an artist's model now,' Theo says.

My eyes jump to meet his. *What?* 'Why didn't you tell me?'

Theo reaches across the table and takes my hand. I let our fingers entwine and look at Vincent. He stares at his own fingers and frowns; his are splattered in yellow and blue paint. I wonder what he's thinking. I wonder if our intimate moment should have been avoided, yet still, this is the sanest conversation I've ever had with Vincent van Gogh. It's almost as if I'm meeting him for the first time.

'Johanna, sister,' he says, unable to meet my eyes. 'I once wanted to paint you in a vulgar position.'

'I remember,' I replied, not turning to see how Theo might be reacting.

'And … and for that I must apologise.'

I look at Theo and his smile beams.

'Now I still long to capture you, but my purpose is to immortalise your beauty,' Vincent says. 'I admire both your magnificence and your strength, and I want others to do the same.'

Theo stands and moves to his brother. He throws his arms around a sitting Vincent.

'They fed you well in Saint-Rémy,' Theo says, slapping his hand onto his brother's belly.

'Unlike you I'm quite fat and cheerful.' The Van Gogh brothers laugh; the sound dances around the inn. 'How I've missed knowing you both.'

'The boy will wake soon,' I say. 'Let's eat.'

'Yes, and later Gachet has invited you to see his many animals. Cats, dogs, chickens, rabbits, ducks, pigeons. My namesake will love them all,' Vincent says, reaching over and stroking his nephew's head.

This is happiness; for too long, we have waited and longed for this normality.

June, 1890.

Leaving Vincent, we talked, with such joy, about the shift in how our brother views me. I asked if Theo had noted any other changes in how men in the art world considered women. He laughed and I glared at him in a way that forced him to apologise!

But then he became entirely animated and outlined a shift he'd considered – among female artists. He talked about how he believes Morisot paints women in the way that they perceive themselves, rather than how men wish them to appear. That through her art she maintains control of her own body or allows her models to do the same. That each self-portrait that she draws shouts to those who view, 'This is me. This is how I want you to see me.' How she disregards the expectations and the needs of the men who stare and how those men are yet to notice.

'If her semi-nudes might attract erotic gaze, then her irregular brushstrokes repel that scrutiny,' he said. 'And other women artists have listened.'

What progress!

Vincent no longer wishing to possess me on canvas – that is progress too.

Dearest Theo,

Sunday has left me truly happy. I am delighted that we are no longer far from one another, and hope we'll have the opportunity to see each other often. I pray that your cough is less bothersome and that you're heeding my advice and resting this week. Enclosed is the list of colours I need you to order.

I've been working a lot and quickly; perhaps this is my insignificant way to express how desperately swift the passage of time continues in your modern life. That said, I've renewed energy and enthusiasm since seeing you all.

I'm currently working on a field of poppies, there's a little finished canvas with mountains and a cypress with a star. Earlier this week I completed the portrait of the daughter of the people I'm lodging with. A young girl wearing blue and against a blue background, you perhaps remember her from your visit? It's on a no. 15 canvas. Before that I accomplished a night effect of two dark pear trees against a yellowing sky with wheat fields. Finally I'm aiming to use the remaining canvas – one metre long by fifty centimetres high – to paint fields of wheat, poplars, a line of blue hills on the horizon and possibly even a train weaving a trail of white smoke through the greenery. I also hope I'll paint Miss Gachet's portrait next week, new canvas allowing.

I'd very much like to come to Paris for a few days over the summer, but for now my art consumes me. One day or another even, I'm convinced you'll find a way to hold an exhibition of my work in a café.

Good fortune for your little one and a strong handshake for you and my sister.

Tout à toi, Vincent

Skull Of A Skeleton With Burning Cigarette

The streets are busy tonight. Carriages race over cobbles, in a rush to deliver wealthy Parisians to theatres, bars, cabarets. Breath and abundance are blown into Paris at night. It's July, and this is my first nocturnal outing in over ten months; the collision of noise and crowds is already too much.

'Mind the—' Andries places a hand on my chest, pushing me back into a doorway as a horse and carriage scoots past.

'*Pardon, pardon,*' Andries says, waving at the coachman as the *fiacre* dashes on. I hear the crack of a whip and a scream of, '*Hé, la-bas!*' as he continues along Boulevard de Clichy.

'Where's your head tonight, Jo?' Andries asks. I glance at him. His oval face remains blemish-free; my brother isn't aging whereas I've gained ten years in less than one.

'The baby screamed all night again. I'm convinced that contaminated cow's milk is poisoning him, but the doctor refuses to listen,' I say. 'Teething. Always teething – that's what he says. I'm going to give him ass's milk instead.'

Andries links his arm in mine and we walk the cobbles together. We dodge couples, my brother bowing to those he knows, others shouting greetings across the streets. I keep my eyes on the stones, not wanting conversation with an acquaintance and fighting all of my instincts to run back home.

Chapter Two

Theo's in The Hague, discussing a painting by Corot with the collector Hendrik Willem Mesdag, and Andries has insisted on a night out together. I told him I couldn't. How another bout of blood loss and another week in bed had left me cured but nervous about being far from the apartment. My brother argued how much he'd missed our adventures and that he'd not take no for an answer. He fails to realise that I heard the mumbles he exchanged with Clara in the hallway. The words 'hysteria' and 'paranoid' that they whispered.

'I'm a mother and my son's unsettled. I can't leave him for long,' I say.

'Clara's looking after him,' he says. 'It's all arranged and my sister of old would have loved this place.' He stops. A black mourning crepe, trimmed with white, decorates a building. A solitary pallbearer in a black cape and top hat opens the door and signals for us to step into the darkness.

'Is someone dead?' I ask, confused that all signs point to death yet I can already hear laughter from within.

Andries pushes aside heavy drapes and my eyes begin to adjust. I cling to my brother, trying not to be overcome by the sudden assault of noise and peculiarity. Large wooden coffins are dotted around the cave-like room. Candles flicker upon them, human skulls are placed on them too. Although it offers the impression of a funeral, the place is packed out with people who all appear to be both very drunk and very happy.

'What is this place?' I ask, gripping my brother. Anxiety bubbles in my belly. 'Am I attending my own funeral?'

'Cabaret of Death,' Andries says. 'It's just opened.'

'But he's drinking out of a human skull,' I say, pointing at a customer. He somehow hears me and raises the skull in the air, as if to say, 'Santé.'

'What on earth is—' I say. My eyes jump around the room. Death surrounds us as if a colossal disaster has occurred during my bedrest, yet women in pearls and men in bowler hats laugh from their bellies. Life is being celebrated; they're all chuckling in Death's face.

'Art and beer,' Andries says. He spreads his arms out wide as if to welcome me to his home. 'Nothing is as it first appears. Rodin loves it here.'

'And Camille?' I ask, unable to hide the flicker of hope from my voice. Andries shakes his head.

'She's stopped sculpting.'

Camille's been erased from the social circle. She no longer exists. Creative women in Paris disappear when their men no longer have use for them. Their stories are left untold.

'Oh my, look at the details,' my brother says, pointing around the murky room. The walls are decorated with human skulls and random bones, full skeletons sit on chairs next to customers. A large candelabra of human skulls hangs from the ceiling. The air is full of stale smoke, the patrons' laughter out-of-place. Death is advertised, death is praised, a guillotine slices through human flesh in a corner.

'The guillotine,' I say. I shudder. I'm unable to hide my horror. 'Is this your idea of a relaxing night out?'

'They demonstrate on real corpses,' Andries says, as if that's explanation enough. 'Now, let's drink a noxious potion from a fake human skull.'

'Dries,' I say.

'It's make-believe, Jo,' Andries says. 'The illusion show later will blow your mind. A woman will change into a skeleton right in front of our eyes.'

'I should be at home with my son,' I say. We're standing in line, waiting to be seated.

'Nonsense,' Andries says. He laughs. 'Now enough of your whinnying. Shall I tell you my news?'

I nod apprehensively.

'I've been looking at the apartment on the ground floor of your building.'

'What? Didn't you say that where I lived was—' He bats away my response with his hand.

'Theo and I are considering starting our own business.'

What? 'He's giving up his job? But he pays for Vincent too…'

'If you and Annie get on, think how wonderful it'll be.'

It would be, but I don't understand why Theo hasn't discussed this with me. Living with Andries in Paris feels almost like a dream and there isn't a single memory from my childhood that doesn't have him in it. To have my brother near me again, for baby Vincent to have him in his daily life... I can't help but smile.

'Are you going to marry Annie?' I say and my brother nods.

'As soon as I can,' he says. 'I asked her to come here tonight...' He leaves the statement open. I think he might be anxious for my reaction. I bat his arm with my hand; *it will be fine*. Time alone with my brother is so very rare these days. We've created new paths and new lives. It isn't that I wish to jump forward into a different existence. Tonight though, I guess I was hoping we could pause time. Rewind two years. That I could be Bonger's sister again.

A monk approaches us, clutching a human skull in each hand. 'Weary travellers. Welcome. Let me choose for you a coffin that will fit.'

'Is he a real monk?' I ask and my brother laughs.

'He plays a part. Nothing is as it seems, Jo. You know that,' Andries says and I do. This place mimics the Parisian art world – nothing is as it first appears and if you dwell too long, your mind will be lost forever.

My brother's arm rests around my shoulders as we follow the monk to a wooden coffin surrounded by chairs. As we sit and I refuse to remove my cloak, the monk places our skulls on our coffin. A bell tolls and a funeral march is played. Some of the customers stand. The monk leads them into a second chamber. Foreboding lurks.

'What the actual hell?' I say.

'Exactly,' my brother says. He's laughing. My concern and confusion amuse him, but then he leaps to his feet and waves his arm in the air. 'There she is.'

I'd not have recognised Annie from our childhood. She's slender, blonde and English-looking, like the girls I've seen in illustrations in books. I imagine her facial expressions mirror how I looked stepping in here a few minutes ago. I watch her, clearly terrified at where she's somehow found herself, avoiding coffins and manoeuvring through the room. She's Dutch in a Parisian world, but, more than that, my brother's thrown her into the underworld and seems to be watching to see if she can swim.

'Jo, you remember Annie. But now she's exceptionally clever and flawless,' Andries says and I hold out my hand.

My brother (and sister?),

Bonger wrote that he was viewing the apartment below you and, as if that were not enough news, that you consider starting business together. That you're to be an independent art dealer thrills me, yet why has this not been a discussion for us brothers? Is it that you're concerned regarding the likelihood of this enterprise's success, when you have both a family and this failed painter to support financially?

Am I to deduce that you're taking the bread from my mouth and feeding it to Bonger instead? Have I done something wrong?

I'm haunted by the inkling that I've become a burden for you, but surely you must know that I slave away daily on my art?

Vincent

July 11, 1890.
Paris.

My dear Vincent,

Forgive my not sharing those early discussions that Bonger and I had, although it's not unexpected for him to proceed at a speed that's unwarranted and to tell anyone who'll listen! However, as quickly as all negotiations began, they have ended.

If I might be entirely honest, I'd suggest that he's already under Annie's thumb. Indeed, he even dared to suggest that my enthusiasm didn't match his, in terms of business. I explained that I've been incessantly exhausted of late and not truly interested in anything other than eating and sleeping. Bonger even stated that perhaps we only desired them living in the apartment below so that Annie would be of use as some form of maid for Johanna. I can't imagine that Bonger would have formulated that conclusion himself and must therefore attribute this shift in him to Annie. I'll leave it with you to imagine how my wife responded, but still our child continues to preoccupy her. The boy remains unable to settle, Jo only just recovering from another week's bedrest and this Van Gogh household is a wearied one.

Yet all that matters is that you know that Bonger has withdrawn from renting the apartment and has pulled out of all plans to run a joint business. He even talks about moving to Amsterdam when he marries. I don't wish to give you additional worry, but I would like to leave Boussod, Valadon & Cie. I'm increasingly noticing that my hours are long – is that not why I'm so constantly weary? – and the pay somehow inadequate, but perhaps I'll discuss these worries with them.

If the business were something I'd considered seriously or if financial matters were pressing, I'd have visited you myself. I hope, my dear brother, that your health remains good, and that if there's anything that troubles you then you'll seek assistance from Dr Gachet. He can perhaps offer something if the melancholy returns.

Give me news of you as soon as you can. I have enclosed fifty francs with this letter.

Chapter Two

Warm regards from Jo, from your nephew and from your brother who loves you.

Theo and Jo

My dear brother (and sister?),

With thanks for your letter and for the fifty-franc note within.

Some days I wish to write to you about many things, but today I do not see the point. Instead I'm concerning myself only with my painting. My canvas has my complete attention and I'm determined to do as well as those other painters who you exhibit and sell daily.

Hirschig lodges here now too. He asked if you could order the attached list of colours for him and I've included my bare minimum order too. Perhaps add his to my consignment, but if you tell me the cost, Hirschig will send you the money.

More soon, and good luck in business at Boussod, Valadon & Cie.

Warm regards to Jo and to my nephew.

Tout à toi, Vincent

From: Dr Paul Gachet
To: Theo van Gogh

Urgent. Come straight away to Auvers. Vincent has been shot.

July, 1890.

The telegram arrived late last night. The banging on the front door woke us.

Theo didn't want me to go with him. He insisted I remain in Paris; the baby is still unsettled, my heavy bleeding only just under control, the horror that he expects to face.

I've no idea if Vincent's alive or dead.

Dread whirls in my stomach. There's no respite; will this be the time that our brother succeeds where other attempts have failed?

My dear Johanna,

I can't quite comprehend what I'm hearing here. My brother crumbles before my eyes and I'm powerless to save him. I'm trying to piece together what has occurred, but there's much that makes little sense.

Yesterday, Vincent ate lunch, as he always did, but then went to the wheat fields immediately. He'd created at least one piece of art every day during his stay here and he was showing no signs of slowing down. At dusk, he hadn't returned and this caused some concern as my brother never missed a meal.

The proprietors of the inn were sitting outside when Vincent finally staggered towards them. It was around nine o'clock in the evening. He was clutching his stomach. Someone asked if he was fine and he mumbled a few words before entering the inn and taking the stairs to his bedroom. The innkeeper, a Father Ravoux, a kind man, felt sure something wasn't quite right. He went to Vincent's room and found him lying on his bed, moaning. He asked Vincent if he was ill, to which Vincent held up his shirt and showed a wound.

'I have tried to kill myself,' are the words that my brother uttered!

It seems that my brother shot himself with a revolver and then fainted. He told Father Ravoux that he 'tried to finish himself off', but couldn't find the revolver. Where could it have gone? Surely it wouldn't have disappeared from his grasp? Vincent claimed that he finally gave up his search and returned to the inn.

Father Ravoux sent for a doctor. It was Gachet who finally came to my brother's assistance and bandaged his wound, before sending the telegram to inform me. But it was Father Ravoux who stayed with Vincent all night. He lit Vincent's pipe and talked to him, even listened to my brother moaning with pain.

When I arrived here I ran from the station to the inn, just as two gendarmes entered the house. Someone had informed them of an attempted suicide. I followed Father Ravoux and the gendarme to Vincent's room. At first my brother failed to acknowledge me, his focus being on Father Ravoux's explanation of French law and the crime that Vincent had committed. No one has the right to suicide, yet my brother argued that it was his body and that he could do to it whatever he wished.

'Did you wish to die?' I asked and Vincent looked at me for the first time.

'Yes,' he said with a smile. 'La tristesse durera toujours.'

Sadness will last forever! Dear Johanna – what will we do?

I thought that he was going to say more, but then he was hit with lethargy and pain. The gendarmes were ordered to leave, and I took a seat on the only chair in his room, next to Vincent's bed, kissing him, our two heads on one pillow.

'I no longer stand firmly on two feet, but I am at peace now that you are here,' he later told me. 'You are the only person in this world who has shown me love.'

He rests now, but my heart is breaking. He appears smaller, wrapped in bedsheets and lost to the world. There is a silence in this room that alarms me. My brother sleeps too quietly; I fear he might not wake and I can't leave his side.

I'll write more tomorrow. Kiss my little boy and a thousand embraces from me to you.

Yours forever and always devoted, Theo

July, 1890.

No letter from Theo today. I've written but received nothing in response. I know that his time and his mind will be occupied with our brother, as it should be, but still I can't rest without news.

After seeing Vincent last month, Theo and I both commented on how well he looked; I thought him cured for once and for all. Now, instead, I miss Theo and I think about Vincent constantly: that he'd never quite grasped happiness, that I'd not invited him to live here, that he'd given up on hope.

I can't bear to consider how truly lonely and desperate he must have been, to deem shooting himself the only escape from his pain. My lone relief is that he now has Theo by his side.

Can I hope that my husband has painted things to be worse than they truly are?

For now, I wait.

I occupy my days with domestic chores and my son. I watch my boy's wonder at all that he discovers in this world – he clutches, he babbles sweetly. Soon our little one will be six months old and I expect it won't be long before he can say 'mamma' quite clearly. I'm covered in a crushing need to cling to our happiness and to share this life, our son, with Theo. We belong together. Yet, for months we've had lingering illness, one after the other, and now our gladness teeters over darkness like nothing we've experienced before.

I long for us all to be back in this nest – with Vincent well again and us all resting.

Irises

Each knock on the door sends shoots of dread through me: fear of a telegram delivery to inform of Vincent's death. Two days since Theo's letter and dread bubbles.

'No news might be good news,' I say to my sleeping child.

'Johanna.' I hear a man's voice. For a split-second I think it's Vincent.

He's not dead. Everything will be fine.

I turn, relief sweeping into me, but then I see Theo standing in the open doorway. His body bowed. His arms wrapped around his too-lean torso.

'Vincent?' I say and I watch as Theo's face contorts. He nods his head. The grief explodes from him; he stumbles and I rush to him. His entire body shakes as he sobs. I grip his arms and help him to the nursing chair. I crouch in front of him, my hands on his knees, waiting until he's ready to talk.

Minutes pass, our son sleeping soundly in his cot, our son unaware. I watch Theo. I listen to how he struggles to breathe.

'I didn't leave his side until it was over,' he says.

I hear how difficult it is for him to swallow. I rest my cheek on his knee.

'He wanted to die,' he says.

I wait.

'He gave up. It wasn't an accident.' He coughs. 'He wanted to die so that the sadness would go away.' A pause. 'He found so little happiness in life.'

Another pause. Minutes pass.

'He fell into a coma,' he whispers, but I don't lift my head to look at him. 'He died around one o'clock in the morning on July 29, but I waited. I made the declaration of death at the town hall.'

'Where is he now?' I ask.

'Still in Auvers. He's in a coffin, surrounded by his canvases. *Irises* hangs on the wall. Its paint is still wet. At the foot of the coffin there are…' Another pause, then a sob. I can't look at my husband. I can't see his grief. 'At the foot of his… His palette and brushes are at the bottom of his coffin,' Theo says, his voice hoarse.

'His true loves,' I whisper and I feel Theo's legs tremble.

'So many bouquets and wreaths. Other artists living in Auvers came,' he says. 'Tomorrow, he'll be buried in a sunny spot…'

Polite society demands women restrain their tears at funerals; I won't be allowed to attend. I don't move my cheek from his knee. I hear his sobs, and my head moves with his tremors. What I would do now to go back to Johanna Bonger: to explain to her the precious beauty of peace of mind, to show her the power gained from being loved, from giving love, to show her the worth of gratitude and truth. I'd tell her to grab happiness. I'd tell her that nothing lasts, that everything passes.

'I should have been kinder to him,' I whisper.

Tears track down my cheeks, snot drips from my nose onto Theo's trousers.

'Why didn't he tell me how desperate he was feeling?' Theo says. His sobs punctuate each word. 'People said he was calmer, that he was healthy. It makes no sense…'

'These things seldom do,' I say.

August, 1890.

Grief covers us all.

Such a great, a wondrous, a remarkable talent. Is it all gone and now buried forever?

Instead I watch the man I love spiralling beyond my reach. Into depth of loss that I won't grasp.

My little family is destroyed. My husband drowns. The love of my life barely recognisable.

Theo's lost, he's desperately ill. Weight falls from him.

He rejects sleep, he rejects food; instead he's consumed with the impossible need to reverse time to save his brother.

Today he refused to hold baby Vincent; he said the name was a curse, that only one Vincent van Gogh could exist in his family at any given time. He looked at our son as if he were to blame for his uncle's death.

I can't accept that any of this is true.

Tree Roots

My husband's back at work. I had hoped new art deals would be a distraction, but instead his artists have been abandoned and rejected. A month on from Vincent's death and while illness consumes my husband, his brother's ghost devours him.

'My focus has to be on Vincent's memorial exhibition,' he says. 'October, maybe November. When the Parisians are back in town.' He wipes his forehead with a handkerchief as he paces unsteadily around the parlour. 'It's essential that the exhibition allows the seeing of my brother's art all together. That's how others will understand it entirely.'

'But not at the expense of your own health,' I say with more sternness than intended. 'Look at you. You can hardly move without falling. You've clearly still got a fever and don't think that you've hidden that new rash.'

'You irritating wretch,' he shouts, the words full of venom. 'This is for *Vincent*. This is *all* that matters to me.'

I step towards him. I need him to look into my eyes and see my concern. 'You know I love our brother, but are his paintings more important than your health? You're close to complete exhaustion.'

His jaw clenches. His eyes are fire. He slaps me. I shuffle

backwards, out of his reach, my palm raised to my cheek to ease the sting.

His breathing's rapid. He looks at his hand as if it's alien and not connected to his wrist. Then he looks at me, his face a picture of disbelief. 'I'm sorry. Johanna, God, Jo. I'm so sorry. I don't know—'

'Never raise a hand to me again,' I scream, but then I watch as Theo folds to the floor, crouching on his knees. His shoulders trembling.

'I don't know who I am anymore. I fear I've caught my brother's madness. It's in the Van Gogh blood,' he says. His eyes are fixed on the parquet floor. 'I've passed it on to our son.' The words are full of desperation and fear.

'I understand your duty to make sure Vincent's talent isn't forgotten,' I say, my palm still touching my cheek. 'But we miss you. Your son, me, we both need you.'

'Sara Voort's written every day for the past week,' Theo says. He's still staring at the floor. 'She says that Vincent killed himself because he loved you.'

'And you believe her?' I'm trying to keep my tone calm. I move my shaking hands behind my back. I don't know how my husband will react next.

'His death makes no sense. Look.' He pulls a piece of paper from his pocket. His fingers tremble. He unfolds the paper, laying it on the floor in front of him. I kneel opposite, still keeping a distance; the wood hard and cold through my skirts. I can't quite read the boxes of facts, but I can see the many arrows to underlined names.

'You think he was murdered?' I say and Theo nods.

'Seventy-five paintings in the last seventy days of his life,' he says. 'Gardens full of flowers, waving wheat, panoramic landscapes…'

'*Wheatfield with Crows* was his last painting,' I say. 'Remember the vicious crows? They slashed into the blue sky. Surely that reflects his state of mind and—'

'That wasn't his last. The morning before his shooting he

painted a *sous-bois*. Full of sun, full of hope. It was found on his easel in the wheat field.' A pause as he coughs into his handkerchief. I wait. 'It's a tangled and otherworldly study of tree roots. Vivid colours, irregular shapes, almost abstract, yet so full of life.' More coughing into his handkerchief. 'There are empty areas of canvas, but that's because it's unfinished. Why start a painting, then leave it incomplete to kill himself? For Vincent, the art was his all. He would have finished the painting before...'

'Could he have been saying that he was happy to die?' I ask.

'That makes no sense to me.'

I shuffle backwards again, away from his anger. 'The desire to take your own life makes no sense to either of us. We can't begin to imagine the torment that drives someone to think death is an escape.'

'Who shoots himself in the stomach? How is that even possible?' His voice rises in volume at each question. He points at different boxes. His fingers tremble, his words slur together. 'All reports say he seemed happy and calm and not at all on a path to self-destruction.'

I stand up, moving beyond my husband's reach. 'None of us can know what was going on inside his head,' I say.

'Why won't you consider foul play?' He glares at me, his eyes searching mine.

'Murder makes no sense. Who would have wanted Vincent dead? Why won't you consider suicide?' I ask. 'The man cut off his own ear. He consumed paint.'

Theo stares at the floor and then he places a hand on his stomach. 'I feel it in here,' he says. I nod. I look at my husband and his detailed diagrams. He's desperate to make sense of Vincent's chaos.

'If he'd wanted to die, why didn't he shoot himself in the head? The angles weren't right, the bullet didn't go through the body,' he says. The words rush out. 'He was shot.' His hand forms the shape of a gun. 'Bang, bang.' The words contain venom. He fires his fingers into the air and I wrap my arms around myself.

'I just know he was shot, but by who? Who would my brother protect?'

'*La tristesse durera toujours,*' I say.

'I know you want me to move on,' he says.

'You're ill, you need help. I want us to take back our lives. The ghost of your brother—'

'He haunts you?' he asks. His eyes narrow and I shake my head a little too vigorously.

'Only what I should or could have done to help him,' I say. 'In the two years that I knew him he—'

'Many came to the interment. What if one of them was the killer? Who had a credible motive? Why did Vincent, on his deathbed, protect his killer? Why would he not share the identity with me?' His words rush into each other. He's not interested in my thoughts on his brother. 'I thought he trusted me with his life.'

I need him to hear me; I need my husband to listen to me. 'You'll never know,' I say harshly. 'But you'll drive yourself to insanity if you keep focusing—'

'I wasn't there enough for him in life, the least I can do now…'

'What did Vincent tell Dr Gachet when he was told that his life could be saved?' I ask, my tone still stern.

'That he'd just have to do it all over again,' he says.

'And yet you think it wasn't suicide that killed Vincent? I beg you,' I say. I move to him and I grab his hands. I hold them in my own. 'Please, Theo. I beg you. Let this go. Together, we can make sure the world knows all about the great artist that he was, but let us be a family again. Please. Better days can come.'

Autumn 1890

PARIS

September, 1890.

Theo arranged for Paul Durand-Ruel to visit here and look at Vincent's many paintings. He was convinced Paul would want them for an exhibition immediately. The entire apartment had to be tidied by ten o'clock and Clara took the baby for a walk to the park.

Poor Paul stood bewildered and unsure how to respond to Theo's frenzied bounce around the room. I tried to calm my husband but he was feverish in his detailed attempts to sell each and every piece of art. I'm sure I heard Paul's first excuse to leave after fifteen minutes. Still the kind man stayed an hour, but didn't even get to view the paintings created in Auvers.

'Vincent's art might be too controversial,' was his final remark, and also, 'I'll let you know within a week.'

Sorrow

W*hat now?*
    That's what I think when I walk into the bedroom.
Two months of him descending, weeks of diagrams and suspects
being drawn on canvas and nailed to our parlour's walls. Now
Theo's sitting on the edge of our bed, my sketchbook open with
letters out of their envelopes and scattered around him. I've
nothing to hide, but the intrusion marks a new spiral.

'Durand-Ruel said a week,' he says. 'He lied.'

'Perhaps he's busy with—'

'A month of silence is a refusal to exhibit my brother,' he says. I
don't reply. I know that's a sore blow and my husband already
teeters on the edge of exhaustion and sanity. 'Our love was never
equal, was it?'

What? The shift in topic throws me. I don't respond; I search
his face for clues.

'I've given notice. I no longer work at Boussod, Valadon &
Cie.'

'You're exhausted. Let me fetch your medicine,' I say, turning
to leave the room.

'Those drops make me literally mad.' I wait. Theo draws in
breath. 'I trusted you. I gave you all of me and *this* is how you

repay me?' he says, pointing at my sketchbook. His calm tone unnerves me.

'What are you talking about?' I ask.

'What will you write today, darling wife?' he asks. 'October 4, 1890, husband discovers I'm a filthy whore?' He growls, guttural, from deep within. 'Just tell me. You and Vincent together. All this time. Is it in here somewhere? Do you still go and visit him when I work?'

Still? I pause.

'Well?' It's a growl.

'What? How? Why would you think such a thing?' I rush out the words as I stand in the doorway, turning my wedding ring on my finger, entirely unsure what to do next.

'Do you laugh about stupid, unsuspecting Theo? At how you trick me with your lies,' he asks, his eyes wide. 'How thoughtless was I to trust you with my heart, my soul.'

I stand as still as a statue. I hold my breath. I try to catch up with the accusation.

'Does every artist in Paris know? All of them laughing at me behind my back. All of them knowing my brother's still alive.'

'Vincent's dead,' I say and I see him flinch. He shakes his head vigorously. I take a step towards him: my instinct is to comfort my husband. 'Nothing happened between Vincent and me,' I say. 'Why would you think that?'

'Did his paintings have messages for you?' he asks and I sigh. I fidget with my wedding ring again.

'I saw you together,' he says.

'Where?' I ask. 'When?'

'This morning. In the kitchen.'

I don't know how to respond. Vincent's dead and buried, Theo's hallucinating; what new storm is this?

'Were you biding time until you could be together properly? Forever?'

'Theo, let me get your medicine,' I say, stepping back towards the door. I'm trying to keep my tone calm, trying to reason with a man who's riddled with disease. Trying to figure out what help he needs.

'I'll never be the person I was before meeting you,' he says. His eyes look down to his shoes.

'And that's a bad thing?' I say. I'm too defensive and his eyes jump back to mine.

'You're blaming *me* for your deceit?' he asks. He slams his fist onto the sketchbook. The bed wobbles, he sways too.

'No,' I say. I hold up my palms; they're trembling. I've existed for two months in this constant state of panic. The husband I knew and loved died with his brother. This reproduction is entirely unpredictable and fake.

'You're always the victim, aren't you Johanna?' he says. He cackles, the sound lacking any joy. Perspiration trickles from his forehead and down his cheeks to his whiskers. He's ill. He's very ill. 'Poor you, entirely innocent, not at all responsible for the decline of the Van Gogh brothers.'

'Let me send for the doctor. He'll—'

'When did you stop fighting for me?' he shouts and I bow my head. 'When did you stop fighting for your son?' I look away.

'I never stopped fighting,' I whisper. 'You're everything.' A pause. 'We can get you help. You're not well. Please,' I say. I take a step towards the bed, but he holds up his hand. He wants me to stay away from him. A fit of coughing prevents any new words. I wait, fidgeting from foot to foot.

'Did you write to him, sharing details of our marriage, about my flaws, about what you disliked in me?'

I shake my head. 'Of course not,' I say. My voice remains a whisper; I'm already defeated.

'My brother sees all of my women as his property, as something that he's entitled to own.' Each word is sharp, each word is coated with bitterness.

'I want you. Only you. I knew you from the moment I saw you,' I say. I try to awaken the man I once knew. My lips quiver. My words vibrate.

He laughs, dismissing my sentiment, but I can't give up on him.

'You changed me. You brought out the very best in me. You showed me how to love. Please, Theo, please let me send for a doctor.'

He glares at me and I see his face altering, his eyes widening.

'Are you planning an escape with my brother? Is it all in here?' he asks. He shakes my sketchbook in the air. 'Has this been going on from before we were engaged? Was Vincent telling the truth? That time, you and him, on Bonger's rug—'

'No,' I say firmly. 'You're all I've ever wanted.'

'Did I vanish from your thoughts each time you were with him? When he was inside you this very morning? How many times did you visit him in Auvers?' The words are slurred and gush together.

'Only that once. With you and our boy,' I whisper.

'Liar,' he shouts. It bellows around the room. He thrashes the sketchbook onto the bed. 'You're a whore. I saw you together this morning,' he shouts.

'Please, Theo—'

'I don't know you at all, do I?' he asks. He jumps from the bed and leaps towards me. He shakes the sketchbook too close to my face, the edge hitting my nose. I try to grab it, but he's too quick. He moves it behind his back, twisting his face into a sneer.

Flushes rush up my neck. 'What do you want me to say?'

'That you're sorry. That could be a start,' he says, his spittle landing on my cheek.

'But I haven't—'

'I'm going to read this and find out who you really are,' he says. He's swaying, clutching the sketchbook and pushing it into my face. I don't move my head. I try to stand tall. My nose stings as the book hits it again. My entire body shakes. 'This person who gains pleasure from destroying the Van Gogh brothers.'

'Theo,' I say. 'Please.' I can't stop the tears. I let them race down my cheeks. 'Read it, I've nothing to hide.'

'You're the only woman I've ever loved,' he whispers. He turns and walks back to bed. I watch him zigzag; waves of exhaustion must keep hitting. 'But I was never enough.'

'You're more than enough. You're everything I need.'

He slumps on the edge of the bed, facing me. He looks more like Vincent than himself. 'What else do you hide, Mrs Van Gogh?' His eyes jump to mine, there's fire within them. 'Is the baby even my son?'

There's a silence: it's eerie, it's full of darkness. My kind, my loving husband's expression is raw and pure. In that moment he's a little boy again, desperate for me to make everything better. I'm face to face with loss. Everything has changed, all that we share has crumbled apart. He's lost his peace, I've lost the love of my life. But, also, I've paused; I've observed instead of speaking. My silence has articulated words that aren't true.

'Of course he is,' I say. The words are rushed, they blend together, they're too late. 'I've never been intimate with Vincent.' My tone's flat. I sound like I'm making excuses. I want to say more, to be coherent and precise, but it's too late.

'You named him after *his* father,' he says. The words have a snap. He growls. Fire burns in his eyes.

'*You* named him after *your* brother,' I say. I fold my arms across my torso. 'I wanted to call him Theodorus, after *you*, after *his* father.'

Silence.

'You're my only love. The father of my child. My future,' I say. The words are punctuated with sobs.

'Future?' He laughs, it's harsh and rasping. 'We have no future,' he says. I see his pain, I see his fear, I see his disgust. I see his hatred too. 'You've taken everything from me,' he says.

He leaps from the bed, throwing the sketchbook at my head. A precise shot; the pain is immediate. It distracts, and in that moment Theo jumps upon me. His strength and energy are unexpected, they burst from his core. He pushes me. My head strikes the parquet. Pain thumps inside my skull. I'm dazed. I'm not fighting back. He drags me by my skirts into the middle of the room; a knee in my chest, a boot on my arm, his hands wrapped around my throat. Tighter, and tighter. He squeezes my throat.

I struggle to breathe. I gasp. My head's about to pop. Too much pain; agony everywhere. I try to shake my head, but his grip's too tense. Perspiration drips from his chin onto my face. He clenches firmer. He's determined.

I've no fight left.

The door to the bedroom bangs open.

'Mr Theo,' Clara screams and baby Vincent shrieks in support. The sounds distract him. They bring him back into the room; he loosens his grip and I wiggle my throat from under his fingers. Clara walks into the room, baby Vincent in her arms, her eyes searching to understand what she's seeing.

He looks up. He sees her and lurches to his feet.

He sways to them, his footing now unsure. He tries to grab the baby. He pulls at Vincent's arms, at his tiny neck, but Clara turns on her hips. She folds over Vincent, protecting the screaming child from his father. He lashes out at Clara – a punch, a slap, a kick, pulling at her hair. He tries to unfold her, tries to get to my baby boy.

'Help,' Clara yells. 'Help me.'

'Theo,' I try to shout, then I try to scream. My voice is scratchy. My throat sore.

I crawl towards them. I sweep a lamp, a chair, books to the floor; they clatter, they smash, I make as much noise as possible.

All of the screaming and all of the din works. Madame Joseph rushes into the room. She drags him away from Clara. She pulls his arms tight behind his back, but still he thrashes out his legs. His entire body wriggles and squirms under Madame Joseph's unexpected strength.

'I'll kill you all,' he shouts. 'You're the Devil,' he says, but then his eyes look to the ceiling. He thrashes his head from side to side, as if a bee's trapped inside it.

Something isn't right. Something's changing. Something inside his head distracts him.

'Make it stop. Make this stop,' he says. The volume's lower, the words are full of pain.

'Shush, Mr Theo,' Madame Joseph says, but he doesn't seem to hear.

He coughs now. He squirms with the coughs. His eyes are closed. I watch, but it's all happening too quickly.

'Let him go,' I shout, the words hurting as they escape my mouth.

Madame Joseph looks at me. She's uncertain that she should follow my order, but I nod my head. That simple movement sends spasms of pain through my entire body. It distracts me for a second and when I look back to Madame Joseph I see her let go of him.

My husband clutches his chest. His eyes still closed. His mouth open.

'Theo,' I scream.

He falls to the floor.

October, 1890.

Theo lives.

    He was taken to La Maison Dubois Hospital, but now he rests in a clinic in Passy.

    He suffers from a disease of the brain. They're saying he's been pushed to madness by his brother's death.

    Doctors suspect he'll never recover.

    I've forgotten what normality feels like.

    I've existed in this storm for too long. Our happiness was far too brief.

Landscape With A Carriage And A Train

'J o.'

I recognise his voice. I turn, my eyes searching the crowd of busy travellers. Just that one word and I'm transformed into an ugly, sobbing mess outside the Gare du Nord. Lord knows what the other passengers must think: child on my hip, no husband, a small trunk dropped to my feet, tears decorating my cheeks. Baby Vincent releases squawks as strangers bang into us both.

I see him. My brother: tall, bowler hat in hand thrust above the crowd, calling me, fighting against the stream of people arriving. I jiggle Vincent to my other hip, trying to smile through my tears, to reassure my son that everything's going to be fine. Andries weaves past the other travellers, with their porters wobbling behind them.

'What are you doing here?' I say, the words stuttering out.

'Heard you were catching the night-train to Utrecht,' he says.

'But who—'

'Clara,' he says, bending over and kissing the top of tiny Vincent's head. My boy reaches out and grabs the lapel of Andries' lounge coat. My brother looks less refined today: blemishes cover his neck, the end bristles of his moustache have refused to be tamed. 'Thought I'd keep you company,' he says, kissing my son's fingers loose. He carries no luggage, a clear signal that he's rushed to be here.

'They've said Theo's condition is much more serious than Vincent's was,' I say.

Andries nods, his eyes jumping to each passer-by, not meeting mine. That starts me off again. Snot and tears galore. I lift the sleeve of my blouse to wipe my eyes but Andries thrusts his silk handkerchief at me. I take it, dab at my eyes and cheeks, then blow my nose so hard that it toots like a trumpet. Tiny Vincent giggles. I hold out the handkerchief to my brother but he shakes his head. Instead he pulls me to him. He plants a kiss on my forehead, before placing his arm around my shoulder.

'We'll get through this together,' he says.

'There's not a gleam of hope,' I say.

I'd tried to see Theo last week, when he was still in Paris, but I wasn't allowed. I'd stood, baby on my hip, pleading for just five minutes with my husband and still they turned me away. They said I needed to allow Theo more time to acclimatise to his new surroundings. From a distance though, through the bars of the iron gate, I could see him in the garden with a nurse. He was stooped, but able to walk, and that both calmed and covered me in sorrow. Foolishly, I left with hope for my husband's full recovery. Five days later and I'm told he's already been transferred to Utrecht, to an institution for the mentally ill.

'Tell me all you know,' Andries says.

'I only knew about the move when the doctor, the one from the Willem Arntz psychiatric hospital in Utrecht, wrote that Theo had arrived there agitated and confused. Apparently he didn't have the slightest idea of either the day or where he was,' I say. 'They've put him in an isolation room.'

'And so you've decided to travel there with a baby?' he asks, before ruffling my boy's blond hair. 'And what do you expect to find?' The station's clock strikes two and Andries bends to pick up my luggage.

'They're saying general paralysis as a result of his syphilis infection,' I say. A wave of shame rushes through me.

'You've all been ill for months now.' I nod; we have.

'But our doctor has said that neither the boy nor I are infected.'

'Do you want me to carry him?' he asks and I shake my head. I need tiny Vincent near me. I have to keep him safe.

Andries turns and steps in the direction of the platform. His pace is a little too quick, I hurry to keep up but I've barely energy to spare. In the last two years, I've lived a lifetime. In the last month I've felt my grip on sanity slipping.

'Tiredness and restlessness have exhausted us all,' I say. 'If Theo could just sleep,' I say, mainly to myself but Andries turns to me. He smiles.

'And you think seeing you will help him?'

'I'm sure of it.'

My brother turns and nods for us to follow him through the crowd. My words echo after me: *There's not a gleam of hope.*

November, 1890.

The visit was a disaster.

We were put in a room – a table and three chairs. Theo was brought in and remained standing by the closed door with his nurse, refusing to come near.

'Look, your son is here,' I said.

He walked to us slowly, eyes on baby Vincent with each step, yet a blank expression on his face. Then, on reaching us, he glared at the boy and shouted, 'I don't know you.'

'Theo,' I said and he looked at me as if seeing me for the first time. Then he threw a chair back towards the door. Dries moved in front of me and my husband released a sound unlike any I've ever heard. A high-pitched scream so very full of terror. My son matched the sound with his own fear and I stood crying, unable to help either of the men I adore.

The nurse rushed to Theo and ushered him from the room.

They've asked that we don't visit him in Utrecht – only if and when reasonable calmness is returned.

Still, I'm frightened that a day will come when I'll forget his face, when I won't be able to close my eyes and hear his voice, when I won't look at our son and long for him to be even half the man that his father was.

What will I tell our boy about his father? How will I ever find enough words to describe a man he'll never know?

Olive Trees

Clara had refused to let her into the apartment. She came instead to fetch me from the nursery and I walked slowly to the front door, silently rehearsing my speech. I've been waiting to face Sara Voort. I knew she'd call eventually. I've prepared what I'd say.

But now all I see is another exhausted and broken woman. Sara's in the middle of the open doorway, I position myself opposite her. I stand tall. Her eyes are cast down, her shoulders droop. Her wrists are bandaged, hiding her latest attempt to cheat life.

Everything I prepared seems both irrelevant and needlessly cruel.

'And?' I say instead, all propriety gone. 'Why are you here?'

'I wanted to ask about Theo,' she says, unable to make eye contact with me.

'He's in a padded cot and, for safety's sake…' I gulp, trying to force the emotion away. 'He's in isolation.'

She looks up. Her brown eyes are puffy and lined with red, her face a blotchy heart-shape. She's exhausted. We're both defeated.

'Pa's sending me away. To London,' she says. Her lips tremble. 'I wanted to say sorry, before I leave.'

I don't respond.

'I considered him mine,' she says. 'He was my first love. I gave myself to him. He said we'd marry... I thought that you stole him.'

'And?' I ask, my hands now on my hips. I'm poised to fight.

'You knew him for such a short amount of time.' She sobs. 'I'm so very sorry for interfering...'

'Please stop,' I say, my shoulders slumping, all fight sliding off them. I step back, wanting to close the door. I don't want her grief too; I'm struggling enough with my own.

Sara puts her hand on the doorframe to stop me from turning away. 'Vincent told me about their cruel game,' she says. 'How he agreed to take me on, just to distract my thoughts away from Theo.'

'That was unforgiveable,' I say, shaking my head. 'But I was never your enemy. I'm not to blame for the Van Gogh brothers' mistreatment of you.'

'I craved his time. But whenever he was with me, his mind was elsewhere.'

'Whenever he was with you?' I ask. I fail to hide all panic from my voice.

'I forced myself into his days. Making up problems for him to solve, reporting lies that Vincent told me. Any excuse to speak to him, to see him, but he...'

I nod for her to continue.

'Theo shunned me every time. He only ever loved you.'

I don't hide my tears. Sara reaches out a hand but I step back.

'You sought to destroy my marriage,' I say. I try to keep my tone neutral, try to hide both my anger and my relief. I'm grateful though, for the truth. 'You dismissed me.'

'I'm sorry. I'm ashamed,' she says. 'Not being enough...' She sobs between her words. 'I longed to be you, but then Vincent hoped for a relationship with you and I thought he could distract you from Theo.'

I bob my head, accepting, understanding too. 'You tried to play the Van Gogh brothers at their own game?'

'They destroyed me, made me ugly.'

'Do you even hear the nonsense that pours from your mouth?' I ask, the volume a little too loud. Sara's lips twist as her expression sours.

'But—'

'No *but*.' I mimic her voice. 'You sought a man who rejected you every time. You knew that, but pursued him repeatedly. That's your truth, but they didn't make you ugly.' I pause. Sara doesn't respond. She watches me. I inhale, I exhale. 'The Van Gogh brothers haven't destroyed you. You chose to play the part of hysterical woman and I was at the receiving end of your manipulations.'

'I know,' she says, her eyes locked on her boots.

'But you're still here, and you're still alive,' I say. 'If nothing else, keep being truthful. Take from this a responsibility for your own actions, decisions and happiness.'

'I'm sorry,' she repeats, the words so quiet that I'm not even sure they were spoken. I hear her grief and it equals mine. The pain, the guilt, the shame, the loss – we're both just about clinging to our sanities. We've both suffered enough.

'You need to respond differently to society's unreasonable demands on us women. Be bolder and braver; learn to rise,' I say. Sara looks at me with an expression that offers a thousand questions. I smile with my tears. 'See London as a new start. I know people there. Sympathetic people. They'll help you.'

'Why are you being kind?' she asks. She's confused. This isn't the narrative she expected, or the one she believes she deserves.

I reach out. 'We're both weary.' Sara moves her hand to mine and our fingers entwine. 'But don't you think we're stronger and wiser because of the Van Gogh brothers? They've changed us both.'

'For the better?' Sara asks and I nod.

I'm the same as Sara; we're both women shattered by our decisions and behaviour. We're both daring to be truthful about who we are.

'You know what I really need, right now?' I say.

Sara shakes her head.

'Someone who'll listen to me talking about Theo, someone who can tell me stories about the man I love.'

'I can do that,' she says. She smiles. 'I loved him too.'

I nod. She did. I move aside, inviting Sara into my home.

Chapter Three

RISE

Winter 1891

PARIS

My dearest Theo,

You died last night.

Three months of longing. Three months of missing you every single day. Three months of writing you letters in my head – words you'll never receive. Now I'm your widow. Now I'll never see you again.

I wasn't allowed to visit you again, instead your doctor has written. The truth scratched onto yellowing paper. You suffered two epileptic fits; didn't regain consciousness after the second. Your heartbeat weakened, your breathing faded and at eleven-thirty yesterday evening, you left this world. And already I envy those who knew you longer than I did. Now, in this instant – I hate them. I can't bear that you loved your brother for all of your life and me for such a tiny amount. But mainly I detest myself for feeling such ugly emotions. But we were in each other's lives for only thirty months. I was your Mrs Van Gogh for merely twenty-one months. I'm just twenty-eight, you were barely thirty-three. Our numbers are inadequate.

And although, in reality, it's already been months since you left us, it seems that today I'm permitted to grieve. Our son is asleep. They think I'm sleeping too, but I can't. Our apartment is too quiet. I'm sure Clara and Madame Joseph stay still as statues, huddled together in the kitchen so as not to cause a sound. They haven't realised that the lack of noise unsettles me further.

But I bought sunflowers earlier. For you. They're in a vase, next to the framed photograph from our wedding day. I look at that photograph and remember how scared we both were about Vincent, about what he might do to himself. Some days his sadness invades all of the joyful moments in our too brief time together. Every artist has a story to tell about my husband. My stories and memories of our trip of love contain so much fear for Vincent van Gogh.

I want to scream, Theo. I want to shout from the balcony. This isn't fair. This isn't how our tale is supposed to end. Why weren't we allowed to finish our love story, my darling man? Where are the good parts that I can cling to? Why does the loss of you invade every thought I have?

I need you. Your son needs you.

In five days, our boy will celebrate his first birthday. You'll never get to teach him everything you know. He'll spend his life searching for you; snatching other people's memories of you and trying to make them his own. I need you to walk in here right now, to scoop our tiny Vincent into your arms, to pull me close, to tell me that everything will be fine.

I don't know how to be Mrs Van Gogh without you. I don't know how to be me without you.

I wish I could rewind our short months together. I'd travel back to that first time I saw you. All rigid, entirely out of place in the swirl and rush of Moulin de la Galette. I remember thinking that you looked as if you'd been carved from wood. Your pristine lounge coat fitted too close to your slight figure. The front buttoned high. Everything about you stiff and unyielding. But still, somehow I couldn't stop looking at you. My first evening in Paris. I was so very lost and full of shame, yet I recognised myself in you. An instant connection. I was almost frightened to blink in case you disappeared.

And that's how I feel now. Too frightened to sleep, but this time because I know I'll wake and have to feel all of this pain, all over again. With even more intensity. With even more longing. With the knowledge that this is real; that I'll never see you again. Our threads spin together, my Theo. We were stronger as one. I already miss the sound of your heart's beat.

How do I say goodbye to the love of my life? When every day, when every glance at our son, will remind me of your absence.

This is wrong. This can't be right.

I'll live your death every day until I die.

Rest well, my darling man. I will forever be your wife.

Tout à toi, Jo

January, 1891.

Our son's first birthday and my husband has already been buried in Utrecht.

Edgar Degas called here today. In our first official meeting Theo spoke of how he'd arrange an introduction and I've lost count of the times I've avoided a meeting.

A kind, portly gentleman, Edgar spoke in rapid French and gesticulated wildly with his hands. We didn't speak about my lack of art but he shared that he no longer paints as his eyesight troubles him. He has an appreciation of photography that Dries would have enjoyed. I wish now that I'd agreed to meet Edgar when Theo was here. I wish Theo could have sat with us and joined in with the discussion. I missed my husband's laughter, his quick wit, his fingers finding mine.

Theo's absence caught me off guard. Poor Degas hardly knew how to talk to a sobbing woman.

Or perhaps he did. He ignored my tears and he spoke at length about Theo's skill and Theo's legacy, while my son slept in my arms.

My dearest Jo,

A quick letter but one that demands urgent action!

You know when I first told you about my moving back to Amsterdam and how you spoke about a desire to leave Paris, to be nearer to myself and Annie? Well, I've found the perfect opportunity for you to be both close to us and to make a living.

Annie has a friend and her parents live in Bussum, about fifteen miles south-east from here. They have a boarding house that they can no longer maintain, and seek someone to step into their shoes.

I've been there today and it's perfect, Jo. Perfect for you and for tiny Vincent. They've had much interest, but I've spoken with them and sold them a merry tale about your intellect, wisdom and charm! I may have also told them how you were recently widowed and how the boy is fatherless. They've agreed to hold off other negotiations until they've met you.

Can you come to Amsterdam? Bring my nephew and stay with us.

Your loving brother, Dries

Poppy Flowers

Clara's in the apartment when I return from Amsterdam. Stew cooks on the stove and she's moved the stacks of paintings from the hallway. She said it helped her keep busy, that she misses Theo too.

'I've decided to leave Paris,' I say, lifting a spoonful of stew from its pan and blowing on it. 'I don't feel at home here. Not now. I've never belonged here really.'

I wait, watching Clara for reaction, fearing she'll try to change my mind.

'When?' she asks. She doesn't meet my eyes, preferring instead to play peekaboo with my boy from behind a handkerchief.

'Two months,' I say. I pause, slurping the liquid and smiling at its taste. 'Will you come with us? We'll live in the Netherlands, near Dries and Annie. A boarding house to maintain.'

Her eyes jump to mine and I see them searching, checking my words aren't part of a cruel prank. 'I was worryin' you'd not ask me,' she says, jumping on the spot with joy. 'Dinner will be half an hour yet.' She scoops tiny Vincent into her arms and spins with him to the doorway. The boy squeals with delight as we walk into the salon.

'I never once considered how immense Vincent's collection of paintings, sketches, and illustrations would be,' I say.

As Theo van Gogh's widow, I've found myself in possession of all of Vincent's paintings and all of his letters too. The quantity overwhelms. I look around the salon. Paintings already cover the walls, the grey and white floral pattern barely seen. Our brother created over two thousand artworks, including around eight hundred and sixty oil paintings in the ten years he was an artist. I now own, all stacked around my apartment, nine hundred pieces of his art.

The piano hasn't been played since my husband's collapse, instead Vincent's sketches are scattered across the keys. Each piece is precious, each piece is rare, each piece is important. The *chiffonier* has paintings loaded on it, some leaning against it too; many of them barely dry. The 'Vincent drawer' is open and the familiar yellowing envelopes, his distinctive handwriting, spill from it; now there's other correspondence too. Hundreds and more hundreds of letters Vincent wrote and received all through his lifetime, so many to and from Theo.

'And I know what I'm going to do with all of this,' I say, waving my hand around the chaotic exhibition and to Clara. She nods for me to continue, placing tiny Vincent onto the floor. 'Alongside the boarding house, I'm going to finish what Theo started.'

'The memorial exhibition?' Clara asks, her features set in concentration. My son creeps beside us on hands and knees.

'And more,' I say, bobbing my head enthusiastically. 'Dries suggested it and I was resistant at first. Convinced it was too daunting a task for me.'

Clara smiles. 'You're the strongest woman I've ever met.'

'And I'm also a woman with no direct experience of selling paintings,' I say.

Clara shrugs her shoulders; she doesn't understand what I'm suggesting.

'Courage in the face of adversity,' I say and Clara looks even more puzzled. Tiny Vincent grips my skirts and pulls to standing. We watch him move around the room, holding on to stacks of canvas, not yet brave enough to take those first steps alone. 'I'll complete my husband's work for him,' I say. 'I'll stick to his plan.'

I'm sure there'll be some who consider me a martyr, but they'd be wrong. I've made a decision – this is how I'll rise. It'll give me a sense of purpose, it'll help me push past my resentment and the grief of what the Van Gogh brothers and I have all been through: the three of us locked together in a painful trio of love, hurt and jealousy.

'Maybe my guilt is for surviving,' I say. 'Maybe it encourages me too.'

'Does that even matter?' Clara says. 'Your boy's already glad he's still got his mamma, and let's not forget that he needs food in his belly and somewhere to live.' She puts her hand on my arm and strokes it gently. 'There's enough sittin' on your shoulders without addin' guilt to the pile.'

I smile; she's a wise friend. 'I've a love of art and I've listened and learned from Theo van Gogh, the finest art dealer in Paris.'

'And?' she says.

'And I'm going to bring Vincent van Gogh's art to the world. I'll let others see his genius. I'll let the paintings speak my brother's story.' A pause and then I add, 'No matter how long it takes.'

Clara claps her hands together, her smile wide and encouraging. My boy giggles from the floor and claps too: a game for him. 'Mr Theo was always sayin' that his brother was a genius,' she says, applauding again for tiny Vincent to copy. 'He reckoned Mr Vincent was destined to be one of the Dutch greats.'

She's right and her support strengthens my confidence. 'That's why I can't let either of the brothers slip into the unknown,' I say. 'It's the only way I can begin to make peace with myself and continue Theo's legacy.'

I thought about Andries' suggestion for all of the train ride home. I've been a Van Gogh for only twenty-one months, but my son's a Van Gogh. He'll always be a Van Gogh. I have a duty to myself and to my boy to push away my sadness, my loneliness too. But, more than that, my brother's right – I have an obligation, a calling, a burden even, to continue my husband's work; to shout out to the world that Theo van Gogh was right to have tireless faith in his brother's art. My husband's devotion to Vincent's paintings was never compelled by sibling duty. No, Theo van Gogh was the first to identify and to comprehend the greatness of Vincent's genius.

I clap my hands and my son releases his grip of a picture frame to copy me. He falls to his bottom, a startled look on his face as he considers wailing. I scoop him onto my hip and twirl until he giggles.

'I'll introduce your uncle's paintings to the world,' I tell my boy. 'I'll attract the attention of major art dealers, of collectors, of everyone. It's what your pa was going to do. What he would have done. Yes?' I ask, jiggling up and down until he giggles again.

'A slight woman with a baby at her hip! They won't see you comin', Mrs Van Gogh,' Clara says.

I nod, they won't. Yet still the irony isn't lost on me that within my grief I've achieved boldness. I'm being forced to rise and step away from the safety of those very things – wife and motherhood – that once filled me with fear and doubt. Yet here I am daring to strive out, not at all on my own merit, as an inexperienced art dealer.

'Mark my words,' I say, wagging my finger in the air and smiling at little Vincent. 'One day, the world will know and admire the Van Gogh name.' I look at my son and he stares at me. His light-blue eyes are reassuring – those eyes and features, his tender nature too, identical to Theo.

Spring 1891

PARIS

The Potato Eaters

'**P**ardon. Apologies for the jumble, I'm packing up paintings for our move this weekend.'

Another visitor to look at Vincent's art. There's been a surge of interest in his canvases. Every day, since the news that the paintings were leaving Paris, unannounced callers have asked to see his art. Now, this stranger and I, stand in my salon.

'We're moving to Bussum, near Amsterdam,' I say. 'The fresh air will be wonderful, but I'll possibly miss seeing Eiffel's tower every day.' I can't help but look towards the window. How we've both grown over these past two and a half years.

'Verkade and Serrurier suggested I call,' he says.

'They admire Vincent's art,' I say, shifting my attention back to my guest.

'Perhaps,' he says. He's my height and twice as round. His top hat still rests on his head. I'm not sure why his fists are clenched. Eyes forward, scowl on face, chest thrust out, the man struts around my salon.

'Although why you'd want to move all of this with you...' He holds his arms out, sweeping around the room and taking in the stacks upon stacks of Vincent's art.

Above the mantelpiece Vincent's *Sunflowers* hangs. On the opposite wall, above the *chiffonier*, there's *Starry Night Over the*

Rhône. Over Theo's armchair *Boulevard de Clichy*. Over the piano *The Harvest*, next to it *Orchards in Bloom*. There are others, too many really; the walls are cluttered with art.

Vincent van Gogh still breathes oil paint into this room.

The pile of letters that Theo and Vincent exchanged sits on the *chiffonier's* folding panel. In the lonely evenings of the month after Theo died, I sorted the letters into an order. I knew that in them I'd find my husband again. Yet at first, I hated that the letters existed, some days I considered burning them and pretending instead that I was the most important person in Theo's life. But evening after evening, reading the letters became my reward for surviving the day. Letters spanning their lifetime together, seeing, hearing and understanding why my husband loved his brother so very much. A chance to be introduced to the Vincent who endured, before illness. The words within them brought me comfort and gratitude, that Theo made room in his heart, alongside Vincent, for me and then for our son. Two months on, when my son sleeps, I translate the words that the Van Gogh brothers exchanged and through that translation I'm breathing life back into the artist and his brother. I'm hearing their story as if I'm sitting in a room with them while they speak their words, just for me.

'I was informed that you wished to get rid of the paintings,' he says. 'I've come to relieve you of them. Shall we say three francs a piece. Same price as a whore. No, let's make it twenty francs for the lot. I could reuse the canvas and—'

'You've had a wasted journey,' I say. 'Vincent's collection isn't for sale.' *And never to you*, is left unspoken.

'You think you'll get a better offer, for the likes of that?' He points to *Sunflowers*; the fourth version, with its little wooden edge and white frame.

'I do,' I say.

His already unpleasant face twists into a sneer.

'These paintings are very rare and very precious. They'll be viewed together and that's when others will understand him entirely.' I hear my husband's voice, I embody his belief.

'It's clear that you're a charming little lady, Mrs Van Gogh,' he says, 'but that you gush overenthusiastically on a subject you know nothing about infuriates me.'

'How kind of you to travel to my home to offer criticism,' I say. I fold my arms across my torso. My eyes lock with his. He looks away first.

'I wanted to see the work of the *great* Vincent van Gogh for myself.'

The arrogant little man mocks me, but clearly he's not realised that I don't have to jump to his demands. I'm not looking to marry him or even to have him like me, and I doubt he's capable of showing respect to a woman.

'And now you have,' I say. 'Please see yourself out. I've an apartment to pack up. So many of Vincent's paintings to look after.' I point to the wooden cases collected in a pile next to the piano.

'And you're an expert on packing paintings too?' he says. 'Art critic, art dealer, art packer, is there no end to your skills?

'There's a carpenter on Boulevard de Clichy. He was taught how to pack paintings by an artist. And he's taught me.'

He tuts. I glare. He won't match my eye contact. It would seem that since losing Theo I've acquired a boldness that makes some men uncomfortable. If all is stripped from you in Paris, don't you only have two choices – to crumble into pity or to fight with conviction? I learned that from Agostina, from Camille, from Clara, from Sara too. I'm a widow at twenty-eight with a child who's barely one: I've nothing left to lose. I've the means to support myself and only my son who I wish to impress. I don't have to play by this man's rules anymore.

'Who are you to criticise me, *sir*?' I ask.

'I am Henri Chevrolet.'

'And?'

'You're blinded by sentimentality. Sell the work, be done with it. Your critical stance lacks—'

'Yet you've perfected yours,' I say, interrupting his rant. 'Tell me, Mr Chevrolet, what is your vast experience of the art world?'

'I'm an artist.'

'And I'm an art dealer.'

'Hardly,' he says. 'Your sorrow seeks to turn Vincent van Gogh into a god.'

'My brother a god?' I laugh. 'You judge me unfairly. Vincent van Gogh was a creative genius and sometimes an ugly man. Yet the world will see his truth and love him for it.'

He laughs.

'Tell me, Mr Chevrolet,' I say. 'One hundred years from now, will anyone remember your name?'

'People are already forgetting Vincent—'

'Have you heard of Julian Leclercq?' He shakes his head. 'Really? I'm surprised. He's a renowned art critic and connoisseur.'

He tuts and scowls. 'I don't require lessons on—'

'Together we're already plotting how to broaden Vincent's recognition. The value of his art is arising.' I'm sounding far more confident than I feel.

He laughs. It's a nervous sound, not quite sure of itself. 'Good luck to you both.'

'Mr Leclercq is a man who persists. I'm loaning him eight of Vincent's finest pieces and there's to be a retrospective. It's only the beginning but Vincent van Gogh is on the brink of—'

'You bore me. An ugly woman who considers herself an art dealer. I've never heard such—'

I laugh. 'Mark my words, Mr Chevrolet,' I say. 'You'll watch me rise. If it takes until my very last breath, one day, every single artist, art lover and art critic in the world will know the name Vincent van Gogh.'

He laughs. 'You're as mad as the earless painter.'

April, 1891.

Did I dream that life with Theo? My too short, heavenly marriage – was it a dream?

I was in love in a way I'd never considered myself capable of being, and loved beyond any expectation I once had, yet now I worry I imagined that sweet man into being. That I slept for the longest of times and dreamed the most wonderful dream.

When I first arrived in Paris, I wrote in my sketchbook that I'd rather be entirely happy for one summer than have to spread it over my lifetime.

I want to erase those words.

What I would give to start all over again.

And still I must. Tomorrow. But not with Theo.

Little Vincent, Clara and I are leaving Paris. A new life. One where I'll continue to develop with truth and kindness, so that my boy won't ever look on his mamma with contempt.

I'm lonely and abandoned, but there's hope too. It lurks deep in the shadows. I've much work to do and a need to maintain my own health for my child – my little angel. Yet still the loss of Theo dances alongside me each day.

Spring 1891

BUSSUM

Still Life Vase With Twelve Sunflowers

'F resh air, quiet village, healthy child,' I say, mainly to try and convince myself that I've made the right decision. Vincent's on my right hip as I press down the door handle and give the door a bump with my left. Clara's behind me, a small trunk in each hand.

The door swings open, hitting the wall and the bang makes Vincent jump.

'Welcome to Villa Helma,' I say. 'Our new home.'

I place Vincent onto his little feet. Mamma called him a late walker, said it was a sign of him being underdeveloped. She blamed the Van Goghs, of course. My son's perfect though. I wouldn't care if he was entirely Van Gogh without a sprinkle of Bonger. He's still unsteady on his new leather shoes. His feet feeling a little too heavy for his chubby thighs.

I speak to my boy in Dutch now. Some days I wonder if he misses the loops and twirls of the French language. I wonder if he's confused about why I've taken that language away from him. I shake my head. My boy's lost so much already in his fifteen months of life.

'Today marks a new beginning, Vincent,' I say, ruffling his blond curls. Vincent takes a step forward, unsteady or even unsure. The open hallway is vast – my voice echoes around the emptiness.

'Welcome home,' Clara says, moving past me and making for the staircase. She's been here for the last two weeks while Vincent and I took time to rest and heal with Andries and Annie. 'Wait till you see what I've been doin' with the little mister's room.'

It takes me a moment to realise that I'm the new proprietor of a boarding house in Bussum. That this is where I'm going to be living. Villa Helma is charming. A spacious home located on Koningslaan. A quiet avenue, a sunny garden, a family home. Except my family is me, Vincent and Clara. No more children are planned, no husband is about to arrive home from a hard day at work. Instead, my son and I will live in this huge house, with its seven bedrooms, and we'll fill our spaces with noise and strangers and artists, and everything else that Mamma detests.

'Knock, knock.'

Vincent plops onto his bottom, releasing a tiny squeal but I don't think he's hurt. My very own guard, he's simply signalling that there's a stranger near. Perhaps the single squeal is a reflection that he doesn't consider him a concern.

'Let me, Miss Jo,' Clara says from up the staircase, but I shake my head.

I turn towards the still open front door. He's standing in the doorframe, his fist poised to fake knock on the wood again.

'Can I help you?' I ask, scooping up Vincent and moving towards the stranger. I stretch out my hand. He hesitates for a moment, then grips and shakes in response.

'I'm Jan. Jan Veth,' he says. 'Your maid said you'd be arriving—'

'Jo,' I say. 'Johanna van Gogh.'

'I know,' he says. 'I live next door. I'm a painter, poet, critic, lecturer – take your pick from any of those.'

And straight away I'm guarded. I exhale a little too loudly. I'm not in the mood for another arrogant man telling me what I should or shouldn't be doing with Vincent's art.

'My home's a salon of sorts. I'd go as far as saying it's the centre of civilization here in Bussum,' he says.

I nod, not sure how he expects me to respond. I'm Theo van Gogh's widow, nothing he's saying impresses me. He looks flustered though. Awkward even. Perhaps my silence is a little too unnerving. He turns and points out towards the street. I shuffle a few steps forward, jiggling Vincent as I do, to peer over him. I don't see anything. But what did I expect to see? An easel set up outside his house?

'I wanted to apologise,' he says. His cheeks are bright red and there's a single drop of perspiration making its way down his long nose.

'For?' I say.

'I'd dismissed Van Gogh's work. I met him a few years ago and the violence in his brushstroke...'

'And?' I say, curious as to why he now feels the need to unburden his guilt.

'It repelled me.'

A deep sigh – here we go again, another man trying to challenge my plans. 'I'm not sure why you're here, Mr Veth.'

'Jan, please.'

I'm keen for him to leave.

'She said you were arriving today,' he says, nodding towards the staircase.

'Clara,' I say. 'My sister.' *Not maid.* He looks from Clara to me, his expression revealing his confusion, but I offer no further explanation.

'And I just wanted to say hello.' He's speaking the words but he's no longer looking at me. Instead his eyes are darting around the empty hallway. He's clearly looking for something or someone.

'Is there something else I can help you with?' I ask.

'No ... I mean, not really,' he says. He's looking at the floor now. Embarrassed to have been caught. But caught doing what, I'm not sure.

'My reaction to his art was regretfully conventional. I'm here to apologise, I was wrong, but also… It's just that … I'd hoped to see more of his paintings.'

'Vincent's?' I ask, unable to stop the smile from spreading.

'My wife told me to wait, but—'

I laugh and Jan Veth searches my face. He's unsure if I'm mocking him. If I'm laughing at him. I step forward, embracing him with my left arm; I'm convinced the poor man wants the tiled floor to swallow him up. Tiny Vincent wriggles on my right hip. He wants to be back down on the floor. He's keen to explore. I lower my son onto his two feet and he totters forward, one unsteady step at a time. I reach down to hold his hand, but he refuses my help. My boy's independent and headstrong; I turn my attention to my guest.

'My brother, Dries, arranged for some of my belongings to be shipped two weeks ago. Clara arranged for Vincent's paintings to be hung,' I say, but I think he might already know that piece of information. I'm back in the Netherlands; Gossip travels faster here. 'Come,' I say. 'Let me formally introduce you to Vincent van Gogh.'

I lift tiny Vincent and lower him in the direction of the living room, and then I nod for my guest to follow me.

'I left some paintings with Julien Tanguy in Paris,' I say as we step into my living room. 'Père Tanguy. Owns a little painting supply shop in Paris. Do you know him? I only met him recently, after Theo…' I don't continue. I'm not ready to discuss Theo with a stranger.

Jan doesn't seem to notice that I've stopped talking. He doesn't answer. Instead, he takes steps towards the mantelpiece. I don't speak. I won't break the spell that Vincent's art has cast upon him. Seeing others discovering Vincent's talent is a new favourite thing of mine. Perhaps I even judge them and count their emotional depth within that first reaction. Jan's scoring high. I think he might even have forgotten to breathe.

Hanging above the mantelpiece is Vincent's *Sunflowers*. Facing that masterpiece, above the large cupboard, is *The Harvest*. Azure blue sky, green tones of the land – you can almost feel the heat blazing down on Arles. If he turns around and looks back over the door, just above my head, he'll see *Boulevard de Clichy*. If I were to step into the painting, into this reminder of our precious Montmartre, rue Lepic would be just beyond the right corner of the frame. Or perhaps he'll look to the left of me, next to the white porcelain shade of the paraffin lamp, where he'll see three of Vincent's Japanese prints. Unusual special effects, expanses of strong colour, but oh the joyful atmosphere that our brother created.

Vincent van Gogh still breathes oil paint into my immediate world. This is what Theo would have wanted: would have demanded. Vincent's the man my husband loved the most in his lifetime. Their letters, their words to each other, showed me that. Some days I like to imagine that they wrote these letters knowing they'd be left behind, knowing the relief that would bring me. Late at night I can read them and imagine the love that would have been bestowed upon baby Vincent – had the Van Gogh brothers been of sane mind and body. I wish I could articulate the comfort that's given me over these last few weeks.

'Père Tanguy had wanted Vincent's *Sunflowers*. Theo had promised it to him. There were several initial versions and replicas, but this fourth version was my husband's favourite. He spent so long deciding to leave that little wooden edge and he chose that white frame,' I say, pointing to the picture. 'I couldn't part with it. It keeps us close to Theo.'

'Vincent's better than I remember,' Jan says. 'I mean I'd heard arguments that he was good, but this…' He sweeps her palm around the room. 'I see his great humility. That he seeks the painful core of things.'

'There are many more,' I say. 'Hundreds.'

'Hundreds?' The word is released in a squeak. He doesn't hide his joy and excitement.

'Not all are unpacked yet,' I say and I see his disappointment. 'Would you like a cup of tea?'

I watch Jan as he hesitates. 'If it's not too much of a bother,' he says and then he notices little Vincent pulling on my skirts. 'Can

I?' he asks and I nod. 'We have five for now.' He bends and picks up my son. He reaches for Jan's moustache. Trying to pull at the auburn hair.

'Vincent,' I say, my tone stern. His bottom lip curls. It's in those moments, in the sulks and the cries, that he looks most like his uncle.

'You named him after the painter?' Jan says, pulling tiny Vincent into a tight embrace.

'Yes,' I say. 'We never expected he'd be our only child.'

I'm crying. Not a sob, rather a slow stream of tears. That happens a lot recently. This stage of my grief is beyond my control, but somehow accepted too. I'm no longer hiding myself from others.

'That tea,' Jan says. 'Let's go to my house. Bring Vincent. My wife would love to meet you both.'

I nod a yes. 'I'd like that.'

Summer 1891

BUSSUM

Dear Mrs Van Gogh,

A quick letter to let you know that I have every intention of keeping my promise to you. Although I am yet to attract the interest that I had hoped, I remain committed to arranging a retrospective that will treat art lovers to the glorious progression of your brother's paintings.

So please do not lose hope. Even if it takes many years to achieve, there will be an exhibition: one that truly celebrates and shows off the work of the great Vincent van Gogh.

Your friend, Julien Leclercq

June, 1891.

A mere blink of the eye since my husband and I sat on the delivery bed in the box room, surrounded by tiny flannel vests and our heads full of questions about our unborn son. Now the child is here but the father isn't!

I'm so tired of worrying and thinking about everything. The duty, the responsibility, the future too – it sits on my shoulders and pushes me down.

I've taken on too much.

I've promised what I can't deliver.

I'm going to fail and let down both Vincent and Theo. They will be forgotten, because of my failure as an art dealer.

Oh Theo, my darling husband – I miss you in our boy's every sound, in his expression and in his movement. I look after him, I care for him with the strength of two parents, but why did you leave us so early?

I read your letters to Vincent again and again. I read each and every word, I read between each line.

We need you so very much. I love you so very much. You were pushing me to be a better person and tonight I worry about who I'm becoming. I worry that I can't succeed in your plan.

I don't think I can do this on my own.

A Field Of Yellow Flowers

We're sitting at the dining room table. Vincent's letters and sketches are scattered across the wood. All food, drink and small children have been forbidden from the room. After three months of settling into the boarding house and being embraced by the local art community, that I've made no progress with Vincent's art has left me flat as a crepe. Jan offered his help over tea on the day I arrived, but I've spent my weeks here filled with housekeeping and adapting to a new routine. Perhaps it's even taken until now for me to admit that I can't possibly fulfil my duty on my own. No one could.

'You can't be so apologetic,' Jan says. 'Use whatever contacts you have, Jo. It's all about gaining a critical following for Vincent.'

Jan Veth's an exceptional man. A talented painter and a poet, so with creative sensibilities, but a critic and a lecturer too. He has wisdom, kindness and integrity in abundance, and has fast become a friend. I've no doubt that his offer to help comes from a place that believes Vincent's art deserves a wide and vast audience.

'You know I left eight of Vincent's finest pieces with Julien Leclercq in Paris? He was determined that there'd be a retrospective and that he'd pull together French art collectors and dealers,' I say. 'But yesterday he wrote that he wouldn't give up.

As if failure were a possibility already. He even said that it might take years to achieve.'

'Years?' Jan asks, pushing his tiny round spectacles back up to the bridge of his nose.

'I hoped there'd be more initial interest.'

Jan nods. He'd hoped that too.

'The task just feels a little too big for me. What with my son and this boarding house to run,' I say. 'I've been neglecting my duty…'

'I've many connections here in Bussum and throughout the Netherlands,' he says. 'Let's coordinate an exhibition of Van Gogh's work, and then another and then again. We can get bigger each time.' A pause, while he considers what he's suggesting. 'We can be clever, show his lesser-known works alongside the masterpieces.'

'To increase the value of those lesser-known pieces?' I say. I know how this works. I smile at that. I adore that Jan now admires Vincent's art, that he sees the genius too. Theo would have liked him. My husband taught me so very much, but thinking about him brings with it an ache in my stomach. A longing to hear his laughter, to feel his lips on mine.

'Do you think it'll take years?' I say, maintaining a foot in the present to stop me spiralling into that past.

'I've no idea,' he says.

'But it will happen,' I say. A statement. I was right to ask for his help; even just talking about it all leaves me less overwhelmed by the task ahead.

Jan applauds to show his approval. His excitement is contagious. 'Loaning the work will get people to know Vincent's art. Loan to everyone who asks.' He points at my piece of paper: a prompt for me to write all of this down. A document that I can refer to when the magnitude of the task overwhelms again.

'And we'll get critics to write articles about every exhibition,' I say.

'We'll keep people talking about Vincent van Gogh and, believe me, in the Netherlands, people will be very interested in his work,' Jan says. 'We'll make it so that there's hardly a newspaper that doesn't say something about him.'

'And what will they say of me?' I ask. 'That I'm full of schoolgirlish twaddle. That I'm at best bombastic and sentimental?'

'And does it matter if they do?' he asks.

I throw my arms out and look to the ceiling, as if tossing a prayer to the heavens. 'Let them underestimate me.'

He laughs but nods at my piece of paper and I quickly jot down a few more notes.

'Once we have interest here, we'll take Van Gogh's work to an international audience,' Jan says. 'You'll establish yourself in all of the art circles across Western Europe.'

I stop writing. I can't even begin to imagine what that would look like. I glance at Jan, to see he's watching me already. Does he realise that he's expecting too much of me? That I doubt I'll ever establish myself—

'What is it?' Jan asks.

'I wrote to the Rijksmuseum in Amsterdam. Theo so wanted Vincent's work in there,' I say, my entire body squirming with the words.

'Too soon though, Jo.'

I nod. 'They declined a loan of any picture by Vincent. I'm sure they had a good laugh about it all.'

'Did you expect any other response?' he asks and I shrug. When I left Paris I was bold and possibly hadn't considered the magnitude of the task ahead of me. Reality's hit and has taken root on my shoulders. Like I'd *expect* anything related to the Van Goghs to be easy.

'It'll all work out,' Jan says. He smiles; he doesn't show even a fragment of doubt. 'Do you still have all of Theo's contacts?'

I nod. I've already written them all down. I lift a few sketches, move a couple of letters, and hand Jan a small notebook.

'Then you'll reach out to Theo's friends, to Vincent's friends and to the many admirers of them both across the globe.'

I write that down too. Jan flicks through the notebook: pausing, smiling, reading the many names.

'Be bold, be persistent. If you have to rent and pay for the gallery yourself, then do it. You believe in his art?'

I nod again. I really do.

'I can contact important dealers in the Netherlands and France,' Jan says. 'Do you know Paul Cassirer?'

I shake my head. 'I don't, but he might remember Theo.'

'Offer him ten per cent but be prepared to rise to fifteen per cent commission on any works he sells. Let him use his reach to place Van Gogh's work around the world.'

'But I don't have a gallery—'

Jan holds up a palm to stop me considering even a hint of negativity. 'You don't need to be based in an art gallery. Use contacts and dealers instead, let them negotiate prices for you.'

A pause. There's a niggle.

'He needs to be in a museum, in a public art collection,' I say. 'It's what Theo wanted for his brother.'

Jan takes a handkerchief from his breast pocket and removes his spectacles. I watch as he gently cleans the lenses while considering my request. 'There are no shortcuts. That could take years,' Jan says. 'It's quite a commitment.'

We let that reality rest alongside us both.

'I'll make it happen,' I say. 'The goal is to get Vincent's work seen and appreciated.'

Jan smiles as he puts his spectacles on again. He approves, he supports me. I'm so grateful for him.

'I have his letters too. They're remarkable. I was thinking...'

Jan bobs his head for me to continue.

'We could include brief quotations alongside his pieces,' I say. 'It's what makes him unique. The juxtaposition of his words and his art. I'll let people access Vincent in every way.'

'Can I read them?' he asks and I nod. 'You'll create enemies. Critics will attack your new methods. They'll focus on your age and you being a woman, say you're trying to redefine art.'

'Let them,' I say. 'They'll dismiss me. And I'll show them they're wrong.'

Jan claps again. 'So you have a plan?' He nods to the piece of paper that's covered in my scribbles.

'Time's on my side. I'll slowly release paintings and drawings into the world,' I say. 'I won't flood the market.'

'I do have one question,' he says and I signal for him to continue. 'Why, Jo?' he says. 'Has anyone ever asked why you're devoting your life to the Van Gogh family?'

I smile. 'Theo always said that his brother was a genius, that he could be one of the Dutch greats,' I say. 'I can't keep this collection just for me. It's my duty. It's what I have to do, in the memory of my husband and Vincent.'

Spring 1892

BUSSUM

March, 1892.

The Kerkhovens living in the far wing of the house, and not needing much from me, clearly lured me into thinking running a boarding house would be straightforward. But yesterday I was incredibly busy with a new family and their five children. Today Mrs Ballot arrived – a respectable Hague lady with the most beautiful blue eyes – and already we've had two conversations about George Eliot. I just know she's going to be a delight of a paying guest.

Yet working brings me the busyness and distraction I still need, and I'm earning far more money than I ever imagined I could. Clara is entirely at home here now and she's an unmatched help with the boy, and with the cooking too.

It's the silence that disturbs me though. Like now: I sit quietly by my lamp, a storm brewing outside, Vincent and Theo's letters in a pile on my lap. Through my window I see the lights shining in other people's homes.

I hate it's been over a year since Theo's death and still I am so deeply alone and abandoned.

But then my thoughts shift to Vincent and I can't bear to think about how often he must have felt this way too. I carry such sadness that now, too late, I finally and truly understand him.

Horse Chestnut Tree In Blossom

We turn the corner and we walk through a small avenue of chestnut trees. There's bounce in my stride today; exciting developments and decisions are being made as we walk.

'So you think it's a good idea? It'll be a selling exhibition of forty-five paintings, forty-four drawings and one lithograph,' I say to Jan Veth.

He runs a finger over his moustache, considering his response. 'Where though?'

'I'm going to hire three rooms on the upper floor of Café Riche in Passage.'

'In The Hague?' he asks, glancing at me for confirmation.

A bob of my head. 'I've looked and there's much space and light for viewing the paintings.' Nerves bubble in my stomach. 'Do you think I've enough time to bring it all together?'

He pulls an expression that suggests he doesn't, but then adds, 'I know better than to underestimate you, Mrs Van Gogh.'

I laugh at his honesty; some days I think he might fear my independence and boldness. Other days he sees how much I've been struggling with the lack of progress, with the too frequent knockbacks and rejections. A few more steps in silence, but my head's full of the enormity of the task ahead. 'I can't quite believe this is actually happening,' I say. 'A large-scale retrospective.'

Chapter Three

'And you're suggesting a run from May 16 to June 6?'

'Yes,' I say. Still walking, I watch as he takes his little round spectacles and rubs their lens with his handkerchief. I know he does this when needing time to consider his response. He holds them to the light, and then wipes where he might have spotted a smudge. 'The Danish artist Johan Rohde has already said he'll pay up to 270 guilders for *Wheatfield after a Storm*. And so many people have said they'll attend one afternoon.'

Jan smiles. 'Excellent news, Jo. You've worked so hard. Theo and Vincent would be proud of you.'

I try to be discreet as I pinch the bridge of my nose to stop my tears. What I'd give to walk around the next corner and see Theo waiting outside the boarding house. My days are so very full: housekeeping, my son, plans for Vincent's art. All of it excites me, yet good things make me miss my husband even more.

Jan and I walk in silence. Spring is here: hope and resurrection after the long winter. Pink flower clusters decorate the branches of the horse chestnut trees, some of the blossom floats with the breeze. I smile as I watch its journey.

'I received flowers and a pleasing letter from Isaac Israëls this morning.' Jan turns to me, raising an eyebrow for me to continue. 'He wrote about how not everything can be painted, that there's a fine line that's easily crossed.'

'Such as?'

'His example was the sun, but he said that when my brother selected items or people within the possible, then that's when his work was remarkable.'

Jan nods. 'Others now recognise what you and Theo already knew.'

'Israëls even compared Vincent to Wagner. And he wants to paint my son. He's invited us to his studio.'

'Be careful with that one,' Jan says and I wave my hand in the air as if to bat away the words.

Clara said the same, but I like Isaac's friendship already. He writes often and seems to be a lonely man who always eats in cafés. I think we might both have been abandoned.

'This is the first step,' Jan says.

For an instant I wonder if he's referring to my correspondence with Isaac and that thought makes me laugh. The sound puzzles my friend. '

'In getting Vincent's work seen and appreciated?' I ask.

Jan bobs his head, observing me thoughtfully as he strolls. 'And how do you feel, Jo?' Jan asks.

'Terrified with a dose of exhilaration,' I say. 'There's so much still to achieve.'

May, 1892.

Verkade and Serrurier visited today. I loved having French painters in my home again. To speak French and to hear news from Paris made me homesick for a place and time that no longer exists. Their appreciation and unreserved exclamations of joy at seeing Vincent's work thrilled me too.

I can't quite believe that I'm finally beginning to achieve this, but news is spreading. My brother's reputation travels across the sea.

So many are travelling to share this show.

They're coming to the opening tomorrow. An actual exhibition of Vincent's art in The Hague.

So much appreciation of Mr Van Gogh's skill and talent; those who once laughed and made him the butt of their jokes are already hiding in corners. I don't think they'd dare to step out with their opinions.

Oh, how the tide turns.

Today, I've sent ten paintings to Buffa in Amsterdam, yesterday I sent twenty to Oldenzeel in Rotterdam, soon there'll be another exhibition in Pulchri and then the largest yet in Kunstzaal Panorama this December. I'm sticking to my plan, and it's actually working. I'm loaning key pieces of art and offering paintings for sale alongside them.

My boy will one day read this sketchbook and he'll judge the life of his mother. He'll know my thoughts, my flaws, the obstacles, the devastation, and also my determination.

What better lesson is there to teach a child: that his mother persisted.

Autumn 1892

BUSSUM

Orphan Man With Top Hat, Drinking Coffee

I wasn't expecting Holst. He walks past me and into the Villa Helma's hallway, flapping a piece of paper in the air and removing his top hat.

'I couldn't wait a moment longer,' he says.

He's clearly excited, yet still I shrug my shoulders like a petulant child. I can guess why he's here and I'm ready for another argument about Vincent's letters. Holst pats a handkerchief at the perspiration on his overly large forehead. I watch as a drop zigzags into this bushy eyebrow.

'About my design,' he says. He shakes his head vigorously, freeing the drop of sweat; it falls to the floor tiles. 'The litho,' he says, waving the paper again.

'Your design?' I say, unable to hide my joy. It's for the cover of the catalogue. Jan and Holst are helping to arrange a Vincent van Gogh Exhibition in the Kunstzaal Panorama this December. 'I still can't quite believe it's—'

I take the piece of paper. I'm caught off-guard; it's both beautiful and poignant. A wilting sunflower against a black background; the word 'Vincent' floats over its exposed roots and a halo waits above the flower.

'My heart aches,' I say, wiping a tear from under my eye. 'Theo would have adored your work.'

429

I look at Holst and he's looking along the hallway, towards the kitchen.

'Would you like a drink?' I ask and he bobs his head.

'I've been talking to Jan,' Holst says, turning and walking to my parlour.

A deep inhalation, then I exhale. This was what I was expecting. 'About including the letters,' I say.

I watch the back of his head as he nods. He observes *Sunflowers* above the mantelpiece.

Since reading the correspondence, Jan's been enthusiastic about my suggestion – that to better understand his exhibited art we'll include quotes from the letters Vincent wrote. Jan's even been suggesting which snippets can accompany which piece in the Kunstzaal Panorama. What I'm suggesting is a first, something the art world has never experienced before; already there's a rush of interest about its potential. Holst remains both vocal and unconvinced though.

'You don't want to appear unprofessional,' he says. He points at the painting. 'The art can speak for itself.'

'My brother's words enhance its understanding,' I say, but still Holst shakes his head. 'I am not without understanding.'

His eyes jump to mine and I hold my stare. Jan told me that Holst considers me a woman who 'fanatically raves without understanding'. I need him to realise that his words have been passed to me and for him to appreciate that his opinion no longer bothers me. Vincent's art and letters need to be exhibited together. Indeed, even Jan agrees that my brother's words illuminate his paintings and that my timing is perfect. I've been listening to artists, dealers and critics; there's been a shift in art and in literature, one that now considers both social and spiritual questions. Vincent was always before his time, perhaps even timeless. His paintings and words already merge. To see his life and his art as one feels right; my brother was unique. I can but hope that Theo would approve too.

'There'll be eighty-seven paintings and twenty drawings

included – the biggest exhibition yet,' I say. 'Already the prices for his art are rising.'

Holst turns to me and smiles. Money matters. This man marks success in guilders paid.

'And when they look at Vincent's paintings they'll know about his labouring, his sorrow, his cutting off part of his ear…' I say.

I hear his tut.

'You have something more to say?' I ask and Holst's cheeks blush red. 'I'm happy to prove you wrong.'

He laughs, shakes his head then holds up his palm in defeat. I can't help but grin.

'And I'm sure you will, Jo,' he says. 'But, first, is there coffee and *koekje*?'

Chapter Four

PERSIST

Spring 1914

AMSTERDAM

~

TWENTY-TWO YEARS LATER

~

My dearest Vincent,

I have been keeping a secret from you: one I hope will bring you much joy.

As you know, since the success of Kunstzaal Panorama, there have always been brief quotations from your uncle's letters in his exhibitions. The juxtaposition of his art and his words have shown many people Vincent's depth: the astonishing artist alongside his remarkable letters. Consequently, people have been intrigued and they've asked for more.

And now I have more.

I've spent so many years meticulously translating and editing Vincent's letters to your pa, and your dear pa's letters to Vincent. And now it's time for the full tome to be read by others. Today in fact! The Dutch and German editions of the book are published. Brieven aan zijn broeder – Letters to His Brother *– exists.*

It's time for me to share the Van Gogh brothers with the world – for everybody to appreciate your uncle's genius fully, for them to have insight into both his process and his glorious mind.

Yet, more than that, now others can read the lifetime of letters that Theo and Vincent exchanged. They can see for themselves the deep and enduring friendship that has shaped my life with you, just as it guided both brothers' lives: the swapping of stories about friends, successes, disappointments, ambitions, and their extraordinary love that endured.

For now though, my darling boy, I enclose this first copy for you.

Your loving, Mamma

Still Life With Pears

We stop outside the big white house at the end of the oak
avenue. Beautiful red roses creep through the bars of the
fence: their heads turn to the sunshine. Past the roses, the garden
plays host to pear trees and more jasmine than I've ever seen; its
smell is heady.

'It's as if the jasmine's a bouquet for one pear tree to marry the
other,' I say.

I've been strolling for fifteen minutes in silence, arm in arm
with my precious boy.

I see him too infrequently of late. In his final weeks of
studying mechanical engineering at the University of Delft, he's
visiting just for the day. Tonight I'll attend a meeting at the Dutch
Social Democratic Workers' Party, where I'll put forward my plans
to co-found an organisation committed to labour and women's
rights.

'I'm going to ask Josina to marry me,' he says.

I'm unable to stop the surprise from splashing across my face.
'That's wonderful news,' I say. I throw my arms around my son
and pull him into a tight embrace.

'Mamma,' he says. He laughs. 'Let me breathe.' I loosen my
grip and we continue our walk. 'I'm hoping she'll come with me
when I move to New York.'

'My son the engineer,' I say. 'Neither your pa nor I predicted that when you were tiny.'

'I doubt I'll ever understand art. I respect it, I respect you, but looking at paintings all day…'

I smile. Some days I worry he thinks he's disappointed me, by not choosing to remain in the family *business*; other days I fear it was a deliberate decision.

'Art simply fails to excite me,' he says. I shrug as I grip his arm closer to me, and lean into my son.

'Are you happy?' I ask and Vincent laughs as he nods his head.

'You ask me that so often, Mamma. And, yes, still, I am,' he says. 'I put my heart and soul into all that I do and I've yet to lose my mind in the process.' We walk a little further in silence, but then, 'It's happening tomorrow, isn't it?'

Of course I knew this was the actual reason for the surprise visit. He's checking to make sure I'm not falling apart, that I've not spiralled into the madness that haunts him.

'They'll exhume your pa's body tomorrow and transport it to Auvers,' I say. We don't look at each other. Neither of us wants to consider what will be unearthed.

'It's been twenty-three years,' Vincent says. 'Are you sure this is what you want?"

I stop walking and look into my son's eyes. I nod. That's all; just a nod. And Vincent bobs his head in response.

Because my son knows that for those twenty-three years not a day has passed that my thoughts haven't strayed to his uncle and his father. Years spent reading, editing and translating their words. Hours and hours consumed in silence yet overhearing the Van Gogh brothers' intimate thoughts, gossip and truth. And those letters offered insight into a side of my husband that existed beyond my reach, my knowledge and my time. How they felt for each other, how they understood each other, is something I'd not fully appreciated when they were both alive; my biggest regret, I wish with all of my heart that I had.

I'm not erasing that the Vincent I knew was riddled with disease, that he stole my joy or that he was difficult to be near. But those letters offer a side to him that I'd not, till his death, had the pleasure of meeting. They explain why my husband adored Vincent, and I'll forever adore Theo. I've lost count of the times I've wept while reading their exchanges, and for the last twenty-three years I've existed through them and with the Van Gogh brothers by my side.

'Their relationship was like no other I've encountered,' I say. 'What better tribute can I offer them? The Van Gogh brothers have brought so much joy to my life.'

'And when you die…' I turn to my son but he's unable to make eye contact with me. 'I hate even talking about this,' he says.

'I'll be here for years yet,' I say, squeezing his arm. 'But then I'll rest next to Johan.'

Vincent stops abruptly. My response has surprised him. 'Even though he didn't bring you the joy that Pa did?' he asks.

'He was a good man,' I say. My husband for eleven years. An insecure and solitary man who existed in the shadow of my love for the Van Gogh brothers. Perhaps my second husband's true strength was in his ability to accept Theo's presence in our marriage. His ghost existed with us. 'I'll rest beside Johan to show my gratitude and to return his loyalty.'

My son nods. His blue eyes, his complexion – his likeness to his father catches me off-guard too often. Theo remains thirty-three while my son races towards that age.

'From tomorrow my beloved Theo will fill the grave adjacent to his Vincent. They'll be reunited, they'll rest side by side,' I say. 'That ivy from Dr Gachet's garden will grow over them both.'

Vincent throws his arm around my shoulder and pulls me into an embrace.

'My life didn't begin until I met your pa,' I say and Vincent laughs. He's heard this too many times. 'Until then I'd lived without truth, existing with my eyes half-closed. Theo taught me to open my eyes, he taught me how to see the truth, how to seek it and how to live alongside it too.'

'Don't worry, Mamma, you've drilled that lesson into me,' my son says and I feel a gentle kiss on the top of my head. 'And so very much more.'

'Eliot's *Mill on the Floss* speaks of how I dream of Theo and Vincent,' I say. '*In their death they were not divided.*'

'From tomorrow,' Vincent says and I nod.

'Now,' I say, leaning in to my son. 'Did I tell you that Helene Kröller-Müller bought another five of your uncle's paintings?'

Vincent shakes his head. 'More?' he asks. 'She owns almost as many as you.'

I laugh. I like that another woman, a wealthy collector with a keen eye, sees my brother's genius too.

'She's bought ninety Van Gogh paintings and one hundred and eighty-five drawings, and I've still to meet the woman,' I say. 'Apparently the social themes interest her and she plans to open her collection to the public.'

Winter 1924

AMSTERDAM

~

ANOTHER TEN YEARS LATER

~

Mr. Charles Aitken.
Director, National Gallery of British Art,
Millbank, London

Dear Mr Aitken,

For two days I've tried to harden my heart against your appeal. I felt as if I couldn't bear to be separated from the picture that was Theo's favourite, that I'd looked at every day for more than thirty years. But in the end the appeal proved irresistible.

I know that no picture would represent Vincent in your famous gallery in a more worthy manner than the Sunflowers, and that he himself, le Peintre des Tournesoles, would have liked it to be there.

So I'm willing to take back The Postman and to leave you Sunflowers at the price agreed.

It's a sacrifice for the sake of Vincent's glory.

I finally feel that my battle has been won.

Yours sincerely,

J. van Gogh-Bonger

Autumn 1925

LAREN

≈

ONE YEAR LATER

≈

~

DIED.

Van Gogh-Bonger,
Johanna, age 62,
a resident of Laren,
mother of Vincent Willem,
passed away on
September 2, 1925.

Widow of Theo van Gogh
(1857-1891)
and Johan Cohen Gosschalk
(1873-1912).

Burial at Zorgvlied Cemetery.

~

Spring 1990

NEW YORK

~

ANOTHER SIXTY-FIVE YEARS LATER

~

Portrait Of A Wife

'Yes, yes, I'm live at Christie's auction house in Rockefeller Center, New York. Vincent van Gogh's *Portrait of Dr Gachet* has just sold for 82.5 million dollars!

'One hundred years since it was painted in Auvers-sur-Oise, during the last few weeks of Vincent's life, the painting is said to be of a doctor who cared for Vincent on his deathbed. And, today, just now, that oil painting's sale has exceeded all estimates.

'Van Gogh, a Dutch Post-Impressionist painter, is among the most famous and influential figures in the history of Western art. With a price tag of 82.5 million dollars, and sold within three minutes, his *Portrait of Dr Gachet* now stands as one of the most expensive paintings to have ever been sold.

'It's miraculous though, isn't it? Some would never now consider that a name that's synonymous with art sold perhaps one or two paintings during his lifetime and that mainly he survived by exchanging his work for food and alcohol. Can we take a moment to consider that?

'Of course, other artists in Van Gogh's social circle appreciated his work, but most of the public only learned his name years after his death.

'It was Mrs Johanna van Gogh-Bonger, Vincent's sister-in-law, who took it upon herself to introduce Van Gogh's paintings to the world and, aside from Vincent's artistic talent, she is entirely accountable for making Van Gogh a name that everyone recognises.

'Yet what do we know of Mrs Van Gogh-Bonger? That she was only part of the Van Gogh brothers' lives from June 1888 to her husband's death in January 1891 – a mere two and a half years – is mind-blowing. That in that short time, she experienced meeting and becoming engaged to Theo van Gogh, Vincent's mental collapse, her marriage, pregnancy, childbirth, Vincent's death, Theo's mental collapse and then his death. A former schoolteacher who stepped in to two and a half years of madness, love and grief.

'After that, aged only twenty-eight, some might have turned their back on the Van Gogh name. But nevertheless, Mrs Van Gogh-Bonger persisted. She spread him over the world, selling at least 195 paintings and 55 drawings by Van Gogh, including *Sunflowers* to London's National Gallery of British Art in 1924, the year before she died.

'To think that when Johanna first arrived in Paris, she wrote in her sketchbook that she'd hate to reach the end of her life and to never have achieved something that was great or even remarkable! An unlikely figure to have played guardian of Vincent's legacy and such a key role in art history, yet the bold, determined and astute Johanna van Gogh-Bonger is noted as one of the greatest art dealers to have lived...'

Author's Note

This novel is a work of imagination, but its genesis rests in a trip to Amsterdam in 2016. Without question, Amsterdam is famous for many things, from its seventeenth-century canal houses to its tulips, Rembrandt, clogs and Vincent van Gogh, and that's perhaps why my three-day trip ended in the Van Gogh Museum. I was already a fan, but for me, this visit was illuminating for reasons that went beyond the usual joy of exploring Vincent's art. During my time in the museum I noted a photograph and a small sign that mentioned the artist's sister-in-law, Johanna van Gogh-Bonger.

It has been well-documented, and many have an opinion on, how Vincent van Gogh died in 1890, almost penniless and with little recognition for his artistic talent. Yet, eleven years later, his work was being exhibited at a major retrospective in Paris and his reputation as a great artist was firmly established. I, like numerous others, had never questioned how that shift in fortune happened. I'd simply attributed this to his brother, an art dealer, or to Van Gogh's artist friends.

After initial research, I discovered that on Vincent's death, and the subsequent death of his brother, Theo, six months later, Johanna van Gogh-Bonger – at only twenty-eight years old – became keeper and advocate of Vincent's immense collection of paintings, sketches, letters and illustrations. I was shocked and bewildered that despite her key role in the growth of Vincent's posthumous fame, Johanna's story had been all but ignored. I wanted to understand why she'd dedicated her life to the reputation of her late husband's brother, and so began my three-year obsession with rewriting Johanna into and alongside Vincent's narrative.

In truth, during my research, I relied on Johanna's sensibilities and voice from her diaries and letters, but facing huge gaps in her archive meant that the novel's narrative arc was unstable. As I'm neither a historian nor a biographer, I had little choice – and much pleasure – in writing an imaginative reconstruction of a brief marriage and the story of how a young widow changed art history. As expected, creative license occurred and it was never more resourceful than having Johanna move to Paris at the beginning of the novel. I could argue that this single detour from fact allowed for a hastier unravelling of plot – alongside comment on Parisian society, on women and on Vincent – but the truth is that Johanna Bonger wasn't living in Paris during that summer of 1888.

Letters from spring 1888 (van Gogh, T., et al., 2005) contained details of Johanna's family wishing to send her to Paris, but Andries was newly married (May 3, 1888) and her family were worried about Johanna's health and her need to recover from an infatuation. Johanna was given 'an honourable discharge on health grounds' from work in May 1888 and she was involved with Johann Eduard Stumpff at that time (van Gogh, et al., 2005). In her diaries, she talked about her lack of willpower and self-control, and how his disinterest and indifference towards her had increased her obsession. The relationship was officially over by October 11, 1888 (Diaries Jo Bonger, 2019) and at that time she even talked about regret and how she'd spurned her own happiness by turning down Theo (who had proposed to her after one meeting). Indeed, on October 15, 1888, Johanna wrote how she wished Andries would find her a post in Paris (Diaries Jo Bonger, 2019) and many other diary entries spoke affectionately about her favourite brother. Perhaps then, this novel offered a creative response to the question – what would have happened if Johanna Bonger had arrived in Paris, in that summer of 1888?

Other fictionalised additions include that although Johanna did read vastly – Victor Hugo, the Dutch poet Nicolaas Beets, Alphonse Marie Louis Prat de Lamartine and Françoise-Alix de Lamartine-Des Roys – she was never an artist, but did have an interest in art (Diaries Jo Bonger, 2019). I gave her a desire to learn technique and about the art world, so that she (and the reader) could explore the domain Johanna would later inhabit. Additionally, there was no Sara Voort, but she is based on a tiny seed of truth. Theo had been having a relationship with someone referred to as 'S' in letters, and he had wanted to break things off, but considered 'a sudden termination was too risky, because it would either drive her mad or "straight to committing suicide"' (van Gogh, et al., 2005, p. 16). The letters showed that Theo did use Vincent to distract women, with Vincent being prepared to 'take the role of the other man upon himself' (van Gogh, et al., 2005, p. 16). Likewise, there was no Clara but her inclusion – indeed Sara's inclusion too – provided voice and researched comment on female friendship and society's view of hysterical women. Additionally, there was no Dr Janssen and no known marriage was arranged for Johanna. I also know little about her relationship with her mother and there were many siblings mentioned in letters and diaries (both Bonger and Van Gogh families), but they have been removed for ease of narrative control (as the number of characters would have been too many and the length of the novel too long).

However, on November 6, 1888, Johanna wrote that she would leave for Paris the following Thursday and was at that time courting Theo (Diaries Jo Bonger, 2019). That was her last diary entry until November 15, 1891, when she re-emerged as a widow.

Consequently, this novel offers a fictionalised account of Johanna living in Paris with her brother, but from November 1888 much of the narrative was inspired by real events and discovered from available correspondence between Bongers and Van Goghs.

Author's Note

There is, of course, considerably more that I could have written about Johanna's life after Theo's death. Yet, as previously stated, I am neither her biographer nor a historian, and, instead, this novel offers a creative account of the remarkable woman who became the guardian of Vincent van Gogh's legacy.

Johanna van Gogh-Bonger died on September 2, 1925 and was buried at Amsteldk 273, in Amsterdam Begraafplaats Zorgvlied. She lays next to her second husband, Johan Cohen Gosschalk, who she was married to for eleven years and not next to her beloved Van Gogh brothers in Auvers-sur-Oise.

Dr Caroline Cauchi

Useful Resources to Discover More About Johanna:

Diaries Jo Bonger, 2019. *Bonger Diaries*. [Online] Available at: https://www.bongerdiaries.org

Van Gogh Museum [Online] https://www.vangoghmuseum.nl/en

Van Gogh Museum, 2019. *Research Project: Biography of Jo van Gogh-Bonger*. [Online] Available at: https://www.vangoghmuseum.nl/en/knowledge-and-research/research-projects/research-project-biography-of-jo-van-gogh-bonger

Van Gogh, T., Jansen, L., J, R. & Bonger, J., 2005. *Brief Happiness*. Amsterdam: B.V. Waanders Uitgeverji.

Van Gogh, V., n.d. *Van Gogh's Letters: Memoir of Johanna Gesina van Gogh-Bonger*. [Online] Available at: http://www.webexhibits.org/vangogh/memoir/nephew/1.html

Vincent van Gogh The Letters, n.d. *Vincent van Gogh: The Letters*. [Online] Available at: http://vangoghletters.org

Thanking

I do hope that I've opened conversation about Johanna van Gogh-Bonger, that I've positioned her alongside Vincent, that she's perhaps been rewritten into his narrative and even that she's reclaimed her importance in art history. Vincent van Gogh's skill and genius as an artist isn't in question here. Thank you, Johanna – it's been a privilege and an honour to spend three years devoted to researching and retelling your story.

Thank you to all of the fabulous team at One More Chapter. The biggest thank you to Charlotte Ledger – editor of my dreams – for your excitement, vision and belief in my writing. There aren't enough words to express my gratitude, but thank you for recognising what this could be and for making it happen. A thank you for Lydia Mason too, whose editorial wizardry matched her passion for this novel. Charlotte and Lydia have been the best cheerleaders and supporters of both Jo and of my writing. Women supporting women is a wonderful thing. Similarly warmest possible thanks to the brilliant foreign rights team at HarperCollins – to Samuel Birkett, Aisling Smyth, Agnes Rigou, Zoe Shine and Rachel McCarron. That Johanna is reaching an international audience is bringing me much excitement and happiness (and many new Smurfs for my shelf).

I'm so very grateful to LJMU for awarding me a fully funded, three year, PhD Scholarship to complete the research for this novel. I'm indebted to Professor Catherine Cole. Her guidance, generosity and belief in my academic ability has reached beyond her pay scale. I wouldn't have completed this research or novel without her persistent guidance, regular encouragement and friendship. So many others from LJMU have supported me as I wrote this novel (and completed my PhD), but I consider myself so very fortunate to have had Catherine Cole, Robert Graham and Emma Roberts on my supervisory panel. I've had three (long!) years of being guided by enthusiastic, reassuring and talented academics. Thanks also to LJMU's Sarah Maclennan, who encouraged me from my initial application to study, through the pandemic and cheered my completion of this research.

Thanks to the historical novelists Doug Jackson, Sara Sheridan, Kate Lord Brown, Rowan Coleman, Jill Dawson, Elizabeth Chadwick and Catherine Johnson, for their generosity of time, expertise and opinion. Thank you to Jackie Jardine, for more than I want to reveal here. Thanks also to my glorious friends – Kat Nokes, Philip Shell, Bernie Pardue, Alex Brown, Dave Roberts (I miss you), Clare Christian, Elsa Williams, Keith Rice, Wendi Surtees-Smith, Rachael Lucas, Keris Stainton, Paula Groves, Richard Wells, Margaret Coombs and Johnny Vegas – for their advice, arse kicking and belief in me. Love to you all.

This novel is about one remarkable woman and is dedicated to another – to Dr Jacqueline Azzopardi. There will never be enough words to explain how much I miss her, but, equally, I feel blessed to have had such an extraordinary woman influence my life. Jaka wanted me to return to academia many years ago and I regret not completing my PhD during her too-short lifetime. I know she would have been the first to shout, 'Prosit Kugina.' I wish, with all the wishes I have left, that I could celebrate with her over a pastizz and a Cisk or two.

And, finally, thanks and so much love to Gary, Jacob, Ben, Poppy, Ramon and Lauren. Thank you for insisting I push through those too-frequent attacks of doubt and fear, thank you for singing karaoke with me, thank you for the constant and unconditional love. I'm so very lucky that you're my family.

Notes

Epigraph

1. *Diary 1,* https://bongerdiaries.org/dagboek_jo_1_section_0

Printed in the USA
CPSIA information can be obtained
at www.ICGtesting.com
JSHW031124090724
66096JS00011B/381

9 780008 641535